Isabel Burning

Donna Lynch

RAW DOG
SCREAMING
PRESS

Published by Raw Dog Screaming Press
Hyattsville, MD

First Hardcover Edition

Book design: Jennifer Barnes
Cover: Steven Archer

Printed in the United States of America

ISBN 978-1-933293-49-3

Library of Congress Control Number: 2008930804

www.RawDogScreaming.com

Isabel Burning

Acknowledgements

My heartfelt thanks goes to Jennifer Barnes & John Lawson at Raw Dog Screaming Press, Carolyn Wells & Al Auckland, Hazel Wells, Patrick Lynch, Rainey Latham, Patrick Rodgers & Dancing Ferret Discs, Rebecca O'Rourke, Magpie Killjoy, Dai Andrews, Frankie Stoner, Cat Mihos, Christopher Danaher, and to the friends and fans of Ego Likeness who have supported this endeavor.

My love and gratitude to my husband Steven, for his encouragement and patience while I lived between our world and theirs.

"...we must acknowledge...that man with all his noble qualities, with sympathy which feels for the most debased, with benevolence which extends not only to other men but to the humblest living creature, with his godlike intellect which has penetrated into the movements and constitution of the solar system—with all these exalted powers—Man still bears in his bodily frame the indelible stamp of his lowly origin."

~ Charles Darwin, *The Descent of Man*

~ a fronte praecipitium a tergo lupi ~

I dream of a canyon. There is wind and water and darkness, and from that darkness arises a terrible desire to throw myself into Her depths. There are wolves all around me, closing in with shining red eyes, and I know that the only way out is through. And I am afraid because She, the vast hole in the ground, is my carnivorous Mother.

I am awake before the impact and every time I am calling for someone. I believe it's for my father.

(September)

I have to admit I was impressed. Every now and then, when the good doctor would remember that I was a person capable of participating in intelligent conversation, he would pour glasses of red wine and enthral me with tales of his time spent in Zaire, as it was called then. He was quite an accomplished storyteller with a voice that flowed from his throat as smoothly as the wine went down mine. Listening to him speak was by far the easiest and most enjoyable part of my job.

Now, perhaps it is a bitter thing to say, but since I'd left my father's house I'd encountered no shortage of self-centred people who droned on and on recounting their fabulously dull victories as though I had no real life of my own. Thank god they were there to save me from my own tedious experiences by allowing me to share in theirs, second-hand, of course.

And this is how it went, time and time again. People were dull and grey, reminding me of the smog-stained windows I'd looked out as a child. In a factory town, everything and everyone is covered in the same filthy sheen.

I'd just about given up the hope of ever feeling any way other than jaded and numb when I met Dr Grace. I would have never believed that I could be content living vicariously through another until I came to be in his employ, but I happily lived that way for some time. Of course, I was much younger then and his wine and words were enough.

Really, just being away from the looming presence of smoke stacks was enough.

He struck me as a curious and solitary man, and I found his tired and worn face to be as captivating as his stories. It may have been those heavenly lines that would be my eventual undoing.

In the first few months as his assistant—he never called me his maid, but he rarely called me by name, either, and I sometimes wondered if he remembered my name at all—it was unusual to see him leave the house, and never did I see him entertain guests. No family ever rang and I didn't ask any questions; no one ever rang me, either. Only the occasional colleague would write or phone, and even that was rare. These exchanges, from what I could hear, were always brief and enigmatic, coolly civilized at best. Dr Grace appeared to be the loneliest man I'd ever met. I imagined him to be suffering greatly beneath his weathered skin, desperate for someone to come along and release him from his isolated prison.

It was necessary for me, in those days, to assign such emotional handicaps and social deficiencies to anyone who intimidated me so that I might spare my own ego. And I should make it understood, before this goes any farther, that no one on this earth knows better than I how incredibly self-absorbed I was, which explains why I immediately believed that fate had brought me to him. I was to be his salvation. I would be the one to free him. It did not occur to me then that he could have possibly been content with his quiet life. I had no way of knowing that his withdrawal from the outside world was not so much a disadvantage to him, but a necessary benefit to society; but I was a naïve girl in those days, greatly lacking imagination.

I recognize that it may be presumptuous for me to assume that anyone should care to hear my story, but believe me when I say there are vital lessons to be learned here. Perhaps they were only meant for me, though I doubt it. I doubt it very much. But there I go, talking about myself again—truly, it's like a sickness—when this time was to be reserved for the doctor. These words are for him.

⨠

The Grace family estate, much like its only heir, was isolated, as the houses in stories like these always are. The Tudor manor lay hidden behind a shallow grove of evergreens at the end of a private, serpentine road. A forest, dense and lush, fortressed the house on three sides, yielding its growth just enough to allow for a clearing, carpeted with fading greens of varying hues. I've been told there is a farm beyond the woods to the east, though you cannot see it from the house. Dr Grace called it modest though it remains the most beautiful home in which I've ever been.

The rooms were like those found in museums, though much less cold and sterile. White walls with mahogany trim were tastefully decorated with paintings and weavings, while a vast array of sculptures lined the various tables and slate sills. The doctor, or perhaps an ancestor, was a collector, and a rather serious one at that. No matter where I stood I found myself encircled by virgins, goddesses, demons and martyrs—religious icons of all denominations—ornate furniture, antique medical equipment displayed as works of art, and books—entire walls carved out into shelves for hundreds of books. The ancient world was alive and well within the walls of the Grace house.

As enthralling as I found the house and its specimens of exotic religions and medicine to be—really, I could go and on and never do it justice—I suppose I should start this tale from what is ostensibly the beginning. And although the story really began long before any of us were born, this is where it began for me.

I met Dr Grace through a referral from the cleaning service I worked for. I was hired by said service on a temporary basis at my own request, having no desire to live out my years in the same manner as the two women who owned the business. I never got to know them particularly well, but could tell enough by observation alone. They were divorced, discarded by their husbands in the throes of mid-life crises for younger and thinner models, a fact that did not at all help endear me to them, as I was also younger and thinner. But after many tumultuous nights in lonely beds, they traded in their tears and bitter chocolates for self-help books and feminist propaganda—nothing too edgy, mind you. No spirit-invoking bonfires or lesbianism or any other such *nonsense*. Before long they had picked themselves up, thrown on some sensible yet fashionable running suits and started a business that put their only real skills—aside from giving me disapproving glares laced with hints of resentment—to work. If they could no longer keep tidy homes for their husbands, then they'd bloody well straighten up everyone else's.

I knew they didn't care much for me from the very start and I wasn't at all surprised when they put me on such a time consuming job. They said it was a large undertaking but it would be worth it for the money and that I should take care to stash away as much money as I could because one day I wouldn't be so youthful and once the sagging began I shouldn't count upon a husband to honour any of the bloody promises he made to keep me and support me through all things, good and bad—including the gradual onset of jowls, the dreaded thickening up through the middle, and that short, kicky hair style that claims to thin you about the face and neck—practical *and* age appropriate, so say all the salons and tabloids. But, that was merely their advice to me and of course I could do as I pleased with my earnings, but it would be a right shame to see me end

up as they did, and I agreed with them wholeheartedly. I suppose I could have
appreciated their advice had it felt even a little sincere, but it was delivered to me
wrapped in a certain smugness that suggested they couldn't wait for the day to come
that I found myself bitter, shapeless, and utterly alone. But in the end I swallowed
my pride and took the job, grateful to spend my days out of their company.

Upon my arrival at the house I understood what they meant by 'large undertaking.'
I always thought those sorts of places came with their own domestic services included,
and expected to be greeted by an elderly butler, but it was the doctor who opened the
colossal oak door himself.

After a few overwhelming moments inside and some brief small talk, Dr Grace
confessed he was actually looking for someone to be a live-in 'personal assistant,'
which didn't sound quite right to me then, either, and with a nervous laugh admitted
his plans of stealing me away from the service, with ample compensation of course.
He said he would have taken out an advert in the local paper but feared what manner
of bizarre soul might reply. I remarked quietly that he must not have actually met
with my employers, then found myself awkwardly trying to explain the joke as he
stared at me with a look of polite confusion, followed by an even more polite and
sympathetic smile.

Kindly ignoring my awkwardness, he went on to explain how this would be a full
time situation and, in addition to caring for the house, he desperately needed someone
to attend to his personal errands. He explained that he was in the midst of a very
crucial project and barely found the time to feed himself any more. I would receive
a weekly allowance and any additional funds required for housekeeping, as well as
private living quarters on the western end of the second floor. Only the kitchen would
be shared, though I would be free to roam in most areas of the house at my own
discretion. If I agreed, there would be a three-week trial period and then, assuming all
was well, he would have a contract drawn up for a year's employ. He sped through the
terms of the arrangement so quickly I believed he must have practised it over and over
again before I arrived. When he spoke it was flawless.

It all seemed simple enough. I needed work, and this was a beautiful place. And
really, what else did I have? A rundown flat, a non-existent relationship with my father,
and no real friends to speak of. All things considered, I should have been ecstatic.
Everything was about to change. But as grateful as I was, there was something familiar,
something torrid stirring inside of me.

I have a secret that I feel would be appropriate to share at this time, as odd as it
may seem, but way down in my stomach lives a creature that is fond of lighting fires. It
does this to make me aware. Sometimes the fires signal me to run, sometimes they tell

me to stay still and quiet. But mostly they just *tell me* and allow me to make my own decisions. In these fires I am shown pictures—rather, flashes of pictures, though most of the time I manage to convince myself it's merely a daydream. I used to try to share these pictures with others, but quickly found that I was cursed like Cassandra, fated to be met with ridicule and stern looks from my parents.

It has been this way since I can remember.

But I have always been filled with red—red fires, red flags and deep, scarlet burning. Red is the colour of things like mistrust and anger. Red is a warning. The idea is a bit obvious, I know, the way that envy is *always* green and cowardice is always yellow and just as orange-yellow is disgust that begins in your stomach but rises to your throat and purple is resentment—though I may have made up the latter—but those reds...they have made it difficult for people who would lie to me; they have made it difficult to lie to myself, though when I do—and I *always* do—I know I will be burned from the inside out.

Of course this *gift* is futile if I ignore it. Only after I have dismissed the fires and run straight into the mouth of turmoil do I wonder why, *oh why* didn't I trust my instinct? If only I had paid mind to the burning, if only I'd acknowledged the flags, if only I'd *just this once* really looked at the picture, remembered the dream, or learned from my mistake, but no...I didn't believe in psychic powers. I didn't believe that intuition was anything other than fear and in that, I was absolved.

So often these gifts are wasted on the stubborn, the skeptics, and the ignorant, and I am no exception. To this day I still don't know what the fire meant to tell me as I made my decision, but it raged for a moment so fervently that I thought I might combust and take that beautiful house and her beautiful owner with me. But the embers have long settled and cooled now. I moved in the next morning.

There is a large tapestry in Dr Grace's bedroom, directly above his bed. It is filled with ancient threads of red and coppery orange. A horned god smeared with the blood of his sacrifice dances through a fire, displaying an embarrassingly large erect phallus. Above him, three figures in white and blue hover like pornographic angels. A barely pubescent girl, nude and aloof extends her hand downward to the god. Beside her a pregnant woman glowing like the moon lounges, nearly penetrated by the antlers below and to her left a mature and indignant woman holds a child in one arm and a spear in the other, in a startling display of strength. All three women sit, legs apart, the first with crimson thread sewn between her thighs, the last two with blue, exposed genitalia. If you press your face to the fabric, you can still smell the old London market wherein the wool and saffron and silks were purchased a very long time ago. Dr Grace lies beneath this each night and releases his dream to weave itself into the pagan scene. He dreams of terrible things.

❦

Our trial period ended without incident. I spent my free time slinking through the house carefully studying his collections. There was an abundance of silence throughout the days so that when the doctor would finally speak, his smooth and sedate voice shattered through the quiet like a car crash. He would always offer his apologies for this. There were other moments when I would talk to myself just to make sure I remembered the sound of my voice. At night I read aloud in my room, much like a child. I was grateful that Dr Grace's bedroom was too far away for him to hear me.

In many other awkward moments, he would enter the room, hesitate for a minute and then leave, as though he had meant to speak but couldn't find the words. I wanted to find my own words in those moments, but my mouth was always empty and dry, so I just smiled meekly and he would smile meekly and that would be the end of it.

Timing is everything to a man like Dr Grace and throughout the first few months the time to get to know each other was never right. In the beginning it seemed like just having another heartbeat in the house was enough for him.

❦

(*December*)

Christmas came, as it always does, and he asked if I'd planned to take a holiday. Having no one to make plans with, I let him know that I would stay, if he so desired. He stated, much to my delight, that he would enjoy my company, as there was no family gathering for him to attend either.

He looked so small for a moment, a bit malnourished and tired. He rarely ate or slept and I grew concerned that he was suffering from a winter depression. Already I fussed over him, surprising myself with such an immediate attachment.

It was just after Christmas that we began our tradition of talking over his extensive collection of wine and spirits. In the beginning this made me a bit nervous. His presence often caused me to feel like I was drowning in a most pleasant way, but drowning nonetheless. I was not at my best anyway; New Years had always been an unpleasant time for me and despite the exhilaration brought on by the doctor's casual banter and attentions, that year was no exception.

I told him about my life in fifteen minutes, trying to leave out the boring details and trite revelations of my twenty-five years. I didn't tell him about the dreams or flags. I didn't tell him then about any of the red things that had been haunting me since I could remember. I kept it light, unemotional. He asked why I had chosen to be a domestic, and I could have told him the truth—that I, just like the employers I'd ridiculed for the very same reason, had no real abilities or useful skills—but instead I came up with the less painful, yet still self-effacing reason that if I spent all my time cleaning up other people's lives I wouldn't have time to clean up my own. He suggested I go into psychology and make ten times the money I made now.

He listened so well, resting his mouth on the fleshy part of his palm, raising an eyebrow here and there at the appropriate moments. When I managed to make him laugh or smile, I considered it a tiny victory. More than once I caught myself becoming entranced by his face, barely remembering to finish my sentences. I never felt comfortable looking people in the eyes, but that night I had to force myself to focus on the heavily lacquered oak tabletop to keep from staring at him. I watched his dark reflection, and pretended that I would turn to stone if I looked upon him in the flesh.

In talking about myself I suddenly became very aware of my own voice, honing in on the cracks and imperfections. This was unexpected, as talking about myself had always been such an easy task. Abruptly I asked him to take his turn. The burning inside of me was becoming too painful to bear.

Dr Edward Grace was not the kind of man you could simply learn about. He was, and is, the sort of creature that must be studied, even dissected. Of course, you can gather bits of information and fact, as I did, though really it was nothing more than a general timeline, and an incomplete one at that.

He said that he was born in 1953. His late parents had no other children. He mentioned flatly that he'd never married nor raised any children of his own. His mother and grandparents, all of whom lived rather solitary lives, raised him in this house, which had been built by his great-grandfather. He said he would forever be amazed at how quiet the house could be at times.

At the height of his medical career he'd been a prominent obstetrician, though he'd begun as a scientist, becoming a leading researcher at a very young age in prenatal pharmaceuticals. Before settling down with a practice of his own, he'd spent five years during the 1980's acting as head physician at a Red Cross sponsored prenatal and women's health clinic in the country known then as Zaire.

He spoke of his love of ancient cultures and religious artefacts, and how it eventually led him to pursue a second degree, this time in Theology, thus sparking such a fascination with African mysticism. I marvelled at the dedication and discipline it must have taken to accomplish so much so quickly. He responded humbly, saying that he'd had nothing better to do.

"People are quick to assume, foolishly, that if you come from money, life is automatically more exciting and fulfilling," he said. "But money is boring. It means nothing unless you do something purposeful with it. So I bought an education."

As quickly as I learned that knowing this basic information and truly knowing Dr Grace were two very different animals, it would still not be quick enough. Had I been listening to the distant crackling of flames in the hollow space between my stomach and my spine, I would have known it that very night. Of course, his voice was far more appealing than the very unmelodic sound of suffocating intuition.

I asked him to tell me about Africa.

His eyes glimmered at the very thought. "My time in Zaire..."

He spoke of the people he encountered, the creatures of the Congo and those far to the south on the Botswana plains, the children he delivered, the unending sky above the clinic that he would stare into after a birth. Never had he witnessed such quiet sunrises or seen such dark night skies. "Even the stillborn are blessed in Zaire, to be released into such a magnificent space. Their path to the heavens completely unobstructed," he mused.

The land had bestowed upon him a gift, so he said, an understanding not to be found anywhere else. In Zaire he learned where the body ends and the spirit begins. I didn't pretend to understand what he meant that night, but I knew whatever his secret was, it brought him more joy than most people ever find. Or at the very least, it had the potential to.

Dr Grace spends many nights staring into the cold black sky outside the large window of his bedroom, scrutinizing it as though it was an inferior replica of the one that covers Africa. The stars are not the same to him here. They are flawed, maybe dimmer. While he understands he cannot transport the stars of his beloved third world, he is consoled by the secret he has been able to bring home. It would be some time before that secret would be revealed to me. In the meantime, the three of us lived in quiet anticipation, Dr Grace, his dreaming, and myself.

(February)

In the midst of all the papers and research and secrecy my life slipped into a comfortable routine. I had menial tasks to keep me occupied throughout the days; dusting the bookshelves and the half million sculptures and valuable trinkets alone could devour most of my waking hours. The cautious method necessary for handling them slowed me down even more, but in this weekly ritual I found myself becoming very familiar with every piece, learning which deity was which and from where and so on. I began to memorize the names of authors and the books they penned, although for the most part I couldn't tell you a thing about the book itself. Regardless, this wealth of useless knowledge fostered my ever-growing delusion that I was extremely intelligent and well read.

Weekly, I would venture away from the doctor's timeless world and back into the realm of the waking dead—the market. I suppose it wasn't so terrible, really. Going out on errands made me appreciate my new home that much more, and I'd get to take the car, which I enjoyed. I noticed that the doctor began to make fewer requests for my trips to Chapel, the local market, but insisted that I purchase only the healthiest foods and ample supplies of vitamins for myself. He had a vested interest in my health habits, drawing frequent examples from his days at the Zaire clinic. The women were often so malnourished and he was amazed, he said, at the toll a simple vitamin deficiency could take on a woman's body.

When he felt I was not heeding his advice to the fullest he would resort to graphic scare tactics, telling me in a most ominous voice of the ravaged conditions in which the local women had come to him. The distended stomachs as a result of starvation, the lesions on the legs and bellies of victims of scurvy, the hair loss and rotted teeth, infestation, worms "of the ring and tape variety," he teased, following it with a sinister laugh and scowling face, the way a grandfather might end any decent tale of terror passed down from the generations.

I would finally relent with amusement and disgust when tales of parasite-ridden colons and intestinal tracts were recounted and Dr Grace would revel in his victory with smug satisfaction. However, this did not negate the fact that I became healthier with each passing day, feeling better than I could ever recall, while he seemed to care less about his own eating and sleeping habits.

The doctor's moods were extreme at times, though not difficult to predict. If I found him in his study, then it was usually best to refrain from any playful remarks or casual gestures. In this room he was cold and withdrawn. Conversely, any humming or whistling on his part could be taken as my cue to incite frivolous banter and silliness. I laughed more in those moments than I had in the better part of twenty years, and although I would have vehemently denied it at the time, an outside party—had there been such an entity in our world—would have surely seen our antics as the obvious flirtations that they were.

∽

The winter sun was pale and ineffective, leaving the darkness to linger on almost painfully. I slept lightly in the Grace house, always feeling the eyes of the gods and goddesses on my body. It was difficult to sleep and dream in purity—as though I'd just come from the convent—with Bacchus keeping vigil over my bed, and I wondered if the placement was intentional. Many nights I would wander through the halls and out to the ivy-smothered courtyard beyond the kitchen. I felt so small in his house and even smaller under Dr Grace's sky. We were so far away from the rest of the world. Only by looking to the south on the darkest nights could I see the dim orange haze of the town rising above the trees beyond the black silhouette of the house. Sitting on a marble bench near a dormant fountain of angels, I would retreat from the motionless eyes of the painted deities inside only to find myself caught in the gaze of another collection of gods above.

There were closer eyes as well, not so distant as the heavens, that watched me on those nights from a large, dimly lit window at the opposite end of the courtyard. They were the same eyes that closed briefly each night under a woven display of fire and blood; eyes that grew increasingly tired of the second rate stars above us.

I suppose I had little room to protest, as I was becoming a bit of a voyeur myself. After my chores were done each day I would read from the doctor's library or examine the artefacts that interested me. It was the cross-cultural imagery that fascinated me the most. Religions formed of unlikely unions. Tribal icons fused with so-called *civilised* symbols of faith.

One painting in particular commanded my attention every time I passed by. It was small and wildly coloured, the way a child sees things—only in crayon hues. The piece featured an astonishingly beautiful and peculiar woman in blue robes, and it took me a bit of research to decipher her title and purpose. I would learn later that she was part Virgin Mary and part *Erzulie*, Mary's *Voudoun* counterpart. She had a star at her shoulder for Stella Maris and stood under the triple moon of Diana. For a collaged goddess, she was remarkable. She was every Mother. She was very old. It gave me chills to stand before her.

When I grew weary of those objects, I turned my attention to the doctor, as he fascinated me even more than his collections. A tiny burst of heat and electricity shot through me as I caught myself staring a little too long into his study one afternoon. I wasn't hidden, but the doctor was lost in his papers and I realised I was in no danger of being discovered. I watched him work so feverishly; the rapid pace in which he wrote left me curious and weary.

He worked this way each day, disappearing for lengthy periods of time into his provisional laboratory. Like Bluebeard's tragically curious wife, I had my forbidden room. At the doctor's request and my discretion, I kept away from the lab. Even the study, which I was permitted to enter, left me uneasy. I made a point of only visiting that room if necessary. More often than not I would linger in the doorway only long enough to get whatever it was I came for, usually just to ask if he was hungry. As I said before, Dr Grace was less kind then, never giving me more than a one or two word response.

So from the living room I found I could see him, or more truthfully *watch* him, working at his desk, far enough away so as not to be intrusive. His lips would move every few pages and he would roll his chair to and from a nearby bookshelf, searching for information. I kept waiting for him to breathe, but he was far too busy to be troubled. Again I noticed how small and meek he appeared, worn down and distant. It was so strange to see him this way when at other times he appeared so tall, well sculpted, and aware.

Men like Dr Grace are not impetuous, they carefully choose their passions. They do not waste precious time on dead end causes or flights of fancy. Any good doctor knows life is far too short for that. I wanted to ask him what he meant that night he spoke of Africa. I wanted to know what provoked such intense behaviours in him these days. I yearned to know what he knew, this secret he guarded so carefully. That he would not share was killing me.

(*March*)

As weeks passed, Dr Grace grew ever reclusive, no longer bothering to return the few calls that still came. He said that just before my arrival he announced his impending retirement from the practice. There were more than enough competent physicians at his office now, he reasoned, and things would run smoothly enough without him. Within the month he officially withdrew from patient care. He made no mention to his colleagues of his unofficial return to research.

Rarely did he come to the dining room for meals any more and on those exceptional occasions he only picked at the food I prepared. One evening, after losing my patience and thus forgetting my place, I chided him on his poor eating habits. With visible irritation, he produced a few bottles of dietary supplements from a drawer and slammed them on the desktop.

"All right then," I said. "So you have vitamins. You can't survive on those."

"I *have* been known to eat on occasion. Just because you aren't there to witness it doesn't mean it doesn't happen. Are you over my shoulder every moment of the day? I participate in plenty of activities that you don't bear witness to, and for that matter, I hired you to assist me with this house, not to be my nanny."

I suppose it was by accident, though I don't believe in accidents any more, that I saw the small opened case in the corner of the drawer, nearly hidden by his papers. Inside was an antique syringe. I tried to turn my eyes from it before he noticed, though by the look on his face I was certain he'd seen. I doubt my troubled expression did a proper job of hiding anything, either.

"I get what I need," he said. "Now may I continue with my work, Nurse?"

The needle made me burn deep inside. Never would it have entered my mind that Dr Grace could be an addict. I'd heard it said somewhere that drug abuse was commonplace among doctors and chemists, but this knowledge did not lessen the sorrow I immediately felt.

"Forgive me for being concerned," I whispered and left the room.

"Let us remember which of us is the doctor here," he called after me without looking up.

I was certain there was a small trace of guilt in his voice and a few hot tears rolled down my face so quickly that they left no trail.

Late into the night, as I settled into my bed, there was a soft knock at my door, followed by an even softer apology. I wanted to answer him but couldn't find the words. We were bickering so much these days, and over what? He owed me nothing; I was not his wife nor mother, but still it felt so unnatural for me not to care. He was a junkie and from the looks of it, beginning to lose control. Isn't that what they'd taught us in school? It begins with experimentation, which becomes a growing dependency and then spirals down to the inevitable demise.

I was growing weary of my concern being met only by sarcasm and quick verbal slaps in the face. Why couldn't he see that I only wanted to make sure that he was well? *Perhaps* that was his real reason for employing me, after all? *Perhaps* he was a man too proud to overtly ask for help. *Perhaps I should make a promise to myself, and to Dr Grace, that I would care for him and aid him in working through his addiction. This would be my new mission. Not to be confused, of course, with my primary mission of saving him from painful isolation.*

But at some point in the night, I stumbled to the lavatory, wherein I caught a glimpse of myself in the mirror. Despite the glaring white light or that hazy film sleep brings to your eyes, I saw myself clearly for the first time in years. I saw my declaration of righteousness and my smug certainty of the situation. I saw the conceit and the self-serving motivations. Then I saw the insecurity, the need to feel useful, the need to have purpose. It was incredibly ugly.

Who do you think you are? When did you become a saviour? I fought the urge to turn away from my own face. *You have no idea about the reality of this situation. He might have been addicted for twenty years for all you know. Why would he turn to you for help? Or he might not actually be addicted to anything at all and if you weren't such a self-centred little prig, you'd realise that and keep to what you're good at—scrubbing toilets and sweeping floors.*

I whispered soft obscenities to the girl in the mirror and went back to bed.

The next night as I prepared to eat my dinner alone—the perfectly miserable end to a perfectly miserable day—Dr Grace appeared in the doorway of the dining room. I had not spoken to him at all that day due to my frustration and anger. I was embarrassed by my thoughts and decided to stay quiet, for fear that I might say something stupid. "I thought I might join you tonight...if there's anything left...to eat, I mean." He kept his hands in his pockets like a little boy.

I let him stand there for a few moments while I stared at my plate, eventually replying that there was. The silent space between our words was painful. He started to the kitchen to fix a plate, but I rose from the table and gently pushed past him. "I've got it," I said, looking at the floor. "Go on. It'll just be a moment."

He remarked, with a smile, that I made for a wonderfully embittered housewife. I wanted to return the smile, but in my head a million words rushed through like wind. *How long have you been an addict what are you shooting into your veins why would you do this to yourself what about your career what about the people that love you what about me?*

The questions came to a sudden halt. This had nothing to do with me. I had tried so hard not to think about myself. Instead, "I would have filed for a divorce by now," was all I said.

"It's said that the good ones are always taken for granted," he replied.

After dinner we had one of our talks and some very old cognac to ease our troubles and all was somewhat right in the world once again.

"Ready, love?"

Those were the words he spoke in my dream that night.

I nodded quickly. 'Love'? He called me 'love', but then again, so did everyone in these parts.

"It's nothing more than an affectation. It doesn't mean he loves you, Kate."

"And please...I told you not to call me that. It's not my name. You're my mother, you ought to know that." I looked around only to see the doctor. "My mother...she's not even here is she?" I felt ashamed and confused.

"No, love. She's *never* been here." He smiled. "There is a gown for you on the chair...I'll give you a moment." He turned his head away.

I undressed in haste and slid onto a sleek red chair with chrome stirrups. "All right then..." I chirped in a ridiculous high-pitched tone that echoed around the cold room. He turned back and I was afraid to look at him directly. Instead I found his reflection in the steel tray table.

He smiled and said, "You can look at me. You won't turn to stone, you know."

He wasn't wearing a white coat like I had anticipated. Just his usual grey trousers and a white dress shirt with the sleeves rolled up. There was a pin on the collar of his shirt. It was a tiny red flag.

His forearms were thin and strong with large blue veins at the surface. One wrapped itself around the muscle of his entire arm. It was punctured with holes that only carpenter's nails could have made. I followed it until it disappeared under his shirt. I still couldn't look at his face.

He instructed me to lay back and try to relax. I could feel my heartbeat in my stomach and I wanted to be sick. I flinched as he put his fingers to my neck and began to palpate.

"Don't tell me that hurt." He smiled.

"Oh no, I just..."

"Merely checking for pearls," he replied.

"How's that?" I asked.

"Swollen glands. I said I'm checking for swollen glands."

"Oh. I thought you said pearls."

"Well, that would have been an odd thing to say, don't you think?"

He moved his hands down to the ties on the gown and wove the ties apart as he informed me that he'd be checking my breasts for anything unusual...like pearls.

I felt my face and neck go hot, which made me blush harder still.

He moved his fingers around the tissue; his face remained stony.

"Everything seems to be in order here...let's move on, shall we?"

I nodded in agreement and closed my eyes as he slipped the latex gloves on his hands and made his way to the end of the table. I felt his powdery hand glide across my foot, pulling it further into the stirrup, adjusting and positioning me before resuming the exam.

I awoke in a breathless fury, drenched from head to toe, and not yet able to identify the quivering in my stomach and throat as a sign of arousal.

I would have given anything to disappear that day. I hid in my room trying to make sense of what I was feeling and how I could have become so depraved. Granted, it had been a long time since I had been intimate with anyone, but this was ludicrous. After hours of shame, I grew tired of feeling the blood rush to the surface of my skin and finally crawled to some make-believe place of resolution. It had just been a dream after all and Dr Grace was the only man I interacted with any more. It was not so strange that certain *feelings* should arise, despite that fact that he was my employer and possibly a junkie. Really, it was just the way those *feelings* manifested that left me disturbed.

I knew I would have to face him that evening and decided the best approach to this would be no approach at all. Dinner would be business as usual, as this was some inane, personal drama he did not share with me. Any bizarre behaviour I might exhibit would only serve to make me look like a dolt, a hazard I carefully avoided in the doctor's presence.

Dr Grace was more congenial than usual that night. I felt a twinge of pity in his words as though he sensed my discomfort. He was cool and proper but a bit more approachable than usual. I was making far too much of a stupid dream.

On his way through the kitchen he invited me to join him at the kingly dining table when I finished with the plates. He grabbed two glasses and retreated to the dining room with a bottle of Merlot. Of all the nights to indulge our casual relationship, I thought, but perhaps he could distract me by talking of Africa. He was so descriptive at times that I felt I had been there. I could see the orange landscapes and the great dome of a sky. I could see the villages and hear the sounds of the people. I could hear the ocean on the jagged coast and hear the screams and shrieks of creatures hidden by the canopy of the jungle. Once, I saw a nature programme on the Serengeti. It showed a sunrise over the plains, scored only by a quiet swell of violins. Maybe it was the light or the melody, but it moved me to tears. It felt like the way you cry when you suddenly realise what you've lost.

I thought about Africa a great deal, especially at night. It would be some time before I realised that his stories left me with more than just an active imagination. I would eventually discover that his words were sparking the creature in my stomach to ignite many fires. Of course, by then it would be far too late to contain them. My red flags of warning were incinerated with each passing day.

At the far end of the dining hall, beyond the great mahogany table stood a cabinet decorated with turn-of-the-century heirlooms. The theme was the Hunt, depicting riders in dark greens, bone whites and browns. A small bronze fox sat erect in the midst of the decorative china plates, and a set of crystal brandy snifters occupied a corner of the cabinet. Above the cabinet hung a relief of the Green Man. His face reminded me of Bacchus on my bedroom wall. I stared at his stone face to avoid the doctor's. This was always the darkest room in the house.

"Are we all right?" His voice was delicate, cautious. It struck me painfully like a needle on bone.

"Why wouldn't we be?"

"You seem tense."

"Oh, no I'm fine." I could feel tears of embarrassment pooling in my eyes.

"Have I done something inappropriate?"

"No, you did nothing, really."

A tear dropped down on to the table. *Why can't we be talking about Africa or the weather or anything except what's wrong with me?*

"What is it then?"

I watched his dark eyes and his thin face. The lines were perfectly placed. The word 'beautiful' entered my mind, softly at first, then violent and sharp, screaming. "I really don't know..."

"You don't know or you don't wish to say?"

I thought about all of the shameful pieces of myself that were surfacing these days. The condescending revelations, the delusional ideas of my purpose, the underlying feelings and desires that laced my sleep and the truth about how little I actually knew.

The tears came quicker as I went through the list. For once I hadn't wished to give a mysterious response, but I simply couldn't find an answer that wasn't vague.

"It's just...I'm not really like this. Really, I'm not."

"Like what?"

Self-righteous, maybe. Or a stupid, insipid brat. But all I could manage was, "A bad person." I quickly covered my face.

"Of course you aren't a bad person! Why ever would you think that?"

I stared at my distorted reflection in the tabletop and shook my head. "I don't know. Please, just never mind what I said. I'm really tired." I wiped my face and promptly forced a weak smile. I regretted leaving Dr Grace feeling responsible for my discomfort and I went to bed that night full of wine and guilt.

He remains at the table for some time, drinking and petting the little bronze fox. He holds it close to his eyes until it is a golden blur. He puts it to his lips, savouring the cold metal; then touches it with his tongue. To keep from laughing he bites down lightly on it's muzzle and holds it there in his teeth until the urge is gone.

I am sick of dreaming.

I was choking in the dust, waiting on a dry plateau under an orange moon. I could taste the grit in my teeth. A tent stood in the distance, the tarp shivering in the freezing desert wind. Red sequined flags whipped violently around on their poles. The stars were brilliant. I pulled my only covering around my face. It was the tapestry from the doctor's wall. When the sandstorm died, I found myself inside the tent.

Dr Grace sat in the corner behind his desk. He asked me what the problem was. I told him I didn't know and I was confused. I'd been trying to write down the song that the violins were playing, the very same one from the television programme, but I couldn't get it right. I don't even know how to play the violin.

He beckoned me to the exam table and took the tapestry from me, leaving me naked and exposed. "There's the problem," he said, pushing my knees apart. This time he wore no gloves.

Between them, pink viscous fluid covered my thighs. With my hand I followed the trail up to my groin. The substance coated my hand, pulsing in its thickest consistency. I looked to him desperate for an explanation.

"It's simply too soon," he said, "You weren't ready yet. Do you remember how it goes?"

"How what goes?"

"The song. How do you expect to write it down when you can't even remember how it goes?"

He collected an ounce of the fluid in a vile, took out his syringe and turned away.

"I remembered it yesterday. What's happening to us?"

He turned to face me, moving in very close. On his arm a series of track marks, red and flared, were exposed. "Don't trouble yourself with it, love. I'll get what I need," he said as he pressed his hand between my legs. A fire burned outside the tent and another red flag went up in flames.

(*April*)

Dr Grace disappeared into his papers again. I delivered two plates of food to his study each day. More often than not, the plates would return to me untouched. Nothing personal, he offered. This irritated me more than usual as I was suffering from a lack of sleep. The dreams were growing stranger and getting harder to recover from. At least three times in the past few months alone I'd had the canyon dream and now these disturbing scenarios featuring the doctor seemed to be the newest trend. I was losing my appetite as well.

"Are you sick?" he asked one evening.

"I'm just tired. Should I bother to leave this plate or should I just take it away now?"

"You look thin. Are you eating enough?"

"Why? Am I foiling your secret plan?"

"What do you mean by that?" he snapped.

"The one to fatten me up and cook me in a stew?" I grinned. "What did you think I meant?" I could feel the smile fading from my face.

"I asked you a question."

"Why are you so bloody concerned about my health? Are you trying to insure that I'll be well enough to care for you when you've wasted away to nothing!"

"You can take the plate away now, thank you, I'll get something later," was all he said.

I stormed to the kitchen and threw the plate into the steel sink. It shattered into several large segments, the food splattering up the side of the basin. I sat down at the small wooden table in the alcove and began to sob, knowing very well that I was a bit too old to be throwing temper tantrums.

Sometime later Dr Grace came into the kitchen. He slid onto the bench across from me, smiling and looking around coyly, as though nothing was wrong. "I'm in the mood for a celebration," he said.

"Really."

"Let's just say I believe I've found what I've been searching for."

"And what's that?"

"I'll tell you if you wash your face. Your mascara is a disaster. Meet me in the dining hall. I'll bring the libations." He brushed his hand through my hair playfully as he left the table.

My heart jumped. He'd never touched me that way before.

"I'm sorry about your dish...the one I broke," I said.

With a kind smile he said it was fine.

"Tell me what you believe in?" He smiled, having asked such a weighty question, then watched with great amusement as I stumbled over my words.

"What do you mean, exactly?" (This had been so eloquently preceded by a series of 'hmms' and 'umms,' a great deal of lip-biting, thoughtful nail chewing, and an intense scrutiny of the ceiling).

"Would you say you are a religious girl?"

I tried to keep the unintelligible noises to a minimum while I pondered this.

"Is this a topic you'd rather not discuss with me?"

"No. I mean to say... *no*, I don't mind talking to you. And I suppose I'd have to say no, about being religious, that is."

He remained patient as I continued to spew out my half-formed ideas.

"Well, I mean...I don't *disbelieve* in an afterlife or spiritual...*things*, really. I just don't follow any sort of organized religion."

"Do you believe in the existence of a soul?"

"I suppose I do," I paused to consider this, "but I have no proof." It was a stupid answer. To believe in something, to have faith, implied that you didn't need proof, you simply believe it to be so.

"No, we don't have proof. Science has failed us there. So all verification aside, what do you feel?"

I took a sip from the paper-thin crystal he'd placed before me and half considered biting it in hopes of creating such a distraction that we'd have to end the discussion at once so he could sew my lip back together.

"I suppose I think that all living things have souls. Rather, I think *I* have a soul, therefore everything else must as well."

My words were, yet again, maliciously exposing my ignorance, but I decided against the glass-biting plan as I'd already broken one dish that evening. Two would've been excessive.

"Fair enough," he replied. "Now, what do you think a soul might be made of?"

I wondered where he was going with this. I shrugged, not liking this question and answer session at all. *What is a soul made of? Painful memories. Ugly truths. Fear. Suicide letters. Bits of ashes, snips and snails. How the hell should I know?* Instead, all I could say was, "Energy, I suppose."

He gave me a curious look and nodded, "Yes, and possibly chemicals—chemicals that trigger all of those intangible pieces of human existence. Memory, intellect, dreams, emotion—all of those wonderful, terrible things we feel. The flutter in our stomachs, the lump in our throats, the weight of the world on our shoulders, the burning in our hearts."

I didn't breathe as he spoke.

"There is a beautiful synchronicity that exists between the body and the earth. Do you know what laylines are?"

I said no, as I'd only heard the expression before, and didn't thoroughly understand the concept.

"Streams of energy that run through the earth and pool in various auspicious places. Or perhaps places become auspicious because of laylines," he chuckled. "The chicken or the egg, right? No matter. My point is that there is a correlation in the human body. I have reason to believe that the chemical reactions that make up the thing we call the 'soul' act in much the same way, and if we can locate such auspicious places in the body, we are that much closer to locating, therefore defining the soul. And there you have the first tiny step into some very unknown territory. Can you even imagine it?" His eyes glimmered wildly.

As he spoke, the apprehension I felt began to melt away. I understood why he had been so revered by his colleagues once. He was thorough and clear in his explanations and kept my full attention in the manner of a great storyteller. I so enjoyed his voice. He continued on for hours, teaching me about energy, eastern medicine, and his further theories of the soul. I thought he would speak of Africa then, but he didn't. Some of his ideas were quite fantastic, but his delivery was convincing enough that I readily accepted it as scientific truth. To Dr Grace, the line between physiology and spirituality was almost non-existent. This was the sort of thinking that created fierce debate in the scientific community, and the doctor had certainly seen his share of criticism at the very mention of the matter, but his response was a concise and solid one. He said, "When you have witnessed what I have witnessed, it becomes undeniably clear that those who would denounce science are trapped by their ignorance, and those who would denounce spirituality have been poisoned by their fear." He paused, smiling very slightly to himself. Then he said, "And I do not consider myself to be an ignorant or fearful man."

I dream of a canyon and then I am awake.

My understanding of the world began to change in the early morning hours, much like a heavy curtain had been lifted just enough for me to see a glimpse of what lay beyond. Or perhaps just enough to show me there was something beyond it to see in the first place. Just before dawn I awoke, confused and drenched from the canyon dream, certain I'd heard wolves crying throughout the night. My mind raced as I wandered to the courtyard, still affected by the nightmare, but more by the doctor's voice.

I'd never minded the grey this early. It could become tiresome day after day, but I derived a great sense of peace from the ashen dawn sky. The air was never cleaner at the estate than just before the sunrise.

I pulled the heavy shirtsleeves over my hands and sat on the marble bench. The cold stone bit my legs through the flimsy pyjama shorts I wore. I'd nicked them from a former boyfriend, whose face had since faded from my memory. Most of them had faded, rather swirled together to create some strange boyfriend archetype. I wished they'd meant more to me, but that sort of wishing only led to more pain, so I decided it best to let them wash away into the background. More than one of them had said I was cold. At the time I preferred the word 'cautious,' but what did it matter anyway? If I didn't care, I was cold. If I cared, I probably would've come off too needy. Either way, I'm certain they all wrote me off as mental at some point or another.

It was a trait I'd picked up inadvertently from my mother (besides being mental)— to do whatever it is you need to do because you simply can't worry how it may affect everyone around you. So perhaps I was cold, but I could say with certainty that I'd never given away more than I could afford to lose. I suppose I'd never given away much at all.

I wondered what time it was in Africa. I wondered how I ended up here. As I looked around at the walls that enclosed the sacred space, I tried to imagine the doctor as a child, playing on the grounds, exploring and discovering. I didn't want to think about myself again for a while.

Beyond the courtyard lay a clearing and a large slate swimming pool. After years of neglect it had surfaced on the lawn like a gaping wound. No longer suitable for swimming, it became the home to a million breeds of fungus and algae, a paradise for birds and tadpoles. Not terribly far beyond that the woodlands began. The trees formed a lush wall across the hilly landscape. Had it not been for the unprovoked fear that welled up in my heart, I might have gone exploring. Never before had I been frightened of the woods in real life, but in dreams there were *always* beasts and holes to consider. So, as beautiful as it was, I kept my distance, not leaving the shadow of the house. Suddenly, I felt exposed. I turned to face the second floor window in time to see a thin shape dart into the interior of the room. He was watching me again and it chilled me colder than the air itself. I tried to hold onto that feeling for the rest of the day.

Dr Grace would continue the prelude to his discovery that evening at dinner. He told me it wasn't the sort of thing he could explain in a few hours. There would be years worth of information to be discussed in due time.

Of course I was eager to find out about the secret he had been dedicated to for so long, but now I had yet another assignment—one that involved me. I needed to find a way to bring up all the spying. Kind soul that I was, I didn't want to embarrass him, so I'd have to be subtle. I needed to steer the conversation in a personal direction and as much as I dreaded it, I was prepared to confess a portion of my own secret attraction. I prayed to find the tact I would need to pull it off. After several false starts, I began a few moments in to our meal.

"You were up early this morning."

"So were you." He hadn't missed a beat. He glanced up at me as he sipped his wine.

I paused, suddenly unsure of what to say next. "I couldn't sleep...I thought I saw you watching me."

Already this was not going the way I'd planned. My anxiety was obvious. The doctor, on the contrary, was perfectly calm. He nodded confirmation, as though it were the most obvious thing in the world.

I choked a mouthful of wine down my constricted throat.

"I only mention it because it seems you've watched me a few times when I've been in the courtyard and I was curious as to why?"

"How do you know I was watching *you*? How do you know I wasn't watching the birds?"

Well, I just assumed since I am terribly self-centred... "Oh. Right. There were birds, then?" My face was starting to burn and I could feel the beginnings of perspiration on my brow.

He smiled and waited. He waited long enough to make me feel sick before he answered.

"No. I was watching you."

Oh thank god... "Right then...anyway. I was just wondering why...you were watching me..." I trailed off, certain that I was going to die of embarrassment then and there.

He finished chewing his tiny sliver of chicken. "For the same reason you watch me, I would hope." His face was stone.

"Oh?"

He took another sip, letting me shift uncomfortably for a moment. He raised his eyes to meet my own. "Sometimes our dreams betray us, you know? Sometimes they reveal sensitive truths that we are a bit too quick to deny in our waking hours."

My hand shook violently as I reached for my wine, which I immediately spilled across the table. My face was burning a deep red and I couldn't speak. He stood up and touched my arm and the blood drained away from my head as quickly as it had come.

"Oh, come now..." He was trying not to laugh. "Goodness, look at you. You're like a ghost! There's no need to be embarrassed." He was still grinning as he dabbed at the spilt wine with his napkin.

"How did you...I mean, how could you know?" My mind raced for an explanation. Perhaps I was talking in my sleep and he overheard. It was the only thing that made sense.

"I meant about the wine. Accidents happen."

The wine. Of course he was talking about the spilt wine. "Right," I whispered. "I think I may have had too much to drink. I'm feeling a little off."

He smiled again. "You haven't had all that much to drink, but I think it's safe to say that in general you tend to be a bit off," he laughed, then straightened himself up. "But perhaps I've been unfair with all this teasing. And I never answered your question. I was watching you because you're a very lovely and unusual girl, and I enjoy lovely and unusual things." His voice was soft and kind. "It's really no more dubious than that."

I breathed out for the first time in several minutes. I still couldn't find my words. He hadn't offered an explanation and as much as I needed one, I was far too distracted by the compliment.

He filled in the space for me. "Would it be presumptuous to say there is an attraction on your part as well?"

"No," I spat out impulsively. I couldn't meet his eyes.

"No, there's no attraction or no, it's not presumptuous?"

"No..." the blood was rising up into my neck again... "it's not presumptuous." I wished he wouldn't torment me this way. I began to feel confused again, though I hadn't more than half of a glass of wine.

"In business arrangements, as a general rule, I think it unwise to indulge such personal longings. However, you must know you are more than just a business arrangement to me. I would never deem it appropriate to share my discoveries with just anyone. I believe we share something deeper or at least, we have the potential to." He smiled and reached for my hand but I pulled it away.

I struggled to prioritise the situations before me. "You haven't told me how you knew."

"How I knew what?"

"What you said about dreams..." I stopped, remembering that we had resolved the issue. Or had I just imagined that as well?

"You had a dream, did you? What was it about?"

I was turning red again and I hated him for it. "If you didn't know, why did you say that?"

He stood up and headed for the kitchen with the wine soaked linen and the glasses. "You know, I'm beginning to wonder if I haven't had too much to drink, myself. I'm not exactly clear on what you're talking about..." he trailed off as he left the room.

I was compelled to follow him, but the fire inside of me was raging out of control, worse than I could ever recall, and I thought better of it. I abruptly called out some excuse about feeling a bit ill, bade him goodnight, and locked myself in my bedroom.

It began as a light scratching at my door, just arrhythmic enough to jar me from sleep. But the scratching quickly turned to frantic scraping, and was soon accompanied by a chorus of growls and heavy, snorting breaths. Of course this was a dream, simply some kind of madness. But this wasn't the canyon or the desert. It was my room, dark and authentic. There was no eerie glow about the moonlight that crept through the window, no soft haze emanating from my skin. It was just me, in my room in a great old house at the edge of the forest. It was only me, alone in a bed with wolves at my door, poised to drag me away.

I crawled to the edge of the bed, thinking that I would make a dash for the lavatory and put one more door between the beasts and myself, but as I lowered one foot to the floor, I felt a rush of cool air swirl around my leg.

The floor was gone and my bed was perched at the edge of a black chasm. I must have screamed, certainly I screamed—what else could I have done? The winds were wild now, drowning out the din of the wolves. A violent gust whipped around me and caught a painting on the opposite wall, snapping the wire from which it hung. The painting, some bucolic landscape in oil, fell into the darkness and was no more.

There was a crashing sound at the door. I screamed at the beasts to go away, then I screamed that they should come in and fall to their deaths. Another crash, and as the door flew open, I heard him call my name.

There were no wolves. There was no wind, no canyon. Once again, it was only me, alone on my bed in a great old house at the edge of the forest, sobbing and sweating and trembling with fear. He swept me from the bed in one quick gesture and cradled me in his arms, rushing from the room as though he was rescuing me from a fire.

He took me to his room and I was still clutching him as we fell onto the bed. I wanted to speak and explain to him what happened, tell him what I saw, but there were no words. He rocked me gently and pressed his face into my matted hair. I closed my eyes and turned my head against his, afraid to look around in case the madness had followed us. As I breathed in deeply against his flesh, I felt a sense of calm come over me. It was the smell of him, triggering something in my bones, a mixture of something old and familiar. It was soap and sweat, twisted up with wisteria, molasses, warm cider, sea salt, scotch and all things sweet and bitter and earthy, all things wonderfully lush and drinkable. Things I must have known in another, happier life.

His eyes were glistening and blood-shot with deep shadows beneath them. I thought of the syringe, which inadvertently led my eyes to his arm, but any bruises he had would have been hidden by the darkness of the room. I could see the shape of his pale body, and the shape of my own body wrapped around him. I lost myself, and had not immediately realised how entwined we were. It felt like the most natural thing in the world.

There is never much spontaneity to be found in the prelude to intimacy. At least there never was for me. There is a certain point right before that first kiss or embrace when you can feel it coming, even without words. In the place where emotional chemistry becomes hard science, there is no room for uncertainty or surprise.

We didn't speak. I suppose there was nothing to be said. He brushed a wet lock of hair from my face, letting his fingers slide across my cheek and I pulled his hand to my mouth, pressing his fingers to my lips, then running my tongue along the jagged ridge of his fingernail. I could taste the salt from my tears on his hand. One of us was trembling; it was impossible to say whom. I nestled my head into his neck again and all I could taste was wine. It was coming from his pores and it seemed to make the room swirl. I felt as though I might shatter into a million pieces and slice through him. When there was no more space left between us, he weaved his fingertips through my hair and dug them into the back of my skull. I kissed him and as I expected, it was devastating.

I awoke in the grey hour of the morning. The doctor was sitting in an embroidered antique chair near the window. His gaze was alternating between the smouldering landscape and me. I felt like royalty on the massive feather bed, wrapped up in the thick, white duvet.

"Did you sleep well?"

"Very." I curled up tighter in the warmth of the bed and smiled, despite the dull ache that ran down my back and into my legs. He was stronger than I thought he'd be and the knotted wooden headboard had been less than kind. I'd imagined him to be the passive missionary type, but I'd been mistaken.

"I'd forgotten how much I enjoyed that." He was blushing as he spoke, reminding me of a young boy.

I sat up to share the morning view. "Last night...there was just so much. Our discussion. That horrible dream..."

"There will be time for that. It's too important to be rushed through. These things are best left to take their own course." He left his chair and sat behind me on the bed. His fingers brushed through the back of my hair. "Are you all right?"

"Yeah, I think so."

"Are you...all right...with this?" He kissed my neck.

"Yeah, I think so." This time I smiled so he'd know for sure.

"Does it bother you that I'm..." he paused.

"That you're what? My employer? Older than me?" I couldn't help but laugh. "Did it *seem* like it bothered me? Perhaps it ought to bother you that I'm just a child, really...a babe in the woods? An innocent..."

"Please," he laughed, rolling his eyes.

"Don't laugh. How do you know I wasn't as pure as the driven snow before last night?"

"Your performance betrays you, my dear. That sort of *advanced* choreography doesn't come naturally. That's years of practice, if you ask me."

"Don't be such a cad."

"A *cad*, eh? Where did you come from? 1947? Are you going to fend me off with your beaded clutch now?"

He lifted my hair and kissed me on the back of the neck before disappearing into the lavatory. I smiled, in spite of myself, in spite of the silly conversation, and in spite of the terrifying start of the night. The grey wash over the yard turned warm and green, and with a subtle gesture of my hand I covered my stomach, determined to smother the flames within.

Once a woman has been intimate with a man, she begins to observe things about him that had previously gone unnoticed. I'd never seen the doctor unclothed until that particular evening, and at night the bedroom was dimly lit, cloaking our details and forgiving our imperfections.

One morning, I happened to wake before him just as the light began to flood the room. The covers had been folded down to expose his thin torso and I laid my head on his chest, listening to the delicate beating inside. My eyes went in and out of focus over his skin. He had several tiny bruises on his arms and faint scars as well, looking as though they'd been there for decades.

Scanning his body, I spotted something strange on his stomach. A bruise, small and dark blue, seemed to spill out of his navel. It was such an odd place for a bruise. As I studied it, another oddity came to my attention—a small bulge just above the mark. As inconspicuous as it was, it looked out of place. My first impression was that it could be a tumour or a cyst, but that didn't ring true. Surely a doctor wouldn't let something like that go unchecked. I lightly ran my hand over the fleshy mound. It was soft and no bigger than a child's fist.

I was startled out of my inspection by tightly wrapped fingers around my wrist. I jerked my head up to see the doctor's eyes glaring at me wildly. After a moment, his face softened as he loosened his grip.

"You were tickling me," his voice quivered and he closed his eyes again.

"I'm sorry, I didn't realise..."

He patted my hair and yawned and stretched beneath me. "It's fine, love."

"Are you all right?"

"I'm just barely awake."

He ran his hand down my back. I looked at him intently for a few moments and he pretended to be unaware. I continued to look at him, expectantly. After a few uncomfortable moments he relented. He put his hand on his stomach and sighed. "I suppose you're wondering about this."

"What is it?"

He shifted under the blanket. "If I tell you now, you won't understand. There remains far too much to be explained."

"You should tell me now if you're ill."

"I'm far from ill. Please trust me. You'll know everything there is to know...in time. It won't make sense if I tell you now. Please..." He touched my face. "Trust me about this."

"I don't think I have a choice."

"No, love. You really don't."

I rolled out of the bed and reached for my shirt. I stared at the tapestry for a moment, remembering the dream from before. I decided at that moment that I did not care for the wall hanging, as I did not care for the Bacchus in my own room, as I did not care for many of the ancient relics in the house. I also did not care for the secrecy. These were just some of the things I had never noticed before we became intimate. In time I would notice many more.

That evening, I set only one place at the table. Dr Grace picked over his food as I took my place at the far end, not my usual chair.

"Is this your best means of protest?"

"What should I do here, *Doctor*?"

"You should be patient. That is a virtue misplaced by your generation."

"Perhaps I could be patient if I had a little more to go on regarding this great mystery of yours. And don't speak to me as though I'm some unruly teenager, please."

He put down his fork and wiped the corners of his mouth. "Very well." He stood up from the table. "Let's continue this in the study," he said, and then walked away without another word.

A small desk lamp threw an eerie, orange tint on the room. He motioned me to a dark brown leather chair as he took his seat behind the desk. The room was so cold to me.

There was no wine here to warm us. No flirtatious gestures, no charming grins, just the doctor and his cold secrecy. Then, like a switch had been thrown, his eyes brightened and he smiled.

"In less than two weeks we will have cause for much celebration. Do you know why?"

I shook my head.

"Beltane. I've decided to celebrate it this year. I've always wanted to, but it's really no fun when you're alone." He kept smiling.

"I didn't realise you were pagan."

"Well, I'm not, really. Its just there are no carnal Christian holidays." He laughed quietly. "You *are* familiar then, with the sabbat?"

"I've heard of it."

"Oh, well then," his face lit up, "let me enlighten you further. The ancient people of our land had the most marvellous holidays. Sex, death, rebirth, reaping, sowing, harvesting, burning... busy, busy people they were. So much more productive and interesting than your standard western fete." His enthusiasm was unnerving.

"So which of those elements will we be celebrating?"

"Appropriately, the union of the god and goddess. By which I mean the sex, mostly." He laughed and went on with the details, still avoiding any explanation of the bruise and protrusion beneath his shirt.

To Dr Grace the god and goddess were parasitic figureheads. Though he did not admit to this in those terms, his obsession with their life-cycles spoke for him—the mating and the birth, the gathering of strength, the way they feed off one another, then the autumnal death of the god and his rebirth through his counterpart. To the doctor, this was not a celebration of the seasons or the harvest. His fascination grew out of a far more literal translation—to die and to be reborn of your own materials, to create oneself again and again. Somehow, the doctor believed, this pattern held the answers. One could not fully understand life until he had known birth and then death.

Reincarnation was not a sufficient means to an answer. Too much is left behind, lost in the transition. Too many memories buried in the ground, and the tiny specks of emotion and individuality blown away with the ashes that once were good, solid bone. Reanimation of dead tissue was not an option, either. Bringing back the dead seemed impractical, and frankly, Dr Grace had never figured out the logistics of such a feat anyway. In the end it, like reincarnation, would offer no solution to the problem of lost memory, not to mention the potential for other types of brain damage. There had to be another way. Of this the doctor had been certain. Some time later, the truth of this certainty would surface under the infinite African sky.

The courtyard was silent and cold on the last night of April. The only sound to comfort me as I waited came from my chattering teeth. The thin slip I wore was clearly meant to be an undergarment, but it was the only thing I had that felt appropriate for the coming ritual. I tried to recall how I'd been persuaded to participate in this madness.

A small bowl sat near the edge of the garden, next to a clay pitcher. Both were filled, but in the darkness I couldn't see the contents. A few small candles burned upon the marble bench. I pulled myself in closer to them to feel what little warmth they offered. My eyes kept falling on the bowl at the edge of the courtyard. I wondered if it contained food. Dr Grace had requested that I fast the day before the sabbat, to purify my system. Perhaps this ritual would involve eating, otherwise it was going to be a very long night.

I heard the light slapping of feet on stone before I saw him in the darkness. He handed me a warm mug. As quickly as I put it to my mouth, I drew it away, repelled by the pungent odour. I made a horrid face and looked up at him.

"It smells bloody awful! What is it?"

"It's part of the ritual."

"Have you tasted it?"

"No, but I'm not required to, thank god." He sneered. "Don't fret...I've had my own gruelling preparations to go through."

"Can you at least tell me what's in it?"

"It will taste worse for you if I do," he said. "Now drink it, before it gets cold and congeals."

After a moment of protest, I took a deep breath and swallowed the bitter mixture. It was thick like cream and filled with tiny, solid bits of twigs and leaves. Far worse than any medicine I was ever forced to take as a child, I gagged as it crawled down my throat. Almost immediately, the doctor handed me a tiny glass of water. It was little more than a thimble full, not nearly enough to chase away the putrid taste that lingered, but it was better than nothing. My stomach turned as the liquid found its way down and I suddenly understood the reason for my fast. Had there been anything in my stomach it quickly would have been expelled upon the ground. I shivered and doubled over, feeling a heat rise internally. Sadly, it did nothing to take away the bite of the external coldness. I felt the doctor's hand on my back, consoling me, as I cried out in pain. He put his arms around me to move me onto the ground, and I managed to utter a few words before total confusion set in.

"Why did you *poison* me?" I whispered. I could feel the burn of acid in my throat.

He wiped my hair from my forehead. "You haven't been poisoned," he said. "The pain will cease momentarily. I promise."

I closed my eyes and at his suggestion, the pain began to recede. A wave of warmth swept over me and I no longer felt the cold stone on my back. I thought I heard music and I sang along until I realised I did not know the words or the tune. It was that bloody violin again—the song from the nature programme. I smelled spring wildflowers all around me and felt soft moss on my skin. I could feel the intense green of the plants beneath me. As the music grew louder, I could hear a voice underneath the song. It was familiar, though I could not decipher specific words. I opened my eyes to see who was speaking. A pale figure stood in the distance. I extended my hand through the warm air that surrounded me. Upon closer inspection, I saw that the palm of my hand had been stained blue. I picked up a small, ornate silver mirror off the ground and held it to my face. Something seemed wrong with my eyes, like that disease—what was it, the one that afflicts the elderly? It didn't matter, in a moment the cloud was gone. A little blue crescent had been streaked across my forehead. The little clay bowl lay empty and stained with blue beside me. So it had not been food after all, and this made me very sad, until the shimmering of broken carnival glass nearby distracted me.

I rolled onto my side to further investigate my newly discovered treasure. The blue paint was all over me, in streaks and handprints. A thick blue line ran from my navel, down between my legs. I wondered if that had always been there and I could not remember for sure. A distant scream turned my attention away from the stains. I had forgotten about the voice and the figure. I wanted to look for it, but I could not move away from my bed of moss. Some time later, the figure approached. This time it was red and breathing wildly. The red, which I can't escape even in hallucinations, seemed to flow in a pulsing motion out of the centre of the shape. I tried to speak, but the breaking of the glass was far too loud and I could not hear myself. The figure was on top of me then. I tried to speak again. I reached into my mouth and pulled a long silk ribbon out. It was a brilliant crimson and I laughed as it slid across my tongue and lips. Finally, I could speak.

"This is my gift to you," I said as I placed it in the figure's hand. It grabbed onto me tightly as it shuddered. "It's all I have," I whispered in its ear, tearfully, "I'm not so good at giving things."

I could taste the salt and copper as its red mouth fell on mine. I closed my eyes again and slept to the plucking of strings, playing in a key I had never heard before.

꙰

The sun was setting when I opened my eyes again. I was twisted up in the soft white blanket on the doctor's bed. My body ached horribly as I tried to right myself. On the pillow and under the damp sheets, faded blue stains mingled with blood. My head throbbed as I looked around for the doctor. I heard running water in the lav, and a moment later he appeared.

"I feared you'd never wake up," he said, smiling. "You must have been dreaming just now. You were crying out something unintelligible right before you came to."

I looked down at my body, not sure of what to say. I must have been dreaming of the canyon again, though my head was too thick to know for certain.

"I've prepared a bath for you. You must be dying to have one."

I nodded my head and he helped me to the bath.

"Do you want me to stay with you?"

I waved him off and tried to smile back at him.

He stood at the door for a moment and then excused himself. The door between the rooms was left opened and I watched as he discarded his robe. A large surgical bandage was wrapped around his chest. The growth above his navel was exposed and seemed to be slightly larger than the last time I'd seen it. He finished dressing and exited the room in silence. I turned and stared into the large mirror in front of me.

The sight of my body repulsed me. I was covered in the blue stain and in blood. I assumed it belonged to the doctor, which would explain the bandage he wore. It sickened me as I realised then that the blood that stained my mouth and teeth was most likely his as well. *Fucking hell, did I drink his blood?* There were scratches on my face and breasts. I turned and looked over my shoulder. My back was also scratched and bruised from the hard stone. There were bruises in the shape of a hand and fingertips along my ribs and on my hips and buttocks. I couldn't believe he had done this to me. A large streak of blue ran across my stomach and was sore to the touch. The worst shock came when I sat down to relieve myself. A burning sensation caused me to cry aloud as the urine flowed over raw tissue. Reaching down to inspect the damage, small flecks of blood dotted my fingers.

Try as I might, I remembered nothing of the night before. I settled myself into the deep, warm bath and began to scrub. It took nearly an hour before the stains were gone and by then, the rest of my skin was as red and raw as my groin. I sat in the water, in tears, periodically rinsing my mouth with water from the tap until the bath grew cold and my fingers and toes were wrinkled and white. I checked myself in the mirror again when I finished the bath. With the stains washed away, the damage did not look as severe.

The large blue streak on my belly was gone now, but the pink tenderness remained. I felt around my navel to pinpoint the pain. I turned my torso toward the light and saw the blue-violet stain in my navel. I thought I'd removed all of the dye. With a piece of tissue I rubbed at it, carefully, but nothing came off. I rubbed it until I could no longer tolerate the pain. It wasn't dye. This was a bruise, like the others on my body and just like the one I had seen on the doctor. I grabbed a towel and raced down the stairs, screaming his name as I went.

He caught me at the bottom of the stairwell. "What's wrong?" He grabbed my shoulders and met my face with his own panicked expression.

"*What* did you do to me?" I pounded my fists into his collarbones, knocking him back slightly.

"It's all right...you're fine...I know you feel a bit rough...it's just scratches..."

"To hell with you! You never said it would be like this!" The tears were streaming now.

"I know...I know, things got a little out of hand. I'm so sorry I hurt you...calm yourself." I thought he was going to put his hand across my mouth and I recoiled. He stopped himself and put a finger to my lips. "Let's fix all this, I can tell you everything that happened last night."

"Can you tell me *what the bloody hell* this is from?" I tore the towel away, putting my hand on my navel. "How could you do this?" I sobbed.

"You don't even know what it is I've done!"

"I trusted you..."

He started to speak again, and then withdrew his words deciding he couldn't feign innocence. He led me back up the stairs and to the bed. He left briefly, giving me time to collect myself before returning with a tray of tea and brandy.

"Shall I taste this first so you'll know I didn't poison it?"

"Save your witty banter for a time when I don't hate you," I hissed, accepting the cup from him anyway. I was shaking from the inside out, as though a cold wind was swirling inside my torso.

I sipped the tea as he fetched an antiseptic from the bathroom and applied it to my wounds. When he finished, he took a brandy from the tray and sat in the chair by the window. He took a moment to gather his thoughts.

"I have so many things to explain to you." He stared out the window into the dark sky. "I tried to find the right time. This will be difficult for you to hear."

"I think it's time now. I need to know."

"You may not feel that way when I tell you." He paused and took in a breath. The fantastic and terrifying story began in Africa, and I laid in the doctor's bed, listening to his tale in utter disbelief.

❧

"It was in Africa that I decided to find scientific proof of the existence of a soul. Faith was no longer enough for me. Watching people, watching children and mothers die…my own mother dead, not even a full day after I left…I needed to know there was more. All the religion, all the spirituality, all the faith in the world, it was never enough to console anyone's grief…or fears. So I went searching. How poetic is that?"

"I went to the holy men, I went to the missionaries; I searched through the desert and into the Congo. I referred back to my own teachings, the years of theology, the holy men of our world. Nothing. Simple faith, that was the only answer they gave. Believe, believe! I began to feel like Thomas, you know? I began to think that I'd have no peace until I put my hand right in the wound."

"Then one day, I met a man, a priest from a Togo tribe. His land was where it all began, in a dead kingdom called Dahomey. He told me I was searching. I suppose he could read it on my face. He said he could help me, if I would help him. His infant son had a sickness of the heart, he said. He had tried to help him, but failed, and the child grew weaker each day. I asked him why he would go against the nature of his ways and come to me, a white physician with my western medicine. In those situations it is deemed the will of the gods if a child cannot be saved, but the priest said he had been compelled by the spirits to find me. So I followed him. We travelled for days before reaching his village. He took me to the child despite the fact that I was not a heart surgeon, but this didn't matter. I was the one he sought."

"Without proper technology I was unable to correctly diagnose the baby's condition. He had a severe murmur—his tiny pulse weak and irregular, but that was the best I could say. The child was to play an important role, the holy man told me. He had a great purpose, unknown to any of us at the time, and but for his eyes, he was like an unremarkable child. I did what little I could for the boy, but I knew, as did his father, that he would soon die."

"What was wrong with his eyes?"

"He had one very dark brown iris and one extraordinarily pale-violet, milky iris. Nevertheless, I cared for the infant in small ways, trying to ease his pain, or at best make him comfortable. A few nights later as I sat with the sleeping boy, the priest entered the hut and bade me to bring the child and follow him. We walked to a clearing near the village, where a fire burned. He said it was now his turn to help me." The doctor paused and darted his eyes around the upper corners of the room the way one does when trying to avert tears.

"But I hadn't saved the child, I told him. He actually laughed and said that he had only asked me to try, and I did. I'd fulfilled my end of the bargain, now it was his turn. He reached for his son and handed me this odd little, musty leather pouch. He told me to go back to my camp in Zaire; a man would guide me. He told me to wait, and if the spirits willed, he and his son would be seeing me within three day's time. I headed back with my guide that night." He stood up and walked to the window, rubbing his neck. He seemed a million miles away. I sat in silence as he continued.

"Three days later, when I saw the priest approaching, babe in his arms, I felt as though something had been set into motion. I don't know how to describe it...things were simply falling into place. I led them into my tent. Incredibly, the infant was still alive. The priest asked me if I had gone into the pouch. I had, but all I found were plants that were alien to me. He explained what they were, where he found them, and what they did. He helped me reduce them to liquid. I assisted him, and going against everything I'd been taught at school, I asked no questions. He was chanting in Fon, I think, and I didn't want to interrupt him. Even when he said we would need another healthy child, the only thing I asked was where I should get one. He laughed and responded, 'Do you not deliver them from time to time?' I said that I did, but I didn't feel any mother would take kindly to my abduction of her newborn. He said the opportunity would arise by the afternoon. I would just need to recognize it, and I suppose you can guess what happened next."

He wore the unhappiest smile I'd ever seen.

"As fate would have it, later that morning a woman died during labour. She suffered a stroke moments after the birth of her son. I had my nurse tend to the body while I stole away with the child, as though I were some sort of fairy tale villain. The woman had come to me alone, oddly enough she had no known next of kin for me to answer to. So I took the child to my tent, and we began the experiment."

"And this nurse—she never asked where you'd taken the baby?"

He was quiet for a minute, staring at me, never blinking. He smiled very slightly. "No. We had a...*special* arrangement."

"Of course you did. You are fond of your *special* arrangements, aren't you?" I felt the burning again, but it was not my intuition. It was humiliation.

"I told you that you wouldn't like this. What did you think I was going to say? How I cheated on my exams at University? That I used to nick supplies from the lab? Anyway, the priest guided me through the procedure. I didn't think. I didn't stop to consider anything, really. I just let the man guide me as he let the spirits guide him. I injected the herbal mixture into the priest's sick child. And as we waited, I remarked that I had not yet revealed to him what I had been searching for. He said I didn't have to. He had seen my desire. He said I wore it on my face. After a few moments he instructed me to extract the fluid from his child's umbilicus. I'll never forget the unnatural way the tiny infant squirmed. The syringe filled with blood and plasma and a substance I couldn't identify. He told me to put it into the other child. So I did. Just like that. I inserted the needle deep into the core of the newborn's navel and pushed the plunger down. The child cried out and I stood back, confused about what exactly I'd done. The priest picked up his own son and blessed him and seconds later his child was dead. A chill passed through me as I examined the newborn I'd kidnapped. I wasn't sure what to look for, until the priest pointed to the orphaned child's heart. I listened with my stethoscope as the infant's healthy heartbeat began to flutter and weaken. The murmur became apparent within seconds, and a few moments later, the second child died, having succumbed to the same illness that was killing the first."

I wiped the tears from my face, in shock. "What are you saying?"

"I'm saying that *a part* of the first child's *being* was transferred into the orphaned child," he paused. "I know...it seemed impossible to me at first, too. I thought it could be a coincidence. I thought perhaps a virus could have been transmitted, but it wasn't. It was something intangible, but real. I was ready to believe anything except the one answer I had hoped for until the priest told me to look at the orphan's eyes, and I *swear* to you, they'd changed. They were the eyes of his son, one brown, and one an opaque amethyst. It's been said that the eyes are the 'windows to the soul', right? Isn't that the common belief? The priest said that was the key. We both knew what I was looking for. And he was satisfies knowing his son had done what he was sent here to do."

"And what was that?" I asked, still not completely understanding.

"He gave me the key. He gave me something to have faith in. He gave me proof... and that's what we all wish for, isn't it?" He finished his brandy and looked out the window again. "Should I continue?"

I nodded and wiped my face with my hand as the fire burned all the way into my throat.

"I hope you can understand that I really had no choice in doing what I have done. I wish I could tell you there were no other casualties along my path. Unfortunately, I couldn't simply end the research with the priest's son. Would an explorer turn his vessel back into the sea just as uncharted land surfaced upon the horizon?"

"That's terribly romantic, but what I understand is that you sacrificed two children in a trial run. How many other people died for your science? How many other children?" I couldn't look at him.

He nodded and turned away from his own reflection in the window. "You know me. You know me with an intimacy that I have not shared with anyone for years.

I am not a monster. I feel some remorse for the details of my work, and if I could have spared any of those lives, I would have, but recognise the big picture. I have saved many more lives than I have sacrificed, I've helped bring so many lives into this world...and when you understand fully what I have found here, perhaps you will see the necessity of my actions."

I shook my head, still turning away from him. He continued, candidly revealing the details of his research. He told me of the infants he stole from their mother's arms, convincing them afterwards that the children had died of viral complications, and therefore could not be buried or burned in any traditional manner, for the sake of public health. He told me of the botched herbal elixirs that resulted in the poisoning of some of the children and countless animals. The trusting women who once idolised him, and later the suspicious glares of the indigenous people as the infant mortality rate of their community began to rise. Sadly, for those people of a third world nation little could be done against the reputable, white doctor. He used this to his advantage, until he began to feel his welcome wearing thin. He feared for his life. Sooner or later, a grief-stricken husband would try to resolve the problem with a machete. The doctor's bones could be easily hidden for eternity, deep inside the Congo.

He left as soon as he had gathered enough plants and information to sustain him. For anything else, he had established a black market contact in Kinshasa who, for the right price, had never heard of Dr Edward Grace.

I finally managed to meet his eyes. "You *murdered* children. There is no justification for that."

His face was unaffected. "Are you even listening to me? Do you understand what I've just told you? I have found a way to prove the existence of the *soul*. I've discovered how to harness it and now there are far too many possibilities, things that need to be done, that I have *needed* to do for a very long time, for me to just throw it all away in a worthless act of repentance."

"How can you say that? How can you say that you don't feel...*evil*...having murdered people?"

"Evil? I thought you weren't a religious person."

I didn't answer this time. There was no way to win, though really, there was nothing *to* win.

"The brutal truth, my dear, is that those children really only had less than half a chance for survival, anyway." His tone became more hostile and defensive. "Have you ever been to an impoverished country? Have you ever seen little children reduced to tightly wrapped skeletons, just waiting to die? Have you ever touched the distended belly of a two year old, with skin stretched so taut that the slightest brush of a hand tears the flesh like tissue paper? Have you ever seen the despair on a woman's face as she realises she does not have the means to feed her family? Or the bruises and welts she will receive as her husband makes the same revelation? When he feels like a failure because his children are starving, who do you think absorbs his frustration? These truths are far more monstrous than I could ever be."

This time he turned his face away from me and for a split second I felt a twinge of sympathy for him. It took all of my strength to hold back my emotions. I felt sick to my stomach. I didn't know which concept repulsed me more, that he could have done these horrific deeds, or that I had let myself develop feelings for this creature. I tried to clear my mind, but between his words and the lingering effects of the drug I had taken at his request, it wasn't easy. I wasn't sure what to say next, so I just opened my mouth and let the words come.

"Tell me why it is that you would wait until after I'd fucked you to tell me this."

"Do you really need me to answer that?"

"Tell me about the thing that's growing inside you." My voice was barely audible.

"I am preparing myself for the next phase of the experiment. We've discussed the theology of the ancient world, the idea of an unending life cycle, perpetuated by two life forces. Male," he gestured to himself, then held his hand toward me, "and female."

I felt my heart sink deeply as I began to see what was unfolding before me.

He went on. "Now that I know there is a way to make the soul tangible, to touch it, see it, as though it were just another internal organ, I want to use it. I want to feel a true life-cycle. That priest, in his primitive ways, knew it to be possible. He knew there was more to the soul than just energy. Priests have been collecting the souls of their dead in clay jars, little *govis*, they call them in Voudou, for hundreds of years. That's all I'm doing, except it isn't just energy. It's a real, solid thing. I can take the essence that is my soul, extract it, and feel a symbolic death. It can then be transplanted into a womb, an organic *govi*, if you will, where I will experience what we all wish to remember. I will be in utero *and* I will be aware. Then I'll be born again, as my soul is delivered and injected back into my body, and biological order is restored. My brain will be functioning through all of this, my body should suffer little trauma, provided the pieces of my soul aren't gone for too long. I will remember everything. I will feel every beautiful moment of it, as it occurs. And I will learn. I will learn the answers to questions that have plagued my family for generations, I will begin to understand mysteries that no human has ever solved. You cannot know how long I've waited for these pieces to fall into place."

My breathing had quickened; I feared I would hyperventilate. Never had I been more frightened. He pulled in closer to me.

"I imagine you've worked out your own special place in this equation."

I stared off into emptiness as I spoke. "I'm the womb..."

"Don't look so traumatized. Do you honestly think I would do anything that would jeopardize your well being?"

"You didn't seem to have a problem compromising my well being last night." I looked down at the abrasions on my skin. Again, the tears came.

"Those hardly look life threatening to me," he quipped. His hand went to his temple, out of frustration. He slouched down deep into the oversized chair. "Forgive me...I just can't convey to you the importance of all of this. It has been my life for so many years. And they have been very lonely years." He laughed quietly. "I sound like a mad scientist, don't I? Like Dr Frankenstein or something—but it's true. I sacrificed everything for this work, and now I'm so close...I need you for this. I've invested all of this in you. I wouldn't sacrifice you to it. I need you to believe that. Help me to become something greater than this shell of flesh. I swear, I will make it worth it for you."

"You are utterly insane. I can't even *look* at you right now," I sobbed. As I pulled away the covers to retire to my old room, the doctor stood up.

"Stay here and rest. I'll go. You'll feel better tomorrow."

No, I'll feel better when you aren't a murderer or a lunatic and I'm not just a body for you to experiment on. I'll feel better when—if—you actually decide care about me...

He put out the light and disappeared into the hallway. "I *do* care about you." He spoke so quietly, quietly enough that perhaps I'd misheard him. I hadn't been speaking aloud. I sat under the hated tapestry, staring past the darkness in the room and outside until pitch black took away the sky.

Sleep did not come for me that night. I had never been scared of the dark, not even as a child, but the darkness that filled the bedroom then was unbearable. Every time I closed my eyes I was plagued by confusion and terror. Lucid dreams crawled through the black that surrounded me. Visions of little children, naked and crying and skewered on the doctor's table, screamed out through the darkness. A faded silhouette of a man huddled in the corner of the room. Devoid of any features, the fleshy being cried out a distant, primal scream, somewhere far behind my eyes and ears. I was certain I saw him move, creeping toward the side of the bed, pulling on the covers with a desperate, translucent hand. I screamed pitifully and threw myself toward the end of the large bed only to once again find the floor beneath me hollowed into a deep, black pit. I crept along the edge of the canyon, whispering to myself as I made my way to the door that it wasn't real. It couldn't be real. I stood naked and motionless against the wall, praying that the embryonic creature wouldn't follow. A cold hand grasped my shoulder, triggering an unholy shriek that echoed through the entire house.

The doctor grabbed me as I fell to the floor, overcome with terror. "What's all this? Were you dreaming?" His face was creased with concern. All I could do was cry. The skin on my face was red and chaffed as a result of too many tears.

"It happened again! The bloody floor…" I couldn't find the words. Instead, I ran down the hall to my old room, and Edward followed. I opened the door to find the room as I remembered it, save for the pastoral painting that once hung on the wall between the windows.

"Where is it? Where is the painting?"

"Don't concern yourself with it. It wasn't such a great painting, anyway," he said.

And with that he wrapped the blanket from his bed around me, and led me down the stairs.

"I fear I'm going mad," I finally uttered after catching my breath.

The doctor smiled tenderly. "It's all in how you perceive it. This doesn't have to be so sinister. In fact, I can think of few things more natural than the completion of a life cycle."

"You make it sound so innocent," I sniffed and choked on tears. "I would hardly categorize this as a school science experiment. You've made no mention of tadpoles or petri dishes."

"I haven't gotten to that part yet."

I curled up in the big leather chair, under the blanket, and took in the details of the room. It was a temple to the African deities. On one wall hung the war masks of the central tribes, spearheads, and wood and ivory sculptures of animals and gods. Another wall held Egyptian icons, ancient images of Re and Osiris, a large painting of a jackal-headed creature and another of the phoenix, and other relics from the rich northern section of the land. There were Voudoun pieces in one corner of the room. A little bag he called a *gris gris* and a small wooden boat lay on an oak table, next to an icon of the deity called Erzulie. He said they call their deities *Loa*. There were boards nailed to the wall with chalky symbols drawn on them. One was an elaborate cross with hatch marks and swirls at the ends and a large heart in the middle. It looked like the front of a child's Valentine. The other was similar, but the heart had a thick, black dagger pierced through one side. It didn't appear quite so loving. Statues of wood and bone, similar to the tribal pieces across the room, stood next to the icon, leering at the holy mother with wide, painted eyes and bared teeth.

In my shaken state, I could not fully appreciate the collection. Of course, I'd seen it many times before, but now my tension grew as I stared into the faces of the unearthly beings. I feared there was no longer any sanctuary for me in the cold house. Dead gods filled up all of my spaces.

The doctor's voice broke my concentration. "You really shouldn't fret. It won't be so bad...you've made no complaints so far."

The blood rushed out of my face. "So far?" I started trembling again.

"You never gave me the chance to explain about your bruise...the one in your navel. It was just the first step in the preparations."

"What did you put into me?" My voice was surprisingly calm.

"Just something to prepare your uterus, the way your body would do, were you to become pregnant. Very innocuous, really..." his voice trailed off.

"You've been keeping me healthy so this would work."

He nodded. "I just wouldn't want any complications to arise."

"So you've already decided that I'll be participating in this madness?"

"It seems to me that you've already decided it for yourself. Now you just have to rationalize it, convince yourself that your reasons for doing something you believe to be wrong are valid. You have to go through those motions the way people do—the way I used to do—before your conscience will allow you any peace," he grinned, despite his sorrowful tone. "You'll learn to work around it, though, just like I did. You'll learn how to let your instinct guide you and not think so much about 'what ifs' and subjective terms like 'good' and 'bad'. Science really doesn't allow for those ideas, you know."

"Are you really so certain of the way I feel, or are you just that arrogant?"

He shrugged. "Tell me I'm wrong."

Of course I was too weak, or my feelings for him were stronger than I imagined. Either way I had no ground to stand on. He knew exactly where I was in the whole process. I couldn't tell him he was wrong. I couldn't imagine saying no to him.

I know how it sounds, having gone through it all in my head again and again. I am a champion of justification and it was easier to allow myself the insanity than to fight to be a good person. That's how my mother handled life, after all. When the world and its complicated trappings became too large for her to deal with, she simply lost her mind and was subsequently absolved of all responsibility. She didn't have to be a good mother. She just had to do what she had to do. I was beginning to understand how natural it was for me to think this way, as well

The calm that Dr Grace exuded was maddening. We sat for hours in the darkened room, contemplating the silence between us. A ray of light quietly spilled across the floor, undetected for some time. I wondered aloud how long it had been there. He said it had been about an hour; I believe it could have been a hundred years. The light made me think of Africa, and I asked him why he'd been chosen; why he'd been so special as to find this knowledge.

"Because I was looking for it, I suppose."

I curled up tighter in the chair, half aware of the doctor and myself as he told me what I thought to be a fairy tale. His voice cracked under the strain of exhaustion as he spoke, like an old phonograph recording. I was too tired to react to anything he said. I just listened and watched through half opened eyes. I believed his tale to be an account of the rite we'd performed. I remembered so little of it; I had no option but to take his words for the truth. When that truth became too difficult to hear, I pretended it was just a dream he spoke of.

The doctor said he had not drugged me in order to begin the first stages of his experiment. He claimed the injection had been an afterthought, which I didn't really believe but didn't have the energy to argue. The tonic I had ingested, however, was part of the ritual, and had been so since ancient times. He, too, had been under the influence of a hallucinogen during the rite. The blue stains had been a simple mixture of berries, and the blood had primarily been his. He gestured to the bandage on his chest. He laughed, slightly embarrassed at his mediocre re-creation of the antiquated ceremony. Since he had no stag to take down, he would have no stag's blood to coat himself in so, being the resourceful scamp that he was, the doctor sliced himself down the centre of his chest. This allowed for the desired effect of the savage struggle between man and beast. The fact that there was no beast was only a minor setback. And I was too exhausted to feel much of anything, even when he told me I'd drank his blood. He said he hadn't asked me to. I did it of my own free will.

I drifted in and out of sleep. I don't actually recall asking, but the doctor offered an explanation for his mysterious protrusion. When his soul was removed, he said casually, it would need to be gathered and contained. Without divulging the chemical and botanical specifics, which probably would've made no sense to me anyway, he explained how he'd implanted and cultivated an artificial placenta-like 'vessel' beneath his diaphragm in which to keep his soul, or whatever sticky mass of entrails we might end up extracting. It was the same sort of 'vessel' that was growing inside my uterus as a result of the injection I'd been given, and when it was time for me to deliver his soul back into the world, I would take a diuretic and he would be reborn. It was as simple as that, he said. Then, as if this explanation weren't fantastic enough, he would occasionally say something nonsensical, which I would accept as gospel, just to see if I was paying attention. He laughed quietly as I struggled to understand his ravings. He was becoming giddy with exhaustion as well. He tugged at the white blanket, which was soiled with blood and berries.

"This really needs to be washed."

"You should have the maid to do it," I muttered and fell fast asleep in the sun-drenched room.

There is a bizarre sense of peace that comes out of resignation. My judgment had been severely impaired as though I were drunk. Still, I tried to hate him. I forced the images of his murderous deeds. I pictured his fingernails tearing over my skin, as I lay drugged. I saw him bleeding on to me and finally, injecting me, without consent, as though I were a laboratory rat. I tried to make these pictures come, I tried to see how far I could push until the anger and disgust would surface. With each attempt, it became more difficult. The ugly truth dissolved into his weary smile every time and I hated myself more than ever.

"Can I trust you?"

I nodded my head. "I've never given you a reason not to."

"Right...very well then..."

If you listened closely, you could almost hear the faint hum of nervous energy that spilled out of his pores. I'd never seen him this way before. I sat on the table in the forbidden room beyond the study. In all of my time in the house that was my first encounter with the laboratory.

"This will happen very quickly, do you understand what you are to do?"

I nodded again, feeling queasy. He explained that I would need to be prepared to take over, as he didn't know quite what to expect once the *extraction* was complete. He imagined one of two things to happen, he told me as he casually stuck me right in the navel with a syringe. ("A mild anaesthetic," he said. "You'll not want to feel it when it's your turn.") Either he would lose consciousness, or he would be overcome with hysteria. Vertigo, delirium, or catalepsy were just a few of the potential side affects. Apparently, the removal of one's soul was no small affair.

As part of my abdomen went numb, I asked him why he hadn't done the same for himself. He replied that he didn't want to miss a single feeling.

The doctor looked like a child as he undressed and climbed into the large vinyl chair. I think it was the expression in his eyes and the tight, painful smile on his face. It was the look of a frightened young boy. I put my fear behind the growing love I felt for him and watched as the fantastic events flickered before me like movie images on a giant, white screen where nothing was real.

I watched the needle go in flawlessly. I'd never injected anything into anyone before. It was fascinating and sickening all at once. He remained steady for a moment and then began to tremble. Beneath his increasingly rapid breathing, I heard him whisper the word *now.* Without thought or hesitation, I reached for the oversized syringe—the kind with a large, cylindrical container attached to the end that is used to extract amniotic fluid from the womb—and pushed it further into his navel. As I pulled on the plunger I could feel the resistance of the unnatural substance, as though it was fighting me. I felt nauseous. His naked body lurched and convulsed as I removed the visceral mass from the sucking wound that had been his navel. He kept grabbing, wildly, at the place he thought my hand to be but came nowhere near it. I stepped back from him in terror, while my mind raced through one hundred possible courses of action. Perhaps it wasn't too late to cease this madness. I could inject the stuff back into him and it was likely he'd never know the difference.

Suddenly, he was still.

For a brief moment I feared he might be dead. I couldn't imagine what the police would think were they to see what we'd done. I'd most certainly be committed. I moved slowly toward his flaccid body and I did not exhale until I saw him breathing as well.

It is terribly difficult now for me to recall exactly what the substance in the needle looked like. Sometimes, when I think of it, it is a cloudy white with thin red threads swirling through it. Other times I imagine it is a brilliant pink, glittering and pulsating. Then there are moments when I remember it as a deep red, as thick as syrup, and nearly too hot to grasp. I suppose it doesn't matter all that much. There are days, even now, that I don't mind forgetting.

What I cannot forget is standing on the cold tile floor, with nothing to warm me but a towel, looking upon his painfully beautiful and partially dead body and feeling a numbing fear travel through my limbs. And I cannot forget promising him I'd go through with it, regardless of his reaction. And I did. I lay down on the table with a substantial piece of the doctor's soul in my hands and put the terrifying, thick steel skewer against my navel. This would be the part of the movie where I put my hand over my eyes, parting my fingers only enough to barely see the nightmarish picture. I pushed the needle against my flesh several times, not nearly hard enough to break the skin. I knew that to do it properly, I would have to use a tremendous amount of force otherwise I'd do nothing more than draw a few specks of blood, which would have been just fine by me. But when I looked again at the doctor, I imagined him to be in a sort of holding pattern, a purgatory of some kind, just waiting for me to follow through with my word. He would never trust me again if I stopped now. He would be so disappointed, and might even send me away, back into a world that was a purgatory in its own right, and suddenly I could understand how he must have felt then, if he could feel anything at all. I would have rather died right there in his lab then go back to my former life and I knew somewhere in his soul, he felt the same. I'm fairly sure I screamed out loud as he entered me, though I don't actually recall feeling much at all, other than a slight sense of relief that I'd kept my promise.

I waited, giving him time to feel what he was searching for. I let him live in me. I watched his body curl into a foetal position and respond to the internal stimuli of my womb, even though we were not touching. He'd been right. Somehow, he was still connected to the viscera I'd pulled out of him. I listened to the primeval noises that abruptly came from his mouth silence themselves as he found the suffocating calm that comes with going home, or back, again. I felt him move against my walls. In my entire life I will never feel anything so amazing or miraculous or horrific as the rapid de-evolution of a human being.

Bleary eyed and dazed, I reached for the diuretic he had prepared for me and drank. It bit my tongue and throat as it went down and I recalled his instruction not to focus on the taste of it. Within seconds, the cramping began. In my panic, I wrestled with the latex gloves, and placed one foot into a stirrup at the end of the table. My other foot slipped from the cold metal bar, and my leg fell from the side of the table. The pain in my belly was unbearable enough, and now my groin burned, having been pulled so abruptly when I slipped. I tried to remember to breathe. It was the best I could do as I induced a miscarriage.

There was no question as to my next move. The discomfort I felt between my legs and in my gut could only be remedied by pushing. It took a minimal amount of work before I felt something slide out in a small torrent of blood and water. I do not know how long it took. They say after you birth a child, you forget all the pain and gory details. At least that is what they want you to believe, though that may be one of the first lies a new mother tells. That she doesn't resent the child is possibly the second.

When it was done, I immediately wanted to close my eyes for a very long time, but there was no time for recovery. I forced myself to sit up and I could hear the cracking of my spine. I nearly vomited when my eyes fell upon the monstrosity pooled in a steel tray between my legs. Mucus and uterine lining enveloped the bloody pink and blue bag that held some unknown piece of the man next to me. I tried to hold it, but it slipped between my fingers like gelatine. It was so small and fragile, not even close to what I'd expected considering that the delivery was much like I'd imagine disembowelment to be.

It is common for expectant mothers to dream of delivering hideous, inhuman offspring. I no longer feared those dreams if my time ever came. My mind could never create a more repulsive image than what lay before me in the form of pulsating, nearly liquefied raw meat. I managed to get a grip around the oozing mass just long enough to draw its contents back into the syringe from which it came.

I slid from the table, slick with fluid and sobbing (actually I don't recall if I was sobbing or not, but given my penchant for tears and theatrics, it seems likely) and stumbled toward the doctor's chair. I briefly imagined slipping and dropping it all to the floor. I hoped for a sense of relief once I made my way to his body, but all I felt was horror. It didn't matter that I succeeded. I knew that in my mind I would forever replay that dreadful scenario in which I fell and destroyed him, even though it didn't happen, the same way I still imagine falling from the high stonewall at Caerphilly Castle, even though I didn't. Daddy took my mother and me to Wales on holiday when I was three and I don't recall anything about that visit, other than Daddy sitting me on the wall of the giant tower. I'm certain he held on to me, as the photograph I had of that moment shows, but I have never been able to shake that terrifying vision of plummeting down the wall of the castle, my father crying out as he desperately reaches for my arm and misses. I imagine my father's grief and I can't help but feel guilty. It was merely an accident, after all, and one that never happened, at that.

I was shaken from my daydream by an inhuman noise that could only be described as a backwards scream. It came from his throat as life flowed back into him and he abruptly became aware of the cold world around us. The eerie, glaring overhead light temporarily blinded the doctor. Moist with sweat and blood, he latched on to me like any newborn to its mother. His hand instinctively grabbed on to my breast, clawing and squeezing until my skin was broken. I held on to him, trying to comprehend what I had done. I found myself half singing words of consolation in an attempt to calm him, even though I was burning with disgust. I felt like a criminal. I wasn't just assisting, I didn't just hold the torch steady or watch for the police. I delivered the fatal blow. It was his idea, but I made it real. I could have run, leaving him to his own perversity, but I didn't. I stayed and committed this most unethical act with him. I wished for darkness to come and hide my shame in the bright and sterile room when I realised why.

I wasn't insane like the doctor; I was bored. I was bored with what life had to offer and even something as unthinkable and repulsive as his experiment was better than what I could make of the world around me, alone.

In a reversal of roles, the doctor wept in my monstrous arms before temporarily losing consciousness. As he lay there barely alive, I realised that I was just as immoral (or was it *immortal*? No, just *immoral*) as he. My crushing sense of guilt was the only difference between us. Edward Grace didn't have the capacity to feel that emotion.

In the next hours, as I remember it, we were addicts going through withdrawal. He shook incessantly, and I vomited to the point of dehydration. I sat him in the bath and let cool water trickle out of the tap. I didn't want to put him into deep water. He was still an invalid and if he slipped under I feared I would be too weak to help him. He hadn't spoken yet, but he had done a good job of walking up the stairs with my assistance. He didn't fight me as I sponged off the oil and blood and bits of afterbirth. He even splashed water on himself, in an effort to help me when the sight of the viscous matter collecting at the drain became too gruesome for my stomach to handle. With my head resting on the toilet seat, I watched him marvel at the running water—amazed that such a thing existed, and *god, how I envied him.* I wanted to see what he saw. I wanted to know what he felt. I wanted him to be caring for me. As I embraced the toilet, covered in blood and every other fluid I could imagine, I really just wanted to be clean. It would take more than a bath to wash away what I had done.

I kept vigil over the doctor, waiting in the old chair by the window. I didn't know what time it was. I wasn't even certain of the day. At best, I could tell it was nighttime. I picked at the embroidery thread that knotted up in intricate swirls on the chair. I would have picked apart the entire chair, had the doctor's whisper not distracted me.

"You did it..."

I could barely hear him.

"Aye. I did it. And now what?"

He looked bewildered and bright-eyed. "I can still feel it..." He laughed and stretched his arms out on the bed, opening and closing his hands, resembling a lazy messiah.

"So, was it worth it? Was it worth the pain you caused those mothers and babies, the pain you've caused us?" I wanted him to say no, of course. I couldn't tell if I was repulsed or jealous. I resented his *awakening.*

He pulled himself up against the pillows, eyes closed, hands gripping the sheets, wincing as his body adjusted to its newly upright position. I held in my breath as his pained expression spread into a wide smile. His eyes opened and flashed like diamonds in the darkness of a mine.

"Every bit..." He closed his eyes again and savoured the beautiful depravity of his answer.

What the fire in me said (this time):

Once we all were chemical pools. Somewhere inside, we know this is true.

Later, we became amphibious. Our mothers remember this even if we do not.

Then one day, we were aware.

We are taught about evolution. How we wallowed around in those primordial hot springs, flowed into the oceans, sprouted some legs, crawled onto the shores, learned how to procreate, and learned how to kill.

We know this is true, but do not remember.

There would not have been words to describe what we felt, and this is accepted by most of us.

But the man on the bed did not just accept it. The man on the bed now has the words.

I was thinking about Sundays. I spent the Sundays of my childhood in the basement classroom of our church, learning about God's love and sacrifices. The adults upstairs would sing and pray and we accepted it all, without asking for proof. God was too big to explain. We just had to believe. And so I did.

I never gave much thought to things I could not explain. I never thought about what made sense or what felt right. I did not question the paradox in it all, and I was never close to God. He was just a word I claimed to believe in. A name to call out to when I needed something I feared I couldn't get on my own. God existed on my terms and was a convenient answer for things I couldn't understand. That was my religion.

Now I lay on the bed, face-to-face with the closest thing to God I'd ever seen and I was terrified in his presence. Throughout time, unspeakable atrocities have been committed in the name of God. His alleged words have driven more than a few men to participate in the destruction of their brothers. In this I found a way to justify what we had done.

When we have nothing to go on but words, we rely on our instinct. We trust our intuition, the creature that lights fires in our guts. This is what I did as the doctor recounted his experience.

I knew something had happened on the table, to him and to myself. Something had been planted inside of me, something had moved, something had changed within him. I knew he was telling the truth.

He said that thoughts became words, words turned to feelings, feelings melted into passion, and passion dissolved into instinct. It was a rather elegant chemical process. His body responded to the botanical concoction by triggering and redirecting the chemicals to the synthetic vessel. They flowed in microscopic strands from his brain and his heart; moved like fluid ribbon from his solar plexus and his extremities. They rushed in from his genitalia and the base of his spine and pooled inside the artificial sac, where I would extract it with the syringe. In the simplest terms, that was how we captured and collected his soul. The extraction was a temporary death. He said it was silent.

He remembered the warmth and the water, the suffocation, the confusion. There was a pressure, but he was not sure if it came from within him or if it had been external. He was blind and could not hear. He remembered crawling out of a pool, scalded and broken. He could taste the fluid as it burned away his reptile tongue. He thought he felt his mother's skin. He could feel how white it was. He remembered the vibration of her heartbeat. I wondered if I had skin like her's.

Then he said that everything was red.

It took a million years for him to see again, and at least that long before his tongue grew back. When his sight returned, it was stronger than ever. He could see everything there was to see. He said he could hear me, hear my thoughts. Everything would be different now; his needs had shifted, though he did not explain what that meant. I didn't understand it at the time, but through his de-evolution, his regression, he shed thousands of years of layers—layers made of fear and disbelief, sheets of skepticism and boundaries and oppressive parameters; the fabric that we wrap ourselves in and use to cover our heads so we can't see the truth of our infinite abilities. He removed the curtain that blinds us to *god* and all of its faces, our own face among them. So when Dr Edward Grace came back, he came back more evolved—differently evolved—than the rest of us. I don't believe we expected his evolution to be larger than his body could neatly and comfortably contain.

Dr Grace knew sacrifice. He knew loss. Now he knew life. He knew creation. He had tasted this in Zaire, played a god to the sick women. Brought them life and sometimes death. All along it had been in his delicate hands. Ultimately, the fate of the people he served was his decision. He liked the way this tasted, letting it flow over his teeth and absorb into his tongue. He fed on the people of Africa and they had sustained him for a while. Now he would feed on the devotion of the tribes of the ancient world. He had travelled the cyclical paths of their deities, and assimilated the face of their sun god.

In the light of the morning everything around us had changed. The house had grown larger and colder, even defensive. The vines that ran through the stones had expanded and thickened. The pine trees beyond the pool had stretched and pushed the outside world further and further away. One by one, the deities arrived like a welcoming committee. We were members of their community now, and they made themselves at home at the Grace Estate.

While Edward slept, I stepped lightly through the rooms, nodding here, smiling there, trying to avoid getting trapped in an awkward conversation with Jehovah, or perhaps saying the wrong thing to Shiva, and so on. The walls of the house were alive and breathing, pulsating rhythms and the chants of tribes echoed through the rooms and halls. At first I thought that the house had come alive because of the experiment, though I came to understand that the house had always been alive and it just took a drastic change in my own soul to see it.

I nearly succumbed to the unmerciful scent of roses. I closed my eyes and gripped the doorframe, trying to collect myself. As though I had no choice, prayers spilled from my mouth in song—

Mother Stella Mary full of Grace who guides me through this darkness oh Erzulie bring me to the light to the serpent to repent in the waters she is in the water in her blue robes in her blue water and the serpent is the sky the blessed virgin serpentine sky...

I remember crawling through the kitchen, suffocating under the mother's fragrant breath, until I finally reached the door.

Erzulie Freda Dahomean Stella Marie protect me from the deep deep red from the Dan'tor from the Ge Rouge and the l'eau rouge there is a star there is a boat in the water for me She awaits in the water for me...

I pulled myself up and stumbled out into the courtyard, past the radiant beauty of Isis and Diana, past the gate, past the peacocks and into the lush green beyond.

There is a boat in the water for me...a star burned in my shoulder and a knife run through my heart...there is a boat deep in the red red water...She awaits in the water for me...

At the edge of the great black pool, those were the only words that seemed to exist. A million tiny creatures swarmed at the green veneer. I reached into the water and collected a universe in my cupped hand. The analogy was trite, but it made me smile as I poured my microcosm back into the darkness.

A moment later, the smile became painful and tight, like wire slicing through and carving out the gorge where I would keep my regret. I laid down at the edge of the fetid water and covered my head with my hands as Leviathan laughed at my naïveté. *I never wanted this...* Though underneath it all, it wasn't true. I'd wanted something this remarkable my whole dreary life. I'd prayed for something amazing. I'd dreamed of darkness and of men like Edward. And with that, the Buddha turned his eyes away.

"Are they biting?" He crouched down at my head and peered into the water.

"What are you talking about?"

"The fish...or any other manner of creature living in this septic hole."

I rolled over to face the pool, mostly to avoid facing the doctor.

"How do you feel?"

"Like I've made a horrible mistake." My eyes resumed the familiar burn that meant tears.

"Like *you've* made a horrible mistake? You only assisted me. This really isn't about you, you know."

"I only assisted you? That's grand. You used my womb, I worked the needle, and nursed you through the whole mess, and now I merely *assisted* you?"

The doctor sighed. "The world just hasn't done a proper job until it has forced you to become a martyr, has it?" He picked up a rock and jerked it across the pool's surface.

"Because I have a conscience, that makes me a martyr?"

"No. Because you believe you betrayed your conscience for me. *That* is what makes you a martyr."

"No, that makes me a fool."

"People do foolish things for love."

"Especially when they've been drugged."

"And now you're a victim. Which one do you prefer, dear? Shall I ring the Pope and arrange your canonization or just send you a sympathy card?"

I pulled in closer to the edge of the pool, close enough to taste the years of stagnation, drawing gnats into my nose and mouth with the smallest gasps of air.

"How about both? Two birds, one stone." He waved his arms in a dramatic presentation. "I can see the card now: *'Our most heartfelt sympathies regarding your poor judgment, O Patron Saint of Victimization and Sacrifice, Our Lady of Perpetual Tears'.* Will that suffice?"

Then he was gone. I heard the courtyard gate slam, then the door to the house.

I let my face fall closer to the foul water, closer and closer until it was submerged under the thick skin of the surface. Warmth and stillness surrounded my head while anger seethed on the inside. All I could see clearly in that underworld was how much I hated him for saying such things, and how much I hated myself for allowing his words to be the truth.

I don't remember if I jumped into the pool or if I just let myself roll off the edge. I was just in, under. I went down at an incredibly slow pace, deeper and deeper into the black syrupy atmosphere. I was still holding my breath when I reached the bottom. My legs spread out over the slippery, algae covered floor. I thought of the canyon and the wolves. I thought of my father and then a moment later I let go of the air I'd carried down from the world above.

Regret doesn't live here. Pain can't breathe in this world. He may be a god up there, but this is my kingdom. I created him in this world. This is mine. Let him destroy what's his...but this is mine. One of a million little reptiles that found his way out... that's all he is. Even as a dead mother I have more than he'll ever see. More than he'll ever know. I haven't lost anything. I'll keep creating. Even as a dead mother I feed the creatures that surround me. They'll live on my skin and when that's gone they'll live on my bones. Dead milk is better than none at all...The god above can starve...

They say when you are dying you will see a glaring white light, and I did, except it wasn't God or the light of the heavens, but the mid-morning sun burning through my eyelids as the doctor filled my lungs with his own air. There was a moment of still silence and then the thick water came up and out with a violent, uncontrollable force. With cold, wet hands he pushed me onto my side as I wretched and struggled. At last, I was empty. Tiny rivers of warm water and mucus fell from my nose and out of the corner of my mouth and then ceased.

"Can you hear me?"

I nodded as best I could. He sat back, soaking wet, breathed out hard, and put his head in his hands. When he looked up again, water dripped from his face, from his eyes. I could barely believe what I was seeing. The realm of tears had always been mine. He held his composure for a few seconds then began to sob out loud.

I was dumbfounded. Before me in the grass sat this incorrigible creature falling apart. A fiend, pale and shivering, covered in weeds and mud and slime, weeping like a lost child. It was the saddest thing I'd ever seen. I found myself weeping with him and for the first time since I'd come here, it wasn't for me.

I wanted to be kind to him in that moment. It really was a beautiful day, too beautiful to be tainted with any more hateful words. The sky was clear and bright and the sun had just finished drying up the morning dew. The air was cool and thin without the aid of any breeze. I wanted to forget the nightmare we were living and start again. Just pretend it never happened. No one knew what we had done, we were hidden away in this place, just the two of us and our little crime against nature. The serenity slipped away when I finally spoke.

"I thought we were gods now...I thought we were immortal."

"So you figured you'd test it? Is that what this was about?" His voice was shaking. He rubbed his face with both hands and looked away.

"No, I just..."

He broke in, exasperated and desperate, "Your *soul. That* is immortal. Not your body. I haven't figured that out yet. You know this." He put his head down again and sighed. His voice fell to a whisper. "Do you hate me so much?" He didn't look up.

"No." It was the truth.

His mouth began to tremble again, then his whole body. He choked out the words. "I thought you ran away...I looked out and didn't see you and I thought you were gone. I came out and I couldn't imagine you got so far and then I realised...I *knew*..." he gasped for breath. "I felt you letting go...you were in the darkness and I couldn't see you but I knew...I jumped in and grabbed for you. I felt your hair twist around my foot and *I thought you were a fucking plant*," he laughed for a second, "but then I felt your head and I thought you were gone..." then trailed off into sobbing again.

It was horrible. My chest ached, my throat burned. As he walked back toward the house all I could see was my father's face, the first time I saw him cry. My father, a sturdy factory worker called George, had always been indestructible, more than human. That was how he was to me then, as little children don't recognize passive and helpless behaviours in adults. So, as far as I was concerned there was nothing he couldn't do, nothing he couldn't control. I can recall the day of my fifth birthday and how my celebration was threatened by a summer storm. I worried all morning.

"Don't fret, Isabel," he drew me onto his lap. *"Do you really think I'd let it rain on your special day?"*

Within the hour, the storm passed over and the sky cleared. I loved him more than ever that day.

A few months later, he told me I was going to have a little brother or sister. I was overjoyed. In the child's eye version of this tale he and my mother spent the next eight months planning and whistling and painting the little sewing room, hugging and kissing each other, kissing me. Life couldn't have been better. With every new stuffed animal and rattle purchased for my impending sibling, my father would match it with a doll or a new dress for me. It was our *secret*; my mother feared he would spoil me and we didn't have an abundance of money. I can still see my father's smile. The one he reserved just for me.

My sister died ten hours after she was born. Later that night, I heard my father come home and softly inform our neighbour Mrs Wilder, who'd tended to me that day, that my mother would stay in the hospital for another day or two, sick with grief. I waited for him to come into my bedroom and comfort me, but he didn't. I tiptoed down the stairs and saw him, hunched over in his big chair, head in his hands. He sat still, like a statue. The little orange light next to the end-table cast a shadow over his body. Then he began to sob in little, high-pitched bursts. It scared me so badly I began to wail along with him. I didn't know he was able to make those sounds. He jumped and turned toward me, just as startled and a bit ashamed. Quickly he cast this aside and reached his arm out to draw me in.

"*Oh, Isabel...*" was all he said.

My sister's name was Kate and she simply couldn't breathe.

I'd never noticed how much the doctor resembled my father until I saw him cry. They wore their hair the same way and had thin, angular faces, similar eyes and hands. The biggest difference was that dead babies never moved Edward to tears.

Pretend that nothing's wrong, pretend this didn't happen. This was my silent mantra for the next few hours. It appeared to be his, too. The day crept along lazily like Sundays do. I didn't know what day it was any more, but I've always hated Sundays for their apathy.

He stayed away from me until dark. Reluctantly, I went back into my old bedroom and lay down. I heard him at the door for a moment, then his soft footsteps padding away.

"Edward?" I opened the door and found a neatly folded letter placed on the hallway floor. I slumped against the doorframe and stared down the long, dim hall for a moment. My eyes went in and out of focus between the sleek, dark walls and the scarlet carpet and I felt a surge of emptiness rush past me. The corridor seemed endless for a second. I opened the letter and forced my eyes to focus.

Dear Isabel,

What you must think. I'm sorry. I cannot imagine your confusion. So easily I forget that while I have had years to prepare for this, you have only had days. Forgive me.

I wanted more than anything to share this with you, for us to achieve this level of awareness together, and revel in the simplicity of it all. Instead, I let you down. I assumed you would feel the things I feel, see the things I see. I understand now how different we are, or at least how different you must feel from me. To you I am a monster, a murderer, a lunatic and an addict. To me you are the true deity, the good mother, life ~ that is you. How you could love me, well, I see why you tried to end it all. And even in that act, you managed to bring forth some goodness in me. The tears I shed for you reminded me that I am at least a little bit human. Thank you for that.

Now here we are. There is no turning back. I want to help you understand what we've become. I want to bring you to your full potential. Let me show you this. Such a terrible waste it would be to deny yourself these gifts. Try as you might to leave this world, I assure you, you will not end. With or without breath in your lungs or a beating heart in your chest, my love, you will not end. Sooner or later I'll be there with you. The kingdom is ours. I am sorry for your pain.

~ E

P.S. In the 1300s, King Edward II took up residence at Caerphilly Castle in Wales. It was there he had a falling out with his bride, Queen Isabella, at which point she went to France with her lover, raised an army and returned, driving Edward from his fortress. I thought you might find that interesting, as you were much too young the last time you were there to understand its history, let alone in this context. I can only hope, however, this does not give you any ideas. France can be lovely, but the streets are very narrow, flats are small and expensive, and the architecture is a bit too gilded and frivolous for my taste.

~E

The good mother. The kingdom is ours. Those were my words, words that drifted through my mind at the bottom of the pool. He claimed he could hear my thoughts when he awoke from the experiment; I didn't believe him then. But he knew. He knew about Caerphilly. He wasn't even conscious when I was thinking about that. There were times before his *change* that I'd suspected that he could hear my thoughts, though I didn't know how or why or if I even believed such fantastic things at all.

There would be many consequences because of the time he spent inside me. He would hear me all the time now and this was just the beginning.

I remembered then those moments since I'd arrived that had seemed like daydreams, moments when I could see things in my head. I could see him, alone in his bed or in the dining hall, or in Zaire. I wanted to have made them up. I was certain that's all they were—my imagination. I was so quick to discount them. I was always so quick to write them off, even before I met Edward. I'd handled it that way my entire life.

I sat very still. Could I hear him? Would I want to know his thoughts? Would he know if I were trying to hear him? It was all too much.

Just stop thinking. You're trying too hard.

But was it my voice or his? It was impossible to tell.

Close your eyes and watch...

At first it was unclear. Blue strands of fibre twisted into knots of different hues. Then there was warmth, like breath, ricocheting back from the soft surface. I could feel it on my nose and mouth. The image began to move further away. It slowly came into focus. Little splotches of colour forming true shapes, like backing away from a Seurat. The breathing became harder and deeper. Then I saw the goddess figures. I saw the tapestry through Edward's eyes. My eyes, his eyes darted back and forth between the young virgin and the expectant mother. He brought our eyes down the wall, over the pillows, and on to his bare thighs. He was kneeling before the tapestry, one hand clutching the heavy oak headboard, the other moving rhythmically between his legs. Then everything went dark as he came, and he gasped for air. Far back inside my head I heard the faintest whisper. *I knew you'd find me here, Isabel.* I crawled back into the bedroom and locked the door behind me.

My sleep was fitful, laced with exhausting dreams, the sort that only anxiety can give. On they went, for hours at a time, but upon waking I found that only minutes had passed. Not surprisingly, Edward was present in most all of the dreams, even playing the role of my father in one of them. I resented him for that. Around four a.m. I woke up in a cold sweat, remembering the taste of him. I sat up in the darkness, disgusted at the filmy paste that covered my teeth and tongue.

"Let me sleep, Edward," I called out to the air around me. *Just leave me be...*

⌇

"I've prepared breakfast for us and there's some fresh fruit on the table. Do you like eggs?" He motioned to the crackling pan in front of him. "I enjoy mine over easy," he grinned, "at least I think I do, it's been so long since I've had an appetite for much of anything."

The sight before me was utterly surreal. I had long since abandoned my position as housekeeper and the kitchen bore signs of neglect. Broken glasses and dishes lined the countertops and various stains decorated the cupboards and the grey tiled floor. Ruddy handprints glinted off the steel refrigerator. There was blood on the French doors, on the stove, and on the bowl of fruit Edward had prepared. The sun highlighted billions of dust particles as it climbed through the east window.

Never had I seen Edward so dishevelled. His hair was wild and greasy and his eyes were like glass. His pants were filthy and torn, blood covered his chest, and he flitted around the chaos like a merry housewife. He'd gone completely insane overnight.

I moved toward him with caution, the way one would approach an injured animal. My urge to scream at him for his perverse mind game was momentarily forgotten, and amidst the ruins all I could ask him was where he got the food.

"I telephoned Chapel and they sent a delivery person." He continued to break eggs on the stove. The pan, already filled, overflowed.

"Someone came to the house?"

"Yes. Didn't I just tell you that? Someone came to the house and I gave him some money but then I...Well, I beat him to death with the skillet, and then I thought it was funny that I'd bothered to give him the money at all. Don't you think that's funny?" He mashed the spatula into the pan and began rooting through the clutter until he found the black pepper.

My stomach flipped. "Please say you're joking, Edward." I swallowed hard to keep from being sick. I stared at the blood on his chest and hands.

He smiled and waited too long before answering. "I'm joking, darling."

"You've got blood on you." I looked down at the pan. A burned layer of eggs coated the bottom. Floating above that was a mixture of uncooked whites and yolk, along with some shells, pieces of broken glass and blood. I reached down to turn off the burner and gently took the spatula from his red hand. He shook some pepper into the vile mess and looked at me. His pupils filled his blood shot eyes.

"You said you called the grocer," I whispered and he nodded. "The phones still work, then?"

He smiled dreadfully and his lip split at the corner. "Yes. For now."

⊰⊱

He wouldn't let me bandage him. He wouldn't let me clean the house either. He followed me from room to room in his mania, disrupting any semblance of order I tried to achieve. I told him to leave me alone. I told him he was driving me mad. He would not relent.

"Why won't you let me talk to you?" He grabbed me by the wrist and spun me around.

"I'm busy. Leave me be." When he whirled me around I saw too many things that I couldn't understand. I saw the blurred figures of people, ghosts, and gods surrounding us. I could hear their ancient, dusty voices travelling through the room and through us, hushed and buried under static at first. When the voices came into audible focus, slicing through us like razor-thin paper, I snapped at them as well.

"All of you...*enough*!" But the chattering did not cease.

"I want to tell you things. I want to talk about last night." Edward tugged at my arm, like an impatient child. His breathing was laboured. "Did you see? I know you did...I know you saw it."

Shut up shut up shut up...

"Bel..." he whined. "Did you...?"

"*What*, Edward..." I lashed at him. "What did I *see*, Edward? Did I see you tossing off, did I see you fucking me in my dream?" I pulled my arm away. "Yes, yes I did... you're little plan to get inside my brain has absolutely *flourished*. You were with me all night long, Edward, penetrating me every way possible and now I understand the magnificent and terrifying scope of your power. You are a god, Edward, and I bow before you and your omnipotent cock!"

He stepped back and raised his brow at me. "Well you don't have to be so vulgar about it."

A pressure began to seethe in my chest. I wanted to hit him. I wanted to beat him until he shattered. I wanted to call someone. For the first time in what felt like ages I considered calling his former colleagues at his office and telling them everything. Maybe I could have him committed. I felt so disappointed that I had lost an opportunity when the delivery boy had come to the house.

But *what opportunity*, I thought—the opportunity to pit some teenage boy against a raving lunatic with extrasensory perception? No, maybe it was just the chance to see a real person again. We could die out here and there would be no one to miss us. The rest of the world could be dead and we'd never know, but someone real had been there and I missed it. That was where the pain came from. I had to stop thinking like this. He'd hear me. I tried to block out the words and the pictures that jumped through my head.

Shut up shut up shut up.

Then I did the only thing I could do, the only thing I ever did. My hands went to my head and I just cried.

He wrapped his villainous arms around me, thin and sinewy and bruised. He smelled terrible. His mouth smelled like death and copper. He kissed my face again and again. The crowd was still. They quieted themselves and watched, waiting for my acceptance, not of their presence, but of what I was becoming.

"Isabel, this could be so good. Let me show you..."

And I was broken again.

The shards of glass remained in the doctor's hand for another quiet day before he finally decided to let me take them out. I had to venture into the dreaded lab to get the proper supplies. I hadn't been in there since the experiment, and as I expected, it made my skin crawl. The fluorescent light swayed above me as I stumbled into wires, casting sickening shadows over the cold room. The stench of rotting bodily fluids lingered as a reminder of my shame. I'd given birth to a deranged idea on the table before me and now it was mine to live with. A deformed and demanding mutated progeny that woke me at night and clung heavy to my breast, sucking out every last drop of normalcy and sanity I possessed. But it was mine and there was no doorstep to leave it on, no river to drown it in. I looked away from the stained table, found the materials I needed and fled the room without looking back.

His hand was puffy and dark purple. The tissue was already trying to reject the foreign glass. I grabbed each piece with tweezers and pulled carefully, one by one. He never flinched, even when I applied the stinging iodine.

"You need a bath," I said.

"What do you need?" His voice was calm and nearly considerate.

"What do *I* need?" I thought carefully for a moment. I breathed in the noxious scent of him, the faint decay of the house. "I need to get out. I need air. It stinks in here. I need open doors and windows. I need to see the sky..."

He went into the lavatory and turned on the water. "Open your windows, and when I'm done we'll have a walk." He seemed almost human again.

"How far does your property extend?" I pointed back into the thick woodland. I guessed it to be about six o'clock in the evening. The sky was turning orange.

"Just an acre beyond the ravine."

"There's a ravine?"

"It runs into an old quarry."

That was the first I'd heard of it. I'd never gone into the woods before. I'd never gone beyond the pool. I feared walking past the dreaded hole, as though something might reach out and pull me in. The thought made me shiver.

"Are you cold? Do you want my jacket? Or are you afraid?"

I hadn't noticed his attire until now. He had a bath, but somehow fallen right back into his tattered trousers. He still wasn't wearing a shirt, but had slipped on a grey and black-flecked suit jacket. He looked like a little boy in his father's Sunday best. He had managed to put on his shoes.

"No. I'm fine, thank you."

"You've nothing to fear in that pool. There are far worse things, you know."

We walked hand in hand toward the forest and soon the house behind us fell off the edge of the earth.

Deep into the woods the children went, searching for berries and wood for the fire, but knowing in their hearts they were never meant to return. Neither admitted to their fear, but held tightly to each other's hand. If they could only keep to the path, never straying, perhaps the angels would guide them through the dark night and deliver them to safety by the dawn...

"Mind the briars, Edward." Instinctively, I pulled him to my side. He was walking right through them.

"Don't stop now, Isabel. I was quite enjoying it."

"Edward...how is it that you can hear my thoughts, but I can't seem to hear yours unless you force it on me?"

"Perhaps you aren't listening."

"I don't know how. I don't know how to hear you. I'm not even sure I want to."

"The sooner you accept that we are a part of each other, the more willing you'll be to hear me." He smiled. "You loved me once. You can love me again." He stopped suddenly. "Besides...you heard me the other night."

"That wasn't by my choice..."

His voice hardened. "It's always by your choice. You'll hear what you want."

I glanced around in the green and grey silence. The tall, thick trees had closed in.

He took my hand to his lips and whispered into my palm. "In fact, I'm quite sure that if I left you here right now, deep inside this woods, with nothing to guide you but my unspoken direction, you could find your way home." He glanced up from my hand. "In fact, I'd bet your life on it."

A deafening tone swirled around my head as his hands collided with my temples.

The trees began to blur away into a tunnel as I hit the ground. When I opened my eyes again he was gone and had taken the sun with him.

I sat in the darkness for quite some time, waiting, even though I knew he wouldn't come. What came instead were the noises: chirping and screeching and fluttering on all sides, louder and louder until I could stand no more.

I screamed out, *"Edward, you bastard...how can I hear you with all this bloody noise?"* There was no response and for a second even the crickets went silent.

The crackling of sticks and leaves in the distance prompted me to stand up and run. It was impossible to tell which direction I was facing. In my confusion I became certain that the forest was both haunted and crawling with wolves and hungry foxes and there would be no escape from the surrounding terror. I was tempted to give in and lie down, just let it take me. At this idea, I slowed my pace. Perhaps it would be better if I stayed here. Perhaps it would be better to die out here than to play along with Edward's game. As I traipsed through the lush, black foliage I started to get angry. With each deep breath I took, the anger increased and before long, I was running again.

"Edward...*where are you*?" Singing aloud. "C'mon, darling...I'm waiting for your *fucking direction...you cunt...*"

I could feel where my feet were to go and as I got angrier, running became easier. So easy, in fact, it made me laugh. I was still laughing breathlessly as I vomited, a result of running too hard.

"Fuck you, Edward..." I sputtered quietly as I bent over and spit. *"Fuck you,"* I said with a smile.

Edward didn't answer, but once again the breaking of sticks behind me did. Again my instinct beckoned me to run, so I did. I ran right to it.

"I swear to God, Edward...when I find you..." I trailed off. Even if he were out here, I doubted very much he'd be afraid of my half-hearted threat. Edward never did fancy poorly thought out ideas. So I did the only thing I could think to do. What I had always done as a child in the darkness of my bedroom, all of those times I needed to ward off the terrible thing that took my sister away. I sang made up songs. I sang wishes and prayers.

You...leave me here among the vines...without a path...far too close to the ravine...

Slowly and softly I went, always making sure the ground hadn't fallen away around me. The wind swirled and echoed to my left. I knew the ravine was nearby. I also knew that if I let him, he would lead me right into it.

Then I was down.

Fast and hard, my face thudded against stone. Not the cold slate bottom of the pit, but something else. It was still too dark to see and I had gone a bit delirious at impact. My face felt wet around my mouth. It's always been funny to me how you don't feel pain until you realise the actual wound. I didn't really feel any pain at all until I spit a tooth into my palm. I propped myself up against the rock that disfigured me and gave up. With a swelling tongue I sputtered obscenities to the quarry, to the stone, and most of all, to Edward. And so it was until I fell asleep in the dirt.

The part of the night came when the pitch-black bleeds away to a light charcoal and you can see again, too late to be night-time, too early to be morning. It was a place in which we had become accustomed to living.

My face throbbed, but I remember feeling relieved. A few hours without the doctor had done a world of good. Even the dirt I lay on felt softer than it had during the night. Small piles of slate cluttered the ground near to my head and I knew the quarry must lie just beyond them. I had come so close, but that was how Edward kept me all along—damaged and clinging to the edge.

Then the ground was humming. With my ear buried in the soil, I could hear a low drone. My mind immediately created a picture of monks, all grey and brown in robes, in a dank and ancient monastery. They were chanting and moving through their catacombs, rumbling praises to their furious and mighty god, rumbling from the bowels and depths of their bellies, thanking God for their poverty and misery and unnatural chastity. I wanted to dig down and unearth them. I wondered what it would take to seduce one of God's children, how many moments of body heat and frustration would pass before the robes and the vows were stripped off. I wondered when it was that I began to think like Edward. The naked monks faded away and I dragged myself along the ground, following the trail of noise below me.

Edward would have been so proud to watch me there, bloodied and delirious, on all fours, belly scraping the ground, sniffing out some primal and guttural moan that coursed through the dirt. He would have been like a proud father at his little girl's first piano recital.

He's not like my father. My father is a good and decent man who would be sickened at the sight of a creature like Edward Grace. He would be so hurt to see me like this.

The drone grew louder. Why had I never heard it before? It was too sick and low to be new to the world. I could hear its layers. I felt like a blind, slick puppy instinctively heading to the teat of the bitch. Maybe animals could hear such noises, but I certainly never had. Whatever it was, it was leading me home. The song in the dirt seemed to be attached to the house like an umbilical cord. Beyond the canopy of the woods the mother that was the terrible manor appeared on the horizon, waiting to feed me, then swallow me whole. The coming of dawn did nothing to correct the desperate grey sky. I thought it might rain.

The mist came first, then the downpour. The grass seemed to thicken and turn a deeper green before my eyes. The peat went to a glossy black, rich and oily with decay. Once this was the swamp from which he crawled.

I staggered past the pool and watched the worlds that lived within it turn to chaos as the rain slammed the vile surface. The hum continued, I could hear it over the rain. At the courtyard gate, I hesitated, unprepared for what I'd find inside. I'd managed to shut him out all night. I didn't want to let him in now, but I rued the thought of walking into the middle of some hideous atrocity. He could be dead, hanging from a beam, sliced across vein, blue and stiff in some wretched position. Or worse, he could be alive, waiting to resume the game, naked and flailing about, ready to tear out my eyes and boil them on the cooker. Perhaps I could ignore him. I could pretend he wasn't even there. Or I could just be insane with him, or kill him myself. Yet among these perfectly feasible options, something I could not consider was running away. I felt so small in the shadow of his house. I felt like I was sinking and the only thing I could do to stop it was open the gate and step upon the stone.

The house was breathing, or so I thought for the first minutes inside, but it was just Edward. I looked around the kitchen for him but found only the disaster he'd created. His breathing came from inside my head. I suppose I had finally silenced myself enough to hear him. He was still alive somewhere in the house. He knew I had returned, as well.

It's time to rest for a spell, Edward.

There was no need to speak it aloud.

I cautiously made my way through the rooms and took the time, while he was still and quiet, to survey the damage around me. Most of the rooms were in utter disrepair. Some only suffered from neglect. Many of his artefacts were broken, but these things hardly mattered any more. What value do statues and pictures hold when you can live among the real thing? He had drawn his own pictures on the walls with mud and what looked like flour. The cryptic mess seemed to be symbols and formulas, mostly, very few recognizable characters. *"ISA"* was written in a circle on one of the walls. What I assumed to be a *"B"* had turned into some sort of swirling language. The rest of my name was transcribed into something ancient and foreign. It made me shiver as I walked by.

In his study, papers were strewn from one end to the other. A thick book stood out among them. I sat down at the desk, listening to the hiss of his breath. I concluded he must have been resting somewhere, possibly upstairs.

Without thinking, I began to leaf through the tattered book, not really focusing on the words as much as the shapes of paragraphs and frantic scribbled lines. Loose pages from other notebooks gently fell from the journal, some very faded and yellowed, compelling me to take a closer look.

When I say that the passages were difficult to read, I refer more to content than condition. They made little sense, at best sounding like surreal dreams and nightmares. The first page was dated November, though the year had faded from the page. The author wrote in a thick, yet eloquent prose a fantastic tale of some ancient myth or legend. From the few legible paragraphs, I gathered it to be, as I mentioned before, a dream or perhaps an excerpt from a bizarre work of science fiction about a female deity that lived in the earth.

> *"It has come to this. I am writing under the cover of darkness for fear that She may be watching. My mother, of course, is always watching...and that is a most dreadful condition in and of itself...but if She is here, and I am nearly certain that She is always here, then I am correct in hiding away in the shadows. I would pray, if I believed for one solitary moment that it would wash away the veil of red in which She has enshrouded this house, but those sorts of efforts are of little use in times like these. Christ...even as I pen these words I can feel the lot of them circling in the hall, those red-mouthed ghosts, my own dead whore of a mother being one of the worst!"*

The next page, far too delicate and brittle to have been jammed so carelessly into the journal, was even older and penned by a different author, not as skilled as his predecessor. In his own choppy narrative, he told a similar unsettling tale of a woman, a mother, who lived in the earth. Any more than that, I don't know. There were no other pages from that man's journal. He had initialled and dated the bottom of the page. The only bit I could understand was an 'N' and the year, 1889.

My fingers ran along the edge of the pages as I read on. It was then I noticed a thin gap midway through the journal. There were three black and white photographs wedged inside.

The first was of a young woman, plain but still pretty. Her teeth were slightly crooked but this seemed to make the shape of her mouth more attractive than not. Edward bore the same trait. Her smile, while engaging, was forced. The stillness of her eyes gave it all away. She had seen something ugly once. She was still seeing it. Even before reading the inscription on the back I knew this must be Edward's mother. In faded, perfect cursive it read:

Rosalie Margaret Grace ~ 1952.

The second was of a man I assumed to be Edward's grandfather. He was stern and weathered and had the eyes of an alcoholic. I could see the doctor in this man's angular face as well. This would be Edward in twenty years, if he were still alive. Scrawled across the back in a less steady hand was the name *Jacob Edward Grace*. It had been taken the same year.

The third photograph had been taken in the house. I recognized the mantle of the fireplace in the sitting room that was now filled with broken African deities. Rosalie sat on a Victorian fainting couch with a baby in her arms. She was staring with glassy eyes in the direction of a frail man in a chair. The man was Jacob. The back read simply '*53.*

I stared at the picture for many minutes. I couldn't see the baby's face in the grain of the film. It was difficult to see it as Edward. He was innocent here. I wanted to ask Rosalie what was wrong, as something clearly was, and I wondered if Edward's father had taken the picture. Then I wondered why Edward had his mother's last name.

"You found my journal."

My heart jumped at his brittle voice. I turned toward the door, but couldn't find any words. I could barely find my breath.

He smiled and moved toward me behind the desk. He looked damp, perhaps with water but more likely with perspiration. His skin was pallid and I could see each rib, clearly defined. He was all gristle and bone.

"I thought you might be sleeping." I tried to conceal my fear and stay calm. I'd let Edward set the tone for this encounter and try to adapt. No sense stirring him up if he was feeling sedate even though I resented that he found me before I noticed him.

"You asked for quiet, did you not?" He knelt beside the leather chair and folded his arms on the desk. He put his head down and cocked it to the side like a little boy. "Looks like you had quite a time of it out there."

I remembered my missing tooth and touched the crust of dried blood on my mouth. He turned his head and let out an insincere gasp as he noticed the photographs.

"Oh, look...you found Mum!" He reached for Rosalie. "My, my...lovely woman she was."

"You look like her." My throat felt like it was bleeding. I tried to clear away the dryness but my nerves drank away what little moisture I could produce.

"That's so kind of you to say, darling...but I think I take after this old chap." He ran his fingertip over Jacob's face.

"He was your grandfather then, your mother's father?" My body slumped back into the chair as Edward pushed his way between the desk and me. He wedged himself past my knee and in between my legs, nearly oblivious to the fact that I already occupied that space. He was silent for a long moment.

"Yes...my Mum's father." He twisted his body around until he was facing me, glaring up at me. With one elbow jutting into the top of my thigh, he casually propped his chin on his hand. "I'll tell you a secret, Isabel...but you must promise never, ever to tell another soul. Do you want to know what it is?' He had the demeanour of a six-year-old.

"Of course," my voice cracked again.

"Promise you won't tell?" He pushed himself up further. His hands gripped the arms of the chair. The muscles in his arms pulsed and his knuckles went white with pressure.

"Who would I tell?"

He crept in closer to my face. "Even if you are threatened with unspeakable acts of torture and mutilation..." his voice grew louder with each word.

"Yes, Edward...I swear..." I could only manage a whisper.

He opened his mouth at my chin and breathed in so hard I thought he might inhale me. I closed my eyes and felt his lips brush across my chin and linger at the red crust on my mouth. With the lightest of pressure he licked at the blood. "Your lips taste of blood and earth," was all he said, followed by a soft, seductive laugh.

"That's not a secret." Our mouths were less than a whisper apart. Between us, the scent was foul. I focused on it to keep from kissing him.

"No, it's not." He pulled back slightly and let clarity rush in. "Jacob is my father." There was a calm resignation on his face. "Rather...he *was* my father."

I opened my mouth, hoping to find a sympathetic word, or something that closely resembled it. My heart sank at the very thought and all I could say was, "How...?"

"Well he's dead now, you see...a disintegrated liver, among other nasty things."

"Not that..." I sighed. "How did it come to that? I mean I know how it happened... but why? How did you find out? Did your mother ever talk to you about it? Where was your grandmother in all of this?"

Edward sat at my feet and pulled his knees to his chest. "My, we're full of questions, aren't we? I must have taught you well." Shifting again, he turned to face the desk and put his head against my leg. "My grandmother, she was called Willamena, married

Jacob in 1936. He was a professor of medieval literature—a very, very intelligent man. He travelled the world's brothels and opium parlours before Willamena came along, lived the grand life of debauchery. A regular Oscar Wilde...only without the writing, the wit, or the homosexuality."

I found myself combing my fingers through his oily hair as he continued.

"Finally he decided to settle down. He married Willa...he always called her Willa. She was young and pretty and neurotic. He was a good deal older than she and I imagine this appealed to him. They had a daughter called Rosalie and would have lived happily ever after, if it hadn't been for his vices, that is."

"Paedophilia and incest?"

He laughed. "No, he was an alcoholic. And mad from syphilis." With his finger he traced a vein on the top of my foot, over and over again. "I think it started during the war. His drinking became heavier and between that and the stress of wartime, Willa really began to fall apart. I believe he must have had Rosalie many times before she finally conceived. Poor Willa became so lost she began to believe that her own husband and daughter were actually a couple. The dementia consumed her slowly... there was nothing she could do for Rosalie. Mum was only sixteen or seventeen when she had me. I don't think she could fathom loving me. My mother that is...Willa always loved me. I'm certain of it."

"Why didn't she run away?" The words came before I could think better of it and I prepared myself for the backlash. His finger stopped mid-trace.

"And you have always exhibited such courage and clarity?"

"Of course not...I didn't mean to say..."

"Yes, well, she loved him. He was her father after all. Are you so certain that you wouldn't have done anything your father asked, out of fear?"

"My father is a decent man, Edward. He never would have entertained such thoughts."

"Maybe so. Interesting how you didn't seem to inherit that trait."

"What's that supposed to mean?"

"We both know how much you love your *daddy*. Are you honestly going to sit there and say you never wanted to kill your mother and marry your father?"

I suppressed the urge to kick him. The implication disgusted me.

"Remember, you aren't the only one inside your precious little head any more. I know you think I look like him..."

"Oh, sod off." *Don't cry...don't cry...don't...*

"And..." he drew the word out as he stood up and bent over me. "...I know you've thought such things while engaging in certain lewd, albeit very satisfying, acts."

"Don't, Edward." My jaw felt tight enough to crack.

He put his hand to his face, "Oh, dear...have I hit a nerve?"

I glared into the corner of the room.

"Prove me wrong then." He let himself fall onto me, straddling the chair, trapping me with his arms. "Come on. I'm up for a little role-play. Hop on and see if you can resist thinking of me as your father."

"You are vile. Don't you have some sort of religious icon you can bang one out on?"

The smile slid from his face and he backed away from me. "Funny girl," he sneered, catching me by the arm as I tried to jump past him. "You could call me 'Daddy' if it would help..."

I tore away from him and his vicious laughter and raced out of the room.

In the abysmal pit that was once a kitchen I realised how hungry I was, and the putrid clutter was not enough to curb my need for food or for sanctuary from Edward. I picked through the mess, trying to keep away from the blood and glittering shards of glass. Most of the fruit in the wooden bowl was rotten and splattered with dried blood. He's already been inside me, I thought, so what difference did a bit of blood make. I found an apple that was not yet soft and ran it under the tap.

"Ow, *fuck me!*"

I spit out the first bite as a searing pain shot through my gums. How could I keep forgetting about that tooth? I supposed it was easy to forget about something that was no longer there. It was the tender hole I needed to remember. I tried again, this time taking the tiniest bite on the opposite side of my mouth.

It was divine. I leaned on the counter, nibbling away slowly and carefully. The only two things that existed in that moment were the apple and myself and even though it made my stomach ache, it was mine and I adored it.

Then I heard him coming.

"Dear heart, I'm home...what's for dinner?" He came around the corner and slithered up beside me.

I moved to the other side of the counter in silence, fiercely protective of my apple.

"Speaking of coming home," he sneered, "How did you find your way back?"

"I thought I was following your 'psychic' directions."

"Well, originally, yes...that was what I'd intended," he paused and scratched the back of his head, "but then, after a while without you here to amuse me, I grew restless and then I realised it was harder than I thought with the concentrating and what-have-you and then, well...quite frankly, I got bored, so I stopped." He shrugged and grinned. "After you stopped screaming blue murder out there it wasn't as much fun."

"So you were just going to leave me out there?"

"You're a relatively intelligent girl, Isabel. I knew you'd find your way eventually with nothing but my love to guide you home. As long as you didn't plummet into the quarry, that is."

"Actually, it was the monks." My apple had dwindled to the sticky core and I threw it into the breakfast nook, which was filled with rubbish anyway. I went to the tap to wash my face and hands.

"We don't *have* monks," he said.

Unlike anything else in the house, the water was fresh and clean. I let my whole head drop into the basin. I drank in the streams as they ran through my hair and around my face. A cold arc of water lashed through the air when I threw my head back and straightened up. Edward jolted back as though the water repelled him.

"You're making a mess!" He rubbed his face and arms with much agitation. "What monks?" His voice was impatient.

"The monks that live in the ground. You know, the ones that chant?"

He looked at me like I was the lunatic. "What did you hear? You heard the laylines, didn't you, the hum of the laylines? That's what you heard." He was wide-eyed and manic again.

I shrugged. "All I know is that the ground was humming and I followed it home."

"Oh, this is magnificent. I always knew they ran under here, but I could never hear them myself!" He was ringing his hands. "This is smashing!" He laughed. "And to think...I felt that you'd been robbed a bit in this affair, but here you are...hearing laylines and such." He grabbed on to me in a forceful embrace, pinning my arms to my side. "I'm so very proud of you, Isabel." I thought he might cry.

I couldn't stand to be in the kitchen any longer. I was exhausted and started up the stairs to try to find a place to rest. Of course, Edward followed close behind, chattering questions and praise all the way. He followed me into his room. The bedroom and lav were surprisingly clean, save for a bit of blood. He must not have spent much time in here.

"Talk to me, love..." he whined. "What key was it in? Did it sound like this?" He hummed a low, bass note. "Or was it more like this?" He tried again, this time even lower. "How loud was it? You *must* tell me."

I sighed, turned on the water in the bath and tried to emulate the earthy drone. "I can't do it. It's lower than I can do, I think."

"Could you find it on a piano?" He looked so expectant.

"Maybe..." I mused for a moment, until I realised the absurdity of the conversation.

"Wait, no...Christ, Edward, will you let me have a bath and rest? Is that too much to ask of you?"

"Yes, all right then. Have your silly bath." He was agitated again.

"Do we even have a piano?"

"Well, we must have one somewhere in this house. Wealthy people always have pianos." He sat down on the toilet seat and huffed.

"Are you planning to watch?"

"I don't very well have anything else to do," he sputtered, looking disappointed.

"Lovely," I muttered. I removed the muddy black trousers I'd been wearing for what felt like years. He stared vacantly at me as I did so.

"Is that necessary?"

"Please, Isabel...after all we've done?" He rolled his eyes.

I continued to undress and looked into the mirror. I was disgusting. My heart sank as I recalled a time, long ago, when I had been pretty. Now I looked ropey and dirty and bruised. My hair, once dark and shimmering was caked and knotted. I was pallid and thin. My lip was swollen and the big, black gap in the back corner of my mouth was all I could focus on.

"Vanity is a sin."

"Then I suppose I'll be seeing you in Hell."

"I still think you're beautiful."

It struck me hard to hear him say it. "Please don't look at me," was all I could say.

I sank into the hot water, all the way under for as long as I could take it. It felt as good as it had back in the days before I became such a horrid beast. Edward was serene and quiet after that. It was a new record for him. How could I feel pity for him when really, I just wanted to hate him? But there he was—an insane genius in filthy trousers sitting on a toilet. A god-like creature who had seen and understood more than possibly any other living person, covered in sweat and blood, picking at the skin on his arm and staring at the marble floor with nothing better to do than watch me take a bath.

"Edward, why don't you join me? I'll help you clean up."

"Can we talk about the laylines?" He looked cautiously hopeful.

"All right...but I can't do the noise, so don't ask me."

He stripped down and eased his bones into the water. He was in worse condition than I. With his back to me, I pulled his head gently into my lap, until he was submerged. I washed the oil from his hair and then worked on his face and body. He didn't fight me. He returned the favour by helping me wash my own hair. We didn't talk about the laylines in that time. We didn't speak at all. We simply tried to cleanse each other of the layers of madness and depravity we'd built up.

It was frightening to feel the chemistry emerging again. He pulled me to his body and I let him hold me there for a long time. I kept thinking that if we both just died here, exactly like this, then it would all be well again. This wasn't sick or painful. It was the way we all wish death to be—warm and soft and in the arms of the person you love.

"I love you too," he whispered.

I closed my eyes until the grey water turned cold, but when I opened them again we were both still alive and we were both still monsters.

I slept next to Edward that evening. We held on to each other's bodies, just to feel some sense of comfort.

"We never talked about the laylines," he whispered.

"You're right. I'm sorry. We can talk about them now if you like," I replied as I nestled my head into his chest. "Why can I hear them now?"

He turned onto his side and propped himself up on the pillows. "You know that everything on earth vibrates at specific frequencies, yes?" He didn't wait for me to respond. "And those frequencies are tonal, just like music. The earth has her own tone, her own song to hum, though it's so unbelievably low, that it's essentially imperceptible to people. Animals can hear the static and energy of an impending storm, and I'd imagine they can hear the subterranean hum as well."

He continued, "Now, consider that two components have crossed paths as of late. The first would be the transformation that you've experienced. This is merely one of an infinite number of things you'll discover with your newly opened mind. You'll see and hear and feel things that have been lurking just beyond perception for an unfathomable number of years. You've no idea how lucky you are, really. Before long, the mysteries will be few and far between."

"The second part of the equation is in the ground, in those concentrated pools of energy all over the world, all connected to each other. People have utilized these spots since the beginning without even realizing why. They've built churches and cities and factories on them. These places have been the scenes of both great advancements and disasters, man-made and natural. If history is to be made anywhere, it will most likely occur on these pools. The lines that connect them act just like arteries or railways, they keep all of that energy moving. And you see, we are fortunate enough to live on a layline. I've never been able to hear it, myself, but I've always felt it and now I know for certain."

"That would mean that there's one of those pools of energy around here, then?"

"That's right. Isn't it fantastic?"

"I suppose so." I didn't want to crush his enthusiasm, but I couldn't see what was so fantastic about it at all. If anything, I suddenly felt terrified of my surroundings.

He was awake as I drifted off and still awake when I woke up. I don't think he actually slept, nor did he need to. I'd come to briefly in the night and watched him through my haze. He was lying on his back, eyes wide open and unblinking. He was perfectly still. For a moment I thought he might be dead, but without looking he gently smoothed a lock of hair from my face. It was the only part of him that moved. I awoke in the morning, before the sunrise, draped across his chest. He was still staring. I wondered if he was even inside the shell of his body. He looked utterly empty.

He never seemed to eat any more. He had track marks on his arms and stomach. I didn't know what he was injecting, only that it hadn't killed him yet. There was a deep, hollow chasm below his rib cage where his stomach used to be.

I remembered my dream from months before. In it he had been living solely on the injections. It had been so disturbing in my sleep, but for some reason now it really wasn't so frightening. I lay on his still body and watched the sun rise up, far away over the trees. He kept one hand on my back, moving his thumb in the tiniest circle every few minutes—so I'd know he was still there.

It was our calm before the storm. Everything was so quiet and surreal in eye of the hurricane, too beautiful to last. For a split second I wondered if this was a way for him to torment me, making me remember how much I loved him before tearing it away. It would only be a brief matter of time before it happened again.

Much to my amazement, the day crept along with very little trauma. I washed our clothes and sheets and began the daunting task of cleaning the kitchen. I found some glue and sat Edward at the kitchen table with the pieces of his statues. He was listless at first and complained that he couldn't concentrate, but after a few minutes he began to work in a more diligent fashion. The kitchen was easier to overhaul than I thought it would be as I ended up throwing most of the clutter into large plastic bags.

"Do we have any cigarettes here? I could really go for a fag right now."

"I don't believe so. I've never seen you smoke."

"Many years ago I did. I'm thinking I'd like to start again." He fumbled with a deity's tiny wooden arm.

I shrugged, "I'm sure I wouldn't know what to do about that."

"We could go to the market."

I couldn't fathom what it would be like to go into civilization again. I stared at him, rather stunned.

"You can still drive, can't you? I doubt I can. Or should."

I nodded.

"We could get you some food and wine, since the food we have seems to have turned." He smiled to himself. "That would be nice, wouldn't it?" He seemed so pleased with his generosity.

"Edward...I don't know if it would be the best thing for you to be out in the public."

"I'll stay with the car." He looked at me with strange eyes. "I presume I can trust you...am I wrong?"

I thought long and hard before I answered. This could be my one chance. There probably wouldn't be another for a long time, if ever. I tried to conceal the deep breath I was taking before I let the words spill out.

"I won't try to run." He would know if I was lying, so I made sure it was the truth.

He stared at me with burning eyes for another moment, and then relaxed his gaze. "Right then." He'd sifted through my head until he found that what I'd said was true. "I'll try to find the keys."

If you factored in the time spent in traffic once inside the town limits, Chapel Marketplace was approximately half an hour from the estate, which was still not far enough away in my opinion. The air was different once we were off his property. As I watched the tall, dense trees that lined the road become houses, people, and signs, I remembered that the world still existed. It was a shock to see faces and bodies that didn't belong to us. These people were moving about their lives as though nothing was wrong, as though nothing had ever happened. I looked over at Edward. He appeared half-dead, but clean, in the sunlight, and was wearing sunglasses and his beige Burberry coat, despite the warmth of the air. I'd found a fresh pair of dress pants for him and a clean, white button-down shirt. He'd refused shoes.

His skin was turning blue.

All those people out there were oblivious to what he was and they couldn't begin to dream of what he had done.

"Can you hear their thoughts, too?"

His expression turned to disgust. "My god, yes...but not because I want to," he sneered. "I mean, just look at them. It's bad enough *they* have to be trapped with their mundane thoughts. Should they be inflicted upon me, as well?" He smiled again. "Be thankful you haven't a gift as polished as mine, yet."

"You may have lost your mind, Edward, but it's nice to see that your elitist attitude hasn't waned."

"As long as I still have blood coursing through these veins, I can assure you it will be a lovely shade of blue."

We didn't speak much as we drove through the town. Edward appeared to be in a meditative state, taking it all in, or perhaps blocking it all out. It was difficult to tell.

I, on the other hand, had to fight my urge to pull over and strike up a conversation with someone at every turn. There was no desire to tell them the whole sordid tale. I just wanted to talk about the weather, about current events…I didn't care. Another human voice would be enough to set me right again, at least for a few minutes. I pulled the car over prematurely, still some distance from the market.

"Why are we stopping here?" His eyes weren't even open.

"Because I want to walk. I want to nod 'hello' to people. I just want to get some sun." I tried to emphasise the desperation in my voice. It came out more like whining.

He considered this for a moment then reached for the door handle. "Let's go then."

I grabbed him by the sleeve of his coat. "I really don't think…"

"Christ, Bel, I'm not a rabid beast. I do know how to exhibit some decorum."

"Right. You realise you haven't any shoes?"

He paused and looked down at his feet. "Well what do you know?" He seemed genuinely surprised.

"Look, Edward," I pointed ahead, "you can see the market from here."

He craned his neck and wrinkled up his face. "Where do you see a market?"

"If you get out of the car you can see it."

He opened the door and got out, cringing as the bright sky assaulted him. "Ah, right…there it is."

"Lovely. Why don't you just stay here, then? You can watch me walk down there and make sure I don't run amok, screaming about what a maniac you are. Is that acceptable to you?"

He leaned back inside the car. "You have fifteen minutes before I come after you and make a dreadful scene in my bare feet."

⥆

The aromas inside Chapel assaulted me as I rushed through the door. Under normal circumstances it would have been heavenly, but these odours were pungent and brutal. The air was full of fish and cheese and fruit and death. I walked past the butchery in a rush, knowing I couldn't bear to look at it. It reminded me of what I'd carried inside my body. For a brief second a gruesome scene unfolded before me of Edward and I chewing at a slick, fleshy cord. There was blood on our hands and mouths, and I started to choke on the imaginary mass. Fortunately, a small queue was forming in front of the counter and my view was obstructed. I continued down the long aisle toward the bakery.

There were people all around. Chapel was one of those places that had existed since the dawn of time, passed down from father to son for many generations. It was charming and antiquated, and the new blood that spread out from the cities into this once small town relished the market. It had become the trendy place to be seen having tea among the University set and young, hip couples that overran the town each weekend. At the centre of it all was Mr Chapel, the only soul in the place that looked like he belonged there. He was a bit antiquated, too, with his ruddy face, knobbly hands, and naive bewilderment about what had become of the simple village of his boyhood. As much as he enjoyed the success his family's establishment was accruing, he seemed overwhelmed by it. He was even forced to hire non-Chapels to help ease the workload. He stood behind the bakery counter, watching the pretentious consumers scuttle to and fro with wary eyes. I waded my way through the horde and into Mr Chapel's view.

"Lady Isabel!" He relaxed his brow and his eyes brightened. He stretched his arms up over the counter and shook my hands. "Where've you been, love? I was beginnin' to think you'd left our little town an' not said farewell!"

"Heavens, no. That's not how I was raised, Mr Chapel." I flashed him a frantic smile.

"Are you still up there at the Grace house? I 'aven't seen hide nor hair of either of you for ages, now." He returned my smile with a sly glance and lowered his voice. "I was beginnin' to wonder if the two of you'd run off together...'til the other day when the doctor had me send my sister's boy, John, up with a delivery." Suddenly his face crinkled with concern. He looked me over for a moment. "You 'aven't been ill, have you?"

"No. Well, I was a little under the weather...but it was nothing serious," I lied.

"You look a hair worn." We both knew his wording was generous. He smiled again. "Still pretty as a picture, tho'."

I nodded bashfully.

"So how is the good doctor these days? I hear every sort of rumour 'round these parts, but I never mind that...seems folks 'ave nothing better to do than wonder about ev'rybody else's business when they should just be mindin' themselves."

"He's well...Mr Chapel, I do hate to cut this short, but I really have to...."

"Say no more. If you don' tell me when you've heard enough, I just keep blowin' hot air! What can I get for you?"

I handed him the crumpled list and he put on his thick bifocals holding it at arms length.

"I'll fetch John and he'll get this together for you right quick." He paused and clasped his hands. "Did you meet John when he was up there? He's a good boy," he smiled to himself. I could almost see the wheels turning in his head. "Twenty years old, he is. Say, I bet you'd really fancy him. I could introduce you, if you'd like." He looked so hopeful.

"Oh, well I'd love to meet him...unfortunately I really am in a bit of a rush today."

The old man tried to hide his disappointment.

"But certainly if he has half the charm of his uncle, he must be a fine fellow indeed." I said, hoping it would help.

He puffed himself up a little, satisfied. "Well, perhaps next time you're in then." He shuffled away yelling for his nephew with a thick, booming voice.

I was getting nervous. Every few seconds I glanced around, praying that Edward would stay at the car, and wondering if he'd even know when the fifteen minutes had passed. He'd since destroyed all of his watches. I turned my back to the crowd and peered into the display case I'd been leaning on. The smell of yeast was suffocating and intoxicating. The din of the mob swirled together and it was impossible to distinguish one conversation from another.

Please, come on then...please, hurry. I closed my eyes and rested my head lightly on top of the case, hoping to make the noise and the odours and the frustration disappear. It was working; a hush seemed to be sweeping over the market. Seconds later I realised that a hush *actually was* sweeping over the market. My stomach flipped as I lifted my head and suddenly, I didn't want to turn around.

"There you are!" Edward threw his arms in the air and looked around to address the crowd. He gestured at the imaginary watch on his wrist and turned back to me. "I am a very busy man, mademoiselle." He shot me a knowing glance. "We did say fifteen minutes, did we not?"

He turned to his audience, most of who were beginning to move on, yet the faces remained focused on us. I'd gone from bright red to white and every shade in between.

He sighed and looked to the crowd, "Good help is so difficult to find these days. A cliché, of course, but true nonetheless."

They were all staring at him with utter confusion. A woman only a few years older than Edward shot him a look of disgust and commented to her husband about the doctor's bare feet and corpse-like appearance.

They knew he wasn't like them. They could feel instinctually, in the reptilian part of their brains.

Faintly offended, he slipped behind me into the queue and remained quiet for several moments. Still embarrassed and flushed, I kept my eyes on the floor, shuffling my feet in discomfort.

"Are you upset?" he whispered with a grin.

"No, just humiliated, thank you." I hissed back without looking up.

"Oh, don't get all twisted up about it. It was only in good fun, right?" He nudged me with his elbow.

"You're not funny. You were supposed to wait with the car, remember?"

"Yes, I remember. I'm not a child, you know. Anyway, I was bored. I thought things might be more interesting if I joined you."

"I should say that you'll certainly be stirring up a great deal of interesting gossip, coming in here like this. I mean, you look dreadful...and you shouldn't even be in here without your shoes. It's not sanitary."

"Having this many people crammed together in one space isn't exactly sanitary either. Do you feel all of that heat? It's coming out of these people—this biomass—out of their filthy mouths, out of their unwashed flesh. It's repulsive, really, when you think about it. Far worse than my feet."

"Brilliant." I rolled my eyes in disgust.

He fidgeted around in his coat for a moment, and then began to assign each passer-by a number at random.

"79...83...42, oh my...91...56...37, oh, what a shame..."

"What are you doing?"

"88. See that man that just walked by, in the blue denim trousers? That's how old he'll be when he dies."

"Edward, that is repulsive. Why would you say such things?"

"I remember when you used to be fun," he sighed.

"And I remember when you used to be human. It must have been dreadful for you, out there in the car that *entire* time. And I forgot to pack the crayons and the obituary page in your grab bag before we left. Perhaps we can play 'I Spy' instead."

He disregarded my comments; his eyes brightened as he craned his neck, peering through the crowd. "First-rate idea! I spy...I spy. Let's see...I spy...with my *litt-le* eye... something that is cheating on his wife," he said in the direction of a passing middle-aged man in a brown hat.

The man didn't stop but glanced sidelong at us as he went. I could tell by the look on his face that he thought he might have heard Edward right, but hadn't a clue as to how a stranger would know his business or why that stranger would feel inclined to make such a comment.

A thin woman a few years older than me approached dragging a four or five year old child by the hand. Edward waited until she was in earshot and quietly took his next turn.

"I spy with my little eye something that cannot seem to control her rage." He gazed vacantly above the little boy. "Though I can't even begin to imagine what it is that he could do that would illicit such violence and resentment...can't say I haven't been there myself, though..." he trailed off as the woman turned and glared at him incredulously.

He remained focused on her, waiting, daring her to speak, but she said nothing. She only looked upon him with a bitter mixture of hatred and shame before walking away, carelessly pulling the child along with her.

"Edward, please stop. This isn't right," I whispered.

"Oh, just one more, all right?"

But when he remarked in an audible tone that he spied something morbidly obese that was going to be dead in two years of congestive heart failure, I reached my limit.

"That's enough. *Get out!*" I spun around, seething and gritting my teeth. "Just get out of here! These people have done *nothing* to you! You are behaving like a madman!"

Again, he looked rather offended. "Well," he sniffed. "I spy with my little eye something that looks remarkably like a humourless cunt."

I was about to respond with great fury when I noticed Mr Chapel, holding the box of food and sundries I had requested. By the look on his face I knew he had witnessed most of the bizarre scene. His nephew stood behind him, wearing a similar expression.

Edward smiled at them both. "Ah, lovely...here it is..."

I fumbled nervously through my pockets for the money I had brought from home. It was also crumpled into a ball, like the list had been. Mr Chapel didn't say a word as he slowly took the money from my hand. He was concentrating on Edward, who was digging through the box for cigarettes.

Without looking up Edward spoke. "Lovely to see you again, Mister Chapel. And how is the family?"

Before he could answer Edward spoke again. "And John—lovely to see you as well. You really should drop in sometime, and not just to make a delivery." He continued rummaging. "You see, John, I work so much—it's horrible really—and Isabel is always alone. I mean, you see how nervy it's making her, though that could very well be a feminine issue, if you know what I mean." He looked up and winked at the boy. "At any rate, I think she would just *love* your company, wouldn't you, Isabel?" He gave me a hard and playful shaking then let go and lit up a cigarette. "Well it *has* been exquisite chatting with you people, but we must be off..."

He sashayed down the aisle, leaving the box for me to carry. I muttered an apology to Mr Chapel without actually looking him in the eye and made my way through the crowd, trying to ignore the reproachful faces that surrounded me.

Edward reached the car well before I. I threw the box into the backseat and slammed the door. We were halfway home before the silence was broken.

"Well, that was amusing." He looked smug.

"So where was the decorum you spoke of? What happened to *'I'm not a beast, Isabel'*? You lasted...what was it, seventeen minutes...before the urge to humiliate me got the best of you? What on earth did you think I was doing in there? Where was the bloody trust, Edward? And what do you suppose that little display accomplished...did you need to make certain the whole town knows you're a fucking nutter? Because I think you've succeeded..."

"I told you, I was bored. Plus I wanted to—what's that phrase the kids are using these days— *'check out'* the competition."

"What? Who? Chapel's nephew? Oh, for the love of god! I've never even said two words to the lad."

"Well it seems he'd have so much to offer...though I imagine he might not be old enough for you."

"Why are you doing this? I didn't even entertain the thought and you know it!"

"Oh, lighten up, Bel. So serious, you are..." He was still laughing.

"Fuck you. You were just showing off."

"You know what they say about ladies who doth protest too much..." He raised his eyebrow suspiciously.

"Fine, Edward. I'm going to leave you for the illustrious life of a Grocer's-nephew's-wife. Really, it's been a dream of mine since I was a little girl."

He grinned and put his head against the window. "Sometimes it's just too easy with you, Isabel."

The moment we returned home a hundred unanswered questions swarmed around us.

Much like a faithful dog, they were eagerly waiting for us at the door. Our collective ability to focus on any given topic was diminishing more and more with each passing day. I knew Edward would soon try to resume the layline discussion with me and when he did, I would barter with him for further information on his family history.

I carried the food to the kitchen and proceeded to open the French doors along with the windows. The house was desperate for clean air.

He crept up behind me as I stood at the doors. "We don't have to play games, love. If you have questions, just ask."

"Can you hear every single word I think?"

"As though they were my own." He put his arms around my waist. He almost sounded mournful of the fact.

"All right, then. How did you come to find out?"

He was still holding on. I could feel his breathing quicken.

"Oh, I believe I was about eight or nine years old when I first began to suspect. They had done a tremendous job of keeping it secret until then, though, really how difficult is it to fool a child? I still believed in fairies and witches at the time."

The thought of Edward believing in fairy tales made me smile.

"But then I started overhearing bizarre conversations. I started to notice subtle mannerisms in my mother and grandfather. Awkward glances, inappropriate body language...things like that. I also began thinking about death a great deal around the same time. You see, when I was very young I'd been told my father was dead, but never provided with details. They always said I was too young to understand. It wasn't until I started obsessing over it that my grandmother, the poor soul, told me the truth." He buried his face in my hair for a moment, giving me chills.

"How were you obsessing?"

"I started writing stories and drawing pictures. Horrid tales of every different death scenario I could imagine. The victim was always the same, some nameless fellow that I imagined looking the way I would once I was grown. That poor man suffered more gruesome deaths than I can easily recall. And my mother...god, how it upset her. I would come into the parlour where she'd be sitting with Jacob and my Gram and begin to read my story. Usually she would tear the pages from my hands and throw them into the fire, whereas Jacob, had he been drinking, would grab me by the arm and twist until I screamed for mercy. Or sometimes he would strike me so hard I'd fall down. I was rather weak for my age and had poor balance..." he gestured to his ear, "chronic ear infections. So, it was quite easy to do and he knew it. And my poor, mental Gram would just sit there, all proper in her pearls and gloves—she always wore her pearls and gloves—and stare straight ahead into the fire, chin quivering...it was the only way I knew she'd been aware. She had her good days, but most of the time she was catatonic."

It should have been the most obvious thing in the world that Edward had been abused, but it never once crossed my mind. Perhaps he was just too far from being a victim any more.

"I suppose Gram figured that if I knew the truth about my father I'd stop writing those morbid stories and therefore give Jacob one less reason to harm me. It was surprisingly rational thinking for a woman in her condition. It's funny...my Gram, nearly an invalid...an emotional cripple, had the presence of mind to try and save me from him. Yet my own mother, who always appeared so stable, could do nothing to stop him... nor did she try. I can only imagine how far gone she must have been to allow it."

I put my head on his shoulder. "What did you do when she told you?"

"I took it quite well, really." He laughed. "I believe I said... 'Oh.' And I stopped writing the stories. Little did Gram realise at the time, I hadn't a full understanding of what exactly it all implied. No one had given me any information on reproduction...no birds, no bees...not a word. The worst part was accepting that the father I'd invented didn't actually exist, and it took a long time for me to erase him from my head. As I got older and started to figure things out for myself, and I came to realise how repulsive the whole thing was."

"Did you tell him? Or your mother?"

"Oh, no. He was dead before I pieced it all together." I felt him take a deep breath. "And as for my mother...well, Gram had bade me keep it a secret from her. I mustn't ever let on that I knew...and I held that promise until Gram died and for many years after." He took another painful breath. "But just before I left for Africa, my mother suffered a stroke. She hadn't long to live and begged me to stay with her. I refused. I came to see her one last time and it was then my secret broke. I told her I knew about her and my grandfather. Then I told her I had nothing further to say and that I had an aeroplane to catch. In my head, I had a million hateful words for her, but decided that she wasn't worth another minute of my time. I'm told she died as I was flying over Spain."

I searched for the regret in his voice. It was empty and I didn't completely blame him for that.

"Have you forgiven them?"

He narrowed his eyes and scanned the empty space before him for an answer.

"As for Jacob...well, he may be beyond forgiveness. Forgiveness requires compassion, the ability to see the perpetrator as a human being, no different than yourself—you who are not infallible and have the capacity for regret—but in him there was nothing even close to that. However, I am what I am because of him and I have trouble seeing where 'forgiveness' factors into it. That I am the incestuous result of a disturbed alcoholic's fancy is merely a fact. Nothing to get all emotional about really."

He let me go and lit up another cigarette. "Now, my mother...Dear Rosalie lived here until her stroke. She was here while I was at University, when I became a doctor, and while I was studying Theology. She was here the entire time, subjected to all the religions, all the theories, all the ethics and morality. That was when I endeavoured to fill the house with a collection of spiritual goods. I suppose I wished for it all to break her, to make her confess her sins and beg forgiveness. I'm not Catholic. I never cared which deity would wear her down first, as long as something got through...but they never did. Not once in all those years did she ever admit to it, let alone say she was sorry. Never in all that time did she ever say *'Forgive me, son, for all the times I sat complacent in my chair and watched him beat you, or scream at you, or try to break your bony little arms. I'm sorry for all the torment it caused you, the confusion, all the trouble you had attempting to understand love and intimacy'....*" he stopped abruptly, after nearly tripping over the words and flicked his cigarette into the courtyard, having divulged more than intended. "Well, what's done is done. She's long dead now," he tried to regain his composure, but refused to look me in the eye as he left the room.

Despite everything, it pained me to see him this way. He was unflappable, always one step ahead of his own psyche. Not the sort to leave a room because he was uncomfortable. Edward was never uncomfortable.

(June)

Though hesitant, summer was creeping in slowly, and we had become extremely sensitive to even the slightest atmospheric changes. The house responded to the new season as well, abandoning her usual cold chaos and turning a bit sluggish and apathetic. Neither the house nor Edward cared for any sort of change that they didn't have a hand in, and the summer air, knowing this, tried her best to be subtle. I simply tried to stay out of Edward's way. He was irritable enough and I sensed that he was still feeling vulnerable. It seemed the more I knew about his past, the further away from me he drifted. I came to him one afternoon waving a white flag and carrying a bottle of wine, hoping to show him that I wasn't trying to take anything from him.

He was lying on his bed when I found him, flat on his back, staring at the ceiling.

I took a hefty swig from the bottle and held it out to him. He rolled onto his side and propped himself up on the pillows and accepted my peace offering.

The wine didn't last long. We argued momentarily, trying to decide who would go downstairs to fetch more. I was losing the battle when Edward discovered a wayward bottle of Scotch that had rolled under the bed during one of our chaotic interludes. It clashed with the wine, but it was better than stumbling down the stairs.

I tried to decide if Edward was as drunk as I was. He seemed a bit silly, but my judgment was impaired. I didn't know if he could get drunk any more. It was very likely that he was just playing along. We laughed until our faces were sore.

"It doesn't look bad, you know..." he put his hand against my face.

"Oh...right." I stuck my tongue into the vacant spot in my gum.

"My apologies. At least it's not right in the front." He looked slightly ashamed.

"Well, it's not as though you made me fall." I stretched out, hanging loosely from the edge of the bed. The room looked so different upside down. As a child I would hang from the edge of my father's reclining chair and pretend I lived in the house that existed on the ceiling. It was a blank and spacious house up there, and surreal, the sort of house that Dr Seuss would build. I smiled, remembering a childhood crush I once had on the *Cat in the Hat*. He caused so much trouble and I loved him for it, much like Edward. I closed my eyes and sighed, holding back bittersweet tears for the things I'd lost and the things I'd unintentionally found.

Edward lay down next to me. "Oh, God...I'd forgotten what a weepy drunk you are."

"What changed?" I continued to stare at the ceiling, which was now swirling. "You don't seem as mental."

"My period of adjustment must be over. I've acclimated to my environment, quite a double-edged sword, really. I suppose I'm more manageable, but I'm also getting bored." He pulled himself upright and polished off the remaining Scotch. "I think we should do it again."

"Oh, Edward...no. Please...I couldn't bear it..."

He pulled me fully back onto the bed. I felt like a rag doll, swaying limply in his grip. "You haven't gotten to experience what I have, Bel, in part because you fight it, but you need the connection, the chemistry. You need more before you'll feel what I feel and I can give that to you. I understand now. I know what I need to do differently this time. I know how to bring it to you. You need to shed your skin."

"It's not a drug...Edward..." I was slurring my words and my thoughts. "We're not addicts." I let my head slump down. "You're going to mess up my organs..."

He picked my head up and stroked my hair. "No, no, no," he whispered. "We're not going to mess up anything. You have abilities now, you have all of these wonderful gifts. I only want to help you learn what to do with them." He kissed my forehead. "And I need you to help me."

I shook my head in listless protest.

"We've come this far. There's really no turning back. Please don't make this harder than it has to be. Please don't try to fight me." He put his hand under my chin and lifted my head again. "Look at me, Isabel." He tilted his head and softened his gaze. "You won't win."

My face was thick and numb with alcohol. I don't even remember standing up and I certainly don't remember falling down the stairs. I only remember the haze of waking up, back in his bed, and the pain. I remember the pain. It was everywhere. The entire bed felt painful. Edward was wrapping my wrist in a long bandage. There was an ice pack on my cheek. There was a pounding that beat through my head and into my neck.

"Well, you needn't worry about me killing you. You'll see to it all by yourself long before I'm *that* insane."

"Did I lose any more teeth?" I winced at the pressure he was applying to my wrist.

"Thankfully, no. If you lose any more, people might begin to think you've come from the east end."

"What's the damage then?"

"Very little, a bloody miracle considering how you fell. Your wrist is sprained, and your face and head are a bit mangled...otherwise, besides your death wish, I'd say you're doing quite well. It's amazing you didn't break your neck. Fortunately, you were so intoxicated that you must have passed out before the fall and gone limp on the way down. You'd likely be dead or paralysed if it weren't for your reckless drinking. I won't know if you have a concussion until the alcohol is out of your system. Honestly, I'll be amazed if you don't."

"If I die before you, do you have any plans to reanimate my corpse?" I grabbed his shirtsleeve with my proper hand. "Oh, please...promise me you won't reanimate my corpse."

"Don't be silly...we've discussed that already. It's just not practical. Besides, you're enough of a mess alive. I can't imagine the trouble you'd be as one of the undead, staggering around, bumping into things, knocking off appendages here and there." He lifted my shirt and pushed lightly on my ribs. "Does this hurt?"

A sharp pain ran through my torso and I gasped for air. "Ah...yes, yes very much."

"Can you move? Shift yourself, if you can."

It was horribly painful, but I complied.

"I don't think they're broken. Just badly bruised. We'll keep an eye on it. Don't go anywhere." He chuckled as he left the room.

In the midst of feeling sorry for myself it occurred to me that the accident might be a mixed blessing. I was in no condition to go through with the experiment now. Soon enough my bones would heal, but this unpleasant event would afford me some time. What did not occur to me was that Edward would inevitably find a way to use my pain to his advantage. In time I would learn that my trust was the most dangerous gift I could ever give him. I suppose I knew it then, but chose to ignore it, in spite of the burning that came from a much deeper place than my damaged flesh.

He returned moments later with his medical bag. "I can give you something for the pain. You'll not really feel it until you sober up."

"I really feel it now."

"Oh, just wait. It will be worse later." He held up a needle. It was the one he used on himself. He pushed it into a small glass phial and pulled the plunger slowly. "It's very strong, but it's the only thing I have that will help. Do you want it?"

"Please." I made a wretched face as he slid the needle into my arm. It was only seconds before the pain melted away. I was swimming beneath the blankets, beneath my skin.

He smiled and smoothed my hair and I forgot to ask what it was that he had put in my veins.

We'd fallen into a terrible routine. Every time I winced or groaned, Edward would prepare the needle without hesitation. I don't recall much from those days and nights, except that he was at my side, bringing me tea and soup, helping me to the bath, keeping me company. I remembered fragments of conversation, though they never seemed quite right, never linear. And I remember the colours of my arm where the injections were administered.

As I began to heal, my thoughts became clearer. One evening he came to me, syringe in hand, right on schedule, but the pain had lessened and I could even move a bit on my own. I knew I didn't really need the medicine and I even said as much. He paused for a minute, then shrugged and began to walk away.

But I called out after him automatically, "Unless you think it's best that I should..."

He came back to the bed eagerly and sat down. "I really think it *would* be for the best."

I offered up my arm and slipped back into a beautiful stupor. "Wha's this liquid madness, anyway?" I slurred and closed my eyes.

He said nothing. I suppose he was waiting for me to fall asleep and I was nearly there when I heard him whisper the words, *'just a little morphine.'* There was nothing I could do as I drifted away.

In the morning I was hungry and I yelled for Edward. When he didn't respond, I kicked at the heavy blanket in a fit and twisted it up with my feet. Everything in the room was causing me distress and I felt sick to my stomach. There were piles of clothes on the floor, empty bottles and cups were scattered about. And that goddamn tapestry above the bed...I despised it more than ever. I kicked the mattress in a fit and rubbed my eyes, fed up with the entire world being a blur.

My body rattled as I sat up. I found one of his shirts in the cluster of fabric on the floor and carefully put it on. The pain was still there, but not nearly as strong as my aggravation and craving.

I stood for an eternity at the top of the stairs, frozen. I hadn't gone down them since the fall and now I could only imagine the first step slipping out from under me (*like falling from the castle wall*), and the cracking of bones as I descended. I took a deep and painfully sharp breath as I moved. Like a toddler, I paused with both feet on each and every step, taking twice as long to reach the bottom, shaking the entire time.

Edward was in his study, reading and smoking a cigarette, all in all looking rather normal. I walked in and stood firmly in front of his desk. He held up his hand, gesturing at me to wait a moment while he finished the passage. Before he could, I leaned in, ripped the book away from him and threw it to the floor. He calmly rubbed out his cigarette in an overflowing crystal ashtray and leaned back in his chair.

"I don't feel well, Edward," I snapped.

"So sorry to hear that. You *look* better, up and about..."

"What are you going to do to help me, Edward?"

He lowered his head and sighed, "Well, I feared this might happen."

"Oh, you knew bloody well what would happen!" I began to pace back and forth, unsteadily.

"Isabel, you have to try to fight it. You don't need it...it just has to work out of your system. Be strong."

"No, Edward, you *have* to help me. Now get the goddamn bag or..."

He laughed, "Or what? Are you threatening me, little mouse? What *exactly* will you do? Are you going to hurt me?"

He shot up from his chair and was across the desk before I could even blink. He grabbed me by my bandaged wrist, twisting it slowly and gently until I cried, then let go and backed away. I held onto my wrist, hissing curses under my breath. Without warning, he lunged toward me again and I screamed as he grabbed a fistful of my hair and nearly pulled me over his desk.

"Let me explain something to you, you *ungrateful little junkie*..." His face was pressed against my ear. His breath felt like fire. "I took you in and gave you a home. I taught you everything you'd ever need to know to pull yourself out of that mundane existence you called a life. You remember, the one you despised so much? I showed you things people only dream of, gave you answers that the rest of humanity has searched for since the beginning of time. And what did I ask in return? Nothing but your cooperation and understanding. But what did you *offer* in return? You fuck me whenever I want. Marvellous! Is that how you show your gratitude? I sacrifice years, people, relationships, sanity for this knowledge...and what do you sacrifice? *Nothing!* Tell me, is that how you say thank you? Is the only thing you have to offer me that gash between your legs?" He pulled me closer to him, and I could feel his heartbeat. "Now you stand before me and *demand* my help...though it isn't really my *help* that you want...it's my supply. *Then* you have the audacity to *threaten* me?" He wound my hair around his fist, forcing my head to turn with it. "I could break you, child. In more ways than you could ever imagine."

After what felt like many excruciating hours, he released his grip and flung me at the wall. I fell to the floor and curled into a ball, sobbing.

"It seems you may have forgotten these things when you hit your head," he said and stormed out of the study.

I was unfurling my aching body when he returned. He threw the needle on the floor in front of me and disappeared again. I was almost too upset and bleary-eyed to find a proper vein, but somehow I managed.

When had the tables turned? The morphine made me dream heavily, even when I was awake. My mind played out the peaceful times I'd had with Edward, omitting all of the pain and fear. It filled the blank spaces with unreal scenarios of a normal life with him. I thought we had a little black cat that we'd found in the woods, but it was only

Edward's black leather medical bag, tossed into a corner. For hours, I sat upon the floor of the study, believing the ugly truth to merely be a nightmare. I gazed at the needle at my feet and a wave of panic came over me as I wondered what would happen when the supply was gone. I had to stop. There was a pounding way back in my head. It was distant and irregular and I couldn't understand why. Then the pounding was at the door.

Half dressed, bruised and utterly out of my head, I stumbled to the foyer. We never received visitors. My adrenaline kicked in and gave me a head rush. "Who's there?" I mumbled, swaying and nearly falling to the stone floor.

"It's John...from Chapel. I've got a deliv'ry for Dr Grace."

"What delivery?"

"Er...the one he telephoned in 'bout an hour ago. It's cigarettes, Scotch, apples, some other things...is that you, Isabel? Can you open the door?"

I swung the heavy door open. The smile on John's face fell and he was unable to conceal his horror. He sat the box at my feet.

"Oh *shite*, Isabel...what's happened?" He reached out to me and I backed away.

"I had an accident...I'm fine, really..." I mumbled.

He lowered his voice and glanced around. "That's no accident you had there... look at your face...Christ...did *he* do this to you?"

"Why would you think that? I did it to myself." I cleared my throat. "How much do we owe you?"

"What's wrong with your eyes?" He looked down at the blue and purple pinholes that speckled my arm. The sleeve was still rolled up. "Isabel, what are those from? Jesus...what's goin' on up here?"

He stood before me utterly bewildered. He was much like a big, dumb animal with his sturdy build and thick reddish-blonde hair. His face was ruddy and meaty, like his uncle's, and the knots on his nose from multiple breaks suggested that he was a footballer, or possibly just a hooligan. I thought he might cry.

"Isabel," he whispered, "what did he do to you? I can't help unless you tell me..."

"John, please...let me pay you, then go. It's not what you think...not at all." I tried to force a smile. "It's quite...embarrassing, really. I got right pissed one night and took a tumble down the stairs. That's all that happened. Really." The words were difficult to produce, even though they were true in letter, if not spirit.

He reached for me again and opened his mouth to speak. Before he could, his gaze darted over my shoulder and he bristled.

"Bel...is this any way to greet a guest?" He put his arms around my shoulders and led me away from the door. "Heavens...why aren't you in bed?" He was drilling a hole through me with his eyes.

"I...was...getting some water and I heard John, here...knocking. I didn't think you heard, so..."

He turned to John, smiling. "Can you believe this bird? Falling down the stairs... she's quite fortunate she didn't break her neck, the clumsy thing..."

I nodded bashfully, as Edward handed John the money. John sneered at him throughout the exchange.

Edward raised his eyes to meet his gaze and turned cold and sinister. "Thank you, John. That will be all for today."

They stared each other down for a moment and the space between them went thick and hateful. They were silent. Edward seemed to grow larger—really the very walls around us seemed to grow larger along with him—until he was looming over John. We were tiny and fragile like hollow porcelain figurines in his presence. Finally, Edward broke him and he took a step backwards out the door.

John glanced at me one last time. "Take care, then...Isabel." He was trying desperately to communicate to me with his eyes. I half-waved and turned away from the door as Edward shut it in his face.

"I didn't say anything to him...about..."

"I know." He picked up the parcel of goods and silently retreated to the kitchen.

By nightfall I was irritable again, dope sick and heartbroken that another full day had passed while I was imprisoned in a haze, staggering back and forth between dreaming and pain, and I was doing it alone. There had been no sign of Edward for hours. I lumbered through each room like a zombie, holding myself tightly to keep from shaking and picking away at my skin. I kept him in my thoughts, hoping his words would prevent me from obsessing over things. I felt guilty, even though I knew this was just another game of control, just another way to keep me dependent upon him.

He told me I couldn't win, and as I broke into a cold sweat, I knew it was true. I would always be addicted, if not to a chemical, then to him. I would always be addicted to the trauma. Once, during a manic episode, he said that we needed the trauma, the devastation, every day to know that we were still alive. We would always need it. He believed there was no greater disease than the boredom of routine, and that mediocrity was a cancer that would claim more lives than any plague ever could. I feared as long as we were together, I would never truly have calm or contentment. I believed that he would see us both dead before granting me that.

I found him in the courtyard. He sat on the marble bench across from the fountain, legs crossed, a cigarette in one hand and a glass in the other. He looked disgusted. The June air was still.

I sat down on the opposite side of the fountain. The warmth in the air had done little to take the chill from the stone. The moon had come up full and cast a long, brilliant white pathway across the garden. I could hear the humming in the distance. I wished Edward could hear it, too.

"Is it time for your medicine, already?" His voice was dead as he stared at the glowing stream of light.

The sickness welled up inside, but I swallowed it painfully. "No, thank you." The words barely came. "I'm trying to fight it, the way you said."

"Then why are you here?"

"I just...I missed you."

"Ah." He exhaled a long trail of smoke and gazed upwards to the sky. "How dreadfully romantic."

"The ground is humming again. Out there...beneath the light." I forced a bit of enthusiasm.

"I wouldn't know."

I put my head down on my knees and wondered if this was real. I wondered if he was as hurt as he seemed or if it was a ruse.

"Do you still love me?"

I knew he would despise the question. The look of revulsion on his face was confirmation.

"Would it change anything, either way?" He looked at me for the first time since I'd sat down. "If I said no, what would you do? And if I said yes...what would you do differently?"

I stood up and went to the door upon realising I had no answer.

"Think what you want, Edward...but remember I'd do anything for you. I've done everything you've ever asked and I know that I've *always* had a choice." Tears streamed down my swollen cheeks. "And I always chose you."

I couldn't bring myself to go to my old room when Edward's bedroom was right there, beckoning me. It was silent and dark, save for the stream of moonlight that spilled across the floor and onto the bed. It made the white down blanket glow like a snowdrift on a bright, bitter night. I felt cold and sick and lost, and there was comfort to be found there, so I curled myself into a ball, nestled into his blanket and quietly sobbed. I was so very tired, but every time I began to drift off, a terrible aching would tear through me, causing me to jolt. I tossed around for hours, crying until my eyes burned and dried up.

It wasn't a bit difficult to find the pieces of myself that we're broken because of Edward. They were jagged spears that twisted themselves through my entire body. But something else, not as easily identified, tunnelled through me as well. I didn't see it until I dragged my bones into the lav for a bit of cold water, where I faced myself in the mirror and recognized the truth. It was the truth I'd inadvertently admitted to in the courtyard. A torrent of warmth and pain and emotion washed over me and I was released.

I've always had a choice...

And in that simple moment, in that simple act of opening my eyes, Edward was no longer the enemy. We were the same.

In the courtyard, Edward began to hear a quiet hum rising above the soil.

He brought the drone of the earth inside with him. It was coming from within him, from the walls, and from the floor. It vibrated the glass window and filled the room with a beautiful nervous energy.

We didn't need to speak. I was in his head, the way he had been living in mine since the beginning. He wanted the same thing I did. I went to him, without regret and by my choice alone. That I was still broken and bruised was of no concern to either of us. We were brutal, clawing and pulling at each other's skin like lions. When there was space between us it was vicious and humid. I feared we destroyed my nerves beneath my flesh, as there were pieces of me that had gone numb.

By morning, we were nearly paralysed. He lay between my legs, resting his head on my stomach. His hair was damp and fine like a child's. It felt like silken threads as I twisted it lightly around my fingers. He kissed my navel, letting his tongue brush around the edge. He pulled himself on top of me again and said he needed to go home.

Edward decided we should wait a few more days before attempting the experiment again. I would need the use of my hands and my wrist had not healed fully. Our carnality would set my recovery back a day or two. The pain was incredible by the afternoon and my craving for the morphine returned.

"If I had known you'd change your mind...that you'd finally come to understand, I never would have started you on the stuff." He held my hand as I shook. "I'm sorry, love."

"It'll get better, I think, after the transfer. We'll have new chemicals then, right?" I tried to look hopeful. I couldn't tell if I was making sense. Edward's expression told me very little.

"Yes...something like that." He grinned.

"My stomach hurts."

He stroked my hair. "All right, then. Be right back."

He brought the needle and took hold of my arm, seeing it in the light for the first time in quite a while. "Oh, goodness...what have we done here?" He sounded like a paediatrician examining a skinned knee, but the look on his face told of something far more hideous.

"I'm not very good at it." I felt ashamed for all the wrong reasons.

He was trying so hard to conceal his worry and lighten the mood, for my sake.

"So phlebotomy is not your forte...not to worry, you have another arm." He administered the injection with very little discomfort. It was a world apart from my own method. He cleared his throat. "Darling...I'm going to give you something else... to help with your arm, all right?"

I was feeling hazy and warm and agreeable. "Mm-hmm...what is it?"

"Only an antibiotic," he paused, retrieving a bottle of pills from his bag. "We just have to try to ward off any infection."

I looked down at my arm with blurry eyes. The colours were spectacular, and fortunately, I was unable to recognize it as my own for the time being.

In the evening a very odd thing happened, something unusual enough to cause the both of us to pause, uncertain of what to do for several seconds.

The telephone rang.

Edward stood before it, staring as though it were some advanced alien machine.

Finally, he picked up the receiver. "Hello?" He said into it cautiously. There was a pause and he repeated it, this time more insistent in his tone. He hung up, looking confused. "There was no one there." He was utterly baffled that something like this could happen.

"A wrong number, perhaps?"

"Well they didn't even ask for anyone in particular. Whoever it was just sat on the line for a moment and then hung up. Who *does* that?" He seemed to take it so personally.

I shrugged, thinking we were investing far too much thought into the situation.

"Well I'll tell you who does that sort of thing...someone with no manners, that's who."

I nodded as his rant continued. "I mean...really, how difficult is it to simply say, 'Oh, pardon me, I must have the wrong number'?"

"It's not difficult at all..." I stopped upon realising the question had been rhetorical.

He turned his eyes toward me. "I know what you're thinking. It was just a telephone call, a wrong number..." his eyes were wild. "But there was something very wrong there." He pointed to the telephone. "It was on purpose."

"Edward..."

"Don't you see, Bel? Why are we standing here even having this discussion if there's nothing wrong? Don't you understand? These things *never* happen around here. Nothing incidental ever happens in this house. Nothing accidental ever happens here, either. It is a very purposeful house, and you know I don't have time for this sort of thing, Haven't you caught on to that by now?"

He darted out of the room and down the hall to the front door. It was still locked. He leaned against the door and narrowed his eyes, as though he meant to listen with them. "It's something external...something's going to change." After a few seconds of silence a sly grin moved over his face. "I think we're going to have company this evening, don't you agree?"

I was about to answer him when I realised he wasn't speaking to me. He was talking to the house.

I followed him back down the hall to the kitchen, asking questions all the while. He paced around the island, arms crossed, occasionally chewing on one of his fingernails. Hearing him internally became increasingly difficult as my adrenaline level rose. I was scared, and for once it wasn't of him.

At once he stopped and turned to face me, with great sympathy in his eyes. "Bel, listen to me. You must be calm. Something is going to happen here tonight, and I doubt very much that it will be pleasant. Purposeful and necessary, but most certainly not pleasant." He put his hands on my shoulders. "I wish I could tell you more, but this is all I'm able to understand."

"Do you think they'll try to hurt us?"

He pulled me to him and rested his mouth on my forehead. He didn't speak aloud.

He'll try. I could feel his smile against my skin.

We sat on the floor of the dining room and waited. We drank a little brandy and it helped to calm my nerves. The morphine was wearing thin, but now I was far too preoccupied to bother. I wasn't afraid for Edward; I knew that between the two of us there was very little that could go awry. What frightened me was the aftermath. How would we deal with potential interlopers? How would we hide all the dreadful things we had done? Until that night we had only victimized ourselves. Now that was about to change.

Edward lifted his head and looked toward the front of the house. "Remember, Isabel...listen to me, know that anything I do or say is just part of this unfortunate little production, and that I love you. Now answer the door, please."

He sprinted from the room and disappeared somewhere in the house. I walked into the hall and stared at the silent entranceway. Answer the door? I heard nothing.

The sudden banging nearly caused me to lose my breath. At once I had some answers. I knew the face that would be waiting on the other side. I drew in a deep pocket of air and opened the door.

"John!" I feigned surprised. "What brings you here at this hour?"

He was out of breath and bright red. I could almost see the testosterone pouring out of him in the little beads of sweat on his brow. The water magnified his pores, creating deep black canyons on his face. He braced himself in the doorway with his massive arms, and as he did, I felt the house grow tense, not wanting his hands on her.

"Isabel..." he took a long painful breath. "We need to talk."

I moved back from the door and gave him room to step over the threshold *(and into her mouth)*.

"I been thinkin' about you since the other day, now. I know what goes on here... I can tell he's been hurtin' you. Now, before you say anythin', let me finish. I seen, we *all* seen, how mental the Doctor's actin' these days, and then I come up here and you're all tore up. Christ, you look even worse now!"

"John...I..."

"Isabel, now listen...I don't expect that you have feelin's for me, but I can't stop thinkin' about you an' it's drivin' me bloody mad thinkin' about him doing god-knows-what to you." He looked like he might cry again. "I come up here tonight to get you away from him. I think I've fallen for you and if I don't do this I'll never forgive myself!"

Before I could speak, he grabbed me and had his thick lips pressed to mine. He smelled like the floor of a pub at the end of the night. His mouth was hot and sticky and I tried with every ounce of strength to pull away from him.

Oh, Christ help me...

John would not relent. He whispered words of slurred consolation into my mouth between each nauseating kiss. I writhed in his arms to no avail. It was then I heard Edward's voice drifting through the back of my skull.

Follow my lead and when I'm done, leave with him, through the kitchen, into the woods. I'll guide you from there... "Well, isn't this cosy." His voice startled John and he let me go.

"It's not what you think, Edward..." I played along, sounding fearful.

He grabbed me by the arm. It looked rough, but he was careful to grab above the infected wounds. "I leave the room for two minutes and here you are, whoring around with the villagers...oh, and look...it's the delivery boy, no less!"

"Take your hands off 'er!" John still seemed a bit confused and he hadn't come at Edward like I'd expected.

"She doesn't mind my hands on her any other night."

John stared at me wide-eyed. "Tell me it's not like that with you, Isabel," he pleaded, with great sorrow and disappointment in his voice.

...Tell him...tell him how I own you...

No sooner than I confirmed John's suspicion, Edward struck me, open handed across the cheek. It wouldn't have been so awful if I hadn't already been bruised. We faked a brief struggle before he let go, calling me a lying whore. I ran to John who was now advancing on Edward. I stayed between them and forced some tears. Edward stood perfectly still, unaffected by the boy's threats.

"John, no! *Please* let's just go...now!" I pulled on his arm, attempting to lead him toward the kitchen. It was much like trying to pull a boulder with bare hands for a moment, but then I could feel the air pressure around us changing, forcing him to move. I looked to Edward, confused, and he gave me a subtle wink. He could feel it too, and he casually placed his hand on the wall next to him as if to pet it, as if to thank her.

Edward had strategically positioned himself in front of the door in the event that the boy might flee, but John followed, reluctantly, not understanding what force was leading him away. I could see the disappointment on his face, as he had come here looking for a fight. Edward half-heartedly called obscenities out at me as I led John into the dark courtyard.

We ran past the pool and toward the woods. John stopped a few metres into the pitch-black forest. "Where are we goin'?" he wheezed. "I can't see a bloody thing."

"He'll be waiting for us if we turn back. We must keep going...please. I can't go back there. He's mad."

"I'll kill the bastard! I swear I would've done it right then an' there if you hadn't dragged me away. I wanted to do it the moment I saw you the other day!"

I knew it was more than the alcohol talking. I knew he meant it. I had to resist the urge to defend Edward. It burned me deeply to hear him threatened that way. What little sympathy I felt for the boy slipped into the darkness.

"John, we *really* must go. He'll be coming."

I broke into a run again and heard John stumbling behind me. My senses were severely impaired. Between the darkness and the sound of wind rushing over my ears, I felt out of control and helpless. The ground was humming frantically below us.

Follow the layline....

And I did. The branches were brutal as we tore through them, slicing at our arms and faces, pulling out threads and hairs. I sped through the brush faster than I ever thought I could go. John kept up, calling after me in the pitch black. The moon's waning light wasn't permitted to enter this space. We were in the bowels of the forest and I knew what lay ahead.

The hum grew louder as we fled our imaginary predator. I could hear it emptying out into nothingness, hollow and swirling. My heart was close to bursting in my chest, sinking and rising under damaged ribs. I could feel something churning in my skull. It was so close...that terrible pool of energy and chaos. The layline didn't run into it...the layline came out of it. Then I understood.

Stop, now!

I threw my weight off to one side and rolled across a bed of vines and stones and dirt. My body slammed into the low ridge of stones with such force that breath escaped me for a second. There was no time for John to follow my lead. The inertia was far too great for him to stop so suddenly. I covered my head as he went over the crumbling wall and down into the quarry.

It sounded like a thunderstorm as a barrage of rocks and slate crashed into the depths. He had taken a bit of the ridge with him. I waited for the quiet to set in before going to the edge. I could hear a strange noise, a raspy, choking sound. He was still alive and not as far down as I expected. I could barely see him, though he was less than four metres below me, grasping a ledge with his meaty fingers, choking out pleas, calling for my help.

The tears were real now and I was overcome by the urge to extend my hand to him. *Just let go, please just let go and be done with it. I couldn't save you if I wanted to.* I can't recall if I said it aloud or not, but he held on anyway, determined to pull himself back to safety. I felt sick as I listened to him struggle so and I lied and told him to hold on while I got help. I could hear his thoughts—*"I'll kill him...I can't die like this...when I get out of here, I will kill him..."*

I remembered the taste of his vile liquored mouth on mine and I imagined him crushing my bones in the throes of dumb animal passion. With a shudder, I turned my thoughts to Edward. I thought of Edward when I picked up the rock. I thought of Edward when I let the rock fall on John's hands, and then onto his face.

I stood at the edge of the abyss, staring into the void until I heard the crashing of bones on the slate below. It was quiet again. Even the humming soil had been temporarily stilled in response and this time it was Edward's voice that led me home.

He was waiting for me in the courtyard. I stood before him with a chilling calm between us.

"I've just killed someone."

There were no tears, no hysterics, no emotions. He took me by the hand and led me inside. There was a bath drawn for me and he tended to the latest collection of injuries. He put me in his bed and lay down next to me. All of this was silent.

"The first time is always unsettling," he eventually whispered.

"I struck him with a rock."

He didn't answer, though I suppose it wasn't really a question.

"I dropped a rock on his hands and it hit him in the head and it killed him."

"No, it was the fall that killed him. You merely helped the whole process along. They'll say it was an accident, you know. They'll say he was drunk and lost his footing."

I stared blankly at the ceiling. I could feel the eyes of the woven goddesses above my head. The maiden and the mother glared down upon me, then looked away. The warrior in the middle held her gaze, burning a hole through the top of my head. I had no place to hide my sins beneath the threads.

Edward continued. "If the police come sniffing around, asking questions, you'll tell them that poor, dear Johnny appeared at our door drunk, professing his love... which of course was tragically unrequited...and then proceeded to run off into the night like a wild man. And that was the last you saw of him."

I muttered nervously in agreement.

"The quarry is far enough back into the property that if they do find his body, there will be no possible way we could have been aware of his...misfortune."

"Right."

He looked satisfied at the brilliant simplicity of it all. "We'll want to find a new market, though."

I put my hand to my head and closed my eyes. "Oh, god...Mr Chapel..." I hadn't even thought about him. He loved John like a son. How could I have done this to him, to John?

"Don't do this to yourself, love. You did what you had to do."

"I considered trying to save him, you know. Does that disappoint you?"

"I know you did. And no, it doesn't disappoint me. It's human nature. But you couldn't have helped him. He would have pulled you down with him, and then where would we be?"

All I could imagine was Mr Chapel's face as he heard the news. I started to breath heavy, trying not to cry.

"Oh, Bel...don't get all sappy about it. Don't waste tears over any of them. John came here under the guise of noble intentions, to rescue his damsel in distress...but really, what prompted it? His undying love for you? He'd only ever seen you a handful of times, and never spoken more than a few words to you. He didn't even know you. The truth is, he saw a cause in you...a fairy tale that he could take part in, affording him the chance to finally gain companionship, despite his lack of social graces. So he gets all worked up on drunken machismo while tossing back a few pints with his mates and decides to come here and play the hero. Really, it was more about his simple ego than it ever was about you."

"You always know just what to say to make me feel special."

"I *live* to make you feel special."

I smiled at him and he kissed my face as though it were just another night.

I was careful of my appearance for the next few days, paying attention to detail, in case the police dropped in. Edward followed suit and kept himself neat and tidy, as well. I covered up my arms with long sleeve shirts and concealed my facial injuries with cosmetics. We nearly resembled normal people. It was fun, like playing dress up. Edward said I looked pretty. It was nice to hear.

We cleaned the house, opened the doors and windows, and gathered up the rubbish. We had clean china and proper clothes. We both knew it would be too good to last, but we opted to enjoy our sterile little life while we could. It felt incredibly unnatural.

In the study, Edward attempted to organize his papers and books. He wasn't about to throw any of it away, rather he stacked things into piles and pushed them around his desk and the floor. I was pretending to help when I noticed his journal again.

Without looking up he said, "Go on, if you want to read it. I have nothing to hide in there."

I opened it, then closed it again and slid it to the side.

"Not interested, then?" He seemed a little disappointed.

I pondered it for a moment. "I think I'd rather hear the story from you."

He looked satisfied with the answer. "Fair enough."

"Well?"

"Well, what?"

"Your story."

"I didn't realise you wanted to hear it right now. Besides, you already know all of the important parts." He turned back to his shelves.

"Do you mean to tell me that in all of these pages, there isn't one tale yet to be told?" I tapped my fingers on the book until he turned around to face me.

"In that particular book...no. Within those pages lives the story that you've been privy to. Unless you have a vested interest in scientific formulas and theories, you'll likely be disappointed in it."

"So where's the good stuff, then?" I asked, scanning the shelves.

"You yearn for something more exciting than our current station?"

I laughed to myself. "I suppose not. It's just that there are these enormous gaps in your history that I know so little about."

"And that drives you mad, does it?"

"Well, I know about your childhood, I know about the Congo, and I know about now, but what about the spaces between? When you were at University? When you came back from Africa? People you were friends with?" I waited for a minute then asked a question I hadn't really considered before. "Edward, have you ever been in love...before me?"

His light smile burned out slowly and was replaced with discomfort. I waited, feeling bad for him, but not enough to change the subject. His reaction only piqued my curiosity. He searched for something to say. I kept my focus on him, listening for any response, inside or out.

Finally he spoke. "I thought I was once, but that was a very long time ago."

"You *thought* you were?"

"Well, I wasn't even sure at the time, I suppose. Of course, I was very young and before we were together I was infatuated with her. It's possible I mistook that for love...but I really don't recall." He looked so far away; I knew it was a lie.

"Who was she?"

He sat down in the chair across from me. I felt like his therapist, what a daunting task that would be.

"She was called Abigail—Abby, to her friends. I met her when I was...oh, say twenty, twenty-one, perhaps? Really, it's been a long time now. She was young, seventeen, and in her final year at the girl's school down the way from University. What was that place called? Saint...something or other..." he ran his hands through his hair and wrinkled his brow as though it pained him to remember. "Well, who knows...some place stuffy and chaste and crawling with withered old nuns."

I suspected he remembered the name, but didn't press the issue.

"She was a wild girl. Not my type at all. I was shy and bookish, very serious, as you can imagine. She had a *reputation*. When she would walk past the common area each day, there was a group of boys that would gather to watch. You could set your watch by those lads, but I wasn't bold enough to join them. I opted to watch her from afar."

"So how did you finally meet?"

"Funny thing, really...she came to me. I'd have never found the courage to approach her. She was this little, fiery creature, not very well read or cultured, really...and I was terrified of her. Needless to say, I could not fathom why she'd been drawn to me...she had a surplus of more popular fellows who would have killed to spend any time with her at all. But that wasn't what she said she wanted. Turned out she wanted someone 'nice and smart,' that would like her for who she was, and not what she did."

He hesitated and I could tell by the subtle movements in his throat that something painful was coming. "So I began to court her. No one understood it—including me— but she seemed content and everything was bliss until, well, until she felt it was time that we were intimate."

"And this was a problem because...?"

"*Because*, Bel...I had never been with a woman before." He seemed slightly bothered that I hadn't figured that out earlier.

"Oh. Well, the first time is always...awkward."

"Awkward would have been a blessing compared to what happened between us. It was awful. I couldn't...the first time we tried. The next time, well...I lost control of myself before I could...well, you know. Remind me again why I'm telling you this?"

I had never seen him this uncomfortable and embarrassed before. Edward was by no means sexually repressed.

He looked at me suddenly. "Well, I have had almost thirty years to work on my technique."

I'd momentarily forgotten he could hear my thoughts.

"Anyway, we were in her bedroom, teddy bears and dolls abound...and I finally got it right. Still, I was not very inventive or coordinated, but at least I had the basic idea and it was everything I'd always hoped it to be. And then her mother walked in. The woman starts screaming, as though she'd walked in on me hacking her daughter to bits with an axe or what-have-you."

"Oh, god. That's *dreadful*. What did you do?"

"I grabbed my clothes and ran as fast as I could back to the dorm. And I never saw her again. I heard her mother sent her away to a boarding school somewhere in Europe." He stared up at the ceiling. "So...of course, one thing led to another and my mother received word of the whole sordid affair. I imagine Abby's parents had pressed her for information about me and with University being so close to town, it didn't take long for Mother Rosalie to find out."

"What did she do?"

"She insisted I move back here. She never fancied the idea of me living at University housing in the first place. And since it was the family's money that afforded me my education, she had something to hold over my head. When I came home all hell broke loose. She berated me constantly, calling me a whore. For the first few months she would barge into my room—the one you used to stay in—and accuse me of all sorts of awful things. Really, she went mad over it for a while—if I spent too long in the bath, if she thought she heard questionable noises in the night, if the bloody floorboard creaked, anything. On occasion, she would intrude while I was dressing and ridicule me, telling me how ugly and evil I was for being a man. And In all my years at school, I was never permitted to see another woman."

He was shutting me out. I hadn't noticed at first, but when I tried to go deeper, tried to hear what he was leaving out, I hit a wall of secrecy. And he knew I was trying to break through.

"That must have been horrible for you...I'm so sorry." I truly meant it.

"She was in an extraordinary amount of pain and had so many years of resentment to swim through. After my...after Jacob died, she was left with me, the constant reminder of the ugliness she'd endured. I imagine the thought of me with a woman, doing the things her father had done to her, was too much for her to bear. And that is where the story ends, although you see why I chose to put Bacchus in that room. I figured it to be the only way to erase the enduring stain of sexual repression." He attempted a smile, but still looked guilty.

We both knew there was more.

"Well, I can't imagine that's the whole story, Edward. I can't be the second person you've been with."

"You didn't ask how many people I'd been with. You asked if I had ever been in love before. There's a difference."

"All right then. How many people have you been with?"

"Does it matter?" He was like stone. Nothing came through. "Since we're playing inquisition, what about you? How many fellows have had the honour of knowing you like I do?"

"Does it matter?" I mimicked back at him.

"No, considering I already know the answer."

"Of course you do." I spun the chair around to avoid his face, "I see now that I can have no secrets from you. You are still superior in your telepathic abilities."

"It's all what you choose to do with it." He looked away. He was beautiful. "Did you love any of them?"

It was a difficult question, more difficult than I thought it would be. I had been in love with one of them. I couldn't say the same for the other five. Suddenly I felt like a whore. Two of them had been little more than one-night romps. Edward broke my thought.

"You know, we weren't in love the first time we slept together. I hardly think that makes us bad people."

"How do you know that I wasn't in love with you?"

"Because you weren't," he proclaimed. "You had a crush. And a rather bizarre one, at that..."

"Please don't start with that again. I never, ever wanted to shag my father. I'd think you were far too pragmatic to be sucked in by that Freudian prattle."

I could feel the morphine chills surfacing again. It was abrupt and unwelcome. I tried in vain to conceal it from Edward. I didn't want him to see how little control I had over myself.

Without words he went for his medical bag. I gazed at him apologetically as he gave me the injection, and all he said was, "Soon, love...it will be over soon."

John haunted me throughout the night. Between his unsettled spirit and the morphine, the hallucinations and lucid dreams were insufferable. He was next to me in the bed, covered in chalky soot. He was at the bottom of the pool, wide-eyed and inflated. In the doorway, and the chair by the window, his head twisted around on a broken neck.

Edward could sense my fear, though he hadn't the conscience to accept John into his own realm. I wondered where he kept all the people he destroyed. They didn't live near the surface of his brain, and I doubted that he even remembered their faces. I curled up tightly at his side and watched him. For some time his eyes were open, empty and fixed on the ceiling in his usual fashion. He would close them periodically and they would flutter and spasm beneath his lids. I struggled to see if he was dreaming, but the effect of the drug was too great and impaired my concentration. He'd given me a higher dose than usual. I drifted in and out of consciousness, finally settling into a place of warmth and rest, and when I did, Edward was there, waiting for me.

The first thing I became aware of was red. It surrounded us, entombing us in a warm cave. I could hear the hum of the earth and a beating drum or a heartbeat. Though my vision was blurry, I tried to take it all in. It looked familiar, like I'd been here many times before. The tapestry covered the entrance of the room. I thought he called it a room, though he may have said 'womb' or 'loom.' There were tissue fibres woven into the walls, strands of muscle and silken red linings. It could have been a loom, though it really didn't matter.

Our skin was soft and iridescent. Our hair was slick with oil. Our lungs, not yet functional, we breathed through a symmetrical series of slits in our necks, much like gills. We had language, communication, but through thought only, as a thick veil of fluid congealed in the back of our throats. There were cords, like damp velvet, attached to our spines and one that ran between our navels, connecting his torso to mine. He was the stronger of the two of us; I knew I needed him for nourishment.

He took my hand and placed two of my fingers on his tongue. He helped guide my hand deeper into his mouth until my fingers pushed and stretched the caul. We had no fingernails yet. The smell of the cave had been prominent from the moment I arrived, but it took quite some time for me to identify it. There was smouldering copper and a viscid, sweet odour, like bread and burnt syrup. I touched my tongue to the wall to associate a taste with the scent. It tasted like salt and sugary metal. I tried to swallow the mouthful of saliva I'd produced, but it collected on the caul and spilled back out of my mouth.

I had so many questions, too many to organize. They came as a barrage of random words and images and emotions. I hoped Edward could find the proper patterns.

He did.

He answered what he could with unspoken words, and for the rest he drew out pictures and equations on the wall with a needle. I waited for the raised white tissue to appear so I could understand what he'd carved.

He wrote primarily in an ancient script, like the one I had seen on the walls of the house. It was swirling and primitive. I could finally understand. Everything he felt during his life cycle, everything he'd ever learned, and every ounce of his instinct was clear. I understood his gifts and his insanity.

He told me I would forget much of this, as children often do. He told me we would be children together and would remind me of the knowledge I'd inevitably lose. We would remember our good mother. We would need to remember that she was red. I wanted her to be dressed in blue, like Mary or peacocks, but she only wore red.

He forced his arms gently into my abdomen, tearing through my shiny, tissue-thin flesh. A rush of air, like in the quarry only warmer, blew past him. He pulled me open and rested his head inside, wrapping the cord around his hand for security. I felt no pain, as we were still hollow inside, save for the sound of wind.

When I awoke, I was bleeding under a hot and dusty ray of sunlight. Edward had left the room, but not before inspecting the situation. There were red coloured fingerprints on my stomach and the sheets. My cycles were irregular these days and I was grateful to see blood. It meant I was still mostly a woman. I was also grateful that I hadn't fallen pregnant. We never used any form of contraception and I expected that Edward was still quite virile, though I believed he could control that, as well.

I cleaned up in the bath and got dressed. It had been such a bizarre night, filled with strange dreams. Beyond my rational thinking, I knew it hadn't really been a dream at all, though it was too early to accept that truth. I also knew that Edward wouldn't allow me my denial for very long. Written on the long wall of the upstairs hallway was a cryptic line—*Out of the egg of the mother*

It looked like rust, but I recognized the medium as my own.

Downstairs I heard a wave of voices. They echoed from the outside and surrounded all sides of the house. Edward was nowhere in sight. In the driveway there were police cars and an ambulance. I ran to the kitchen. The French doors were open and off in the distance I saw shapes emerging from the forest. I rushed towards them in a panic. One of the shapes was Edward. As I approached the group, Edward stopped and extended his arm to me.

"What's happened?" I was breathless, terrified.

"Detective Inspector Moorely," he gestured to me, "This is Isabel Scott."

He nodded. "Dr Grace has made an unfortunate discovery, I'm afraid. He rang us early this morning."

"There's a body in the quarry." He said delicately, keeping a firm grip on my shoulder.

"Oh, god..." My fear made for a convincing act.

Edward continued. "I was having my morning stroll and I went down to the gorge and that's where I happened upon the poor lad." He rubbed the space between his eyes. "What a dreadful way to go."

The Inspector spoke up. "I've got some men down there now, removing the body. I fear it may be a young man that went missing a few days ago...can't be sure till I get a closer look." He turned back toward the woods.

"Who do you think it might be?"

He pulled out a small notebook and leafed through it. Policemen were swarming around us. The Inspector gave them a nod and they dispersed towards the woods.

"A report was filed on a John Wheaton. Worked over at the marketplace...he was one of their people, Mr Chapel's nephew, if I recall correctly. They said he never missed a day of work before."

Edward and I exchanged quick glances and he began with much dismay, "Oh, dear. John came by here a few nights ago. He was our delivery boy."

"Did he come on business?" Moorely began writing.

"No, actually. He came to see Isabel."

My muscles tightened.

"Unbeknownst to either of us until that evening, John had apparently grown quite fond of Bel. He showed up at our door, highly intoxicated and quite aggressively revealed this to her."

"Is that what happened, Miss Scott?"

I nodded mournfully.

"What was the nature of your relationship to Mr Wheaton?"

"I only ever talked to John twice, maybe three times. At the market and when he would bring packages."

"And what did you say to him on the night in question?"

"Well...I told him that I was flattered, but that he was drunk and should perhaps go home. I didn't feel it was the best circumstance for us to talk about the matter. He was being rather aggressive and I didn't want to stir him up by flatly rejecting him. However, he persisted, so I tried to be kind but firm in telling him that I didn't share his feelings."

"And why was that?" He was still taking notes, not looking up or acknowledging that his question rang a bit personal and inappropriate.

"Well, I..." I gave Edward a desperate look.

Edward cut in with a hushed tone, "Inspector Moorely, she's involved with me. This is not a well known fact to the good people of this town, as they do love their gossip." He pulled me in closer. "And while I see no need to hide it from you in light of this tragic situation, we certainly would appreciate your discretion in this matter."

Moorely nodded and closed his book, looking at the two of us in a different light. It was warm in the yard, but not yet hot enough to warrant the sweat that was beading on his brow.

He cleared a mass of phlegm from his throat. "So what happened after he left? Did you see where he was headed?"

"No. He stumbled down the front stairs and disappeared. I assumed he would head back home. I never thought he'd go through the woods."

"Well, if it is indeed Mr Wheaton, I reckon we'll have a pretty clear idea of what happened to him. That quarry is a dark pit in the daylight. He never would've seen it coming in the dark. What a shame," he said with rehearsed sincerity.

I noticed how greasy he looked. The way he stared at me made me feel sick and hateful. I didn't trust him at all.

A young officer came through the brush, calling for Moorely. They had recovered the body and were bringing it out into the open. I had to bury my face in Edward's shirt, only half-pretending to be too horrified to look upon the body. Edward put his arms around me and patted my back with contrived consolation.

"There, there, now...it's all right..." he crooned as the officers wandered by, each one trying to look as though they actually had an important and very official job to perform.

Edward watched as they rolled the victim's body out from the shade of the leafy canopy and into the bright sunlight. His eyes were sparkling and gleaming with excitement as they came into view. The rest of him was utterly still. I turned to face the crowd of uniforms. They pulled back the sheet and at once there was silence.

I wanted to look away, but I was not the same fearful child who ran from all things ugly any longer. I gazed upon John's dusty remains and faced what I had done. His neck was broken. I didn't care for the way his mouth hung open, giving him a double chin. I could see only half of his tongue. Later, Edward would tell me that he'd probably bitten off the rest.

"That's him," Edward informed the officers in a cold and clinical manner.

After a few additional moments of questions and red tape, the carnival began to break down and disappear, piece by piece. Edward and I stood in the garden, arm in arm and watched the chaos filter out.

He looked around, squinting at the sky and said, "A lovely morning, don't you think?"

I took a deep breath of clean air and agreed.

We sat in the courtyard watching the grass grow, feeling a bit more relaxed now that things were out in the open.

"That was quite a bold move, ringing the police."

He lit a cigarette and shrugged. "It had to be done. We couldn't go on each day waiting for the cavalry to arrive. John could've been back there for years before being discovered. Not to mention that our names would have most likely come up at some point. Surely he told someone about his affection for you and his disgust for me...I simply wanted to go to them before they came to us."

"How did you know they wouldn't come in the house?" I thought of all the bizarre things they would have come across, the broken things, the drugs, the books, and all of Edward's scrawling on our walls.

"Because they weren't going to."

"But what if they had?"

"Oh, I don't know. I imagine I would have had you bludgeon them with rocks and throw their bodies into the quarry." He flashed a devilish grin and blew smoke out of his nostrils.

"I didn't throw John into the quarry."

"Technicalities, darling..."

"Though I must admit, I would have enjoyed watching that cunt Moorely take a fall."

"That would have been glorious. You could have lured him to his death with your feminine wiles."

"I don't ever want that man anywhere near my wiles."

"I think he really fancied you. Good thing I've been able to hide you away from the world for so long now. I bet you're quite the heartbreaker."

"Yes, you are very lucky, old man that you are, to have me. I am young enough to be your daughter, after all."

I sat down between his legs and leaned back, gazing at the stone cherubs that were imprisoned in the rim of the fountain. It was filled with rainwater and leaves and muck, but the baby angels appeared arid and raw, staring vacantly back at us. They were desperate and aching for something—perhaps clean water, perhaps something deeper.

The older angel that formed the uppermost tier of the fountain looked mournful in her stony gown. She reached towards the heavens with one hand as though she were pleading with God to release her from the decrepit ruins and take her home. I wondered if there would be cherubs on John's gravestone. I imagined not; adornments such as angels came at much too high a cost.

"I wish the fountain worked properly." I rested my head against his knee and played with a tiny, white pebble. It looked like a tooth. I missed my tooth.

"That fountain hasn't run clear since I was a child. You know, I always found that infernal pool unsettling...it was more for ornamentation, anyway. I can't recall any of us ever actually swimming in it. Who even needs a pool in northern England? But this fountain...this was my tiny oasis on the warmer days. I never meant to let it get this dreadful."

He stepped over me and crouched down next to it, dragging his fingertips across the surface, staring at his reflection in the black water. It was a boy's face that stared back.

Edward worked all day on the fountain, clearing the mire and repairing the valves and pressure tubes. As he cleaned, I could hear him humming, only pausing long enough to mutter words of comfort and apology to his heavenly charges. I couldn't imagine how or where he would've learned to repair a fountain. I prepared a bowl of fruit and opened a bottle of wine for us to share as the sun was setting. He appeared at the doors, gleaming with excitement and sweat, wiping his hands on his pants.

"Come see what I've done."

In the courtyard, a brilliant, clear stream of water flowed down the angel's robes and into the basin below. It made a lovely sound.

"Oh, Edward...you did it. You fixed it."

He stepped back from it, bursting with satisfaction. "I really did do a remarkable job, didn't I?"

"It's just wonderful. How did you figure it out?"

"There are answers to every puzzle. You just have to look for them."

"Of course," I said, rolling my eyes. "I forgot what sort of illuminated being I was dealing with."

"That, and I consulted a home repair book that had been collecting dust on the shelf since the 1980s."

The flowing water made the house feel bright and alive, like it was taking its first breath of fresh air in years. The cherubs looked healthier, decades of filth gone from their eyes and mouths. The angel found her purpose again. It was terribly romantic, the two of us, lounging next to the cascade, listening to the water and crickets in the lush darkness, feasting on wine and fruit. It was enough to make me temporarily forget that we were murderers. Those were the most difficult times—when I would remember what we'd become.

We lay there in the courtyard until the sickness came calling, as it did each and every night. Without words, Edward took me inside and administered the temporary cure. The veins in my arms were damaged, so for a while he used the tender space behind my knee and when that was ruined, he stuck me between my toes. The last coherent thing I said was, "I'm so glad the fountain's clean now. At least *something* in this house is."

In the morning, Edward sat beside me on the bed, surrounded by papers. The smell of cigarette smoke shook me from my nightly coma. I nudged him with my foot to let him know I was awake. Outside, the sky was grey and thick. It had been raining for hours. He didn't say good morning.

"I have some bad news...for you, I'm afraid."

"What is it?"

"I can no longer give you morphine. At least, if we wish to go through with our plan." He was unsympathetic, just factual.

I staggered to my knees and felt the bruises from the needle. "But you said I could do this until the experiment and that it would be all right because I wouldn't need it once we we're done!" I was on the verge of tears.

"Well, I was mistaken. Please don't wrinkle my papers."

"So that's it, then? You get me hooked on this stuff, then take it away, knowing very well how awful it will be and the best you have to give is *'don't wrinkle my papers'*?"

"What do you want me to do...trash the whole thing so you can get your fix? You know that's not an option, Bel."

"No, Edward. We both know whose addiction is more important, here. Forgive me for assuming that I might mean more to you than science. I must have forgotten myself."

"This will be the best thing for you, really. Your behaviour has been atrocious ever since you began this routine. One minute you're fine, the next you're worse than a spoilt child."

"Oh, that's brilliant, Edward. And I wouldn't know a bloody thing about having to tolerate erratic behaviour. I'm *so* glad all that's over with now that you aren't using anymore...oh, wait...I'm mistaken. You're still a junkie, aren't you, love? You still wait for me to nod off before you shoot up whatever it is you're addicted to, right?"

"I thought we'd come to an understanding, I thought we'd finally made a connection. Or was it just the morphine talking? Though I can't imagine you'd be able to fool me...you're hardly a complex creature."

Before common sense could intervene, I slapped him hard across his jaw. It was as involuntary as breathing. His eyes closed and didn't move, but I didn't wait for a reaction. I scrambled to my feet and headed for the door, but came to a sudden halt as I realised the futility of running. I turned to face him; I didn't need to turn very far. He was already behind me. He hadn't made the slightest sound.

A storm was surfacing under his skin. I could feel a terrible rage filling up the air around him. His veins were pushing their way out and his muscles twitched one by one. He pulled my arms behind my back and trapped them there, pressing me against him to the point of suffocation. I closed my eyes and focused.

Edward, I love you, please...I didn't mean to hurt you, I'm not like her...I love you and I'm not like her and you're not like him...you're nothing like him...she never said she was sorry, but I am...I'm sorry...please...I'm so sorry...

He relaxed, just a tiny bit at first, then more as I recited the silent mantra. Finally, he let go and backed away.

He stared directly into my eyes with enough intensity to cause me pain. "Clever," was all he said.

It would be another long and silent day.

I was ill and had a fever by ten o'clock that night. I didn't dare call out to Edward. I'd have to face this alone. That would be my punishment. I knew he was right about me, about the drug. It was all so confusing. I knew I was changing, becoming more like Edward but I still had so much of my own skin, my own self. I felt that my beliefs and ethics were weak compared to Edward's. I admired him and feared him. I wanted to be like him or perhaps *be* him, but hadn't the stomach for it. I felt like a failure. In the end, I was nothing more than a child, lacking experience and will.

The cramping in my gut was tremendous. Every few minutes I would run to the toilet and try to vomit. There was too little in my system and I ended up heaving and lurching dry air. It was wearing me down rapidly. I rested my head on the edge of the bath feeling sorry for myself. There was no one to hold my hair out of the way, no one to rub my back and tell me that I'd be all right. I wished my father were there.

He always took care of me when the winter flu set in. Through all the years of colds, stomach aches, and fears, he comforted me when my mother could not. As I began to grow up, he would do the same during the times of heartbreak and confusion. He was a saint. He faced the difficult task of explaining the changes I experienced as a young woman. He was terrible at most of it, but that he tried to help me understand at all was more than most fathers do.

After my sister's death, my mother fell useless. She never recovered from the loss and my father filled the gaping void that she left. A few months after Kate died, my mother began to slip away. She would tear through the house looking for the baby. She would claim she laid her down somewhere and lost her. She'd rip apart the dressers and chests, the wardrobes and cabinets in vain. My father would be at work and I was the only one there. I'd try to tell her that Kate wasn't there, Kate was in heaven, Kate was gone, but I was just a little child and practically invisible to her. The times she could hear me, she accused me of taking Kate and hiding her away out of jealousy.

"Kate's not in heaven, you only wish she were dead!" she'd scream.

My mother was finally taken away two years later. My father had to telephone the doctors himself. It was the most difficult thing he'd ever had to do. She lasted four years and two months in the asylum. She hung herself on New Year's Day. I never knew if that was an intentional choice, just to ruin the holiday for us forever, or mere chance.

She wore the cameo brooch I had given her during our final Christmas visit. The same brooch she barely acknowledged at the time. I suppose it had meant something to her after all, though I never knew for certain if she meant to put it on that last day to hurt me or let me know she loved me. I didn't want to know.

I felt for Edward because of this. I understood his inability to forgive his mother for her mistakes. I understood why he used me as a substitute for all mothers, why it was so necessary for him to do what he'd done. He was right in believing that I'd done the same to him. I still needed my father.

I'd not seen my own father for eight years or so. The day I left home was the end of our life together. By the time I was seventeen, my father had become a shadow of the man he once was. He had given me everything, playing the roles of both parents. He had very little in his life, save for me. I begged him to go out, meet people, find a hobby, anything, but the more I pulled away, the more he latched on. He couldn't bear the thought of losing me, too, he'd said. I loved him dearly, but I was young and selfish and imagined my life with him in the years to come. I was terrified of becoming an old maid, eating a quiet and boring dinner with him each and every night in our little house, which was filled with the frilly and stale memories of my dead mother and sister.

I would twitch when I'd think of the uninspired conversations we'd have, only interrupted by a ticking clock and irritating chewing sounds. I knew in my infinite seventeen-year-old wisdom that I would grow to resent him if I didn't get out and live a life of my own. The day before I left, my father submitted one final plea for me to stay with him. The conversation started calmly, but our words grew heated and it concluded with him telling me that if I left then, I should never return. This was the ultimate betrayal in his eyes. He was about to lose the last real piece of himself.

It broke my heart, but the next morning I walked out our door with only two suitcases. That was all I needed, it was everything I had accumulated since my mother left.

I searched for years for the thing that left me feeling empty. I went through myriad flats, jobs, and men, never finding the unknown variable until the day I arrived at Edward's door. I feared I was on the verge of losing it all again.

How I hated the sickness. The only comfort was the cold marble bath against my face as the convulsions returned. I crawled on all fours, resembling a sick dog, to the bedside and collapsed, pulling the blanket to the floor and over my head. At some point during the night I awoke, ill and disoriented. I panicked as I realised that I was still on the floor, under the heavy covering and Edward had not come in and tucked me into his bed, as he had been known to do.

With a submissive voice I cried out for him. It came like a question. A cold hand extended itself from the edge of the bed, open palmed. I hadn't expected it, I didn't even hear him come in and lay down. I watched it for a moment with uncertainty. In the silence, one finger beckoned me to grab on. I put my hand in his, accepting the invitation. I was soaked with the sweat from the internal fire that had consumed me throughout the night, but gathered the temperature in the room had dropped a good deal since the sunset. Edward was naked and lying on his side, the fine hairs on his skin standing at attention and as sharp as razors. His eyes were closed.

"This is the worst of it." His words broke the stillness of the room.

I responded by shaking uncontrollably. I didn't want to open my mouth, fearful that the dry heaves would return. It was murder on my ribs. He continued the conversation without me.

"It's funny. I just assumed your mother was dead, but I never gave much thought to your father, other than to make the occasional off-coloured joke at your expense, as you don't think about him very much, yourself. Until now."

"How is that funny?" I whispered, breathing out hard, trying to overcome the nausea and thoughts of my parents.

"It just portrays you in a very different light. Perhaps there are more layers to you than I thought." He sounded slightly amused.

I pushed out another deep breath and whispered, "I don't want to discuss this right now. I'm having a difficult night."

He ignored me. "I'm thinking that three days should suffice to get you well and ready to give it another go. I think that gives you plenty of time to pull yourself together, don't you?" He wrapped the blanket around himself and offered a portion to me.

I shook my head and said I was too hot, despite the shaking. My punishment wasn't over yet. He enjoyed seeing me this way. He enjoyed being privy to my nasty little family history, my ugly secrets. He liked me uncomfortable. So much, in fact, that he was becoming aroused by it all. I could feel him moving around, rubbing himself against the covers. He enjoyed that I knew of his perversion and that it only made matters worse.

I rolled away and tried to shut him out. He lifted up the back of my shirt and pressed his hand firmly against my back, first on my ribs, then over my spine. He walked his fingers over my bones, as though he were checking to make sure they were all there. With every movement he applied more pressure, digging his fingertips in deep, then pushing his groin against my lower back. Each time I convulsed I could feel him, as hard as stone, press into me harder still. And with each spasm, he would breathe heavier and deeper. I buried my face in the pillow while he got himself off to the quick and painful movements of my body.

Eventually I fell asleep. It was a deep, human sleep and I was grateful to lose the large piece of time. It was time that would not be spent in pain and sticky humiliation. I dreamed in normal fashion throughout the night, the sort of dreams that were laced with bits of reality, but overall strange and surreal and ultimately forgotten in the end, except for a few incidental details. Only the last dream before waking left me disturbed and unable to sleep again.

There was a dinner party in the dining room of the house. The room was longer and thinner than usual. Edward sat at one end, far away from me, next to a young woman with thick, red hair and full lips. She wore a red, lacy robe that concealed very little and I could see the slope of her breasts beneath the fabric. He was holding her hand under the table as they drank their wine. This infuriated me, but I had other guests to entertain and didn't want to make a scene.

My mother was there, a few places away and she seemed smug about the whole ordeal. She wore the Christmas brooch in her hair, glued to a barrette. She had too much make-up on and I was embarrassed for us both. She hadn't bothered to conceal the purple bruise about her neck and that bothered me, as well.

Moorely sat to my right, shoving food into his mouth and letting half-chewed pieces slide from his lips and cling to his oily face. He kept smiling at me, his teeth large and stained, pasted with the remains of his meal. He found this very amusing.

Edward's grandmother, at least that's who I assumed her to be, sat at my other hand, proper and still. She wore a string of pearls and her white gloves. Her plate was empty. She glanced down next to my plate and sighed. Putting her hand on mine, she whispered with great concern, "Oh, dear...you forgot your gloves."

My arms and hand were mutilated, riddled with scabs and holes. There were shimmering slivers of broken mirror embedded in the sores. Edward's syringe sat neatly in between the two silver forks, looking quite natural in the formal setting.

She leaned in closer and said, "Go on, dear...you need to eat."

A long strand of pearls had been coiled on my plate. I picked it up and cautiously put one in my mouth. Moorely watched closely as I bit into the tiny ball. The first one crumbled into sandy grit and tasted like the sea. With each bite, they became harder to consume. I broke my tooth and it fell onto my plate. I looked up at Edward, feeling like my heart had broken as well. He paid me no mind and continued to let the red-haired woman fawn over him.

His grandmother patted my hand and said, "That's all right now...never you mind."

She picked up my tooth and put it in a little beaded coin purse. It left a bloody stain on her glove. I swallowed the pearls, one by one, until my stomach ached.

My mother finally spoke. "It's just going to grow," she said, staring off into space, "grow bigger and bigger, that pearl in your stomach...grow bigger and wiser...it's just going to grow to despise you, Kate."

Edward finally looked up. He glared at my mother and slammed his wine glass on the table. "Christ, woman...that's not Kate. Kate's in the quarry. That's Isabel. Didn't you learn anything at the hospital?"

My mother sat back in her chair and pouted to herself. Her bruise had turned into a velvet cord. It looked far too tight to be comfortable and I asked her to take it off. She complied and threw it at my plate. Moorely laughed again, spitting saliva and wet crumbs on the table.

Edward stood up, ignoring the woman now, and walked to my seat. Her mouth and nostrils were pink and raw; she looked as though she might cry. He stood behind me, reaching around my shoulders to my plate. He picked up the velvet cord and put it to my mouth, letting me bite into it. It was tough and juicy; it tasted like bland fibre and flower petals. My stomach turned as the liquid ran down my throat. Pearls and blood and some unknown fluid that reminded me of semen and morphine filled my mouth and spilled onto my plate and all over my dress.

Edward muttered something I could not hear and crushed the crystal glass in his hand. He selected a long, jagged shard and slid it right into the back of Moorely's skull, effortlessly, as though his head was made of thin tissue paper. Moorely looked confused, but rather undaunted. He continued to chew his food in a most uncouth manner.

My mother stood up from the table and yelled in a shrill voice, "Really, Kate...you never should have eaten my baby!" She stormed from the room, disgusted.

Edward's grandmother picked the pearls out of the milky pool of blood and placed them gently in her tiny purse.

She leaned in once more and said in her frail, sweet voice, "He really is a good boy, you know. His mother used to love pearls, too."

It was still dark when I opened my eyes. My skin was smooth and soft, the way it feels after a fever breaks. The sickening sweet odour of my shirt and underwear prompted me to search for cleaner clothes in the grey masses of shadow on the floor. I could taste the wretched cocktail of bacteria and stomach acid in my mouth. Beneath that, my tongue retained the memory of all the flavours from the dream.

I found one of Edward's shirts and traded it with my own. It smelled of musky smoke, but was far better than the one I had soaked during the night. I brushed my teeth furiously, trying to clear my palate. It was a deep-rooted taste, layers thick and too many years old. It was the taste of death and guilt and sex. It would be impossible to simply rinse it away. I crept away, down the stairs in the darkness, hoping that the sunrise might change things somehow.

A nearly empty bottle of vodka sat alone, collecting dust in the back of one kitchen cabinet. I had been rummaging through each one, looking for something to mask the terrible flavour. I gagged while it burned its way through my tongue and gums, peeling off the layers of germs and disgust, more than willing to accept the toll it would take on my stomach. I noticed a bulge in the breast pocket of the shirt. A crumpled pack of cigarettes carrying the comforting smell of Edward. I pulled one out and lit it off a flame from the stove. It tasted like burnt potting soil but I welcomed it as it covered up the vile taste of everything else.

As magnificent as the sunrise was that morning, it failed to make any difference at all. Things like sunrises belonged to Edward. This was his world. I merely lingered inside of it.

≈

The only working clock that remained in the house was a German-built monster, the sort that exposed its internal skeleton of gears. It hung in the study, visible from the hall. At two minutes after ten in the morning, the telephone rang. I didn't really want to answer it, but calls came so infrequently that curiosity got the best of me. The moment I laid my hand on the receiver, I knew what waited for me on the other end.

"Good morning...Miss Scott?" It was Moorely, seeping through the line.

"Yes, Inspector. How can I help you? Did you need to speak with Dr Grace? I think he may be sleeping still..."

"Oh...er, no actually..." he sputtered, "I'd like to talk with you. Can we meet in town?"

"Forgive me, sir, but today's really not good..." I gasped aloud and quickly covered the receiver with one hand as Edward had appeared without warning in the doorway. He gave me an exaggerated nod and mouthed the word '*Go*'.

Puzzled, I agreed to meet Moorely, alone, at the park. He would expect me at eleven-thirty. Again he stumbled over his words as he said goodbye.

"Why, Edward? I feel like wretched hell. Why do I have to meet with that pig?"

He sighed and walked to the kitchen. His voice echoed down the hall. "Isabel, why do I always have to spell these things out for you? Why is it that even though you have the same extraordinary intuition as I do, you are never privy to the bigger picture? Pay attention, girl."

I lumbered into the kitchen. He was in the alcove, smoking and drinking pale pink water from a burgundy stained crystal he hadn't bothered to rinse. I sat down across from him and took another one of his cigarettes. He seemed amused by this.

"Pay attention to what?"

He leaned forward, reaching his arms across the table, lighting the cigarette for me. "What is it that you and I do here?"

I shook my head with agitation. "Oh, I don't know. Stagnate and fester?"

He dropped one hand onto the table with a thud. "No, Sunshine. We affect change, hmm? Does the concept ring a bell?" He snipped, blowing a cloud of smoke into my face.

"What does that have to do with sending me off to spend time with that cunt?"

"Well, frankly I'm bored. Sitting around and watching you tremble has become tedious. It will be two more days before we can do anything to change that. You hate Moorely, I hate Moorely...think of the fun we had with John. You said yourself that Moorely needed to go. Let's have some fun. Be creative, Bel. *Affect change.*"

"God, Edward! What's wrong with you? We can't just go around killing off people because you're bored! And just so you know, this is not fun for me."

He rolled his eyes. "Darling, Moorely dug his own grave from the first day. He's going to ask questions. He senses something is *off* around here and he's not going to let that go. Not to mention it's an excuse to see you again. I promise you, had you declined his invitation today, there would have been another tomorrow. We have to end this before it starts, so what's the harm in having a game of it?"

"And how do you propose we account for yet another body in the quarry?"

"Who says he'll end up there? I never even suggested we should kill him. That was your idea, my sweet." He grinned and raised one eyebrow with satisfaction.

"I'm not having this conversation with you any longer. I have to get ready." I stood up and stumbled down the hall, aching and anxious and sick to my stomach.

Edward followed me upstairs. As I washed my face I could hear him in my old room, rustling around in the closet. He returned with two of my dresses and a pair of black heels. He held each one up to me, trying to decide which one suited me best.

"This isn't a date." The dresses were simple, but designed for a party, not a mid-morning police questioning.

"Come on, Bel. Work with me here. We need bait." He paused to study the dresses again. "You're planning on wearing make up, right?"

I ignored his question and looked at the dresses. One was a very tight, black cocktail dress that I had only worn on one occasion. The other was an emerald green silk slip dress with an embroidered ivy pattern. It was slightly less formal. I stripped down and snatched it from his hand, slipping it on my unwashed body. I didn't have time to bathe. I turned around and let him zip up the back. The dress was very tight.

"Good, good...no knickers. That'll work him up nicely." He attempted to keep a straight expression.

"Bugger off. I don't know which one of you is a bigger cunt." I walked back into the lav to fix my face and hair.

"That filthy mouth of yours is only going to turn him on more, you know," he called after me as I slammed the door.

He was waiting in the foyer with the car keys. He smiled as I walked toward him. "You look smashing."

I gave him a nasty fake smile.

"Now, remember...if you need me, you know where to find me." He kissed me lightly on the forehead.

"Edward, why is it that you trust me now? How do you know I won't run?"

He smiled and I heard his voice in my head, clearer than ever: *Where could you possibly go?*

It was unseasonably warm then, even for summer. The sun was spending less time than usual hiding behind England's infamous grey veil. I wore a thin sweater anyway, to conceal the track marks. They were healing now but anyone with any knowledge of drug addiction, such as a member of the police department, would have no doubt as to the cause of the myriad scars and bruises. It took incredible restraint to stop the constant habit of rubbing my arms and face as well, but at least the convulsions had finally ceased.

I drove past Chapel where the usual crowd was eerily absent from the sidewalk. The doors were closed. A cardboard sign hung crooked on one of the doors. In black, shaky letters, it read *'Closed Due to Family Emergency'*. I fixed my eyes straight ahead and blocked out Mr Chapel's old ruddy face. It disturbed me how easy it was to do.

I spotted Moorely sitting on a bench by the duck pond. The park was quiet, only a few people wandering about. I didn't know what day it was, though I gathered from the quiet that it must have been a workday. As I approached, Moorely stood up clumsily, a paper cup in each hand. He still looked greasy, but seemed to have gone to great lengths to place each slick strand of hair where it belonged. He wore a light blue button-down shirt, the kind with short sleeves, and a brown tie. His pants were flecked with some unrecognizable shade of grey-blue-brown. I realised as I stumbled through the uneven and grassy terrain in my uncomfortable, strappy shoes that Moorely was indeed an ugly man, though not necessarily because of his appearance. Granted he was always sweating and carried a bit of a potbelly, but it was something internal that made him so repellent. Something slimy leached out of him, far worse than perspiration. I assumed I would learn more about it soon enough.

I feigned a smile. "Good morning, Inspector. Or is it Detective?"

He handed me one of the paper cups. It was filled with lukewarm tea. "Morning, Miss Scott. Actually it's Detective Inspector, but you may use whichever you prefer."

We sat down, his eyes glued to my dress. I stared at a duck as it teetered by. I had forgotten about normal world things like ducks and park benches.

"You look very nice, Miss Scott."

"Thank you. Please, call me Isabel." I hated offering him that invitation, but tried to adhere to Edward's grand scheme.

"All right then, Isabel." He slurped his tea like a child slurps at a soda. "You may call me Rupert."

He was staring at my feet now. I wanted to shove a pointy heel into his eye.

"Very well, Rupert. Or should I say Detective Inspector Rupert?" I laughed insincerely. "So what did you want to talk about?"

He cleared his throat and snapped out of his foot fixation. "Right, well...let me start by saying that this is off the record. That's why I had you meet me here, rather than the station. So, if you would, please let's keep this between us."

"So this isn't about John, then?"

"No, not really. Well...in a way, I suppose, but not directly. I'll be honest with you, Isabel. I've been talking to some people throughout this investigation and I have some concerns."

"Concerns?"

"Well, seems that people have seen some strange things involving you and Dr Grace. Seems that John didn't visit you the night of his accident just to tell you how he felt about you, according to his mates."

"That's odd, he didn't say anything else," I lied, looking confused and leaning in closer.

He broke a hard sweat, activating a strong aftershave or cologne, nearly causing me to sneeze. I had contracted from Edward an allergy to all things tasteless and offensive.

"His friends seemed to think that he was concerned for your safety. He told them that he thought the doctor was...harming you, somehow."

I laughed. "Harming me? Rupert, Edward did tell you that we are involved, did he not?"

He nodded his sweaty, tomato-like head.

"With all due respect to the dead, I really have to wonder if John might have been looking for a reason to dislike Edward, given his feelings for me. Granted, Edward and I never openly discussed our affair, but you know how people can talk. John may have felt jealous of Edward. Isn't it possible that he could have been exaggerating the situation to his friends, in order to justify his intentions?"

"Well, certainly, that could have been the case. However, there are some other stories going around."

I gave him a puzzled look.

"How would you describe Dr Grace's...mental state these days?"

I pretended to give it some thought. "Edward is a very passionate and eccentric man and this is a rather small town. Eccentricities are often misunderstood by the people of rural areas, but I can assure you, Edward is not mad, if that's what you think."

I knew Edward's sanity would be brought into question and had rehearsed a response in the car. I smiled, pleased at my delivery.

"I heard about an incident at Chapel's. Perhaps you could shed some light on that for me?"

"At Chapel's? Really?" Then I laughed, this time throwing my hand up and resting it on his knee for a moment. "Oh, yes...that. Well, it's a little embarrassing. I simply *can't* believe how people gossip around here." I lowered my voice. "Edward and I had some wine with our lunch that day. Now, he's not normally a big drinker, but I think that day he got a bit pissed and, well...we had a little scene in the market. It really wasn't all that remarkable. Though now that I think back, I suppose it did seem unusual."

He looked at me, uncertain how to take my answers. I needed to act fast, distract him before he attempted to find any holes in my story.

I put my hand on his. "Inspector Moorely...Rupert...I think it's very kind of you to take time from your busy schedule to check in with me. You don't often find that kind of personal interest in these unfortunate situations. You are a very sweet man." I gave him a coy grin. "Your wife is a very lucky woman."

"I...er, well...I'm not married, but thank you," he choked out the words.

"Not married? I find that difficult to believe. It's so hard to find good, mature men, like yourself, that are unattached."

"You seem to, er, have a liking for older...mature...men, yes?" He was squirming now.

"Older men know how to take their time with things. Young men tend to be a bit too self-centred and impulsive."

I thought he might suffer a stroke. His breathing was rapid and he was wiping his brow with a handkerchief.

"Tell you what, Rupert. Why don't you come up to the house tomorrow evening for dinner? That way you can spend some time with Edward and me and perhaps put your mind at ease about everything. Also, I'd like to repay you for your kindness, going out of your way for me like this. Please say you'll come." I tilted my head and brushed his leg with my foot.

"Yes, well...all right," he muttered nervously. "Are you sure it's no trouble?"

"We'd be delighted to have you. Say seven?" I stood up. "Thanks for the tea. See you then."

He nodded awkwardly and sputtered something unintelligible. I noticed he didn't stand up, so I held back my disgust, nodded and sauntered off to the car, fully aware of his eyes on the delicate movements of my dress the entire way. I needed a bath now more than ever between my itching arms and the greasy residue I picked up from Moorely. I collected myself, rolling down the window of the black sedan, hoping to clear away the pungent scent of his cheap cologne.

So there would be a dinner. We would need food, but even if Chapel had been open, I couldn't bear to show my face there. My guilt for John had dissolved, but Mr Chapel was another story. The next closest market that I knew of was even farther north than the estate and I wondered if the Moorely game was worth the trouble. I contemplated just going, getting it done and out of the way; certainly Edward would know what I was up to. After a moment, I thought better of it and decided to telephone him to let him know of my plan. Better safe than sorry with Edward. I found some coins in the dash of the car and ran across the street to the call box. The telephone rang three times before he answered. I barely said hello before he responded.

"I want to come along. I'll be outside." The line went dead.

He was kicking stones around the driveway when I arrived, pacing back and forth in front of the wide stone stairs. He opened the door, lunged across the seat and kissed me hard on the lips, then settled back into his side of the car and smiled.

"Well, I think I....

He cut me off, putting his hand up. "You did a magnificent job. At first I could only hear you clearly, but then I managed to tune Moorely in as well, like I could see him through you. Your thoughts are much stronger to me. It's difficult to focus on other people when you're around," he explained.

It made me feel good that he was so pleased with my work. "So what now? How do you envision our dinner plans?" I paused, mulling over the whole idea. "I mean, is Moorely even worth this trouble? Perhaps we ought to leave this alone."

"Do I detect a pang of sympathy for dear, old Rupert?"

"No. Well...I don't know. He really seems harmless, just sort of pathetic and...icky"

"Bel, were you not listening to him? He knows much more than he lets on."

"I can't really hear other people. Usually just you." I resented that to a small degree.

"Then trust me when I say that the pig-headed fool is thriving on the rumours he's heard about us. When he's not indulging in his own sexual fantasies about you, he's formulating all manner of theories about our relationship and our involvement with the former Mr Wheaton, our relationship to each other and any other nefarious equation in which he can connect us. Don't be so naive." He lit two cigarettes and handed one to me.

"Right. Well, you still haven't told me...what's the plan? If we aren't going to kill him, then what?"

"I told you before, Bel...be *creative*." He drew out the last word with a lilt, as though it were part of a song.

"I haven't the energy to be creative any more. I just wish we could be left alone."

It came out with unexpected contempt. I softened my face and turned my attention back to the road. Edward cocked his head and made a soft noise in his throat.

"What was that for?"

"What?" He seemed taken off guard. "Oh, nothing. It was just odd." He gazed out the window. "For a minute there, you sounded just like your mother."

Immediately, I had to choke back the tears. "What would you know about it?"

He was right. I did sound like her. After a few long moments of silence he put his hand on my leg and lightly tugged at the fabric of my dress. "I think green may very well be your colour."

The excursion to the market was uneventful. Edward was impressively restrained through the entire trip. He remembered to wear his shoes and didn't try to make anyone cry. He even held my hand as we walked through the aisles and he stood quietly in queue while I paid for the groceries.

Edward's mind was racing the entire way home. It was impossible to follow the non-linear train of thought as it sped through his skull. I gave up trying to read him after about twenty futile minutes. It made me nervous to even be next to him when he was like this. I knew he must be plotting Moorely's fate and hoped he'd clue me in before the next evening. By the final stretch of the drive, I was feeling like hell again and wanted more than anything to be home and out of the glaring sun.

I tore through the house the next morning, trying to prepare for Moorely's arrival. Edward made no mention of his plans, so I thought it best to set things up in a normal fashion. The house had seen worse days, but there were still telltale signs of lunacy peppering the rooms. Perhaps the Inspector would think nothing of cryptic messages written on the walls in blood after all. Edward put a stop to my domestic frenzy when he saw me sizing up the rust coloured stains.

"Just leave it, Bel. Leave all of it," he said, casually waving his hand at the wall as he passed by. His face was buried in a science magazine he'd purchased at the market. He didn't look up, even as he walked down the stairs.

I called after him, "Edward, we need to discuss this."

I found him downstairs, in the kitchen. He was still reading his magazine and thawing the venison on the counter. "*Edward*?" I persisted.

"What's that, love?" He finally looked up, seemingly unaware of the topic at hand.

I sighed impatiently, "I'd just like to know what I'm supposed to do with Moorely. You don't want me to cover our tracks. So what does this evening hold in store for us? Are we giving the man a delightful evening of dinner and conversation or are we putting him in his grave?"

He placed the magazine on the counter next to the frozen slab of meat. "I thought we might try to expand our horizons for a change, " he smiled. "We aren't going to murder him. That would be far too risky, but the gears in that smarmy little head of his are still grinding away. So what do you do with someone who hasn't the sense to leave well enough alone?"

I shrugged, unsure of where he was going with this.

He reached across the counter and gave me a playful tap on the end of my nose and said, "It's simple, dear. We discredit him."

Edward had been lurking around inside the inspector's head ever since their first encounter. It was not so easy when Moorely wasn't around, but Edward was careful never to miss an opportunity. He filled me in on the inner workings of Rupert Moorely. He fancied himself a clever and sly man, and perhaps he would have had us fooled into thinking him an ally if we were, say, under the age of ten. Edward came to the conclusion that it wouldn't be too difficult to ruin Moorely's reputation, as the only people who took him seriously were a few of the moronic underlings from the department and the local gossip hounds. In the eyes of the moderately intelligent,

Moorely undermined his own credibility every time he opened his mouth and spouted off his fantastical hypotheses. He was an arrogant, small-minded man that needed to be forcibly removed from his pedestal.

I liked to believe that part of Edward's desire to destroy Moorely resulted from jealousy. I wished that perhaps Edward couldn't stand the thought of another man fantasizing about me and that was the impetus of the plan. In truth, however, it had very little to do with me. The ugly reality was that I had killed for Edward and now I wished for reciprocity. There was no doubt that Edward was capable of murder, but when he killed, it would be for his satisfaction alone.

I suppose the inspector had committed no crime, though in Edward's eyes simply being a nuisance could be considered a capital offence. I carried with me the notion that Edward was a sociopath, a brutal killer without the ability to feel remorse for his actions, despite the fact that I'd never actually seen him commit murder. He had killed in Zaire, but saw that as a scientific necessity, and though he had orchestrated John's death, I carried out the deed. Despite this, something inside of me indicated that the trail of dead that led to Edward was much longer and deeper than he would admit. He claimed Moorely would not necessarily end up as another casualty at our hands. I wasn't sure I believed that.

The detective might have been allowed to continue with his personal investigation if it had not been for his decision to try to uncover Edward's history. He talked to the doctor's former colleagues and even attempted to track down some of his patients. The patient files were kept confidential, but it had not been a challenge to locate some of the women once the news of John's death went public.

A few of them voluntarily met with Moorely, eager to find out current details about the enigmatic doctor and the body discovered on his property. They used the opportunity to recount their own experiences with Edward, exaggerating and twisting Edward's unusual methods and bedside manner. They all seemed to have a vested interest in his personal life as well, offering up their own accounts and opinions of his relationship with 'the help,' as they called me, though to my knowledge I'd never met any of them. It would have been obvious to anyone but Moorely that each of these women were determined to believe that they had been the first to notice something 'strange' about Edward. At no point during these questionings did any of them stop to point out that Edward was not on trial, nor was he under suspicion for the death of John Wheaton. It seemed that most of the town was ready to convict Edward of everything from simply being elusive to causing the summer's unusually high temperatures.

Apparently, the locals didn't appreciate Edward's need for privacy. They felt betrayed by his retreat from their community and labelled him an outcast. One jaded woman, whose three children had been delivered by Edward, seemed surprised by the presence of a woman in his life, claiming that she'd always taken him for a homosexual. Edward noted that this woman had always been quite *fond* of him, despite her husband and children, but he had not reciprocated her advances.

In the end, Moorely came away with very little usable information from the women, though to hear the doctor's story from those who had been in such intimate situations with him served Moorely's desire for gossip just fine. Edward's ex-colleagues had been less receptive to Moorely's questions and theories. In general, they kept their answers short and factual, shying away from the more private details of Edward's personality. They almost seemed slightly embarrassed of Edward, as though he were a skeleton in the closet of the medical community.

It was in one of Edward's oldest associates, however, that Moorely stumbled across a potentially dangerous wealth of knowledge. Dr James Hausner had known Edward since the early years at University. They had ended up in various internships and residencies together and even entertained the thought of going into a joint practice until Edward decided to go to Africa. At that point, James moved to a neighbouring town, where he set up a practice of his own. To say they were best friends was not quite accurate, as they shared more of a mutual love of science and medicine than an interest in cavorting around town as mates.

Nevertheless, James was probably the only man Edward had ever felt a connection with. They paired up throughout the years, when circumstances allowed, in several research and development projects, each becoming published and prominent scientists in their own right. It had been some time since they had spoken, due to Edward's gradual retreat from society. The final straw for James had been Edward's decision to give up his practice in order to embark on the 'mysterious' scientific and spiritual quest that had originated in Zaire. There was vague talk of bizarre experiments, cryptic Russian research papers, and the use of unknown, and more importantly, unapproved 'medicinal plants.' There had even been hints, rumours of illegal activity and highly unethical practices, though no one ever specified exactly what these activities were. Edward refused James any further information on the matter and the two went their separate ways shortly thereafter.

While Hausner couldn't provide the detective with any concrete evidence of illicit behaviours on Edward's part, he did have access to some of the lesser-known facts about the doctor's private life. He knew pieces of Edward's childhood, his miserable existence with his mother, though nothing of the atrocity that was Edward's genetic history. Hausner knew a bit of Edward's social history—ex-friends and lovers—but only to a point. He knew only what Edward wanted him to know.

These things were fine. Edward didn't seem too troubled by it. What bothered him was that before Edward had become completely reclusive and secretive, he had shared some of his early beliefs and theories with his partner. These were ideas that could easily show Edward in a questionable light.

As Edward revealed Moorely's designs, I realised that this was the first time he'd ever mentioned a Dr Hausner. He was hiding something from me. Whenever he did this, my efforts to read his thoughts were futile. He was very good at this trick, scrambling unspoken words and throwing me off his tracks, much like a radio picking up several frequencies at once. It gave me a nasty headache. I suspected that whatever it was that Edward was hiding from me, Moorely had gotten wind of it after meeting with Hausner, or at the very least knew Hausner's interpretation. I cursed myself for not being more adept at hearing other people. Moorely could have information I desired and he would be here in a few short hours.

I offered to prepare the meal. Edward declined, saying that he would take care of it. I followed him around the kitchen, making a pest of myself. It had been ages since he cooked and I didn't fully trust that he wouldn't destroy the kitchen in the process. He shooed me away, telling me to get ready for our guest. The black dress had been placed upon the bed. I took a shower and whored myself up, the way I knew he'd request. The clicking of my heels on the wooden hallway floor gave away my position as I headed for the kitchen. Edward intercepted me at the doorway. "I *told* you, it's under control. Go wait in the dining room and look pretty."

"Why all the secrets, sweetheart?" I craned my neck, trying to see what damage had been done in the room beyond.

"Once again, Bel, you look tremendous," he crooned, changing the subject.

"I look like a prostitute."

"Nonsense. You have better shoes. Now go..."

Reluctantly, I strolled into the dimly lit dining hall. I seldom won these petty battles of will. The table was set for three. He had done a decent job of it, even lighting candles throughout the room. The darkness of the decor made it look like a cave. I fidgeted with a few wild strands of hair that refused to pile up on the top of my head. I didn't care for my neck being exposed this way. It would be too easy for the wolves to find my jugular, and the wolves would be out tonight for certain.

The linens were folded into elaborate floral shapes on the china. As I toyed with the one in front of me, inspecting the folds and twists, I heard a clinking sound on the plate below. Pearls. A long silken strand coiled down, falling from the cloth. The memory of a kind and ancient voice flowed through my bones. They belonged to his grandmother.

I stared at the beautiful little orbs in fear and remorse. I wanted so badly to touch them, but they terrified me. I was afraid of choking.

"You should try them on." The voice came suddenly. It amazed me the way he could move without a sound.

Before I could respond, he had the choker at my neck, fastening the delicate gold clasp against the top of my spine. "They look lovely on you." His voice was soft and gentle. "Go see."

He held my chair as I rose, weak-kneed and stunned. The necklace burned against my skin, one of the pearls boring a hole into the soft hollow above my sternum. I swore I could smell the sea, and not the Irish Sea or the North Sea, either, but some place warmer and deeper.

Edward stood behind me at the hall mirror, urging me to look. I let my eyes fall in and out of focus at first, not wanting to see ourselves in sharpened detail. He placed his hand softly on my back. It felt frozen, but his touch triggered something in me and forced a clearer vision. For the first time in many months I looked. I looked hard and deep at the two beings that faced us. I looked past the make-up and the fabric. I looked past the flesh that I had taken for granted too many times. Living with Edward had aged me. My skin was still clear, save for some scars and bruises, but all the things beneath seemed older and worn. I could see my bones surfacing under the dress. Edward let me look at him, too. We were becoming the same, evolving back into something ancient and pure. We were related now, like fathers and daughters, mothers and sons, brothers and sisters. Despite his need to push forward with the experiment, Edward had already been successful in his initial goal. We had moved forward to the sky as gods and back to the swamps as reptiles. The cycle was set in motion.

Edward was right. Willa's pearls did look lovely. He said she would've wanted me to have them. With animal instinct, Edward turned his head toward the door. An obtrusive knock echoed down the long hall a second later. Harsh reality replaced the ghost images in the mirror and I saw what Moorely was about to see. There was Edward, pale and sinewy with a calm and vicious spark in his eyes. In myself I saw a junkie in a sheath of satin cloth draped over bones; black kohl weighing down my eyes in an attempt to camouflage the dark circles below.

I held out bare arms, "Edward...I need my sweater..." showing him the bruises and panicking.

"Not this time, love."

❧

The three of us stood in the foyer for a brief moment. Moorely wore a brown tweed suit. I stood before them both with an insecure smile, arms crossed tightly. After the initial pleasantries had been exchanged I suggested we retreat to the dining hall. Much to my surprise and dismay, Edward proposed I take Moorely to the sitting room instead, as dinner was not quite ready. I shot him a look of confusion. The sitting room was filled with the broken fragments of religious icons and some of Edward's earliest and most aberrant wall sketching.

"Edward," I maintained the forced smile, "I think our guest might be more comfortable in the dining room."

He smiled back. "Come now, darling. You know it's not proper etiquette to entertain at the table before the meal is served. Honestly, Inspector, sometimes I think she must have been raised by wolves."

He directed Moorely toward the sitting room before I could protest further. I glared at him as he gave me a light shove behind the Inspector. I heard him laugh to himself as he departed to the kitchen. Once inside the room, Moorely stopped and scanned the space. He cleared his throat loudly and slowly backed into a chair. I sat across from him, still smiling until I remembered the gap in my teeth. Even though the hole was far off to one side, I didn't usually smile this wide any more. Now I found it difficult to control due to my discomfort.

"You have a very...interesting house," he said with an ugly grin.

"Yes, well, Edward has very unique taste."

He twisted around in his chair and gestured to the marks on the wall. "This is unusual. What is it?"

I smiled again, "That's art."

"Art."

I nodded. "Yes. Very avant-garde, don't you think?"

I could tell by his face that he wasn't sure what that meant, but didn't want to appear ignorant. He studied the primitive scrawl with a deep and introspective gaze. "Oh, yes... very avant-garde, indeed. Though I've never really been much of an art... person."

He seemed rather satisfied by his empty response. Quickly, he turned his attention to the collection of broken icons on the end table. "What happened to your figurines, there?"

"Pardon?"

"Looks like they're broken."

"Oh, I see what you mean. Actually, that's how they're supposed to be. It's a concept piece, really."

He cocked his head and looked closely, trying to see what I saw. "I'm not sure I follow."

"Well, I think what the artist was trying to convey was a...commentary on the breakdown of... ancient religion at the onset of Christianity and the rise of the...Roman Empire." I hadn't the faintest idea of what I was saying.

"Oh." He was utterly lost. "Ah, yes, I see it now."

"Would you care for a drink...Rupert? May I still call you that?" I gave him a coy glance.

"Thank you. G and T, if you don't mind. And please do call me Rupert."

I excused myself from the room and ran to the kitchen. Edward was sitting in the alcove, laughing to himself.

"Yes, this is hysterical. Laugh it up," I whispered spitefully.

"Bel, I had no idea you had such an astute understanding of the art world." He barely got the words out through his snickering. "Or the rise and fall of religion in ancient Rome for that matter."

"Shut up. Where do we keep the gin?" I ripped through the cabinets.

"We don't keep it at all. I find gin to be a tad *pedestrian*."

"Consider the source of the request." I poured a glass of wine for Moorely, instead. "This seems too good to waste on the likes of him." In my flustered state, I almost didn't notice that the kitchen was surprisingly intact. I feared what this meant. "Edward, did you actually fix anything for dinner?"

"Of course. I'm not completely worthless, you know. It's on the table. Go fetch our friend."

We gathered around the table. Moorely was squinting, trying to adjust to the dim lighting. He looked hopelessly out of place, his cheap suit clashing with the fine china and antique silver. He seemed disappointed with his wine. He remarked that he wasn't much of a wine drinker. Edward responded that white wine didn't really go with tweed anyway. It was better suited with a nice poly-cotton blend. I stifled a laugh and Edward cleared his throat as he lifted the cover from the silver platter that gleamed from the centre of the table.

The raw venison lay quivering on a garnish of lush greens. It was purple, barely warm and marinating in a dark crimson pool. I turned my head away with an involuntary grimace. Thin slivers of apple and oranges had been artfully placed around the uncooked flesh. The white meat of the apples had been dyed to a vivid pink and the oranges resembled a candied sunset, turning from bright red edges to pink to a pale citrine at the rind. The blood absorption left the fruit plump and viscid. A basket

of grainy bread beckoned, promising to spare me from the animal corpse before us.
Again, Moorely only looked confused.

"What is this we're having, Doctor?"

"Venison." He cut into it, shearing a red and blue-grey slab onto Moorely's plate.

"Can't say I've ever had it like this. But I'll try anything once, eh?" He chuckled
and tucked his napkin into his collar.

"Yes, you certainly would," Edward replied under his breath.

"Pardon?" The Inspector raised a brow.

"I'm sorry? I was lost in your thoughts, forgive me," Edward carved a slice for
himself. He knew better than to offer any to me. "This is how they prepare it in northern
France," he lied in a most factual tone.

"Come again?" The Inspector questioned, obviously derailed by Edward's responses.

"The meat, my good man. *This is how the meat is prepared in the north of France*,"
Edward repeated very slowly and deliberately, slightly raising his voice as though he
and Moorely were speaking different languages.

Edward caught my eye with a wink as I tore apart a chunk of bread and ate it dry.
It was a challenge to stomach even the simple grains as I watched the two of them
devour the mass of barely dead muscle. At least Edward exhibited some manners,
cutting the flesh into tiny pieces and chewing each bit with care and patience. Moorely
on the other hand was worse than I could've imagined. He was loud and violent in his
consumption, gorging himself on the raw deer, slurping the rapidly congealing blood
through his teeth. A repulsively pink bit of gristle adhered itself to the corner of his
mouth. I stared at it with a sickening loathing, thinking that it would never go away.
Unfortunately, when it finally left the deep crevice of his lips, it was only to cling to
the edge of the crystal glass. Somehow, this was even more repugnant than when it had
been dangling from his face.

He nodded to Edward, smiling and chewing, revealing bloodstained teeth. Edward
nodded back and gently placed his knife and fork down. He dabbed his mouth with
the napkin and took a sip of wine. He seemed to genuinely enjoy his gory culinary
experiment. Sitting there in the flickering glow of the room, the irony of the situation
amused me. I looked at Edward and thought of his quest to discover the primitive
beast from which he had emerged. Yet through it all he was proper and cordial in his
mannerisms. He had not forgotten etiquette. I turned my attention to Moorely, tearing
through the flesh like a true carnivore, thousands of years away from the advent
of social graces—Moorely, who represented Everyman—Moorely, whom society
accepted as the median, the average. I wondered how it was that the human race had
wondered so far from its path. I would've preferred a hundred lifetimes of Edward's

savagery to another second of Moorely's faux humanity. Just as I was thinking that I couldn't bear another moment of Moorely's revolting display, Edward intervened and the game was underway.

"Rupert, I hear you've had the good fortune to meet my dear, old associate, Dr Hausner."

Moorely's chewing slowly came to a halt. I could almost taste his bewilderment. It was laced with just enough fear to make me feel better about Edward's vague plan. Moorely attempted to hide this with transparent nonchalance.

"Hausner...Hausner..." he muttered to himself, eyes searching through the air. "Oh, yes! Dr Hausner. Fine gentleman, he is. I take it you've spoken to him recently?"

Edward chuckled softly, then abruptly stopped. "No." His face went hard and cold. "Not for many years, now...which is why I find it so interesting that you'd go to the trouble of tracking him down."

Rupert crinkled his nose then relaxed. A glimmer of hope flashed across his face as he decided Edward must have been joking. He smiled again, pleased by his stellar reasoning. "How did you know about my visit with Dr Hausner, then?"

Edward savoured a tiny sip of wine before responding. "The same means by which I know about your meetings with my former patients."

Moorely wasn't smiling now. Before he could speak, Edward unleashed the flood. "And by the same means I know about your little fixation with my Isabel."

Rupert's normally ruddy complexion was vacillating between various hues of white and red. He opened his mouth to object, but Edward was quicker.

"While I can't say I'm thrilled by the way you pleasure yourself to thoughts of my dear girl night after night, I must tell you that I think it's wonderful that you've been able to focus your attention onto someone a bit more...mature."

I looked at Edward, my expression indicating that I was almost as stunned as Moorely. This was brilliant.

"I really don't know what you're getting at here..." Moorely stammered, incredulously.

"I'm curious...how did you ever get your busy little hands on the photographs of those unfortunate children?" He paused, focusing on Moorely's guilty eyes. "Oh, yes. That's right...that depraved clerk at the department in East Manchester. He was your *inside man*, if I'm not mistaken?"

The Inspector was shaking, glancing toward the doorway, searching without hope for the opportunity to run. I had to give him credit, though. He had enough sense to know that running would be futile. He knew this instinctively, the way we know not to run from the wild dogs as they eye our throats.

"Who... who have you been talking to, Grace?" His words were hushed.

"Talk, talk, talk. That's your problem Mr Moorely. With you, it's always about words. You spend your time talking and end up believing that it gives you the upper hand. Truth is found in the ability to quiet yourself and listen. I know what I know because *I listen*."

"I'm not sure what it is you think you know about me, but I can say one thing for certain...I have heard quite a few interesting things about you, Doctor. Things I feel it is my duty as a servant of the Queen to look into."

It was like watching a tennis match. I turned from Moorely to Edward, eagerly waiting for him to take his serve. Before he did, he took care to break the line of secret communication that connected me to Moorely. Whatever it was that Hausner told Moorely must have been tremendous for Edward to guard it so fiercely.

Poor, poor Rupert Moorely. Edward mentally eviscerated him with each statement. He started from the beginning, running down the list Moorely kept in the darkest corners of his brain of every sin, each humiliating secret. He recounted every pathetic lie Moorely had ever told in hopes of convincing people that he was something better than a socially-inept, closet paedophile.

It took nearly an hour for Edward to exhaust the inventory of shameful events. We relived, in agonizing detail, the time Rupert brought his doting mother along to dinner with one of the few women who ever consented to date him. It was the first and last date with that woman, after Rupert permitted Mrs. Moorely to cut his meat into bite-size portions for him. He was twenty-eight at the time.

We learned about the countless jokes the others in the department committed against the Inspector, the deeds always going unpunished, as it was more difficult for Moorely to react and admit defeat then to just accept it and laugh along as though he had been in on it from the start. Moorely seemed to incite this sort of behaviour any time he was around a pack mentality. It had been that way since childhood.

Child pornography aside, the only other thing Rupert Moorely was guilty of was being self-serving. Mother Moorely had always seen to it that little Rupert received whatever little Rupert wanted. Neither could understand why the rest of the world wasn't party to that arrangement. Mother Moorely had devoted her entire life to shielding her son from the ugly truth, and in the course of one evening, Edward would destroy all of her efforts. By the time he got to the tale of Moorely's disastrous first sexual encounter, the man was on the verge of tears. As much as I despised him, there were moments where things became a bit too painful, even for me, to hear.

At least once a day, Rupert Moorely could be heard saying, "You have to wake up pretty early in the morning to outwit this ol' chap," or some such trite nonsense. He was quite fond of this idea. The part of Rupert Moorely that did dreadful things such as tossing off to photos of children only existed in the privacy of his own bedroom. This was not the Rupert Moorely that solved crimes or loved his mother. This was the secret Rupert, who really did no harm. The secret Rupert never left the house. No one was ever supposed to know about the secret Rupert.

Poor, poor Rupert Moorely. He sat quietly, sobbing over a bloody plate. He was broken, nothing more than an overgrown child, yearning for the comfort of his mother's teat. It was a fascinating thing to watch as Edward twisted the umbilical cord that Mrs. Moorely never cut around Rupert's stubby neck. I half wished him a quick death; a bullet to the head, to end his misery, because I knew Edward too well. The night was still very young.

"The difference between you and me, Mr Moorely, is that I acknowledged my weaknesses, and sought to change them," he explained. "Whereas you waste your tedious days convincing yourself that you posses no weakness at all."

He took my hand, outstretching my arm and putting my fingers to his lips. Moorely furrowed his sweaty brow, straining to make sense of the elaborate design of scars on my skin.

"You see, Mr Moorely, even the objects of our desires carry weaknesses and flaws. Tell me...does she wear these marks when you think of touching her soft, clean skin?"

He gave no response and refused to look at my face.

Edward carried on, "You fancy yourself a hero, don't you Mr Moorely? You believe you came here with the intention of insuring Isabel's well being. The unfortunate Mr Wheaton did the same. The both of you came into my home expecting to save Isabel from me, loathsome creature that I am, but what you find is that the only thing this woman needs saving from is herself. I must be frank with you, Inspector. I am more than a little offended by your motive. Do you see a cage? Shackles? Do you see her as a captive? Or perhaps it is not so much about her safety and more about your longing to feel like a saviour. Or could it be, at the very least, your wish to have her for yourself. It was that very sort of thinking that put John Wheaton in his grave. Let me advise you that it will be your undoing as well."

A tiny spark of power ignited inside of Moorely. He lifted his head and straightened himself.

"You murdered that boy, didn't you?" He scowled at Edward and did his best to disguise the fear.

I spoke for the first time in more than an hour. "No, Inspector," I said confidently, "That was me."

He spat out an incredulous laugh. "What's this now? Please...a little thing like you? I can hardly imagine you throwing a big boy like that into that quarry." He was still chuckling.

"Well, I didn't so much *throw* him in. Really, I just led him to the edge. He took care of the falling all on his own."

Edward smiled to himself. I'd made him proud. It was the only reason I would have ever confessed.

Moorely stood up, wiping his face with his sleeve, eliminating any trace of tears and defeat.

"I thought as much of you, Grace. Didn't trust you from day one. I guess Dr Hausner was right to wonder about you." He turned to me. "But you, *Miss* Scott," we were no longer on a first name basis, "I misjudged you completely. It's not very often that I'm wrong on this sort of thing. I suppose I was blinded by your softness. Very deceptive, you are."

"Are you going to arrest us now?" I put my hand over my mouth, suppressing laughter, giddy with adrenaline.

"You haven't left me much choice, really. I don't know who you people think you are, inviting me here, bringing up these preposterous tales, trying to humiliate me! Then you actually have the nerve to laugh and joke while you *confess murder*? You people are mad!"

I nearly fell out of my chair in a fit. Our laughter infuriated Moorely. He slammed his fists on the table and began barking orders for us to cease. This only made it worse and resulted in Moorely breaking his glass in a rage.

Edward immediately regained his composure. "Well, that was uncalled for."

"Very uncivilised," I muttered.

"I'll tell you what's uncivilised. A pair of addicts torturing and killing innocent people for fun. *That* is uncivilised." His face resembled an over-inflated red balloon, ready to burst. "Mark my words...I'll see to it that they put you away for life," he seethed.

"I really don't think you will, sir," Edward said sympathetically, wiping a tear from his eye.

"And why is that, Dr Grace? Are you going to kill me as well?" He took care to accentuate the sarcasm in his voice.

"Heavens no, Inspector..."

"Trust me when I tell you, Grace, that I have more than enough on you now to see you in the madhouse."

Edward raised an eyebrow, looking smug and a bit guilty but it was hardly a defeat. "Touché, Mr Moorely. Though I should note that there is no institution in this country that could possibly be more confining than the existence you call your life."

He sniffed, hoping to counter Edward's barb with an equally witty retort and looking to the ceiling for the words. They weren't there.

"And while we're on the topic of institutions," I chimed in, "where is it that the courts prefer to house paedophiles these days? Prisons or asylums?"

"I should think it would depend on the type of paedophile..." Edward answered.

Moorely rolled his eyes. "Back to that nonsense, again?"

"I wonder if the locals will see it as 'nonsense' once word gets out..." I mused.

"There is no word to get out. I've done nothing wrong! You people have no proof!" The red hue of his face complimented the bulging blue vein running up his forehead.

"Mr Moorely," Edward began in a whisper, "do you know what your mother is doing right now, at this very moment?"

He narrowed his eyes into little slits and shot Edward an icy glare. His eyes were a startling pale blue. "How *dare* you even mention my dear mother."

"She's crying."

"I'm warning you, Grace..."

"She's crying because right now the boys from your department are in her house... in your room...collecting the photographs you hid under the access panel in the floor of your closet. You know the ones, Mr Moorely...the photographs of three young boys, none of them a drop older than nine, unclothed, wearing only shame on their fresh, pink faces."

"That isn't possible," he quivered.

"I'm afraid it is. I know because I rang them while you and Isabel were talking art, earlier. An anonymous tip was enough for your henchmen to investigate the charges. They didn't seem very surprised by my allegations. It was almost as though they were looking for an excuse to ruin you. It would appear your men aren't as loyal as you thought."

"You're lying. This is a farce. This isn't possible." He rambled on in shock.

"They'll be waiting for you, with your mother. She's desperately trying to make sense of this. Her heart is weak enough without this added stress. You may want to consider going to her now, while you still can. I fear she may not be long for this world." Edward's voice was hypnotic, soft and serenely terrifying.

"Oh, God..." he looked around the room frantically, utterly confused, searching for the rationalisations. "I never hurt those children, you know. I only looked. They never knew. I never touched a child, not once. I couldn't find the harm in looking. I'm not like him, you know...the man who took those pictures..."

"You're wasting precious time."

"I...I don't know...what'll I tell her? Oh, God..." he was panicking now, crying like a child.

Edward walked over to the trembling man and placed his hand under his wet chin, lifting his head with an almost tender touch. He spoke softly and gently.

"You'll not have the opportunity to tell her anything if you don't go now. For once in your miserable life accept the truth of what you really are. She won't be able to soften the blows the world delivers to you any more. Be a man, Moorely. You know what you need to do."

And for the first time in his all his years, Rupert Moorely resigned himself to his fate. In silence and he walked down the hall and out the door.

He could barely catch his breath as he sped down the road. The world was whipping past him without mercy or consideration, going much too fast for him to make any sense of it all. He'd never really harmed anyone, had he? After all, he'd never set out to be the way he was. These sorts of things just happen, like thieves in the shadows. You don't see them coming, but once they're upon you, what is there to do but submit? And it wasn't as though he were a homosexual. He liked women and girls just fine, of course. There were several well-worn stacks of pornographic magazines beneath that access panel as well. Hundreds of them, really. It was just that after a while, a man can get bored with all those fleshy curves, all the same poses and parts page after page. A little variety, that's all he was really after. All he ever wanted anyway was to be like other men, what with the way they talked and the things they did. But he wasn't. He knew it, his mother knew it, and now everyone would know it. And the real tragedy for poor Rupert Moorely was that he'd never come to understand why. He couldn't see how it was that he was so different, and he couldn't understand how it came to pass that instead of doing his job properly, he was racing away that very moment from two criminals, based on nothing but their word, which in all probability meant nothing, because a criminal's word never does, but despite these things, there he was, confused and uncertain of every single thing he witnessed and believed. No, the world was rushing all around him now and there was no sense to be made of it any more.

Poor, poor Rupert Moorely. His frail and withered mother would be dead within minutes of his return. He requested to go upstairs before the officers lead him away. He said there was something he needed to do. Moments later, he followed his mother to the great unknown with a gunshot wound to his head. He had purchased the weapon for protection, to keep her safe, so they would always be together. It's funny how things such as these work out.

❧

We lay in bed that night, curled against each other. I was full of adrenaline, which made me very chatty. Edward was more affectionate than usual, kissing me on the mouth every few seconds.

I proceeded to talk around his mouth, even as he climbed on top of me. "What's it like to be inside a person's head when they die?"

He groaned and put his head down on my shoulder, obviously bothered and frustrated.

"I mean, what do people think about when it happens? Do the thoughts just stop or does the chemistry linger on for a bit?"

Finally, he gave in. "I'm not sure how to describe it. I would think it's different for everyone."

"How was it for Moorely?"

He thought for a moment. "Cluttered at first. Though I'm fairly certain that was when his mother died. Just a cluster of images, quick flashes...in no particular order. When it was his turn, it was very clear and simple. Again no words really, just pictures; slow, soft, calm pictures. For such a violent death, it was remarkably quiet."

I nodded, satisfied by his answer and he pulled my leg over his hip and pressed against me. He moved in to kiss me again and I put my finger to his lips, obstructing the path.

"Oh...I have one more question."

"For the love of god, Isabel..." he complained. "What now?" This time he didn't let go.

"What was it that Moorely knew that you didn't want me to know? Your dirty little secret with Dr Hausner?"

"Surely you recognize the quandary that question presents."

"Come on. Is it really necessary for us to have secrets any more?" I kissed him and ran my finger down his chest to his stomach. He flinched and tightened his grip on me.

"That sort of behaviour will get you many things...an answer is not one of them."

"All right then. I'll find out on my own."

"That's fine." He didn't look too concerned.

"Don't underestimate me, sweetie. I learned from the best."

"Right..."

"Oh, why won't you tell me?"

He sighed again. Whining could, at times be effective, not because he sympathized, but because it tired him and forced him to decide if it was worth the struggle.

"Fine, Bel. I'll make a deal with you. You tell me a secret, and if it's something I don't already know, I'll tell you. How's that?"

"That's hardly fair! You know all of my secrets. I've told you practically everything and anything I left out you know anyway, what with you being in my head and all."

"Then it will prove to be a challenge. I guess you'll find out how much you really want to know this information. Now, please, Bel. I'm not getting any younger..."

I kissed him and pulled myself up to straddle him. His razor sharp hipbones cut into my thighs. When he closed his eyes I looked him over as best I could in the darkness. Something was different about him. He looked the way a snake looks right before it sheds its skin, cloudy and worn. The manic glimmer he usually possessed was dull and opaque. He was preparing to change. The experiment would happen tomorrow whether I was ready or not.. I was still having pangs of sickness now and again, but the withdraw was waning and becoming more tolerable. The former Inspector Detective Moorely had been a sufficient distraction from the discomfort and I supposed I would be well enough to carry Edward again.

A rainstorm rolled in under the blanket of night. I gazed out the huge plate of glass, seeing nothing. On the darkest evenings, looking out that window was much like staring at a motion picture screen before the opening credits. The only sound was heavy water on stone.

What secret did I have? Something he wouldn't know. I forced my thoughts to a tiny, invisible whisper. It proved to be ineffective, but it was something I'd never tried before. As I sifted through my memory, hoping to unearth some long-hidden deed, Edward followed right along, checking off each thought before I could complete it fully.

"No, already knew that one," he'd say, keeping his eyes closed. Or, "That's old news...I've known about that for ages now."

"I thought you were asleep," I scowled at our reflections in the empty window.

"I don't so much sleep as lay dormant," he mused.

"I'll never be able to come up with something. Why won't you just tell me so we can move on and you'll never have to hear me go on about it again?"

He placed his hand on my face and just smiled. There would be no confession tonight and probably not for a long time to come. Whatever it was, he kept it locked far away from the surface and there would surely be many miles of hell between it and me.

He would say there was no pain. He never remembered it, but I always did. He never remembered the moments he spent as an invalid, pissing and drooling on himself— the exhausting hours after the experiment when he was helpless and barely alive. As difficult and tiring as it was, these moments belonged to me. I was alone with my thoughts and a useless bag of bones that would quickly grow into something beautiful and terrifying. But until that happened, the kingdom would be mine. The king was dead; long live the queen.

He couldn't hear or see me. He couldn't touch me if I moved away. He couldn't manipulate or threaten me. I cherished this brief period of time when he was nothing but flesh and fluid. I took advantage of this opportunity to be cruel without consequence. Nothing too blatant, no permanent damage done. They were just petty, self-serving games to sate my resentment towards him. I fondled him, quickly losing interest, as he remained flaccid and unresponsive. I stuck him with a needle, first in the thigh, then in the neck. I was tempted to put it in his eye, but decided the risk was too great. The needle was thin, but it would surely bruise and I thought better of it. I was never very good with a needle anyway and there was no telling how he would be when he awoke.

Instead I tested the limits of his flexibility, bending his fingers back as far as they would go, pushing a little farther each time. His hands felt like rubber. It brought back memories of my mother's wake. A lacklustre gathering, I think there were only eight or nine people there. It was the first and last time in my youth that I didn't feel afraid. I went to her coffin and peered in. She looked like a painted whore, thick with foundation and pink rouge. Pink was an awful choice for her. They should have let me do the make-up, since I knew how she wore it before her days at the asylum better than anyone else. There was a choker around her neck, one that reminded me of Willa's, but the pearls were fake. I didn't linger on that for too long, as I'd only end up feeling guilty. My father purchased that choker before the services to cover the repulsive marks on her neck. I knew he wished they could've been real, but it was the best he could afford. I wanted to tell him not to feel too bad about it. She didn't deserve something as nice as pearls in life, let alone in the grave.

As I played with Edward's fingers, putting them in all manner of unnatural positions, I recalled her fingers and how one was left twisted away from the others. I remember some mouldy old relative, a beast of a woman, whisper my name sharply as I reached in to bend the finger back to its rightful shape. And I recalled the scandal it caused amongst the sparse group as I quietly told her to fuck off. It was *my* mother in

the box and if I wanted to touch her, that was my right. My father was too grief stricken
to punish me. I can't imagine how hard it must have been for him.

I opened Edward's mouth and put my finger inside as far as it would go, feeling
the texture of his throat. His breath was cool and moist. I hesitated for a moment,
fighting back the urge to be sick then put my mouth on his. Lightly, at first, trembling
and dizzy from the shock of it all. I let my tongue fall in and licked his teeth and the
roof of his mouth. I kept thinking how wrong it was, every bit of it but I liked him
half-dead. Under the sterile light, he looked like a cadaver sprawled out on the vinyl
chair. I don't know what came over me, what hideous desire compelled me to bite his
lips and tongue and face. I split his bottom lip open with my teeth. The way his blood
burst into my mouth reminded me of biting into a cherry tomato.

I wondered if he had any idea. Would he still think me a good mother? God knows
the sort of things he'd done during my various states of unconsciousness. He should be
grateful that I lacked the physical capability to violate him the way he'd surely done to
me. I bit him again, this time harder on the edge of his jaw and he stirred. I slithered off
the chair and wrapped myself in a towel, still shaking and aroused. He wasn't the only
one capable of such low perversion. There was something very satisfying about that.

His colour returned suddenly and when he opened his eyes he seemed more aware
than the first time. Something was different about him. Something was different about
me, too. Through the stony wall I could hear the humming ground. He sat up with ease,
shimmering and glistening. He looked stronger, more detailed and in focus. The whole
room was sharper and clearer. He touched his lip and examined the trace of blood on
his finger. I clenched up and backed away behind the steel table as he grinned.

"Having a little fun?" he whispered.

I looked at the cold floor in silence. I tried to read him. He seemed more amused
than angry.

"I was just...trying something," I said in a small voice.

"Wicked girl," he said with a coy little smile.

"Are you angry?"

He stood up, swaying a bit at first. He stretched his arms out towards me and I
went to him.

"Of course not." He nestled his face in my hair, taking a deep breath. "How could
I possibly be angry at the light of my life, my ray of sunshine, the mother of my child?"
His arms tightened around me, preparing for a reaction.

I lost my breath for a second. "What?"

"I saw it, Bel. I felt it inside you. I wasn't alone in there." He stroked my hair and I
began to cry. He rocked me back and forth, keeping his hand on the back of my head.

"This is a wonderful thing, Bel..."

"How can I be? How would you know already? It's only been since last night that we..." I sobbed.

"Well, I think it must have happened before last night, silly."

I pulled away for air. It was too humid between our sticky bodies to find any.

"But...I just...I was bleeding!" I cried.

Edward smiled with sincere empathy and tilted his head. "Surely you know that doesn't always mean anything. Many women experience breakthrough bleeding or sometimes one last cycle within the first weeks of pregnancy. It was shorter than usual, remember?"

He was right. It only lasted a couple days this time. He was right about all of it and if anyone would know for certain, it was him.

"I know you're frightened, love. Come now, don't cry."

I let my head fall onto his shoulder, weeping harder than before. I couldn't imagine what this would mean. What sort of parents would we be? We were murderous, callous creatures. Edward wasn't even human any more. How would we manage to raise a healthy, normal child? I didn't even know where I could go to have a baby. I was too young to have a baby. Would Edward want to deliver it? Would he ever let it out of the house?

"Slow down, Bel...there's still time to sort these things out."

I nodded and tried to calm myself. A second later a terrible thought occurred to me.

"Oh, god...Edward, the experiment! What if we messed it up?" I shrieked, grabbing his shoulders. He wrapped his hands tightly around my wrists until I released him. He seemed confused.

"Darling, the experiment is done. We couldn't have messed it up."

"Not that...the baby! What if we messed up the baby with the drugs and the experiment?"

"Oh. Well, I hadn't really planned for this. Though I doubt any damage was done. It's really very small at this stage, just like a tiny little jellyfish."

His lack of concern horrified me. A *jellyfish*? Edward was not a light-hearted man by design. How could he not take this seriously?

"It's not just a chunk of tissue, Edward."

"Actually, right now it is."

"What about its soul?"

He sighed and rubbed his eyes. I was wearing him down. "I don't know, Bel. I don't control these things. I'm not God."

I wiped my eyes and stared at him with desperation. "Yes, Edward...yes, you are."

"When the baby finishes school you will be sixty-four." I stared off into space. The sitting room was bitter and cold and Edward had wrapped me in a blanket and brought me tea. By the time I drank it, it was bitter and cold too.

"That's right, love."

"When the baby is thirty, you'll most likely be dead."

"When the baby is thirty, it won't be a baby any more."

"How am I supposed to take care of a baby by myself?"

He glanced around the room with pretend suspicion. "Do you know something I don't?"

"I mean when I'm fifty-five and the baby is thirty and you're dead." I suppose I knew I was making no sense. I didn't really care.

"I plan on being around for quite a while, Bel. No need to make any arrangements with the undertaker just yet, all right?" He smiled and tucked the blanket under my feet.

I watched him carefully until tears welled up and blurred him into the carpet.

"Don't die, Edward. Please don't ever leave us."

"I'm working on it, love."

"Why didn't it come out of me during the experiment? Why didn't I miscarry?"

"That's a good question."

"Well?"

"I don't know, actually. Perhaps this is something that is meant to be. Perhaps it's a miracle or fate or some such thing."

"What," I laughed. "Like a gift from God?"

"Well, it's a gift from something. Maybe God, maybe something else. I really don't know."

"I thought you knew everything."

"Think what you like. If I knew I'd say as much."

"We'll send it to school, won't we?"

"I'd imagine so."

"I never went to University."

"It's not everything, you know." He was downplaying it for my benefit. He must have sensed some embarrassment in my voice.

"My father never could have afforded it."

He continued with his consolation. "College was very stressful—stressful and lonely. It wasn't the best time for me, really."

"What about Abby?"

"Hmm? Oh. Right...well, that was fairly short-lived." He quickly looked away. There was something with this topic that always seemed to cause him discomfort. I paused and listened for a moment. He was scrambling his thoughts again.

"You don't like to talk about her."

"No. I really don't."

"You never think about her either."

"Not really."

"Does it hurt you that much?"

He shook his head. "No, it doesn't hurt. I just put that away a long time ago."

I waited again, listening closer, trying to pick up the slightest hint. Something was wrong. "Why are you lying?" I was treading on dangerous ground now and I knew it.

He raised his head and stared at me with amazement. "Lying? About what?"

"About her."

Through the static in his head I could hear a remote voice. It would break apart, every few words but I was in there now. I could see his tattered words and ghostly pictures. Amidst the cluster of mangled images I saw a woman with no face.

"Stop it, Isabel," he whispered angrily.

"I can't. I'm sorry..." I had come away from the experiment stronger than before. I was catching up to him by tiny measures.

"This conversation is over now."

"Why doesn't she have a face, Edward?"

"I don't know..." He was losing his composure. It pained me to see this happen, but I struck anyway.

"It's because you made her up, isn't it?"

Silence. Not even a breath, just long, cold silence. He stared back at me for the longest time. I couldn't tell if his glassy eyes were challenging me to push him further or if they were warning me to let it go.

"All right, then. I made her up."

There was a collective exhalation and we both turned our eyes away, blinking away the dryness. He went on.

"There was no Abigail. There was no one while I was at school. I made up the whole story."

"Why would you do that?"

The static came back. Louder and thicker than before, and when instinct said to let it go, I should have listened.

"I really don't know. I mean…I told you about my youth, how humiliating it was. I suppose I didn't want to appear like any more of a…"

"Of what? You didn't want to seem like more of a freak?"

"Exactly," he whispered.

You're lying again… "Edward, please. After everything we've done, you were afraid of looking bad because you didn't have a girlfriend at Uni?"

"Sometimes it's the little things, Isabel. Sometimes it's all in the details." He glared at the floor and cleared his throat. "I'm going to get cleaned up now. Are you staying here or going to bed?"

"I think I'll sit awhile and try to figure out what the hell is wrong with your head."

"Then I suppose I shouldn't expect you any time too soon, eh?" He forced a smile.

As he left the room I noticed that he was wringing his hands nervously, hurrying away down the hall. I heard him whisper to himself, then fade away. I didn't want to know what he said and, in time, I would wish that I never heard anything at all. I felt a burning in my stomach, a feeling that I hadn't experienced for months. The creature that used to light the fires in me had died, probably from neglect. But now there was something else. The jellyfish already had a little spark of its own.

The first thing I noticed was that the lighting was wrong. The sun was gone; it couldn't be to blame. I'd closed my eyes, just for a minute or two in hopes of relieving the strain and pressure. The side effects of the experiment were relentless. When I opened my eyes again I found myself in a faded old photograph, I found myself in 1953.

"Why didn't you finish your tea, lovely? You'd feel better now had you finished it."

"It's too bitter."

"Sugar isn't good for the little ones."

It was a sweet, matronly voice, brittle and soft. I looked around to find its source. Willa sat in her simple wooden chair by the fireplace, white-gloved hands folded neatly on her lap.

"I'm scared, Gram." I knew she'd understand.

"It's normal to be frightened. We all get the worries when our time comes. Dreadful thing, it is," she mused.

"I'm too young."

"Nonsense. You are a grown woman. Why, my Rosalie was much younger than you when she had Edward." She smiled the sweetest, kindest smile I'd ever seen.

"Who do you think she'll take after? More like Edward or more like me?

She laughed, "Oh...it's all the same, really."

"I think she has my intuition," I said proudly.

"There's no question." she beamed.

"Oh, Gram..." my smiled faded, "Edward and I, we've done terrible things."

She gave a mournful and knowing nod.

"Please say the baby will be ok."

"Ah, love...it's the way of this family. She'll manage...she'll manage just fine. She has your strength really, the strength of two, so never-you-mind that. She'll have a hundred spirits to protect her. Now...what do you suppose you'll call her? Have you given it any thought?"

"I don't know. I'll have to talk to Edward." I smiled at her, full of love and trust and then I knew. "But I think I'd like to call her Willa."

"Oh, my..." she sighed in her sweet little voice, drawing her hands to her mouth. "I'd like that."

"Isabel?"

As I jumped, the natural colours of the room washed in. Willa was gone.

"Did I frighten you? Were you sleeping?" Edward put his hand on my leg. Some of the lines on his face had been rinsed away.

"No...I don't know...I didn't hear you coming." I was so confused. "Are you getting younger? You look..."

"It's late. I thought I should take you upstairs."

I let him help me up. I was still shaking and a bit bewildered. As we climbed the stairs I asked him what he thought of the name 'Willa.'

"How do you know it will be a girl?"

I shrugged. "Just a feeling, I suppose."

"Then I think it should be nice to have a Willa in this house again."

"I'm not so sure the first one ever left." I grinned and turned to Edward, expecting him to return the smile. He didn't.

Later he would ask me what I meant by my comment on the stairs. His voice came out of the darkness so abruptly.

"I don't know," I said. "I just think she's still around. I feel as though I know her."

"Do you see her?"

I hesitated. His tone indicated that I shouldn't say yes.

"You *do* see her, don't you?"

"Maybe just in dreams. It's difficult to tell sometimes."

"Does she speak to you?"

"I'm probably dreaming it when it happens. Why?"

"What, exactly, does she say?" His voice was more impatient this time.

"Edward, what's wrong? You said you loved your grandmother. Why would it bother you if her spirit was still here?"

He sat up in the bed, kicking the blanket violently. "Dammit, Bel...what does she say to you?" I could feel him shaking.

"Well, she's yet to tell me any of your secrets, if that's what you're afraid of."

In one furious motion he hoisted me up and slammed me into the headboard. The knotted designs in the wood burrowed into the soft spaces between my bones.

"Whatever it is she tells you..." he shoved his finger at my face and searched for the words. Breathless and nervous, he quickly became aware of himself and shifted back, taking some of the anger with him. He carefully peeled my spine away from the wood and released me into the pillows beneath.

"She's not well, you know. She may try to tell you...things." He was fighting back tears in his wide eyes. "It may not even be her."

I was not so successful. He'd scared the bloody hell out of me. "She tells me it will be fine," I sobbed, making sure to stare through him. "So she must be mad."

(August)

Never had I witnessed Edward in such a state. The laylines were growing louder and didn't help the situation. We were nothing but frayed nerves and still reeling from the shock of chemicals and the presence of the child. Edward resented me now. He had pushed the bitterness aside at first, wanting to be excited, but his true feelings surfaced and were impossible for him to ignore. The thought of me sharing a connection with his dead grandmother and the advancement of my preternatural abilities served as a vehicle for his irritation. Both of these developments pointed to the same conclusion; I was one step closer to uncovering his great secret. We were on an even playing field now and it was a turn he'd not prepared for.

Then, as it was apt to do, the house slipped into a state of madness. The vibrations did not cease for days, the humming was deafening at times. The rooms became sick and violent like rabid animals, driving us to the yard, sometimes even in the dead of night. We blamed this on each other. Edward claimed I was doing it on purpose, just to hurt him. I maintained it was his jealousy seething out and infecting the very walls. He laughed and said the idea of him being jealous of me was preposterous. He blamed me for the laylines, too. The precious din that he once deemed golden was now a terrible curse that I had unleashed upon him. The noise interfered with our unspoken communications. It was nearly impossible to hear him and for the first time since the original experiment, he could not hear me either. Fragments of thoughts and words slipped through every now and then, but it was no longer enough to allow him the upper hand. Paranoia was eating him alive.

I don't recall what specific thing, if any, brought me to that place, but I made a decision one terrible morning, one that I had never had the courage to consider before.

I decided to leave.

I packed nothing but a few changes of clothes and the little bit money that I had saved months before. He met me at the bottom of the stairwell, uncertain of my intentions.

"What are you doing?"

I hesitated, not looking him in the face. If I looked, I feared I'd lose my nerve. "I have to go."

He let out a tiny, sceptical laugh. "What do you mean *go*? Go where?"

"I don't know. What I *do* know is that this house has gone hateful, you've gone hateful, and it can't possibly be healthy for the baby. You lie to me, you are abusive, you are dripping with guilt over some mystery that you won't tell me and I am at my end with it all. It's not just you and me any more and if you can't find the compassion in that cold heart of yours to love me or your child, then I need to go." I brushed past him, still staring at the floor. He caught me by the arm.

"What are you going to do to stop me, Edward? Kill me? Kill your child?" I looked up at him, squarely in the face as I said it.

He was wild and confused. "Do you truly think I could do that?"

"I don't know any more and that's precisely why I need to leave."

"Bel...don't. I'm sorry. Don't leave me now. Please...everything is different and I don't know what to do. You remember the last time we did this, don't you? Don't you remember how things were difficult at first? We just needed time to acclimate to the gift. Then it was good. Remember? But I can't hear you right now, I just need there to be some quiet and then I can hear you and you can hear me and we can be good again."

"*Good*, Edward? When have things *ever* been good? In the downtime between murders? The minutes between the injections and the violence and the ghosts? Was that what you meant?"

"That's not fair, Bel," he said softly.

"Normal people, *Edward*, don't need to hear one another's thoughts to be together. It's called *trust*...the concept of which you are obviously unfamiliar. Or is it just something that's too pedestrian for you, too *mundane?* Let the commoners dally with things like trust and love and happiness and stability! To hell with it all! We don't need any of that rubbish! We have *morphine* and *perversion*! We have each other...*the only people in the fucking world that would have aberrant freaks like us!*

"Bel, no," he whispered.

"Do you know what I see a year from now? I see one of us watching the baby while the other drags some poor soul to his death, then comes back and plays mummy or daddy, as though nothing ever happened. I see us taking turns holding her while we shoot up."

"That's not how it would be." He seemed so wounded

"Really? So what will happen between now and then when some random cunt makes the fatal mistake of questioning you or offending you or looking at you three seconds longer than you prefer? Are you prepared to let it go? Or when you decide that our child is too common and boring for your taste and should be altered...the way you altered yourself, the way you altered me?"

"That's not why..."

"No? You mean to say that the real reason for these experiments isn't to compensate for your feeling small and weak? Why did you become a doctor; why did you try to become a god then? To make the world a better place? To help people learn? No, Edward, it was all for you. It's always been for you," I cried over the noise.

"I did this for you, too," he whispered. I could barely hear him.

"How can you say that?"

"I don't think I could begin to explain it to you right now. I wouldn't know where to begin, but I swear to you, Bel, that all of this...the experiments, the tests, the sacrifice...it's all been for us."

"You don't think you could explain it right now? Well, when exactly did you plan on explaining? What was all that prattling on you did about ancient rites and life-cycles and evolution? I thought that was your explanation!"

"It is, but there's more and I can't...I did this so we'd be strong. I did this to make you strong...I can't explain..." He covered his face with his hands.

"No, of course you can't. But I think I can. How does this sound; I was just body parts for you! You could have used *anyone!* Why did you have to pick me?" I drew my hands across my wet face. "I thought...I hoped that perhaps you could have loved me as I was, but you had to change me, because I bored you. I don't know what I am any more!" I heaved and sobbed. "I'm so sorry that you grew up the way you did. I'm sorry about your mother and your grandfather. I'm sorry about your loneliness and pain. But I had pain, too, Edward. My mother killed herself and my father disowned me! I feel like the smallest person in the world sometimes, but I have never used these things to justify the kind of pain and death that you have inflicted upon people on two continents!"

He stood before me, speechless and perfectly still.

"But if you think for one second that I will allow you to seek retribution for the crimes your parents committed against you at the cost of this child's safety, then you are gravely mistaken. I would see you dead before you ever touch this baby or me again. Now get out of my way."

And most repentantly, he let go and stepped aside. And just as I had done to my own father, I walked out. This time, I had only one bag to take with me.

I walked for some time, trying to get as far away from the noise and chaos of the Grace house as possible before collecting my thoughts. By the end of the day, just before nightfall, I had made it to the other end of town, taking the long route around the north end to avoid the prying eyes of any locals, in particular, avoiding Chapel and the guilt I'd convinced myself to bury.

I watched the sky change from a pale blue to a dingy grey as I came to the south end of town. This was so familiar. I had grown up not far from there. It was all coming back quickly, the streets and shops and little row houses. The factories along the waterfront stained the air and emitted a filthy, burning smell. As I wandered, the businesses gave way to small family row homes and before I realised my path, I found myself on the outskirts of my old neighbourhood.

I suppose it hadn't been the worst place to grow up. When I was very young, before I knew the difference between people like the Grace's and people like us, I happily played with the neighbour children, running the length of the canal, or at least from Cook Street to the alley behind David Sawyer's house. Some of the children, including David Sawyer, were permitted to wander farther, but that was as far as I was allowed to go. I minded that rule for many years, until one day I was double-dared by Glynnis Carroll to walk all the way to Singer Road. I never cared much for Glynnis. She was a bossy little prig on her best day and why we ever tolerated her, I couldn't say. Singer Road was a place that none of us kids were permitted to go. I'd heard the tales of ladies who marched up and down that street, letting men do filthy things to them for money. Glynnis claimed that she'd heard a man stabbed a lady there and threw her body into the canal. She said that she went down there a few days after the alleged incident and came across a torn pair of frilly knickers. This information left the rest of us mildly intrigued and a little nervous, but we all knew that Glynnis was a tremendous liar and there was a very good chance that it never happened at all.

So I ran with my grubby little crowd and did all the things children do until the year that my mother was taken away. After that, they treated me as though I'd been the one who'd gone mad. When Max Littleford's birthday invites went out to all the kids but me, I thought that it might have been an oversight. Max and I were never best mates, anyway, but then the same thing happened when Georgina Kelly had her party, and I knew I was officially cast out. I found out later that Glynnis had told them my mother's insanity was contagious and I probably had it as well. David Sawyer was the last of the group to sever ties with me. It wasn't easy for him, as near as I could tell. We'd been as thick as thieves until then. I think he knew the others had betrayed me, and that he was about to do the same, but the peer pressure got the best of him and in the end, there were no more birthday party invites from him either.

It only got worse when my mother killed herself. There were whispers on the street and at school about it for weeks after. Some of my former friends sent sympathy notes to our house, the sort that your parents make you write. David was the only one of them to come to the wake, along with his mother and father and a covered dish of Shepard's Pie. The only thing he said to me the whole time was, "I'm sorry your mum's gone." Actually, if I remember correctly, he didn't so much say it to me as he did the floor.

The next week, my dad sent me to return Mrs. Sawyer's dish. Once there, she asked me to wait a moment on the doorstep, and I overheard her say to David, "Isabel is here. Why don't you go say hello to her?" David replied with an exasperated whine, "But *Mummy*...do I *have to?*"

She replied sharply that yes, indeed, he did *have to*, as I had no other friends and no mother. He informed her that we were no longer friends, and she informed him that we would, indeed, be friends whether he liked it or not. I don't know if he ever came to the door or not. I ran home before they finished the discussion.

But this was ancient history. I wondered why I would even bother to think of it. Perhaps it was because it was getting dark or because I was pregnant and desperate and alone. I didn't know what would happen next, standing there at the end of my street. I half expected David to come running out of his house, or stupid Glynnis to be jumping rope on the walk, or Max and Georgina to ride up on their three-speeds, but they didn't. A car drove by, and a dog was barking beyond the row, but there were no children to be found playing anywhere.

I could see my father's boxy house. There was a light in the window. I must have let an hour pass, just wandering down the street to the canal. I even went as far as Singer Road. With its hypodermic needles and empty bottles of gin, I gathered not much had changed since I'd left.

I had no idea what would happen if I knocked on his door, but I turned and headed back anyway. It was getting cool now, even in summer the nights could be cold. By the time I'd reached our front walk, I was beyond hesitation. *Just go on*, I thought. *It can't be any worse than where you came from*. I tapped lightly on the old, weather-beaten door and held my breath at the clinking of the latch.

"Isabel?"

"Hi, Daddy." I was weeping before I got it all out.

He took me in his arms and rocked me back and forth. Some feelings never change, I thought. Several minutes passed with only the sound of my sobbing before he sat me down on the couch. We looked each other over. Eight years had not been so kind to him and he thought the same of me. I lied and said he looked well. He told me the truth.

"You look awful, Isabel," he said as tenderly as possible. "Where've you been all this time?"

"Just north. I didn't get very far when I left you."

"Are you hungry? Or can I fix you some tea? Did you walk here, you must be exhausted." His face was creased with a million trenches of concern and confusion. They were permanent fixtures now, as was his white and grey unruly hair. I couldn't believe how time had ravaged him.

I tried not to look around the room too much. I knew exactly where everything was; he'd not touched a thing since my mother died. I knew there was a picture of her on the end table, next to the telephone. There was another picture next to it of the three of us, taken when I was four. The little porcelain ducks and ballerinas and cats and turtles were all in their proper places. I had played with them so many times as a child that they had become real to me. I forced myself to look at them now. They were dead and frozen, suspended in mid-play and motion. All time had stopped in this house the day my mother hung herself. I wanted to smash them, if only to free them from the prison in which she'd put us.

He brought me some tea. I focused on his hand as he gave me the little china cup. He had Edward's hands. The tea tasted exactly the same as it had years ago, bland and tinny. I smiled at him as I sipped. God, how I wished I could telephone Edward. He really did resemble my father, only younger and stronger.

He tried to make small talk. "So what are you doing with yourself these days?"

Not 'why are you here after all this time' or 'what the hell happened to you,' just 'what are you doing these days'

"Daddy, I need to talk to you. I don't even know where to start."

"Oh? Well, what is it?" He shifted uncomfortably in the old armchair.

I put my head in my hands. "I don't know. Everything...I want to talk about you and me and Mummy. I want to tell you about the horrible things that have happened since I left, the man I've been living with."

He looked so uncomfortable at the very thought of such a conversation. "This man...you say you and he been living just across town, then?"

I tried to breathe and not choke on the words. "Daddy, I'm going to have a baby."

"It's a wonder we've not crossed paths before now."

"Daddy, did you hear what I said?"

He let out a deep sigh and rubbed his face. "Aye, I heard you." He shook his head slowly. "This man you're living with...he's the father, then?"

I nodded.

"Are you and this...man...having troubles? Is that what brings you here?"

"No, well...yes, you could say we're having troubles, but that's not why I came."

His face creased even deeper. "I'm not sure I know what to do for you, love. Do you need money or..."

"No, Daddy. I don't need money. I just...I don't know. I just needed my father."

He looked guilty at his suggestion. "I'm sorry, love. But I have to say I don't think I ever expected to see you again. Not a day has passed in these years that I haven't thought about you or missed you, but I don't know..." he put his head down.

"Don't know what, Dad?"

"I don't know what I can give you. I have to be honest with you...the day you left I had to set myself that you were gone, and never coming back. I love you so much, Isabel, but I just couldn't bear the pain."

"What are you saying? You can't be my father now, because I grew up and went on my own? Is that it?"

He kept his head down and confirmed the question with his silence. I was in shock. The dam broke and there was nothing I could do to prevent what followed.

"I can't believe this, Daddy. You have kept this house a stale shrine to a woman who abused us and left us! She tore apart our family and ruined you and you've sat here for years, pining for her, holding on to her ghost! Meanwhile, I move an hour away and try to start my own life and you wash your hands clean of me? *She's* the one who's dead, Daddy, not me! *She's* the one who can't come back! I'm your fucking daughter! I'm still alive!"

"I know...I know it's wrong," he cried meekly.

"Did she even love us at all?" I sobbed.

He shook his head. "I don't know. I never knew."

"Well, I know I love *you*, Daddy. I'm the one sitting here now, telling you that I love you. What did she tell you as she was swinging from that pipe at the hospital? Did you think she loved you then?"

"Oh, Isabel...please don't say things like that."

"It's the truth."

"*Fine*! She never really loved me! Is that what you want to hear? Is that why you came, to get me to say that? You could've saved us both the trouble and never come back. You already knew the truth."

"But did you?" I whispered.

"Of course I knew," he sighed painfully and searched the ceiling with his eyes, looking for a way to tell me. "She...your mother's heart was with someone else."

"Someone else? Who? When?"

"Ah, God...before you were born. Your mother met him when she was working at University library. We had just gotten married and I knew but I...I didn't want to shame her. She was a good woman. I don't know what happened. It was like she believed they shared some sort of connection. She tried to stay away from him, but she loved him too much. It's funny, though...the thing that hurt the most was that he didn't even love her and he made no secret of it. I could've accepted it if he thought half as much of her as she did him. She would have gone off with him, but he only really had one love...his studies and his work. So after some time, she settled herself with me. We had a few good times, Isabel, the three of us, before Kate, but her heart was always with that boy."

He was breaking my heart. "Oh, Daddy, why didn't you just leave her? Were you so concerned with her reputation? What about your pride? You could have walked away."

"It wasn't as simple as that. I loved her. People do foolish things for love. Which brings me to the rest of it." He was shaking now.

"What's that?" Something terrible was about to happen. I could feel the fire.

"I love you, Isabel. I always have. I love you and I loved her, but he left her, broke her heart. He got her with child and I just couldn't leave her. She would have been alone. I couldn't let her raise a baby alone...I couldn't let her raise you alone."

I put my hand to my mouth and leaned back. I felt like he'd punched me in the stomach.

"Isabel, please hear me out...you were *always* my daughter. I raised you, love. I never resented it. I never looked at you as his. You were mine, if not by blood, then by spirit. I promise you that."

After a long, painful silence I spoke. "Did he know? Did he ever know he had a child?" It was all I could think to say.

"Aye. And to his credit, he checked in on you when you were just a baby. He paid the expenses when you were born. His family was very wealthy. He even arranged for the doctor, someone that wouldn't 'ask too many questions,' as it were. The father of one of his schoolmates delivered you. He sent money on your birthdays and at holidays. But as to your mother, well...once you came along, he had no more use for her. As much as I hate to admit it, I hate to give him the credit; I believe he loved you. It was just Emma he didn't carry anything for."

He sat back and let his shoulders fall a bit, the weight of the secret gone. He sighed and asked me if I wanted to know his name.

The burning was unbearable. I could feel it in my mouth, scorching the back of my teeth. I probably had a million other questions to ask him. They were swarming and churning around on the surface of my brain, but I didn't say anything else. I didn't have to because I already knew the truth. I didn't need to know his name. It lay just beneath my skin. The blood was gone from my head and had pooled in the pit of my stomach. My hands tingled and my throat tightened. The fire was raging and it would consume me. The room became a dark and swirling tunnel, and it was the last thing I saw.

I woke up to the glaring, white-green glow of hospital lights and the beeping of a monitor. My father (I'll call him George, to avoid further confusion) sat next to the bed, wringing his wool cap in his hands.

"Isabel? I'm here, love." He moved in closer and took my hand.

"What happened?" I imagined I'd been hit by a train from the feel of it.

"Guess it was a lot to hear at once. Plus with you in your condition and looking so worn and thin and all. I'm so sorry, love. I should never've kept all that from you. I've been wrong about so much for many years now. I hope you can forgive me." He looked away, quickly changing the subject. "The nurse, she says it was nervous exhaustion you collapsed from. Oh! But they said the baby should be just fine, so don't you worry about that." He smiled grimly. "The nurse said you'll need to have a proper exam as soon as possible, though. Just to be certain."

My stomach turned at the mention of the little creature and George pulled me onto my side, shoving a little plastic pan under my chin as I vomited. Too early for morning sickness, this was hideous, vile disgust that I choked on. He stroked my hair and wiped my face with a tissue.

"They say they want to keep you overnight, just to make sure you get the rest you need. Do you want me to ring your...friend, I mean the baby's father for you, so he won't be worried?"

All right, go on and telephone him then. Just ask for Edward and then we'll all know how it came to be that I am carrying my father's child. And while you're at it, ask him to tell you about the murder and the drugs and the other crimes we've committed against nature...

"No. He's not expecting me back tonight. I don't want to see him right now, anyway."

"All right then. You just get some rest. I'll be around if you need me." He smiled again and put out the ugly light.

"Daddy?"

"What's that, love?"

"So, he knew my name?" Of course, I knew he did.

"Certainly did. Your mother even insisted that he have a say in naming you..." he looked ashamed, "...since you'd be given my last name, she said it was only right. So he came up with 'Isabel.' That was all right by me. I liked it well enough... 'Isabel.' He said it was a name befitting of queen. He even came to visit you once or twice when you were very small. I doubt you'd ever recall it, though."

"No. I don't remember it at all."

The vivid pictures came when I closed my eyes. In blazing colour and detail, my mind bombarded me with pornographic films of Edward and myself. I could taste him and smell him and feel him under my skin, deep inside. He knew, with every kiss and every touch, he knew. I twisted around in the starched sheets, pulling the cocoon tighter and trying to move away from myself. A terrible shaking consumed me and I screamed and thrashed the bed, tearing and ripping the wires and tubes from the surrounding web of machines. I did not stop screaming, even as three nurses restrained me.

George could do nothing to calm me. The nurses were just as useless. They pleaded with me, for the sake of the baby, to calm myself. *Think of the baby...this is no good for the baby...no, you worthless beasts, what's not good for the baby was being created...he's not good for the baby...the baby is an ungodly product of unfathomable sickness!* But I was fully aware of myself, making the conscious choice to scream and fight. Sometimes the shrieks were of laughter, sometimes rage and disgust. And there was contempt...so much contempt. I remember chewing on the sheet, trying to destroy it and digest the fabric. There was so little they could do because of the pregnancy. A mild sedative was the only option. I had them all running around in a state of bewilderment, completely oblivious to the cause of my outburst. This amused me to no end until they had to pull George from the room and I noticed the fear in his eyes. I felt bad for a moment, then decided that I was owed this for the years of secrets and lies. And really, what better place to lose one's head than in a hospital? It saved everyone a great deal of trouble.

They sent George home around two a.m. I voluntarily calmed myself long enough to assuage his guilt and allow him the opportunity to go home and rest. In the end I had to beg him to leave and get some sleep. In truth, I didn't really feel like talking to him or having him hovering around the room, trying to atone for his sins. I also didn't want to risk blurting out the devastating truth during one of my episodes.

Exactly twenty-seven minutes after he left I was compelled to start the screaming again. Only this time my ranting wasn't just random vowels and vocalisations. They were words—words unfit for a mother-to-be, or so a nurse told me.

At three a.m. they moved me to a ward where my behaviour would be a bit more socially acceptable. I didn't care for that end of the hospital; the nurses there were not as kind or compassionate. They carted me off to a soundproofed isolation room that smelled of urine and informed me that I could be hauled back to a regular room when I decided to behave myself. I did not decide to do that and spent the remainder of the night in stale darkness, drowning in the stench of ammonia.

By morning my throat was raw. There was no more yelling to be had for me and that made me sad, so I compensated by whispering scratchy insults at the nurses. I was removed from the isolation room, despite my actions, when a young Scottish man on some sort of hallucinogen was wrangled down the hall, kicking and screaming and spitting at the staff. I hoped he liked the smell of piss, as it would certainly be buried deep into his hair by the time he got out.

At six a.m. I reluctantly drifted off for a bit. It was abrupt and dreamless and that was just fine. At seven I woke up and immediately wished I'd never opened my eyes.

Edward sat in a chair at the end of the bed. He had one leg casually slung over the other and was still wearing his overcoat. He was filling out a form on a clipboard. A bundle of white lilies had been tossed on my legs, tied up with a pale purple ribbon. He was humming a quiet tune as he read.

"Wha's that?" I slurred.

"Wagner." He kept reading, occasionally jotting something down on the paper.

"Not the tune...what're you writing?" I felt like I had no control of my mouth.

"It's a release form. I'm taking you home."

"The hell you are."

"Don't start. It's bad enough I have to fill out these dreadful hospital forms. I detested them when I was practising and I detest them now."

I kicked the bundle of flowers at him as hard as I could. They crashed into his legs with a soft rustling and quietly fell to pieces at his feet.

"The nurses told me you were being an absolute terror. They weren't joking, were they?" He resumed the humming for a few measures then stopped again. "You know, I really enjoy Wagner. Now *there* was a man with questionable morals," he laughed. "Consider yourself lucky. He never knew who his real father was at all. It's painfully obvious if you listen to his operas. He was known to be less-than-chivalrous with the ladies, and the men, for that matter. The way he toyed with King Ludwig...scandalous! That poor, dear man..."

"Shut up." I regretted wasting my energy on the staff.

He put the pen to his mouth, thoughtfully, ignoring my request. "Now what do you suppose I should put here on the line that reads: *'Relationship to the Patient'*?" He laughed to himself.

"How did you find me?"

"I followed the incessant yelling. You could have called the dead with that ruckus."

"How fortunate for me. I got you instead."

"Well, it *is* quite fortunate for you. They wanted to keep you for an evaluation. Within the week they'd have you shipped off to the asylum and my thinking on that is, 'why go off to that wretched pit of madness when you can live in your own private little hell at home with me?' You want to play crazy, dear heart, you can do it at home and not waste the time of these fine mental health professionals." He let the words drip out of his mouth.

"You're a maniac."

"Don't you think it might be good for us to go home and talk?"

"Oh, that's right..." I sighed. "If we talk, then you won't be my *bloody father* any more!"

He put his finger to his lips and shushed me. "Really, Bel...there are sick people here. Show some respect, please."

"Where's my father?" I yelled.

Edward flashed a look of confusion, then grinned. "Oh, you must mean George. Your doctor telephoned him to say that you'd be returning home and that you will call him when you are able. He was a bit persistent at first, but eventually he consented once he understood your need for some time to yourself."

"My doctor didn't tell him that. You rang him, didn't you?"

"According to this form, I am your doctor. I'm assuming responsibility for you. It's only right, when you think about it."

"You're a fucking obstetrician! Not a psychiatrist!"

"I am an obstetrician and general practitioner. And you are pregnant and obviously in a fragile state. The doctor sees fit that I should be able to handle things from here. So, it's me or the asylum."

"I'll take the asylum."

He slammed the clipboard down on the arm of the chair. "Well then maybe you can stay in your mother's old room."

"You need to leave."

He pretended not to hear me. "You'll not be going to that dreadful place. The nurse will be in shortly to prepare you for the ride home."

Somehow, Edward had a way of saying things and making them so. There was no point in arguing. He wanted me with him and that was the only way it would be. Suddenly I felt like a five-year-old.

I shuffled into the dead house, half aware and completely sickened. The chaos had fizzled out while I was gone, leaving behind little disturbances and sparks of violence. The house and I were the same right now—tired and drained. *See what he does to us?* I whispered to her. I don't know if I said it aloud or not. It was too quiet now. I could hear the rushing of blood through my head and hands and feet. I thought I might burst and evaporate into the walls.

As he paid the taxi, I wandered sleepily through the dark hallway and caught myself in the mirror. I looked like him. I had never seen it before. My hair was clumped together on one side, where I had laid on it and let it absorb the tears and saliva throughout the night. I was greasy with sweat and I smelled offensively sweet, like Chapel's bakery, and of sterile, blue chemicals. Beneath that was the smell of the diseased. But despite all of this, I looked like him.

I slammed my head into the giant hall mirror before he could stop me. "Look! I'm *bleeding*! I'm bleeding and it's the same as you! I'm spilling *your* blood!" I couldn't help but laugh hysterically as he reached out for me.

"Just like you've always wanted. Christ..." frantically mopping at my hairline with the sleeve of his coat. "Lie down before you pass out."

"I need to use the telephone please."

"I'm sure it can wait."

"Seven years bad luck for me. Seven years." I grinned.

"Dammit, Bel. Why did you have to do this here? I can't see a thing." He was feeling around my forehead and scalp for shards. "God knows how many slivers you're laying on. I need to move you."

"I need to call my father...my George. He'll be worried." I couldn't see clearly for the red syrup in my eyelashes.

He picked me up and carried me towards the kitchen. The light would be better there. As we passed by the telephone, I screamed and twisted around in his arms, nearly knocking us both down. Above my screeching Edward snapped at me, hoisting me back up into his chest so he again had a firm hold.

"*Jesus* Christ, woman...have you lost your mind?" He was covered in long streaks of blood.

"You're responsible for me now! The form says so! I'm all yours...I always have been...all yours...seven years..." I faded out into hushed crying.

He placed me at the little table in the alcove and continued to wipe the blood away with a dishtowel. He said it wasn't as bad as it looked, considering the copious amounts of blood. He said all those tiny vessels were infamous for their gushing.

"Why do you insist upon doing this to yourself?"

"Because I can't do it to you."

As it so happened, I had been mistaken in thinking that I'd have to control my rage toward Edward. I took to hitting him in random and uncontrolled fits of disgust and confusion, and he made no attempts to stop me. He didn't even try to shield himself from the blows. He'd just sit still, in a seemingly meditative state, while I screamed and pounded my fists into his chest and back. When I'd exhausted myself, I'd lie down and cry until I fell asleep. Then Edward would quietly go to the courtyard and have a cigarette or six. There was never any mention made of those incidents after the fact. I suppose it was easier for him to take since he could see them coming. Eventually, my desire to beat him bloody died down. We both knew the futility of it, or any other act of retribution that I could think of. There was nothing to take this kind of pain away, but he let me take what I thought I needed anyway. It was as close to an apology as he could give.

He let me telephone George. I kept it brief, giving the poor man enough information to relieve his conscience. I told him I was feeling better, I'd merely had a 'breakdown' but I'd patched things up with my 'boyfriend' for now, and I just needed to 'get some perspective' and some rest. I would keep in touch and perhaps I could visit again once everything settled a bit. I thanked him. That part was for him, I had little to be thankful for as far as I could see.

I found Edward in the study. I sat across from his desk, closing my eyes and hoping for the pounding to cease. "So now what?" I asked him.

"What?"

"What should we do?" I was too weak to be anything but tranquil. I felt detached.

"What is there to do? I love you. We're going to have a child together, remember? It would appear that there aren't too many options."

I was incredulous. "Are you actually suggesting that we just carry on as though nothing's wrong?"

"Well what's your idea then? Do you plan to stop loving me? And what about the baby? Are you going to abort her?"

"I *can't have* this baby," I hissed.

"This is ludicrous. I can't believe what you're saying. You walked out on me because of her! You've already named her, for god's sake."

"If I have a shred of decency left in me, I'll not bring it in to this world. Just think of all that could be wrong with it."

"I turned out all right. And don't call her an 'it.' You were the one who was so certain that she was a girl."

"*Ha!* You turned out all right?"

"Do you see any deformities? A tail? Webbed toes, perhaps? Are my eyes set too close together?"

"It doesn't have to be visible. You're completely insane, for one thing. I suppose you'll say that has nothing to do with it."

"Royalty used this method for centuries to keep the blood pure. Of course, it has its problems, but they usually don't manifest for many generations. And even then, it's not like this sort of thing creates defects. It's a matter of what recessive genetic defects are already present in the parents. If you and I both are carriers of a certain disease, then there is potential for complications. Otherwise, we have a decent chance of having a relatively healthy child."

"A *relatively healthy child*? I don't want a *relatively* healthy child!" I mocked. "I want a *completely* healthy child!"

"That's unrealistic, Bel. *No one* is guaranteed that."

"I want you to help me get rid of it."

His face fell. "I won't."

"Then I'll find someone who will."

"I'm sorry, love. I can't let you do that." There was genuine remorse in his voice.

"Well it's not really your decision, now is it?"

"And it's entirely yours? She's my child too, you know."

"*Well so am I* and this is the most horrendous thing a father could ever do! I swear I'll see us all dead before I allow you the chance to ruin her like you ruined me!"

"*Bravo*, Isabel. You really should take these theatrics to the stage. You'd do quite well." He stood up and paced to the other side of the room, presumably to put a safe distance between us. I could have taken it as a warning to calm myself, but it only prompted me to push him closer to the edge.

"Think about it, Edward. Think about what sort of man you are, what sort of father you'd be."

His eyes were all sharp edges.

"What's wrong, Daddy? Have I struck a nerve?"

"Don't call me that. You have no idea what sort of father I'd be because I've never actually been a father to you. And you have little room to talk of what sort of man I am when really, you are just as responsible for all of this as I. Perhaps even more so."

"You've got to be joking," I laughed. "How is this *my* fault?"

"It's not an issue of who's at fault. Fault implies something negative. All I'm saying is that we don't really know what would have happened between us if you hadn't initiated a physical relationship."

I felt my chest collapse under the strain of disbelief. "What are you talking about?"

"Isabel, I remember that night so clearly. I remember every detail. You were in such a state. I reached up to brush a lock of hair from your eye. Do you remember what you did then?"

I didn't want to answer him. I wanted to hit him in the face for reminding me. "Yes. I remember."

"Well?"

"You know what I did."

"I know. I want to hear you say it."

There was no use in crying. There was no point in letting the blood rise into my face; no point in allowing my chin to tremble. I would have to face this sooner or later anyway.

"I kissed you."

He nodded and moved toward me. "Then what did you do?"

"I'm not doing this any more. I feel sick."

"Bel, I want to hear you say it. Then what did you do?"

I attempted to push past him, but he held onto me. I couldn't tell if his embrace was one of aggression or of comfort.

"Bel, if you don't say it, I will and I'm quite certain I'll include more detail than you'll care for. But I want to hear you say it and I want *you* to hear you say it."

"Fine. I kissed you and pushed myself into you until I could feel that you wanted me as much as I wanted you, then I fucked you until neither of us could move and I…I loved it. *Every disgusting second of it*. Is that what you wanted me to say aloud? Is it better now that it's out there for us to relive?"

"I only wanted you to admit that you wanted it, too. I never said I didn't want you. But I never would've considered initiating something when you were so distraught."

"As my *father*, you never should have considered initiating anything, ever!"

"What do you want me to say, Bel? We wanted each other. We both felt it."

"You know what the difference is between us, though?"

He took a deep breath and leaned on his hands against the bookshelf. "What's that?"

"That night in your bedroom, only one of us knew that I was your daughter."

I wanted those words to burn him so terribly, and for a second they did. Though in the end it wasn't much worse than a cigarette ember falling onto his hand. Edward's reality was quite different from mine. He had the disturbing ability to override matters of conscience. He had done it many times, and 'our little situation,' as he had referred to it in the taxi, would be no exception.

"I know what you're trying to do and it won't work."

"What's that?" I snipped.

"You believe that if you can provoke me enough, I'll hurt you and cause you to miscarry. Do you really think I'm that simple?"

"Why do you want this child? I mean, truthfully?" I couldn't break through to get the answer on my own. "Is this just another experiment to you?"

"*Life* is an experiment. Aren't you the tiniest bit curious as to how she'll be? What brilliant gifts she'll possess?" He spoke with great enthusiasm at the very thought.

"Or what monstrous qualities she might inherit. Or the emotional scars of an incestuous bloodline."

"Honestly, you are such a pessimist."

"And what happens when she gets older? Old enough to have children of her own?"

"She's my daughter, for god's sake. I'd never touch her."

"*I'm your daughter!*"

"Yes," he sighed, "but I didn't raise you. The only familial bond we share is a genetic one. In my heart, you have always been George Scott's daughter. And until yesterday, your heart told you the same. Are you so quick to discount all the years he devoted to you?"

"That doesn't matter!"

"No? Who took care of you when you were sick, Isabel? Who bought you presents and gave you birthday parties? Who cooked your dinner and read bedtime stories to you? Who saw you through school and cared for you after that wretched mother of yours wrapped a cord around her neck and stepped from her nightstand? It certainly wasn't me, you know, and I'll bet that all those things mattered a great deal to you then."

He looked disgusted with me. It was the most unselfish thing I'd ever heard him say.

"I didn't mean that George didn't matter. Of course he mattered." I wiped the tears away. "But he told me you loved me then. He said you gave us money and visited me a few times. If you didn't think of me as your own, then why did you do those things?"

He lit up a cigarette and drew in a deep breath of smoke. "Of course I cared for you, but the help I gave to your parents was really more a sense of morality than a desire to have a family with your mother. Believe it or not, I once possessed morals. Well, at least more so than now. Your father worked extremely hard for what little you had. The money was for you and George. Not her. I never loved her. She was mental then and I knew it would only get worse. I pitied your father. He didn't deserve what we did to him."

"If you didn't care for her, why did you have the affair?" It was like listening to a twisted Grimm's fairytale.

"I suppose I was desperate to know what it was like...to be with a woman. Your mother was very fond of me and made it easy. I wish I had a more romantic tale to tell you, but that's really all it was for me. We carried on for only a few weeks. For myself it was an outlet for my years of frustration and well...we've discussed what life with my mother was like, but for her I guess it was much more emotional."

"George said she loved you. Even after you left her, she never really let go of you. I think that's why she couldn't really love me and Dad...George..."

"Dad. You've always called him Dad."

∽

It was terribly difficult for me to maintain my contempt for him as we talked. I considered that he might be toying with me again, buying my compassion back intentionally, but with every kind word he had for George, I questioned that theory. And that we both shared the same loathing for my mother only helped his case. George saw her as an angel, but Edward and I were not so blind to her ugliness.

I could recall some of the better times, especially when the focus lay on George, but now I made sense of the darker days spent with her, even before Kate. I was so young before Kate's death and the memories have that cluttered, hazy feel that little children often create when they can't fully understand something. George had worked so hard to shield me from it; Mummy has a headache, Mummy's tired, no, Mummy isn't mad at you, she's just had a dreadful day. Mummy spent much of her time being unhappy, sometimes the wind was enough to make her cry.

Edward said she was a mess from the start, obsessing over him, using the sex as a distraction. She fancied herself a brooding intellectual, but was not much deeper than a puddle. He said it was rather embarrassing, listening to her post-coital ramblings, her amateur philosophising. She imagined herself a worldly and sophisticated woman trapped in a mundane world that could never understand her. Her menial tasks at the library filled her with a smug confidence, and she took it very seriously. But my mother was the daughter of a factory worker and to a factory worker she was married. How she detested her grimy little life and the way the walls held on to the filth no matter how hard she scrubbed. She detested George for coming into her life before Edward and she detested me when I failed to be the glue that would bond Edward to her. The only one she didn't hate was the one who got her pregnant and walked away. And again, it's funny how these things work out.

He could see inside me with sharp clarity now that the laylines were back to normal. Scenarios filled my head, ones that made me feel ill. I saw them together, substituting my face with hers. I got lost in it somehow, swelling up with shame and jealousy. I forgot myself, forgot the reality of the situation and found myself hating her more than ever for having gotten to him first! *He loves me, after all...he never loved her.*

He told me not to torture myself with it. He said it was nothing like what we had, and that I was nothing like her.

That I could entertain these thoughts was absurd, but they would not go away. This whole thing was absurd. It simply did not feel real. That I still didn't completely despise Edward did not feel possible. Nothing in my entire stupid life had ever been this wretched. My dead sister, my mother swinging from an exposed water pipe on New Year's Day, the science and the chemicals, the gods and the murders and the monks in the ground. Suddenly, I could understand all this. But who Edward was, and where we came from, left me devastated and beyond understanding.

He showed me a photograph. It was hidden away, deep inside a pile of dusty books, but he knew exactly where to find it. It made me feel hollow to look at it.

Edward didn't look much different, only younger and not yet so insane, perhaps. The black and white film rendered him severe, with great black spaces where eyes should be and sharp lines in his cheeks. He was so beautiful it scared me. He was crouched down, a long arm wrapped around a little girl with a china doll face and winter coat. A little white dog sat obediently at his other hand. The buildings behind him were decrepit and grey against the pale, empty sky. I knew this distant place from my childhood and I knew the dog.

"I don't remember this."

"Well, you were just a little thing. I think you were three. That was the last time I came to visit." He sounded sad.

I tried to force a smile. "I remember that dog."

"God...that wretched mutt," he grinned slightly. "Your mother's dog...what did she call it? It's been so long...Blizzard? Snowball? Who knows?" He rolled his eyes.

"Snowy. She called it Snowy."

"Right," he drew the word out. "Snowy." There was a great deal of contempt in his voice, the way he spoke of all things beneath him.

We both sat in silence, Edward staring past me, me staring at the photo.

Finally, I spoke. "He was a stupid dog." It was the only thing I could think to say. Edward agreed.

(September)

The house had been quiet for weeks. We were becoming the same entity; the house was living vicariously through us. I knew from the first day that I would never leave and I still know it now. We were growing too large for the dimensions of the house and would have to resort to living in the stone. This realisation crept up on us; we'd never seen it before. We had no concept of what we'd become.

During the early and mid months of the pregnancy I would crave the cold stone, laying face down on the floors and clinging to the walls. Food did not comfort me; I only wanted the cold. Edward had developed the strange and fascinating ability to alter himself from the inside out, changing his heart rate and body temperature at will. It took practice of course; it wasn't the sort of thing that one learns overnight. Buddhist monks spent lifetimes on these practices. I thought of the monks in the ground when he said that. I was beginning to love them again.

At night, he would cool himself down and let me lie against him. Sometimes he would just touch the tiny lump in my stomach with icy hands, which was a great help on those rare and uncomfortably warm late summer days. I never realised before how spoilt I was for England's usual chill. In any other year it would have been colder by September.

He'd tell me stories when I'd become restless. One night we lay in the darkness and he began in a gentle whisper: "A long, long time ago, in China, the earth would tremble and shift and break apart, as it still does today, and the people were terribly afraid of being swallowed by her. The people would pray and pray for the earth to calm herself, but still she would shudder and tear apart unmercifully. So one day, a brilliant man decided that if he could not stop the earthquakes, then perhaps he could learn to predict them. He made a contraption of bronze with a pendulum and a delicately balanced bar. The bar had a dragon at each end and each dragon held a tiny ball in its mouth. Below the dragons sat twelve frogs in a circle, their gaping mouths tilted to the sky. When the earth would first begin to move, so slightly that a human couldn't feel it, the pendulum would shift and one of the dragons would drop the ball into the frog's mouth. Which frog ate the little ball depended on which direction the earth was shaking, and the brilliant man could warn the people of what was to come."

"I love that story."

"It's a shame the quarrymen didn't have any dragons and frogs," he whispered.

"What are you talking about?" My eyes were growing so heavy.

"Nothing, love. I'll tell you that story soon enough." He kissed me on the forehead. "Now go to sleep."

The dirt was my other favourite thing. I longed for the smell of it, the soft feel of the velvet black peat. Something about the deep green of the moss against the coal black soil nearly brought me to tears. The dirt seemed to spill in through the doors like little tendrils. I thought it might be a gift from the house or the land, maybe the monks. I spent many afternoons digging in the garden, inhaling the heavy smell of earth and turning the sprawling landscape into a minefield.

"Tell me when you reach China," Edward would say each day and we would laugh and I would dig and we would simply pretend that nothing was wrong.

In a sense, nothing really was wrong. That was what we decided, though we never said it aloud. There was much left unsaid.

I collected things from the ground in jars. Stones and twigs, the occasional bit of dull, weathered glass or tiny bird bones. I treasured the bones the most. They had their own special jar. I kept the jars lined up along the windowsill in the kitchen. When I wasn't digging I would rearrange the jars in order of colour or alphabetically by content. Edward was calm and quiet these days, observing my strange habits in silence. Whatever my reasons, he understood the necessity of it and did not discourage me.

I didn't understand why I had to do these things. It seemed to be the desire of the little creature I carried, and whatever she wanted I would obediently provide. It was the very least I could do for her, considering what was waiting for her on the outside. I kept this thought in a far away corner of my brain as it implied a problem and as we both knew, nothing was wrong.

For her I would not only collect the bones, but also on occasion, suck the marrow from them. It was repulsive to me and even Edward found it a bit unnerving at first. Not long after that I began to ingest small portions of the soil as well. It tasted much like you'd expect: gritty, musky, slightly salty and metallic. Better than the marrow though and far easier to get to.

When she compelled me to drink from the fountain in the courtyard I complied, but when she turned my eyes to the great black pool, I quickly put my foot down. Edward joked that she might be trying to poison me. This left me more than a little unsettled, and by All Hallows Eve, I'd come apart again.

(November)

The ground had frozen through and I couldn't dig, and I'd had enough of the cold for awhile. My hair had grown long and ragged and the weight seemed to drain out of my face and slide directly to my belly. My clothes were becoming too tight for comfort. My fingernails grew much too quickly and my eyes were constantly bloodshot from ruptured vessels. My feet and the back of my legs displayed pale blue spider web patterns. I could feel the swollen veins pushing up and out. I half wished they would just burst through and let me bleed out.

I was full of complaints over the most trivial things. I hated the house and she hated me. The smell of it made me sick and I took to cleaning and bleaching every surface that would endure it. I thought about a television programme I saw once about an American cleaning service that tends to the homes of people who'd been murdered. They had this amazing sawdust-like substance that absorbs and congeals blood and other fluids. According to the programme, dried blood will become toxic again when mixed with most liquids, so for safety's sake the men use this stuff. This fascinated me and I wished I had access to such things as I scrubbed away at the plethora of red stains. I wondered what would happen if such a substance were injected into a person. I imagined the blood coagulating and expanding the arteries and veins until they tore open. I saw the colloidal blood falling away from the split veins, all the while retaining the tubular shape, like long reddish-brown whips of liquorice. I suddenly could relate to Edward's yearning for experimentation. I wished I were as callous as he. Now, I can't recall if there ever was such a chemical, or even if I ever saw such a programme. It's possible I imagined the entire thing.

In any event, Edward fussed over my misuse of poisonous cleansers until the day I walked in on him just as he was sticking a needle in his arm. He didn't say too much after that. I didn't ask him what it was then. I know that sometimes it was morphine.

I asked him about it later and all he'd said was, "Does it matter? I can barely feel it any more. It's just a routine now, something to help me make it quiet for a bit."

He sounded saddened by this and I believed him. It really didn't matter any more, and I don't think he'll ever die. He's beyond that now.

Some days were worse than others. Some days I contemplated drinking the bleach. Edward would stand guard over me on those days. I resented the fact that I couldn't even kill myself in private had I wanted to. He'd know and he'd stop me.

I thought about the quarry constantly. I dreamed about it almost every night. I longed for it, to be in it. Standing at the windows looking out into the woods, I would be moved to tears just knowing it was out there, calling for me, demanding that I bring it the child. Edward would sweep through the room and draw the curtains without a word. This would prompt me to spew a stream of obscenities and curses at him, to which he would respond with only one calm word: *'No.'*

❦

I dreamed that from the edge I could hear its cries echoing through the swirling winds.

I moved closer to see and a tiny avalanche rolled down the side, throwing clouds of dust and ash into its face. It let out a little choking sound and carried on with the wailing. I ran back to the house as the clouds rolled in. Bloody dots trailed behind me across the courtyard and into the kitchen. The soles of my feet were riddled with hundreds of tiny holes. From the doors I could see the property, needles strewn about carelessly. I called for Edward, irritated by the habit in the first place. He came in from the hall carrying a little grey cat. It had a collar made of pearls.

"Look what I found in the quarry. Can you believe someone would just leave it there like that?" He nuzzled the top of its head.

"I can't take care of it any more."

"Nonsense. You are one of the good mothers."

"Look at my feet. I'll be sick now."

He came toward me and handed the cat to me. I reluctantly took it and held it at arm's length.

The winds came and within seconds the little grey cat had disintegrated into a pile of ash onto the tops of my feet. The pearls broke apart and rolled away in all directions. I watched as they fell into the mouths of several bronze frogs.

"See? Now do you see?"

"Oh...poor Kate. Poor, poor Kate. Best not to speak of this to your mother. You know..." He put his hand to his temple, pretending to fire a gun.

I nodded. He went to the floor and began to eat the ashes from my feet.

Edward rolled over in the bed to face me. "Good god. Where is that coming from? You'd think you were carrying the Anti-Christ."

I rested my arm across my eyes. "Close enough."

Edward jolted up. His lips tightened and he shook his head in disgust. "Has it ever occurred to you even *once* in your selfish little life that I might have feelings? That perhaps after a while names like *'monster'* and *'lunatic'* might be a bit tiresome to hear? I know what you think of me and, frankly, I don't know how you could've ever claimed to love me. Do you think I don't know? Have you *ever* considered what that does to me?"

"You are so far beyond empathy, I can't imagine you even remember what that is, so don't dare tell me that I don't consider your feelings. And anyway...what happened to that *primal being* that lived on instinct alone? Compassion is for men. You've been something else for quite a while now. Everything you know is raw."

He kicked the cover from his legs and gave an exasperated sigh. I waited several minutes before speaking, letting us both take in the silence for a moment.

"Why, Edward? Why did you want me this way?"

He twisted around to face me again with absolute sincerity and spoke as though it were the most obvious thing in the world. "Because Isabel, you're the only pure thing I've ever created."

I've never understood how he could do that. How he can find just the right combination of words to burn me. I think he does it to destroy me. They are terrible, beautiful words and I live for them. I am sickened by the way my heart jumps when he speaks to me, when he touches my face or smooths my hair. I flutter and shake when he gets near me or says that he loves me. This sickens me because it will not fade, even now, in this ugly light that has revealed him, that has revealed me. I am just like him.

In my head, I made a list of all the things that were different now. Kate had been my half-sister. Edward's mother was my grandmother and Willa, my great-grandmother. Edward's father was both my grandfather and great-grandfather. I went to Edward with this list. He simply nodded and said 'yes' after each revelation. There was pity in his eyes. This information was a given to him, but it was new to me. I hadn't considered any of it before. I continued listing throughout the night.

"You will be her grandfather too."

"I suppose so, though she'll never need to know that. George Scott is the only grandfather she'll ever need to know."

"I'm not actually related to the Scott's at all."

"No, you aren't."

"I don't know my medical history any more, then."

"I do. Are you concerned about something?"

"I was afraid of cancer. It's all over George's side of the family. Now I don't know if I should be afraid of that any more."

"We don't have a history of it. Grace women typically have bad hearts or strokes."

"What else?"

"Mental illness, but that could've been as much a product of abuse as of breeding. Your mother had her own problems in that regard."

"I'm well beyond fearing mental illness."

He shrugged, somewhat indifferent and distracted, "What can you do about it, anyway?"

Every once in awhile Edward would shift. The reality of our *situation* would seep in and drive him to the needle. Watching him was difficult. I craved it still. He knew this and yet made no attempt to hide it from me, which felt like a deliberate twist of the knife. I hated these times when Edward would slip, threatening to lose control. Watching my gut stretch and expand made it real for him. There was no denying what he had done.

Upon entering my old bedroom one afternoon, I found an antique bassinet placed by the window. It was dusty and the linens were yellowed, but overall it seemed sturdy enough.

"I intend to clean it up a bit, then we can get some new whites for it."

I hadn't heard him coming.

"Was this yours?"

"I suppose it was," he replied vacantly.

(December)

Edward wanted to examine me. We'd let the first trimester and nearly all of the second slip by without a proper check-up. He insisted that not another week pass without an examination. I didn't want him to do it but he was adamant about keeping me from another doctor. I certainly couldn't go to his former practice. We argued for nearly an hour before reaching a compromise.

"Would you let me see Dr Hausner?"

"Hausner? He's got to be 150 years old by now. He'd one foot in the grave when I was young."

"No, his son."

"James? Why do you want to involve him? Especially after he told Moorely god-only-knows what about me."

"You don't know that he even said anything at all. Moorely could've been bluffing. And anyway, it's all out in the open now. At least, it is between us, so where's the harm? It's the least you could do and if you say no, then you're just being cruel."

"I don't know, Bel."

"Come on. He's got an office with proper equipment, I'll bet."

After much complaining on my part, Edward finally agreed to call Dr Hausner. I bit my nails as he rummaged around for the number.

"What's the matter with you?" He snipped. "I'm the one that should be nervous. You've nothing to be nervous about."

"I don't know. I'm nervous for you then."

"Right," he muttered as he found his old tattered address book. "I don't even know if he'll be at this number any more, so don't get your hopes up."

"If Moorely could find him, we certainly can."

He dialled the number. While he waited it seemed as though he was holding his breath. He grimaced and scowled, closing his eyes and pinching the bridge of his nose to relieve the tension that was expanding in his skull. Then he opened his eyes and gasped in a tiny puff of air before speaking.

He must have gone through half of a pack of cigarettes in the course of the conversation. I sat curled up in a jittery ball, fingers in my mouth, chewing on hangnails throughout most of it, just listening. He told Hausner I was his daughter and that the child's father had left *(yes, yes...it is a shame)*. He kept validating the call, saying more than once that he could imagine how strange it must be for him to do this and *yes*, it would be a good idea for the two of them to sit down face-to-face and talk. I'd never heard Edward so agreeable, tons of 'yes's' and 'certainly's' and 'of courses.' He seemed almost submissive to the words that came from the receiver.

"Well?" I blurted out before he got the phone back onto its cradle.

He flinched at my brusque demand, not yet fully recovered from the exchange.

"We're meeting him tomorrow at eleven. Merry Christmas." He chewed on his bottom lip, staring off absently.

"Why are you afraid of him?"

"Afraid?" He raised his brow and shot me an indignant glare. "I'm *not* afraid."

"All right then."

"Isabel," he let out an uneasy laugh, "I'm *not afraid* of James Hausner. We were colleagues once. It's just that many things have changed since I saw him last."

"You've changed a great deal, I'd imagine."

"Yes." His voice was tight and arrogant. "Time will do such things to a person."

I nodded slowly. "Right. Time. But you know what I think? I think you're afraid. I think you are afraid that you'll look at him and remember what you used to be. I also think you're scared that you might slip and forget which role to play. You're terrified of what he'd do—rather, what he'd think of you if he knew about us. You will look at him and see how far away you've drifted from everything."

He glared at me, completely still, his cigarette turning to a long cylinder of ashes. "Are you finished?"

"You can read my mind. You tell me." I walked away, not waiting for a reply.

That night it was Edward's turn to dream of unpleasant things.

He talked with a young man in the kitchen. He was an attractive man with grey eyes, a less sharpened, lighter version of Edward. His mouth was quite different, though. He had thick, lush lips, closer to a woman's mouth than a man's. Edward called him James.

He warned Edward that the news was not good. The baby was chewing a hole through its umbilical cord and soon enough would sever itself from me. He feared that it would begin to eat through the womb and there was nothing that could be done.

Edward suggested abortion.

"Well, it's not as though I can just kill it, you know. I'm not God. Who among men is qualified to make such a decision?"

"I'm making it. I won't see my daughter dead!"

"Oh, but you will! Which of your children do you love more? You want to be God...then you choose. You can't keep them all, Edward."

He slid a scalpel across the kitchen table. Edward caught it by the blade and it slid through the flesh of his palm effortlessly, like tearing through silk.

"Go on, now." James motioned to the French doors.

"Please. I can't do this, " he whispered mournfully.

James was gone. In his place sat a dishevelled old man, Edward's father. He'd been drinking.

"You pitiful son of a bitch. Do as you're told or I'll snap your arm!"

Edward squeezed the scalpel blade tighter until his thumb separated from his hand and dropped to the ground.

"You're just as bad as that whore of a mother of yours..." his father slurred.
"You better go before she does something foolish."

Edward peered into the courtyard. His mother, in a violet dress, was fishing through the fountain. She reached in with both arms and wrapped something up in her hem.

"Mother, your petticoat is showing." Edward lowered his eyes.

"Oh, Edward. Why did you do this? Do you see what I had to do now?" She shook her head and cast her eyes to the heavens. For a moment she looked like the stone angel on the fountain.

"What is it? What do you have?"

He rushed toward her as she let her dress fall. The unborn child rolled out of the fabric and hit the ground with a repulsive slap. It was blue and flaccid.

"Oh god..." he dropped to his knees, momentarily forgetting his mutilated hand.

"Well, what did you expect dear?" When she spoke, only one side of her face moved. The other drooped, void of control or expression. "You'll be wanting this I suppose." She handed him the purple umbilical cord.

He made a guttural sound, somewhere between a growl and a sob. He took the cord and held it to his cheek.

"Would you have made the same choice?" The voice came from his mother, but it was not hers.

When he looked up, it was me. I was wearing her dress. I smiled at him and kneeled down to meet him.

"Well? Who do you choose?" My hair was soft and styled in waves and pin curls off to one side. Just like she used to wear hers.

"I don't want to choose," he sobbed.

I kissed him on the mouth. "If gods must choose then so should you. You are the father, after all."

His eyes were wild. It had been so long since he dreamed in the bizarre altered state that passed for sleep. He broke a hard sweat.

"It's all right, Edward. It was just a dream." I patted his ropy, tousled hair, wiping the beads of sweat from his brow. "You *do* remember dreaming, don't you?"

He rolled away, pulling the sheet over his head and curling up into himself. By morning he seemed back to his usual self, arrogant and ready to eviscerate anything that challenged him, including Dr Hausner, if necessary.

There was little he could do to improve upon his junkie-genteel look, but what he lacked in appearance he compensated for in demeanour. He held himself up tall and walked without hesitation down the street towards Dr Hausner's office. I dragged myself behind him, weary from the drive and the increasingly heavy burden of the creature inside me.

This town looked exactly like our own. All the towns in these parts looked the same, especially around the holidays, all quaint and Charles Dickens. We finally came to the whitewash two-story office where Edward did not pause before entering. There was no turning back now.

In the closet-sized waiting area, he did not remove his sunglasses or coat. He drummed his fingers on the arm of the chair and furiously bounced his leg up and down with tiny jerks. I threw my hand onto his knee and pushed down hard. He stopped and stared me down for a moment, then proceeded to tap his foot on the floor a billion times. The receptionist peered up from her desk sheepishly. Another woman, a patient, glanced from behind her tabloid with curiosity and unease.

With an insincere smile, I turned to Edward. "Settle yourself, Papa..."

He returned the smile. "Sorry, sweetheart. Daddy's nerves these days..."

"Miss Grace?" A cheerful lady, who looked as though she had a sack of potatoes strapped beneath her nurse's garb, appeared at the door with a chart. "Come on back, love."

"I'd like my father to come as well."

She glanced at Edward, an odd look on her face. She caught herself mid-stare and forced a polite smile. "Well, come on then."

The nurse led us back through a maze of passages to a scale. She weighed me *(a tad light for someone at your stage)* then herded us into another tiny room. She took my temperature and blood pressure *(lower than normal...have you had any difficulties?)* She was such a nice lady. So nice, she pretended not to notice the tracks on my arm, though she'd discreetly alert the doctor in the hallway. She left me with one of those stiff paper gowns that rustle loudly with the slightest motion and suggested that Edward step into the hall while I changed. To my surprise, he did so without protest. As I undressed I heard the voices of the two estranged doctors. I crept to the door to listen, but heard nothing more than clichéd formalities and small talk.

I opened the door slightly and climbed onto the exam table. Dr Hausner swept in and towards me with an extended hand. "Well. It's just lovely to meet you. The last picture I saw of you, you were just a baby!"

He looked like he did in Edward's dream, only more weathered. Still very handsome, though. Edward jumped to my side, placing an arm on my shoulder. I could feel the jealousy seeping through him.

Mind yourself, father...remember who you are...

He squeezed my shoulder, digging a jagged fingernail into my skin.

"It's a pleasure to meet you. Ed...my father has told me so many kind things about you."

The small talk went on for too long, fizzling out awkwardly several times before stopping completely. Again it was suggested to Edward that he wait in the hall, this time by Dr Hausner.

Tell him you want me to stay...

"I don't want to do these tests alone. I'm a bit nervous, really, and I've no one else."

"I'll be calling the nurse in, which should help put you at ease," Hausner offered.

"I'd rather you stay," I said, looking at Edward.

"Are you certain? I think you should have privacy," Edward played along.

"It's nothing you haven't seen before," I smiled as the colour drained from his face. "What with you being a doctor and all..."

Hausner was oblivious. He smiled at me and said, "Well, I don't get many grandfathers in here but if it's what comforts you, then it's your decision."

I looked up to Edward and nodded and he took his place at the head of the table, all the while brushing the hair from my face. I closed my eyes for the initial exam, unable to tolerate the sight of one doctor in my body while another lingered in my head. I was beginning to wish that I'd never suggested it. I resolved things by shutting down for many minutes. In the back of my mind, the last thing I heard was Edward's self-righteous voice: *This was your idea, darling...this was what you wanted...*

It was during the sonogram that I came back into my body and opened my eyes to see the screen. How doctors could decipher anything with those machines was beyond me. I could hear the muffled thumping and I saw movement in the form of a grainy whitish blob, larger than I had anticipated, against the gravel-like background that was my womb. It reminded me of the quarry. I strained to make sense of it, as my eyes weren't trained to see what the two doctors saw.

"Oh my god," Edward whispered.

"You see it, too?" They nodded at one another. "Listen. You can hear them both."

"Both?" Then I could hear it—one heartbeat, strong and prominent and then behind it like a muted echo, another. My own heart began to pound hard enough to cause me pain.

Edward's eyes sparkled in the flickering light of the screen. "Twins, love. Do you see?"

Tears streamed from my eyes while Edward traced the outlines of the foetuses. He outlined their tiny heads and hands. He showed me which was the girl and which was the boy. He pointed out their feet and their spines. I wanted to die.

We piled into Hausner's cramped office when it was done. The walls were filled, cluttered really, with gilded certificates and degrees and honourable things. Mountains of papers and folders and books littered every corner, much like Edward's study.

I felt sore and greasy and a little sick. Hausner handed me a tissue when we sat down. He and Edward chattered on for several minutes, saying nothing of importance.

"Are they conjoined?" I barked loudly, interrupting their petty exchange.

It jolted Hausner back to the topic at hand. "Sorry, Isabel. I just can't tell you how..." he looked at Edward with an uneasy grin and a bit of disbelief. "Well, never mind that. The twins...no, they're fraternal. Everything looks just fine so far. The female is a bit stronger than the male, but they both have a little way to go yet."

I nodded, wiping my face with the tissue.

"Will you come back in four weeks? I'd like to keep an eye on things for you."

I wondered if Edward was once this kind and earnest.

"I'll see that she comes back," Edward interjected before I could answer.

On our way out I heard the men making vague, insincere plans to meet again outside of the office. As Edward headed out the door, Dr Hausner said my name and made a subtle gesture for me to come back.

"Isabel, I know this must be a great deal for you, especially without the babies' father. If you need to talk or anything, please call on me."

I thanked him and he nodded, holding the door for me. Edward looked on from the far end of the waiting area. We both knew what Hausner had left unsaid. He saw the track marks and the unhealthy state we were in. Edward was like a corpse still, and I could not conceal my fear and unhappiness. Hausner knew in his gut that something was very wrong. He'd known Edward for too long, he knew the path his estranged friend had begun to walk years ago and could only imagine what had become of him since.

When he talked with Moorely, he'd expressed his concerns for Edward's mental state. He'd said that Edward was not a man to be taken lightly, his theories could at times be unnatural and unethical, and his actions were presumed to be methodical and extreme. I couldn't decide if I was relieved or not that Moorely had left me out of their conversation. But as it was, Hausner sensed a terrible problem and he was only touching on half of the truth. I wondered what he'd do if he knew. There weren't any scenarios that Edward couldn't resolve by sinister measures, and James Hausner had no idea of how powerful Edward had become. I hoped he wouldn't test it. I rather liked the man.

Edward was none too pleased with my innocent affinity for Dr Hausner and decided to torment me at every turn. His remarks were sophomoric at best, but my tolerance was low and he managed to rattle me anyway. He knew very well that while I thought Dr Hausner was attractive, I was nowhere near attracted *to* him. All the way home he spewed out venomous insinuations that perhaps I had enjoyed the exam a bit too much.

"That's the best you can muster?" I replied. "How disappointing."

"Don't you find him a bit girlish? I don't remember him being so effeminate."

"I hadn't noticed." *Just keep your eyes on the road. Don't let him pull you in again.*

"I'm curious. Who do think is more gentle with you?"

"I wouldn't begin to know how to answer that. You've never examined me and I've never slept with Hausner."

"Well, hands are hands, skin is skin. How was it for you with both of us there, together?"

"Please don't be so vile. I didn't want you there in the first place. You insisted."

"I didn't want you seeing another doctor in the first place, but *you* insisted."

"Oh, as though I can demand anything of you."

He huffed and stared out the window.

"Do you know what I think?" I continued.

"This should be brilliant."

"To hell with you. *Anyway*, I think you allowed me to see him so you could get a little thrill of your own, watching another man touch me as you sat there playing the caring father, all the while knowing our filthy secret. I think you completely got off on the whole situation."

"Well done Agatha Christie! You have outwitted me this time, unravelling the mystery and discovering the motivations behind my questionable deeds."

"It's no mystery to anyone that knows you that you're a sick fuck. Hausner thinks so too, and he doesn't even know the half of it. Frankly, I'm disgusted that you could take such a beautiful moment and make it so ugly."

Edward laughed for quite some time before he could speak. "That's the funniest thing I've ever heard you say! You'd cut those babies out of your womb and toss them in the quarry if I gave you the chance. *A beautiful moment*...that's magnificent." He shook his head, smiling with disbelief.

"I don't hate the babies."

"Of course you don't."

"How could I *hate* them, Edward? I'm their mother. This isn't their fault. I'm just afraid."

"Of what? James said they were doing fine. Normal little foetuses. I saw them. They're perfect."

"I don't know..."

"You've got a doctor now that isn't me. You'll most likely have a safe delivery and if something should go wrong you'll have a hospital full of professionals to help you. These were fears of yours and now we've resolved them."

"It's not that..."

"They never have to know, Isabel. They never have to think I'm anyone other than their father..."

"That's not the problem, either!" I started to cry again.

"Then what the hell are you afraid of?"

"I'm afraid of *them!*"

"Who?"

"The *babies*! I'm afraid of the babies!" I slammed on the brakes and skidded to a halt along the wooded road.

Edward reached for me as I flung open the car door and ran into the forest weeping.

"*Isabel*!" He jumped out after me. I ran only a few yards before realising the futility of such a manoeuvre. I stopped and let him bear down upon me. He grabbed me by the arms and held me still for a moment. The cold mist of our collective breath surrounded us. The only sound besides the breathing was the crunching of dead leaves beneath our feet as I staggered about in his arms.

"Christ, love...calm down...calm yourself. Why on earth would you be afraid of the babies?" He was composed and quiet now.

"I don't know..." I whispered tearfully. "I just am."

My fear grew at the same rapid rate as the little creatures I carried. I didn't want to eat or sleep. Food made me sick and sleep only brought dreams of unimaginable terror. Something horrible was happening to me and there was nothing I could do. Edward knew; he could feel what I felt. He saw the dreams and the thoughts that plagued me, but he cast a blind eye. He was determined to have his children and refused to see the threat they posed to us both.

Dr Hausner, on the other hand, became quite concerned with my emotional state — prenatal depression, perhaps, though the babies were still developing normally, he told me. I cried endlessly and Edward would plead with me to tell him what he could do to make it stop.

"Do you want to talk with James about it?" he offered up one morning.

"Talk about what? About you and me, about how I'm afraid of my own children? He knows I'm having troubles from the last appointment."

"He thinks you're depressed. And yes, I think you should tell him about your fear."

"What if I slip and say something about us?"

"I'll be right there to help you. You won't slip."

"I wish you trusted me."

"Darling, *you* don't even trust you. I'll ring James."

Dr Hausner met with us the next morning.

"Isabel, I want to help you and I'm glad you came to me," he folded his hands on the desk, looking like a school's headmaster," but I need you to be honest with me about some things."

"All right," I meekly agreed. I felt like a child. Edward sat by brilliantly acting the role of concerned parent.

"Are you presently taking narcotics?"

"No."

"Have you taken any narcotics since you became pregnant?"

"No." I believed it might have been true, but I couldn't remember for certain.

"When was the last time you took narcotics?

The way he said '*nar-cot-ics*' made me twitch. He just kept saying it, clicking it around his mouth, and driving me mad.

"Beg your pardon?" I felt like the chair would suck me in.

"The track marks on your arms. They are from intravenous drug use, correct?" He was very matter-of-fact about it. All I could do was blush and nod and stare at the green and brown-flecked carpet.

"Don't be embarrassed, Isabel. Remember, we're here to help you."

"It's been many months since Isabel stopped using," Edward offered. "I'm quite proud of her."

"What was it?"

"Morphine," Edward continued as I sank even further into the chair.

"That's not a popular street drug. Did you have a script?"

I looked to Edward for the answer. He took a deep breath. "No. I gave it to her after she took a spill down our staircase. She cracked her ribs and fractured her wrist and I felt it was the best thing at the time. Only after she healed, things began to get out of control for her and..." he glanced sidelong at me, "she began to steal it from me."

You son of a bitch, you bloody lying cunt...

"Why were you treating her at home? Why didn't you take her to the hospital?"

I looked to Edward again, this time a bit more secure and smug. *Good...call him on it...good, good, good...*

Edward kept up a solid facade. "In general, I don't trust hospitals. I felt that I was able to accurately diagnose and treat her. You are familiar with my credentials, James, if I'm not mistaken." He smiled.

He knew it was rubbish, but smiled and said, "Of course. I'm simply trying to get all the information. So what did you do when you discovered her problem?"

"I took the drug away and set her off '*cold turkey*', as it were." He sneered as he said those words. Edward detested slang. "The withdrawal was difficult, of course, but absolutely necessary."

"And how was her emotional state after the withdrawal?"

"She..."

"Christ! I'm *sitting* right here! Why are you talking around me like I'm *bloody invisible?"*

"I was only trying to give the doctor an accurate account of it. You were hardly in a proper state at the time, I doubt you remember much."

"I remember enough."

Hausner cut in, trying to ease the tension that spilled between us. "Isabel, would you care to add anything?" he asked kindly.

"No." I tried to collect myself. "I just wanted to let it be known that I'm capable of answering your questions as well."

He agreed with a slight smile. "Have you considered counselling? I know some very good people..."

"No." Edward and I chimed in at the same time.

"I mean...I don't feel comfortable with many people and I'd prefer to talk to you. But I don't want to talk about the addiction or anything else from before."

"Before what?"

"The pregnancy. All I know now is that I'm feeling things that I don't care for."

"Such as?"

"Fear."

"Surely you realise that fear is perfectly normal."

"I'm afraid of the babies."

He smiled again, this time with pity in his eyes. "Isabel, it's normal for you to feel afraid. You have no guarantees in childbirth or child rearing that all will go smoothly. You have no guarantees in life..."

"That's not why I'm afraid."

"She doesn't trust them," Edward volunteered.

"I see." He sat back and looked up for a moment, considering the information.

"Isabel, do you recall us talking about how a pregnancy can cause emotional turmoil?" He tilted his head and gazed at me with obvious pity.

Yes, you condescending prick... I nodded. "Of course I do. But this isn't it."

"How do you know? What's your basis for comparison?"

"I know in my gut. Something's wrong with the babies."

He sighed. "Isabel, listen to what you're saying. We've done tests. We've seen them and they're normal. Don't you think any problems would have shown up in the results?"

"Not if it hasn't happened yet."

Edward cast his eyes down. Hausner looked to him for help but he feigned ignorance. I didn't need to read his mind to know what he was thinking.

"You know what..." I stood and gathered my coat and bag, "let's just disregard this entire conversation, all right?"

"Isabel..."

"No, really. Thank you for your time. Just let me know when my next check-up will be. Edward?" I motioned for him to collect his coat.

"Go on ahead, love. I'll be right there."

Edward and James carried on for several minutes. I tried to clear my mind to hear Edward, but it was too cluttered with fear and heartbeats and mixed signals. The way our *gifts* waxed and waned was too much to bear at times. It was like being adrift in the sea. When my head was above water the words were clear, but with each swell I would sink under momentarily and hear nothing but the muted tones of the creatures around me. These days I spent my time trying not to drown. Outside, I asked what they had talked about.

"He maintains that you are suffering from prenatal depression. He does, however, have concerns that it may develop into a psychosis of sorts...delusions of paranormal abilities, psychic visions and what-have-you. He thinks you should seek counselling, for both depression and addiction." He lit a cigarette.

"And what did you say?"

"Not much, really. I just listened. He's a good doctor, you know. Very observant."

"How's that?"

"He wanted to know how long I'd been taking the morphine."

"Well, look at you. It's not so hard to tell."

"He also wondered why you called me by my first name on this visit."

"*Oh, bloody hell.* What did you say then? Did you explain that I'm...you know, still getting used to the idea of you being my dad after all these years?"

"I told him I really wouldn't know and perhaps you are going mad after all."

He laughed and took me by the hand. I tried not to be saddened by this. Every time Edward was happy it only meant that he would have further to fall, and every time he fell he made certain to take me with him. So I tried not be saddened by the death of certainty and stability. We'd never have them again, though I suppose we never really had them to begin with. I imagine it's possible to miss something you've never had, though I'm not sure how. I looked to the sky. There was going to be a storm.

⋙

The rain and thunderclouds finally rolled in at two in the afternoon and lingered overhead well into the next morning. We stayed awake, watching the sky light up above the forest. Edward rested his head in the sunken space between my breasts and belly all the while.

"So what now?"

"What, what now?"

I placed my hand on the underside of the bulge and felt around. It felt cold and empty, nearly lifeless.

"Stop fretting. They're fine." He put his mouth back on my stomach. "You're just fine, aren't you? Your mother is being so daft..."

"Can't you feel it, Edward? Why can't you see that something's not right?"

"The only thing that's not right is your head. I half think you're trying to will them harm." He closed his eyes and nuzzled his head against them.

I knew he was lying. He probably knew more than I did. He wasn't going to tell me and he wasn't going to let me break through the static, either. Whatever it was he was hiding, he knew it was terrible and would only turn me against them more. There would be no resolution tonight or any time soon. I closed my eyes and remembered my hunger for the dirt. Edward remained fixed upon my torso until sunrise, keeping watch, protecting the children from me. His eyes remained open throughout the night.

In the morning I drew a bath for myself. Edward agreed not to hover over me, but warned that he'd be only seconds away were I to have any sort of *accident*. I was grateful nonetheless for the privacy, even if it was conditional. Just as I'd settled into the hot water I heard Edward dart out of the bedroom, then the faint ringing of the telephone downstairs. I leaned back into the deep water, coming very near to relaxation for the first time in ages. My stomach was still small enough to stay submersed in the water, but just barely. I felt a slight movement and wondered if perhaps the babies could sense the change of environment. I spread my fingers out over the mound and began to whisper to them.

"What's going on in there? Everyone tells me that the both of you are just fine, and I do hope they're right. But I need to feel it from you, all right? Can you help me?" I took a moment to breathe. "I'm sorry, babies. I'm sorry for all of this. There are so many things...you don't know. Or maybe you do. Maybe that's why I'm afraid." I drew my legs up as close as they would allow and put my head down towards the water. "I can feel you in there, Willa. I suppose we'll still call you that. What should we call your brother?" I waited, as though she might answer. "Maybe you know why I can't feel your brother? I know he's there, I saw the both of you and they said you were fine. Are you in there, little boy? Are you ok?"

I tried not to panic. Speaking to them for the first time was so alien. I didn't know these tiny people. They were just strange little beasts floating around inside of me. I had always heard that mothers feel the needs of their children, even in the womb. I wanted to feel it, too, but instead I felt like a vessel. It didn't feel as though my babies needed anything of me except for the dirt and the hollow cavity in my torso. I was just a holding cell.

"Guess who that was." Edward sat down on the edge of the bath.

"Dr Hausner," I replied automatically.

"Do you know what he wanted?"

"To meet with you?" I stared blankly at the tap.

"I'm thinking of a number between one and three hundred-thousand..."

"Shut up."

"He's coming here this evening."

"Is that a good idea?"

"No, but it would have seemed suspicious to refuse him. Especially since I have nothing to hide." He smirked.

"Is this going to end badly?"

"I suppose that depends upon who you ask."

I closed my eyes and took a deep breath.

"My god. How any child of mine could lack a sense of humour is beyond me. That must've been your mother's doing. She could siphon the fun out of anything."

"What about the house?"

"The house is fine. You've sterilized every visible surface."

"Did she ever come here?"

"Who?"

"My mother. Did you ever bring her here?"

"No. Christ, Rosalie would've eaten her alive."

The house would have eaten her alive.

"Oh."

"Don't do this to yourself, love. We've been through this."

She wasn't strong, like you.

"Did you talk to me before I was born?"

"Isabel..."

Every chance I had.

"It's all right. I already know. I'm just talking."

He put his head down. "I had to stay away, for you and for George. What a mess it would have been if I had insisted on being around."

"It might have been better."

"Oh, Bel. You *can't* really think that."

"I don't know what I think. My mother might have been happier. She might not have resented me."

"Bel..."

"I know. She was sick. I know every reason you could possibly give as to why it never would've worked. I know that *what if* doesn't really matter, anyway."

He leaned against the wall and tilted his head back.

"I keep thinking about the photograph." It was burned into my brain and would stay there forever.

"We were different people then."

"I suppose we were," I whispered mournfully.

"Really, it feels like a different lifetime. It's not so awful if you think about it like that."

"Did you ever think this would happen? Back then, I mean."

"What? *I can't wait until she's older.* What do you think I am? A paedophile, like Moorely?"

"You let things...happen between us. I know I did my part as well, but...you knew who I was."

"Yes. We've been through this, too. My wicked design." He knelt down next to the bath and reached in for my hands. "The experiment never would have worked with someone else. Your genetic material was vital. But even more, I *knew* you were the one person in the world that I could make understand the importance of it all. And I so desperately wanted you in my life. This was never to hurt you." He kissed my hands.

"Did you ever think about what it could do to me? Did you care?"

"Does it matter if I say yes or no? It's done. Though I have to ask...if I've done so much damage, then why are you still here? Why do you still let me touch you? Why didn't you run when you had the chance?"

"When did I ever have the chance?"

"When I left you in the woods. Or when you ran John Wheaton into the quarry. Or when you met Moorely in the park. Or ran away to George's. *Four times*, Isabel. Not to mention the time before the experiment, before I was in your head."

He was right. Again. It amazed me how someone so insane could understand things so clearly.

"And really, you could have left any time you wanted. All you needed to do was click your heels, Dorothy. You were free to go at any time. You've always been free to go."

"There were times you came for me." My arguments were losing strength.

"I came for you because you allowed me to. And really, what did you expect me to do? I love you. I don't *ever* want you to go."

I kept my eyes on the water. I couldn't look at him.

"I'll tell you something now, because I think it's time you know. You think I planned it, that I brought you here. You think I tracked you and arranged the whole thing. But I didn't. I didn't need to. The paths you chose brought you here, like I knew they would. This is your home, Isabel. You are of the earth and the stone and the slate that built this house. And you are a Grace. This is the only place you could ever really be." He spoke with tremendous sadness.

"Do you know how long it's taken me to convince myself of personal responsibility? Do you have any idea how hard it was for me to believe that at the end of the day, my place in this world was my decision? Not my god's, not my mother's or my father's. It's mine. Every day it's mine. But now, you want to tell me that it was in my genes or my bones or whatever that I would come here, that this place drew me here simply because I'm your daughter? Where's the free will? Where's the choice?"

Edward laughed, almost unhappily. "You're not wrong, Bel. That's all true. But like I said, you may have been drawn here by something greater than yourself, but each day that passed had the potential to be your last day here. Yet you stayed. You made the decision to stay the moment you first arrived, remember? Between genetics and free will…I wish I could tell you which is greater, but I doubt very much that there is only one answer."

After a long silence, all I could do was change the subject.

"George said you named me."

"I did," he whispered. "You were my little Queen Isabella and I…"

I nodded. "And you were King Edward. Thank you for not giving me a stupid name. Though I'm a bit surprised you didn't give me a name from your family."

"No, love. I didn't want to do that to you."

He left me alone for a while. I wasn't going anywhere and we both knew it. I lay down on Edward's bed and tried to clear it all out of my head for a bit.

"What troubles you, precious? In the chair by the window, Willa held tight to her little handbag. The room was grainy and colourless, like the sonogram.

"Something's wrong with the babies, Gram, and no one believes me. Even Edward won't acknowledge it."

"Oh, dear. He can be so stubborn. It's just like these Grace men to think they know it all. But who knows a child better than its mother?" She smiled.

"They won't help me. They keep saying everything is fine, but I know it's not."

"When you hush all the voices in your head, what do you hear?"

"They say there are two babies, and I saw them, but I only feel one. I don't understand."

"You go back and make them check again, then."

"It's the boy I can't feel. I know it sounds terrible, but I feel like she's done something to him."

"You know, dear, that you can't help him."

"Then it's true. She's killed him, hasn't she?"

She tilted her head and sighed. "It's not always so easy to find that bond with your own children. It's not like they say. Sometimes, you have to allow things to happen... if it's for the best."

I gave her a puzzled look.

"Well, just look at Edward. If I had tried to stop Jacob, Edward wouldn't exist and neither would you. And then we wouldn't be able to have our little talks."

I shook my head, still not understanding her reasoning.

"Sometimes, dear, a lady has to make...unpleasant...choices in order for things to be as they should."

"I see."

"When the time comes, you'll know just what you need to do. There's more than one way to be a good mother."

"Bel, wake up. James will be here shortly." He looked around the room suspiciously. "Is everything all right?"

I sat up and nodded. My head felt thick.

"Willa's been here, hasn't she?"

I shrugged. "Perhaps. It could have been a dream, just the same."

"Is it ever a dream?"

I shook my head. "Do you think everything happens for a reason? I mean, that sometimes you have to do difficult things in order to keep things right?"

"I don't know, Bel. I do believe in free will. I believe that you set your own path and that right and wrong are arbitrary. What exactly are you asking me?"

"What about when you were in Africa and you had to kill those babies? Did you do that just because you wanted to or because it was necessary to get you to this point? And how do you explain the priest? If it's all free will, all your decision in your own hands, then how do you explain signs and omens? How do you explain this house? The way it's haunted, I mean?"

"I don't know. What I do know is that there is no place in life for regret, because you always have the ability to choose."

"Did those babies in Zaire have a choice?"

He narrowed his eyes and quietly told me to get dressed, then headed downstairs. I hadn't meant to be inflammatory. I felt it was a legitimate question and by his silence I knew he did as well. It was no victory, though. I knew that everything that happened in Africa indeed happened for a reason. I knew that it all meant something. The priest finding Edward was not just a random event. I knew, the way that man knew, that there was something greater than the lot of them, revealing a path that it desperately needed them to travel. Maybe we do have free will and maybe right and wrong are arbitrary to the universe, but to us mere mortals, there are things that feel right and things that don't and we will forever be throwing ourselves at the feet of higher beings, begging them to show us the way, despite what out intuition tells us.

I was into his shirts now, as I had no maternity clothes. I refused to buy any of those atrocious rags in the fat lady shop that we'd visited on our way to Hausner's office one day. We did, however, find some sleepers and little socks and what-have-you for the children. After the enigmatic chat with Willa I wondered if it would be an issue much longer. For all I knew, I could be dead by morning and so could the babies. And for Edward not to know...something must have changed. I think I was happier when Edward knew my every move before I finished thinking about it. I may have been trapped, but at least I knew what to expect. Now, only pieces of my thoughts were getting through, or so it seemed.

I made myself scarce upon James' arrival. I thought it might be good for him and Edward to have some time to talk alone. I didn't mind, considering I was hearing the whole conversation through the wall between the dining hall and the sitting room. I sat on the floor of the dark sitting room, twirling long and knotted pieces of my hair around my fingers, and staring vacantly at the remains of the Voudou alter. Sometimes I was certain that those icons used to be mine. I was convinced, at times, that I knew the ceremonies and the language and the reason for it all. It lay just on the tip of my tongue. It tasted like cinnamon and bourbon. It tasted red.

Through the wall, Edward weaved a fantastic and completely false tale of how we reunited and all the ups and downs of it. He confessed to his 'little morphine problem,' making sure to accentuate remorse and regret in his voice. He even spoke a bit of Africa to fill in some spaces and add an air of legitimacy to his story. Hausner still had questions. He asked about Moorely and the whole body-in-the-quarry incident. Edward waved it off like a little bit of fluff, claiming ignorance to any real details. As it turned out, our involvement in the Wheaton-Moorely accident-suicides was minimal.

Hausner wanted to talk about Edward's theories and studies, but Edward made it nearly impossible. He ran the most eloquent circles around James' questions, causing the poor man to lose his train of thought at every turn. These were the moments that impressed me the most. They also terrified me. I doubted I would ever know if Edward was truly an ally, albeit an erratic one, or if it was all just one brutal hunt. He was a master of dehumanization and we were all mere experiments to him. He does not feel the loss or suffer consequences because he refuses to feel pain. He has learned to neutralize it, break it down into fact and truth and remove any emotional element. He is a sociopath. I have seen him, at times, portray a human in distress or discomfort, but this only goes so deep. It is a convincing act that he has perfected at the expense of many, but beneath it lays a black, swirling hole where a spirit once lived a long, long time ago. All that lives there now is annihilation and wind. He is much like the quarry.

I stood in the doorway for several seconds before the doctors looked up. There they were, pretending to be two old friends, pretending that Edward wasn't lying through his teeth and that both had really wanted this meeting. Hausner was just fine with this, also pretending not to notice how amiss the situation was. He'd even brought a present—a gift basket with some more accoutrements for the babies. I was 'the daughter of one of his oldest friends,' after all and this visit had been of a 'personal nature' and 'with the holidays drawing near' and what-have-you. The degree of deception and denial between them was remarkable. I thanked Hausner for the gifts and calmly stated that I wanted to go to his office immediately. I politely told him that I needed to see the babies.

"See? They're fine. Just as fine as they were two days ago." Hausner pointed to the screen.

"Yes, I see. Something's still wrong, though."

Edward stood in the corner, visibly irritated.

"Isabel, I don't know what to tell you. Every test we've run has come back normal. What more can we do to help you through this?"

"We could put her on a high dosage of Thorazine. That would certainly help *me* through this," Edward remarked.

Hausner replied that he didn't see that as a reasonable solution. I wiped the cold gel from my stomach with a corner of the paper gown.

"All right then. I guess we're done," I sighed. It was futile to protest any further.

"Please try to relax, Isabel. This incessant worrying isn't healthy for you or your children. If you calm your nerves and take care of yourself, everything will, in all probability, turn out fine."

"All right..." I whispered as the doctor helped me up... "you'll see."

When I looked at Edward, the little hairs on his arms and neck were standing at attention.

"You just can't leave it alone, can you?" Edward moaned as I wandered through the house restlessly, until well after midnight.

"What do you want me to say, Edward? I know something's wrong, I know *you* know something's wrong and I can't prove a bloody thing. Hausner's tests aren't seeing it."

Edward paced around the foyer, still fuming at my stubbornness. "Why...?" he stammered. "Never mind." I could see him suddenly making a concerted effort to control his frustration. He inhaled deeply, relaxing the creases in his face. "Are you hungry or tired or anything?"

"No." I considered what it was that I *did* want, besides impossible answers. "A stroll," I finally concluded. "I'd like to take a stroll in the woods."

"It's the middle of the night."

"I'm aware of the time. I want to watch the sunrise."

"You can do that from the courtyard."

"I want to watch it from the quarry."

"I'm *not* taking you out there, Isabel. Do you think I'm mad?"

"Yes, but that's got nothing to do with this. Anyway, I'm going out there with or without you. Unless, of course, you plan to restrain me like some sort of prisoner."

"What...and lend validity to your fantastical view of our relationship? No, thank you. You can let yourself in and out of your gilded cage any time you please."

"Yes, yes...free will...blah, blah, blah...Are you coming or not?"

I could hear the arguments swirling around his head but he bit his tongue. "Fine. Get a coat or something."

It was dreadfully cold at the top of the quarry, but we sat quietly until right before sunrise. He'd brought along an old, moth-eaten quilt to keep me warm, but I wasn't worried with it. About the time my nose and fingers began to turn pink, he wrapped the blanket around my shoulders and I knew he wasn't as annoyed with me any more, at least for the time being.

Sitting there so close to the edge, the calling was hushed. It almost had me, almost had the babies, in its maw. There was nothing for it to do but wait quietly with us. We were at the western end, the end closest to the house. The sun rose and was almost immediately swallowed up by clouds, not that it mattered as deep into the woods as we were. The sun had little power in here, at best creating lacy illuminations on the ground. The trees kept this place hidden and cool, but the birds still knew precisely when to start screeching and chirping despite the grey.

Before Edward was born and even before Jacob's birth, the quarry was mined for slate. A river had carved out the adjoining ravine a thousand years before. Rainwater still collects at the eastern-most corner, creating a translucent green pool, far deeper than it looks. Natural steps sink into the little sea like a Roman bath. A bed of broken slate sprawls out from it, creating a stony-grey beach over most of the floor. That is where John Wheaton died. The walls are high and unmercifully smooth. There is nothing substantial to hold on to, nothing to break a fall. It is a giant echo chamber and the wind is painfully loud and sharp. At night it is a void. The house was built, in part, with slate from the ancient quarry.

"How do you get down there? Besides accidentally, I mean."

He peered around the rim and shrugged. "I couldn't say. Perhaps you *don't* get down there."

"The miners must have had a path."

"It's been quite a few years since that."

"Well, what about the police? They must have found a way down to retrieve John."

"They had ropes and pulleys and the like. Didn't you see all that equipment they carted out of here that day? Not to mention this hole is prone to sudden changes which, by the way, is another reason to stay out of there."

"How so?"

"The land back here...I don't know. It's just different from when I was a boy. If it can change that much in forty years, I can't imagine how much it's changed over the centuries."

"I wish I could've seen it then."

"Sometimes my Gram would have these little bursts of clarity, for no apparent reason...no trigger...and she would randomly begin talking about when she was younger or when my mother was just a girl." He smiled at the thought, forgetting for a moment how painful his memories could be. "Anyway, she told me once about when my mother was young and she used to take her for walks to the quarry until Jacob scared them both half to death. He said that when the quarrymen first started mining here that it was still very much a true ravine." He pointed off toward the eastern cliffs. "All of that, over there, was open. You could see where the river kept on flowing for quite some distance before it began to fill up with soil and taper off. So the men were working there, at the deepest point, when something shifted. The ground collapsed and buried some of the men alive."

"That's dreadful. Was it an earthquake?"

"I doubt it. There are no fault lines around here that I've ever known of."

"No fault lines, but there are laylines."

He nodded.

"So what happened after the accident?"

"Nothing. Just business as usual. Quarrymen were thought to be expendable. They live in the dirt and die in the dirt and in the morning the ones that lived to see the day go into the cities and towns and grab the sturdiest boys they can find to replenish the crew. Popular opinion used to be that it was a shame the vast majority of vagrants are so sickly otherwise they'd be perfect for the job. They've all one foot in the grave anyway, but...no, there was no fuss made, really. The truth is that it was more than just another labourer's task, though. It was an art, as delicate as it was brutal, and those men, those artisans, died not because they were careless but because the earth takes what she needs. Anyway, that was the year our house was built, before Jacob was born. Gram said that she and my mother thought it was so peaceful back here until that drunken bastard ruined it for them, scaring my mother like that. He ruined everything good for them." He stiffened his chin and sighed. "But it changes every year. The water is deeper than when I was young and more of the cliffs have eroded away."

"It's getting bigger, then?"

It's getting bigger, just like him. He is the ravine...

He said nothing. He just kept staring at the eastern wall rising up from the green sea.

...Or maybe just like you. You've been growing, too...

I didn't know from whom the thought came.

"Isabel, you can't go down there. Don't be a fool. You'll kill yourself."

"And what a shame that would be."

"Do you have any idea how tedious you've become?"

"And yet you still follow me." I smiled at him as we rounded the edge to the northern cliff.

"You're almost six months pregnant. You've got two lives in there. I suppose I should just let you scale down the cliff, anyway? Would you like me to run back to the house...get you a brandy and a pack of cigarettes while we're at it?"

"There's got to be a path. Even if it has eroded a bit..."

"And what do you intend to do once you're down there?"

"I intend to see what it is that I've been dreaming of my entire life, what I've fallen towards night after night."

It was treacherous enough without Edward yammering away below me. I kept trying to block him out and concentrate on my footing. The path—which I knew existed all along—was narrow and steep, barely recognizable as a footway. At times the decline was nearly vertical, placing me almost directly above his head. A few scattered tree roots jutted from the walls every few feet, providing a small amount of help. It was better than nothing. John should have been so lucky to go off this side. He might have had a chance here.

Closer to the quarry floor, Edward crouched down and grabbed onto the lowest root. There was barely enough room for both of his hands, but he managed to lower himself down, landing with a dusty thud on the jagged bits of slate below.

"Reach down for that root." He held his arms up. "I'll have you. Just swing yourself down, carefully."

As I dropped, he grabbed me around the hips, my stomach pressed against the side of his face. I held onto his shoulders as he turned away from the face of the cliff, searching for a secure place to put me down. In those brief seconds I spent up in his arms, I saw him in black and white, holding me close to his face, breathing me in. I was tiny next to him. When he put me down he seemed to go on forever, tall and strong and more powerful than anything else in the world. I did not know his name or why he smiled at me or why he wouldn't really say goodbye as he walked away. I cried that day, reaching out for him from my mother's cold arms. I don't know why. I only knew I wanted to be with the strange man that held me so tight and kissed my face for those few, brief seconds.

Even though I was standing, he held on tightly, still supporting my weight. He was not so much taller than me now. He put his face next to mine and breathed in again. There are no words to explain how it felt to remember him that way.

The air was foreign inside the quarry—warmer, without the bitter wind that tore across the top of the abyss, and less stagnant than I'd expected. For all the howling and whining I heard from above, it was surprisingly calm this far down. It was really beautiful, the quiet and expansive beach of stone and a shimmering lake. It was a brilliant teal from this angle. It seemed greener from above. It was also incredibly still.

Edward and I were frozen in an embrace. I wanted to pull away, but it was impossible, so I opted to break the tension instead.

"I must be heavier now."

He didn't release his grip or break his stare. "Not by much." He let go and stepped back, smiling sweetly. "Go on then. Do whatever it is you came to do." He walked over to the spot where John had landed, bent down and inhaled the chalky ground on which the boy died.

The lake was the most fascinating thing I'd ever seen. I stood at the waterline, trying to gauge the depth. I'd heard the waters in the Mediterranean and the Caribbean were like this, blue and green and deceptively deep. I almost remembered them, I suppose from a dream. I could see the bottom; it was only slightly cloudy, but I knew it was secretly further down than it looked. I tossed a small piece of slate in and watched it fall in slow motion. It took an eternity to reach the bottom. I was home in this pit and suddenly I realised that I hadn't come here for myself. I'd come here for the pool.

"There's a pool up at the house, you know, just as stagnant as this one. You could've saved us the trouble."

"It's not at all like this one. I can't explain it." My eyes were glued to the perfect natural steps just below the surface. There were two of them and then a straight drop to the floor. "There's something in there."

He peered over my shoulder. "Really?" He sounded bored.

Before I could think better of it, I had my shoes off.

"What are you doing? It's winter."

"It's fine, watch." I stepped onto the first ledge. "It's not cold. Not even a little," I laughed.

"You're out of your head." He crouched down suspiciously, dragged his hand across the surface and shrugged.

Edward never cared for me being right...about anything. I took another step.

"Would you please come out of there?"

"Why?"

"I don't like you being in there. It isn't safe."

"What's wrong? Are you afraid I won't want to leave?" I turned to look at him. "Are you afraid of the water?"

"That's doesn't even make sense."

"If you're not afraid, then come stand with me."

"I have a better idea. Why don't you get out of the water and we'll go home?"

"I can't. I know you think I should, but I just can't."

"Where's your sense, Bel? It's bitter out here."

I could hear Edward's muffled voice calling for me as I drifted down into the rainwater pool. It was a different world down there, a million worlds away from the one above me and certainly different from the old, reeking pool behind the house. Everything was jade, even my skin. The water was clean enough not to sting my eyes. I turned and kicked back up to the surface. Edward was sitting at the edge of the stony beach, picking through the rubble.

"Does the world make sense now?"

"It's beautiful. You should feel it."

"No, thank you. I prefer not to catch pneumonia," he sniffed. "What's down there, anyway?"

"The decaying corpses of quarrymen."

"Lovely."

"What do you think is down there? Slate and algae and dirt, mostly."

"Well, why didn't you say so? Dirt and algae, imagine that!"

"It's not that. There's something else."

There is a boat for me...

"Just like there's 'something else' wrong with the babies?"

"Never mind."

"And speaking of the babies...you really must come out of there. We can't afford for your immune system to shut down. Especially now with there being three of you and all."

He stretched out his arm and bade me to take it. Instead I pushed away from the steps.

"Bel...that's enough."

"Don't speak to me as though I'm a child, Edward," I huffed, treading the water. My clothes were growing heavy on my arms and legs. "I know how to take care of my children."

There's more than one way to be a good mother...

I took a deep breath and raised my arms, spiralling back down to the bottom, away from him. It seemed my only escape from Edward, going underwater. Not that he wouldn't follow me if necessary, but I was protected here. It felt like mine.

This time under, I made it farther down. The walls were smooth like marble with patches of plant life—still green and warm, despite the depth, this truly was another world. I swam in the direction of the far wall, a new terrain to explore. As I moved in toward it, I extended my arm, reaching for the shimmering facade. It was a bit darker here and colder, and I thought myself to be closer to the wall than I was. The closer I swam, the farther away it moved. The pool was most definitely not this wide. I assumed my perception to be faulty in the darkness. It felt like being drunk, so I headed up for air. At least that was my intent. But of course, in a moment, I was lost. I could hear nothing but the thud of my pulse rising into my head. Then came the vibration. It came from all around me, this shaking and humming. Like the monks, like the laylines. It ran through here, just as we'd thought. It caused the earth to cave in on those men. It created this sea of rain.

I was still. The water became colder in a heartbeat. Something dark was gliding toward me, but I remained suspended in the absinthe-like water. I did not kick or struggle even as she grabbed on to my legs. I still can't remember if she had a face, but if she did, it was the face of all mothers. I can recall an orb, perhaps a belly, if it was her front that I saw, but it could also have been a shell on her back, like a giant tortoise. Or perhaps even a cocoon. I felt fingers and nails, but then again it may very well have been tentacles or some manner of wispy appendages. Her touch was soft, but strong enough to keep me at her will. She pulled me down to her and I could feel her drag an arm across my stomach. She lingered there for a moment, cradling my belly and I could not tell where I ended and she began. She placed her strange mouth over mine and breathed into me. Her breath tasted like copper and spice and I could feel something soft falling across my tongue then down my throat. A sense of arousal was sparked within me until the spice began to burn my lungs. It was painful, but I could breathe. I saw her clearly as she held me, but the moment she released me, nearly whipping me to the surface, she began to fade from my memory.

The one thing I remembered for certain was that the humming had come from her. The layline began inside of her, like a long red ribbon spilling out from her mouth.

I did not tell Edward right away about the creature in the quarry. I figured he'd know the moment I came up, gasping for a breath, but he said nothing. When I climbed out of the pool, shaking and immediately struck with the winter air—which I knew would only be worse once we left the pit—he asked if I was all right. I had been under for a while, he said. He expressed nothing but irritation as he hoisted me, cold and terrified, out of the ravine and remained quiet all the way home.

After I'd thawed, Edward asked me if I had found what I was looking for.

"You know, don't you?"

"Of course I know."

"You don't let on that you can hear me much these days."

"Then why are you still cautious with your thoughts?"

"Because you never know, I guess."

"You *always* know."

"What was it, then?"

"She's the mother. That's what she is to you, what you want her to be. Right? I don't know what she'd be to me."

"She ate those men. Swallowed them whole," I said as though I'd known her for a million years.

"All the more reason for me to stay away."

"She wants the babies, I think."

"Perhaps. Or perhaps you want to give them to her."

"Perhaps they'd rather be with her than here with us."

He put a hand under my chin and turned my face up to his. "If that's what you need to believe in order to assuage your guilt, by all means..." he rubbed his hand down my cold cheek. "But don't think for *even one second*, love, that I don't know how readily you'd throw our children into the mouth of that stagnant bitch if I gave you the chance. You rest up now. You've had a busy morning." He kissed my forehead then walked away.

I had a frightful dream in which Willa appeared, but she was not herself. She was silent and cold, her eyes covered in an opaque sheen, like cataracts had claimed her sight. She blindly reached for me from the chair and opened her mouth as if to speak. No sound came. I noticed that her teeth were gone and her wrinkled fingers appeared long and tendril-like, her nails like pearls and shells. I was afraid of her in this sinister manifestation, but it was, after all, only a dream.

When I opened my eyes, I thought she was still in the chair by the window. I closed my eyes and opened them again, this time seeing the blanket that Edward had carried with us to the quarry draped about the chair.

"It's about time you figured it out," Edward muttered, semi-conscious.

"It was just a bad dream."

"All right..." he mumbled.

"It *was*."

"I said all right."

"You don't mean it."

"Fine, Bel. Go back to sleep."

"Why would you imply something like that?"

"I haven't implied anything. I was simply resting, minding my own business."

"But you started the whole thing with your '*it's about time you figured it out,*'" I mocked in his pretentious accent.

"You were going to say something about it anyway."

"No, I wasn't," I lied.

"Yes, you were. You woke up and sighed that sigh you always do whenever you're troubled by these little nightmares."

"You think you know everything, don't you?"

"Fine, Bel," he sighed and threw his arm over his eyes.

"Sometimes you are so selfish. You know how I feel about Willa, how much she means to me."

Edward sat up, twisting and writhing until his torso and shoulders cracked, relieving some of the tension in his joints.

"It's a trick, you know. It isn't even Willa any more and I doubt it was ever her at all. She's got you fooled."

"You've hated me talking to her from the start. Sometimes I think that you don't want me to have anything that makes me happy. Not one single thing that's mine."

"Fine, Bel. Don't listen then. I'm at my wits end with you anyway. You're..."

"More trouble than I'm worth?"

"Oh, what rubbish. I didn't say that."

"But you thought it. You don't care about me any more. You just want to see what your offspring will be like. Well, I'll tell you what they're like!"

"Stop."

"They drain me of everything. They make me sick and sore and miserable. All they do is suck up my energy and my sanity and make me wish I were dead, so at this point I'd have to say they take after their father."

"Bel, enough. You're just a bit high strung..."

"Don't you *dare* try to trivialise this! I can't believe you'd have the audacity to say that after what you've done to me. Wait...no, I've forgotten who I'm talking about. Of course you'd be so condescending, " I laughed. "That's quite all right, though. We'll see how arrogant you are when your precious beasts come into this world bearing the stamp of all the ugliness you've collected throughout your entire life. When you see it on those tiny creatures in such a concentrated mass, how proud will you be then?"

"I understand why you despise me, but how can you hate them so much? They've done nothing."

"No, Edward. It's already begun. She's killing her brother. I don't know how, but she is. He's almost dead. And when she's born, she'll not stop. She'll try to take me, too. I don't know why but you know what I'm saying is true and you deny it. You'll let her hurt me, because once she's born you'll have no more use for me. And despite all of the hideous things you've done to me, none of them have been so... so..." I couldn't think of any word that might possibly affect him.

"Bel..."

"...heartbreaking."

He looked hurt and puzzled, but I went on anyway.

"I thought we were in this together. I thought you wanted us to go on for all eternity, learning and watching the world change. I thought that deep down you would be my ally and would love me unconditionally. But now I'm seeing things clearly. It's all been wrong. *I've* been so wrong."

He reached for me but I pulled away.

"How much longer do I have? Will I die giving birth or does it happen later?"

"It's not like that. It's not at all what you think."

"Then tell me. Reassure me. Prove to me that I'm wrong."

"I need you to trust me."

"Right." I wondered if I'd even have to wait for the children to kill me, or if I'd die of fear before then. I wish Edward could have told me what really lay before us, for as terrible as it was, it was still not as painful as waiting to die, alone and betrayed.

I never knew for sure if Edward was actually persuaded to give in to me, or if he just grew tired of my voice. Either way, he telephoned Dr Hausner and made arrangements for yet another sonogram.

Hausner doubted that anything had changed. I said nothing. He and Edward studied the screen for a moment and listened for the heartbeats. I closed my eyes, immediately falling into a lucid dream.

I held the hand of my son as we wandered through the forest. He was so beautiful and slight, like a sparrow. He stopped and pulled his hand from mine. *"You can't go with me. I have to do it by myself."*

How a voice so sweet could rip through me...but I did not cry. I knelt beside him and he kissed my cheek. I wanted to make one final plea for him to stay with me, but there would be no other path this time.

The child pushed my hair behind my ear and whispered, *"Tell Papa that we know. And be careful of the red."* He left me then and went on his way to the ravine. There was nothing I could do.

Edward turned away before Hausner finished his assessment. Edward knew. He didn't have to listen or look any further. Hausner tried to find his words before facing me. He only got as far as "I'm sorry." Edward kept his eyes to the floor. The boy was dead and since this was old news to me, I said nothing.

It really *was* a dreadful situation, despite the serenity in the exam room. Hausner gave Edward and me a few moments alone. I suppose he wanted us to talk, or for Edward to console me, or something. We didn't. He sat next to the table and we just looked around the room. I watched the lump in his neck wriggle under pale skin with his every tiny swallow and futile attempt to speak. When Hausner returned, he suggested that we look at our options, but as it turned out, I didn't have any. One baby was dead and there was no way to remove it without killing the other.

I think Hausner was waiting for some emotional response from me, but I sat up and quietly dressed.

"You'll want to take some time to...accept this. Some time to grieve," Hausner suggested hopefully, nodding his head.

"No. I'm all right, really. I could scream and cry and carry on, but it wouldn't change anything. I'll still be carrying a dead baby."

"You still have another child to care for. Another reason to take care of yourself. She needs you."

I hoped this was making him feel better. I think he was taking it harder than I was. Hausner put a hand on Edward's shoulder. This struck the both of us as odd, healthy people were rarely inclined to touch Edward.

"I'm very sorry. I don't have grandchildren myself, but I imagine this will be a difficult time for you."

"Thank you, James." He turned his empty stare towards me. "I'm quite certain we'll do whatever we need to do in order to get through this."

Edward had known, just as I'd known, that the boy would die. I couldn't understand why he pretended nothing was wrong and that I was paranoid. Later, he would tell me that the pieces hadn't fit together enough for him to understand then. It was a peculiar thing to say, but it was the closest he could come to admitting that he was saddened at the loss of one of his own.

He whispered to me all night, thinking I was asleep. He said he was sorry that I had to keep a dead child inside of me. Then he just said he was sorry.

I really didn't have too much to say in the following days. I did think about it all quite a bit—the quarry and the water and the dirt. I tried not to think about the babies. Edward was quiet, too. Many times I would pass the study or the dining hall and see him sitting and staring, never blinking. I might have thought it was shock, but that was a far too human condition.

There were no words, spoken or otherwise. Just stillness. The connection wasn't gone, just switched off. So I would sit, sometimes next to him, sometimes across the room from him. Sometimes minutes would pass, sometimes hours. It may as well have been years.

When I finally spoke again, it was to ask questions that I had desperately tried to avoid, as though the only way to set them into motion was to speak of them. What would happen to the dead boy? Why wouldn't I miscarry both of them? Would they have to remove him separately from the girl? I didn't want to say any of those words, but the fear of the unknown outweighed my discomfort and loathing.

Edward sat still in his leather chair as I went down the list of worries. Void of any expression, only his eyes indicated that he could hear me. After several anxious minutes he finally gave a response, though not the one I'd wanted.

"Sometimes the earth does odd things, you know?"

"What are you talking about?"

"Your quarry. I didn't want it to be this way, but these things happen for reasons, Bel."

"Edward..."

"There are places in this world that want nothing more than to consume us. We live in one of those places."

He stood up and came toward me, bending down to rest his ear to my bloated stomach.

"I hoped it would all end when my mother died, but I should have known that it wasn't over. The minute you came back into my life, the moment I touched you, I should have known," he laughed sadly to himself. "I thought I could evolve away from it. I thought by bringing you here, having you assist me in the experiments, that we could break free from it. Of course there was a risk, with you coming here..."

"What are you talking about?"

"I'm talking about who we are. Since this house was built, the Grace family has belonged to the quarry. We've cared for her, fed her. This is her house and her land. She's grown with each passing year. I don't know exactly why or how, all I have are some incomplete journals that belonged to my ancestors. But I do know she's driven us all mad, with her laylines and hauntings and visions. She's driven us to all the terrible things we've done..."

"Edward..."

"Think about it, Bel," he smiled painfully. "You've dreamed of her your entire life. But you almost got away. You weren't a product of incest. You had half of a chance to be free of her if I hadn't been so damn certain that I could transcend her and everything else in this world. I came so close."

There was nothing to say. I couldn't deny what I knew to be true. I suppose somewhere under my skin, buried deep in my genes, this knowledge had existed all along. Edward placed his hand on my stomach. "This is our price. This is what we must pay for the knowledge we have. She knows it and she's offered up her brother so that she might live. And she'll live to serve the quarry." He pressed his lips against my shirt, and lowered his voice. "Clever girl. She's just like me."

I pushed him away. He was beginning to make sense of it all and it was worse than I ever could have imagined.

I hid under the blanket, away from the many theories and puzzle pieces that loomed above us. There were so many things, ugly and mythical and old. Every time I thought we'd managed to achieve a new awareness and were finally granted clarity, another bit of chaos would come smashing through the window, tearing its way through us, leaving yet another mess for us to clean up.

Edward spoke of a price to be paid (the closest thing to regret he could offer), but he was only half right. There was a price, there were consequences—always consequences, but it wasn't our son's life. It was that perpetual mess, the constant shattering, the mania we'd set into motion. It whirled out of control now, growing far bigger than any of us. Even Edward, who had managed to advance higher than his mortal birth would have naturally allowed, was finally beginning to see the vast scope of what we'd done. And finally, he knew fear, even if it was only in tiny increments.

In my dream the quarry was hungry again. Edward and I lingered at the edge, tossing pearls into its terrible mouth.

"This isn't so bad," I offered hopefully.

"Really, Isabel...I can think of nothing worse. Sometimes you are such a stupid creature."

"They're only pearls."

He stood up and brushed the dirt from his trousers. "That's just like you, isn't it?

Only seeing what you want to see." He crouched down to the ground again, muttering under his breath, "Stupid thing..."

"That's not true. I see things as they are, plenty of things. Ugly things."

He responded with a mean little laugh, gesturing to the hole before us.

Then I saw a city rising from the water. I saw pillars of flesh and spires of twisted bodies. Glittering entrails wavered like flags and hung like storm-ravaged telephone lines. Great stalagmites tore through the floating dead, impaling them and carrying them toward the sky. I was stilled by its presence.

"Do you see?" Edward whispered, dropping another pearl into the lake. "Watch, now."

With a delicate splash, the little ball drifted below the surface, and returned as a buoyant, shimmering corpse.

"Oh god."

"Well, now it's done. We'll have to keep feeding her," Edward released an airy sigh.

I turned to run and found myself in a tent on the outskirts of a West African village. Rich cloths and tapestries lined the floor and hung from the support poles. There was a table, much like the one in Hausner's office, covered in soft blankets and pillows, but the cold steel beneath could not be entirely hidden. I moved towards the entrance and drew the tarp aside. Outside, a group of small village girls giggled and ran about, twirling long red ribbons in the air. They were beautiful and dark, with high cheekbones and ashen hands.

"You really should lay down, dear." The frail voice of Willa crept upon me from inside the tent. "It's not over yet."

I couldn't face her. My eyes remained on the girls, now aware of my presence. Their ribbons fell to the ground as they became still. They reminded me of a murder of crows.

"What does it want?"

"What's that, love?"

"The quarry. What does she want?"

"She just needs someone to feed her, the way you and my grandson once did, and the way we all have, somehow. Edward's great-grandmother took care of her so well, giving her all those miners. My Jacob and Rosalie didn't take to it as easily. They gave her more in spirit—more in pain—than proper bodies, but she fares well enough either way. And then my dear Edward...just like his father, more souls than bodies, but one does what one can. Thank heavens for your daughter. She'll see that our mother eats, when you no longer can."

I closed my eyes as the truth slammed into the back of my head. When I opened them again, one of the girls had come toward me. She stood before me, jutting her underdeveloped hip to the side, and pulling her necklace across her pink and brown lips. It was my necklace, Willa's necklace. She licked one of the pearls and laughed before running back to her friends. She carried herself like a prostitute. The child couldn't have been more than eight. I looked to the sky and saw the head of a Chinese dragon eating the blood-red sun.

I didn't have to tell Edward. He knew. Somewhere inside his reptile brain he knew.

The presence of the creature that masqueraded as Edward's grandmother grew stronger each day. I would see her in every corner and breaking through the dusty rays of light. I could feel her come upon me, nearly threatening, until Edward would move in, displacing her. If he couldn't see her, he certainly felt her.

This was our Christmas—isolated, cold and haunted. We were so distracted with this terror that we paid no mind as one year drifted into the next.

<hr/>

(January)

For the first time in a million years, we discussed options. He didn't dictate or demand, and I neither refused nor caved to his suggestions. What we should do…he knew no better than I.

When we spoke of "dispensing" with the child, the terrible thing that looked like Willa would react violently, throwing the house into her familiar state of chaos. Edward said the house had reacted this way since he was a boy. Of course, it wasn't at Willa's provocation in those days. He blamed Jacob, or his mother, or even the quarry. Now it was dear Gram. I wondered if we would have our turns at it when—*or if*—we died.

I begged Edward to take Willa's pearls out of the house. I could no longer live with them and I imagine he felt much the same. The ground was frozen beneath the snow, but he managed to dig just deep enough to prevent us from finding them again after the thaw.

So the house would quiver and groan, breathing in that heavy way which only serves to command one's attention. She was like a spoiled teenager then. There were times when the rooms would be sick and angry, and winds would tear through the halls, tossing the mirrors and artefacts to the floor in a fit. The wires would strain and the pipes would creak, crying out through the taps and shorting the lamps. The snowstorms were relentless, though I imagine that was only coincidence.

Despite the madness of the house, it was comforting to feel Edward on my side for the first time in ages, or perhaps ever. Immediately he corrected me, saying that it wasn't the first time he'd been my ally. The day he'd come to visit, when I was very small—the visit of which there was a photograph—he had been my ally then.

"You wouldn't recall this, I'm certain, but when I held you, when your mother and George were fumbling with the camera, I told you that I was sorry. I whispered into your little wool cap how sorry I was that you would stay with your mother. 'I'm sorry your mum may very well be crazy,' I said, 'because I know what that will do.' I wished upon you strength and hope and all of the things I prayed for myself when I was a boy."

"You remember that after twenty-odd years?"

"Of course I do. I remember everything that had to do with you, until your mother went completely mad. She wrote me with news of everything you did. I like to think that she genuinely wanted me to know all about you, but I suspect she used it as an excuse to contact me."

"Oh."

"It doesn't matter, though. I knew when you took your first step and when you started talking. Your first word was 'fish.'" He laughed for a moment. "I haven't a clue as to *why* that was your first word, but that was what you said, nonetheless."

I couldn't help but smile.

"Eventually the letters stopped coming. I knew something must have happened. I worried about you a great deal and after awhile I rang your house. George answered but he wouldn't tell me anything, except that you were fine, and really, that was all I was concerned with anyway."

"Then why did you leave me? If you were so worried? If you cared so much about my first words and my welfare?"

"You know, I've often wondered if George hadn't been in the picture, whether I might have taken you. But the only place we could've gone was here and trust me when I tell you that you had a better chance of surviving your mother than you would've mine. And George *was* there. I knew he'd take proper care of you."

I smiled, trying not to be sad or sickened. "I guess things have come full circle then. You have me back and we are fighting the same fight. It's funny how things like that work, don't you think?"

"Funny? No...It's not funny. It's completely anticipated."

What horrific torture it was, those moments when the lines were so blurred and I looked upon him with utter confusion. What terrible thing lives in my soul that I can feel such a passionate desire for him as he tells me of the innocent and tender way he loved me when I was a child and when he was only my father? It did not occur to me until later that this was most likely one more of his attempts to dissolve any tiny remaining spark of my mental stability. And worse than knowing it to be a twisted game, was the certainty that everything he said was true.

⨪

(February)

I felt like the universe this morning, but at present (in this dream) I am mean and beneath the current.

The winds were quiet at the edge of the canyon, which was unusual, but I could hear the low, soft growls of the wolves behind me. It was a hypnotic rumbling, so much in fact, that I did not hear them come upon me. It took several bites before I could realise fully what was happening, before I understood that they were eating me alive.

It was the pulling and pinching of my skin more than the piercing that caused me to cry out. The beasts tore at my back and my thighs. With dripping muzzles and calloused paws, they pulled me to the ground and flipped me onto my back. I grabbed at their beautiful grey coats...there was nothing else I could do. There were too many.

I thought of covering my face until I could see that the wolves were huddled at my torso. This was the prize, the most coveted meat. When the blood came, the pain receded until I felt nothing but the softness of their fur and the heat and saliva. I could only hear their growls and cries, and I could only see the grey sky above the canyon.

It was the absence of pain that afforded me the strength to pull myself up after the wolves had filled their bellies with my flesh. And I suppose it was the delirium of blood loss and the shock of being half-devoured in the forest that led me to fall.

"Bel...wake up..."

I expected to hit the water with devastating force; I have no basis for comparison, I'm usually awake by now.

But the water was soft like the wolves. It flooded the cavity that once was my stomach and womb and still there was no pain.

"Isabel..."

I am calling for my father...

"I'm right here love. Wake up. It's all right, don't be frightened..."

I could still feel the water all around my legs, and then the sickeningly dull cramping.

"I fell asleep...oh my god..." I lost my breath in the wave of a muscle spasm. "Oh, *fuck...*"

"It's all right, Bel." He placed one hand on my head, smoothing back my hair; the other was on the underside of my belly. "Mind your breathing, love. You're going into labour."

It was an exceptionally difficult delivery, one that continued throughout the night and into the next evening. Edward had me walking around the room at one point, which was a most unpleasant activity for us both. He maintained his calm and patient demeanour as I kept forcing us to the floor. It was mostly involuntary; my legs felt numb and I was certain that the weight of my pelvis had tripled over the previous hours. It was becoming impossible to stay vertical.

Eventually, after Edward gave up on keeping me upright, I curled myself into a ball and rolled partially under the bed, the way a dog will steal away into a cupboard to deliver her pups. I stared into the darkness underneath the bed for hours, entranced by the painful contractions and fear, feeling quite wretched and sorry for myself. I was completely unaware of the hour until Edward lifted the blanket from the other side, letting sunlight spill into my pitiful burrow. I tucked my head into my chest as he peered under the mattress.

"Do you think you might want to come out now and let me take a look?"

"No, I don't think so," I muttered into the dusty carpet.

"You can hide under here as long as you like, but she'll still come out sooner or later."

"I feel I should tell you I've decided not to go through with this."

"I see," he said softly and unconcerned. He'd heard this a million times. "Christ, it's filthy under here," he muttered to himself.

The blanket fell, interrupting the stream of light. Seconds later, his hands were gripping my hips as he pulled me from the safety of the floor.

"*Hey*! Stop...what the hell do you think you're doing?"

"I thought I'd get you up and we'd go dancing. What do you *think* I'm doing?" He dropped me on to the bed with a less than graceful thud. Immediately I rolled onto my side, curling around my throbbing gut as tight as I could manage, resisting as he tried to pry my legs from my stomach.

"Will you *please* stop acting like a half-wit?" he snapped. "This is getting tiresome.

Now roll towards me, please. I'm about to stop being gentle with you."

"That's lovely. Is that how you spoke to the women in Zaire?"

"No, other than abducting, experimenting on, then poisoning their children, I was extremely cordial to them," he sneered. "However, none of those women tried my patience quite like you do."

"I apologize if I'm taking up too much of your time...perhaps you have another pregnant daughter hidden somewhere in the house that you need to tend to? Or maybe she's not yet experienced that special relationship that daughters and fathers seem to share in this house and you need to get to work..."

He grabbed me by the wrist, yanking me toward him with one quick motion. "Perhaps *you'd* like to do this alone," he hissed, "because in about two seconds I'm going to walk out of this room and leave you to deliver these children by yourself."

Children. The tears came uncontrollably and seemed to soften Edward's threatening gaze.

"You forgot about the boy, didn't you?" he sighed.

I shook my head, sobbing in pain and sadness. "Please...don't leave."

He rolled his eyes. "I'm not going anywhere. Now, let's take a look. I don't think either of us want to see you back in the hospital."

The children, rather, the girl and what remained of her brother were born at dusk. There was surprisingly little blood or gore, even with the presence of a lifeless, half-formed foetus. Edward attempted to keep him from my sight, but I insisted upon seeing him.

They came out at nearly the same time, the girl holding the boy at her side, pulling him along with her as though he were her ragged toy doll.

He laid the children at my breast in silence. There was no crying from any of us. The girl was quiet and aware, more so than seemed normal. And the boy of course, was stillborn. Edward helped the girl to my breast, instructing me on how to feed her. He attempted to take the boy from my arms, but I held his cold body closer until it was clear that I wasn't letting go. The girl was refusing me. Edward repositioned her every few seconds, but to no avail. I suppose this should have upset me to some degree, but really, I felt no sadness over it. I asked Edward to take her.

"I think you ought to hold her for a while. Just her. I'll take care of our...the other one." He cleared his throat and looked away.

"I can't hold her right now. I just can't..." She wasn't our daughter, just as we had known. I don't think she was even human. Not in the way that Edward and I were 'no longer human' in the traditional sense, but in some ancient, alien way. She belonged to the quarry, and that came as no great surprise.

I held on to our son as Edward took the girl away and carried her across the room. Still, she had not uttered a sound. I studied what was left of the dead child. He merely looked unfinished.

"What are we going to do with him?" I whispered, holding him close to my face. He was covered in tiny hairs, like down feathers. His fingers and toes were still slightly webbed.

"I thought we'd bury him. We haven't too many other options. The ground is frozen, so it won't be easy. I'll have to find the pickaxe..." he muttered.

"If we bury him, we ought to name him, don't you think? He ought to have a name."

When he turned around there were tears in his eyes.

"If that's what you want," he sniffed.

I examined the tiny creature again. I haven't a clue what I was looking for; some spark or glimmer of life, maybe some early indication of personality. I tried to think of a meaningful name, something appropriate or symbolic. I tried to ignore the fact that the tiny thing in my arms was just malformed tissue and demised organs.

"I think he looks like a 'Gregory.'"

Edward nodded absently. "I like Gregory."

He knew as well as I that Gregory didn't look like *anything*. He was not much more complicated than a piece of meat. I'd chosen the name at random when I realised that I might as well be naming a sirloin. I'd never even known any Gregory's, but I carried on just the same, content in my denial.

"What about a middle name?"

He rubbed his temple and took a deep breath. "I don't know, love. Whatever you like."

"What's your middle name?"

"Nicholas," he said weakly.

"I like 'Nicholas.' Gregory Nicholas Grace." I was satisfied with that.

"What about this one?" He gazed at the baby in his arms. "What do you want to call her? I imagine 'Willa' isn't at the top of your list any more."

"I don't know. You can decide."

His face suggested a sense of disappointment and frustration. "Bel, please hold her again. I need you to at least *try* to be her mother. She's an infant. Infants need their mothers."

"Let's take her to the quarry then."

"Isabel!" he snapped sharply.

"She doesn't need me. She doesn't even want my milk."

"She doesn't *know* you. You didn't hold her for more than a minute or two. How do you expect a bond to form between you when I'm the one holding her?"

"A bond? Edward, we talked about this. There isn't going to be any bond. She's not like us."

"She's a baby, Isabel. She's our baby. You just gave birth to her!" he shouted, then quickly collected himself, remembering the child.

"She may have lived in me, but she's not our daughter. We know what she is and why she's here. Don't you remember what you said?"

"Of course I do, but now here it is. She's real and she's done nothing to warrant abandonment. She's done nothing wrong."

"She *murdered* Gregory!" I shrieked, hoping to cause some stir of emotion in the girl, but her only reaction was to dart her blue-violet eyes toward the direction of my voice. "Look...she doesn't even cry! What sort of newborn in the midst of all this yelling doesn't cry?"

"Or maybe, *just maybe*, Gregory died. Maybe he was just stillborn due to any one of a million possible complications. Maybe you're just as mental as I and all of this is in your head. Did you ever think about that? Maybe there's nothing in the goddamn quarry! What if we imagined all of it?"

"Is that what you really think...there's nothing in the quarry? It's all just been delusions?" I was nearly laughing in disbelief.

"Well it's possible, isn't it?" It was almost hopeful.

"Of course. It's possible that you and I and your mother, father, grandmother and your great-grandparents have all suffered from the exact same delusion. It's possible that a small army of people have died at the quarry merely by coincidence. And it's also possible that you've taken about all you can of this madness and have slipped into a state of denial. Now, what do you think is more likely?"

He didn't respond as he laid the child in her bassinet. He checked her over once more, presumably for abnormalities, though he would not admit to it. When he was done, he came to the bed and sat down.

"Let me see the boy." He reached for the bundle in my arms.

"He has a name."

"Fine. Let me see Gregory, please."

After some hesitation, I handed the child to him. He traced his finger over the boy's partially formed head and torso, looking carefully at his skull and what would have been his neck. I would not have given him to Edward if I'd known it was the last time I'd see or touch him.

"He knew. He told me in a dream," I said.

"Who knew?"

"Gregory. When he died, he spoke to me. He told me to tell you that they know and he told me to be careful of the red. I don't know what that means exactly, but that's what he said before he went to the quarry."

"The red?"

"I think the thing in the quarry is red. It's all been red—my dreams, the warnings, the pain and anger. He was warning us."

Edward took him away moments later. I immediately resented him for leaving me alone with the other baby. He hoped that I would eventually break and go to her crib. I couldn't believe how passive he had become, how quickly he'd given in to her. I lay in the bed, exhausted and afraid, staring at the bassinet until I fell asleep.

There wasn't as much pain in walking as I'd expected. I just felt dry. The bed was a mess, though Edward had the foresight to lay out several thick towels to avoid ruining the mattress. As I gathered them the child began to gurgle and softly caw, sounding like a sick bird. Ignoring her, I continued to clean up the remnants of the birth, throwing the towels to the floor and pulling the sheets from the bed. The caw was growing louder and coming in more frequent intervals until it ascended into a full-fledged cry.

I felt a tiny pull in my chest. Dropping the covers to the floor, I turned towards her. Maybe she did need me. Maybe we were wrong. Maybe none of it was true and Edward and I had indeed succumbed to our delusions and paranoia. Or—and this was the likeliest of scenarios—it was a trick. She was crying to gain my compassion, the clever thing. Unfortunately for her, she hadn't the slightest idea of what a monster I could be.

"Oh...so *now* you cry," I sneered, approaching her crib.

She looked normal for a brief moment, crying and jerking her little fat arms and legs around in the air. But there was something in her face, something contrived. She seemed to have her eyes opened the slightest bit, as if to make sure that I was still there, as though if I weren't, she'd not waste any more energy on tears and sobs.

"I'm not falling for it, you know. I don't feel bad for you."

She carried on with her yowls, her cheeks growing redder by the second.

"I tried to feed you, but you'd have none of it. So I suppose you'll just go hungry for now."

The pulling sensation inside my heart returned when she still did not stop. I felt as though I could burst into tears myself.

"*Stop crying!* You aren't really upset! It's bad enough your father's taken my son from me, now I should have to listen to this bloody noise, as well! *And you don't even mean it!"* I put my hands to my face and clasped them together to keep from reaching in and strangling her.

"Do you know where your father is right now?" I lowered my voice. Tears were rolling into my mouth now. "He's gone outside, gone searching in the dark and the snow for a place to bury your brother, the little brother that *you* murdered. We have to put your little brother in a hole in the ground, just like when we buried Willa's pearls..."

At once the room was dreadfully silent. She'd stopped wailing without the tiniest snivel or hiccup. We stared at one another, without a sound or a breath. She squirmed a bit, throwing her arms about, but still did not cry or look away.

"What did I say?" I whispered. A terrible salty taste arose from my throat and the skin around my neck began to tighten. Then, as I choked on grit and sea water, I understood. *"We buried Willa's pearls."*

I found Edward in the kitchen smoking a cigarette. Beautiful Edward in a bloodied shirt. Beautiful Edward, weary and broken by the sight of his children—all three of us. Beautifully inhuman, incestuous Edward, sitting in the dark, waiting for the next storm, the next ghost, the next shattering memory.

He did not seem surprised when I told him his daughter's name was Pearl.

He buried our son at the edge of the forest. The grave was rather shallow, but he placed a piece of wood over Gregory's body to keep the animals from digging him up. Edward thought it best to simply wrap him up in a cloth instead of building a coffin. It would be a while before the wood would decompose and this way, Gregory would go back to the soil faster. Of course, the ground was frozen and blanketed in several feet of snow so none of this would matter until the spring thaw, a fact that for some reason induced much sobbing on my part.

Edward refused to allow me outside for the burial. I was in no condition to stand around in the bitter cold, he said, and it took him forever to dig the hole. Anyway, someone would need to stay inside with Pearl. I was livid at the suggestion—that I should miss my own child's funeral—and what was worse, I had no idea with whom to place the blame.

"It wasn't *really* a funeral, you know," Edward curtly explained when it was done. "It's not as though I'm ordained. I just buried him. Please try to calm yourself. I'll make us some tea, all right?"

I was still crying uncontrollably as Edward stripped out of his frozen coat and boots. His hands were red and cracked and the skin around his nose and mouth was a shocking pink. His hair was frozen into little, stiff spears that hung just above his eyes.

"I don't want any bloody tea!" I snapped.

"Then why don't you try to rest? You've got to be exhausted. You just spent the last twenty hours in labour..."

"How can I rest? Do you have *any idea* what this feels like?"

He straightened up a bit, tensing his shoulders but keeping his eyes on the floor. "Of course I understand what this feels like. They're my children, too. I *do* have the capacity to feel pain. I *do* understand loss, you know. You aren't the only one who's ever lost something."

"That's funny. I thought you needed a conscience to feel things like that. I suppose I was wrong."

He shot up from his chair with unbelievable force. "*How dare you question my conscience?* I was right there beside you...*inside your head*...feeling the pain as you felt it, feeling the fear so I could understand what you'd need from me when it was done. I never left your side or pulled away while you delivered our children. I forced myself to feel your grief while you held our dead son and I forced myself to accept your reluctance to nurture our daughter...*because I understand your fear.* Now, what I would like to know is *where the hell were you while I was wrapping our son in a fucking bed linen and burying him under a metre of snow?* Where were you but in here by the fire crying your *selfish little heart out over your own misfortune?*"

"I...I was here because you told me not to come outside with..."

"*No!*" He slammed his fist into the doorframe. "I'm not talking about your body. Why weren't you *in my head?*"

I couldn't speak. I put my head down on my knees, trembling and wishing I could disappear.

"You left me alone out there in the dark and in the cold with *our dead fucking child.* You didn't feel the bitter wind slicing through my hands as they went numb and could barely hold the *goddamn shovel*! Do you know what it feels like to cry with the wind and snow battering your face? It feels as though your eyes will freeze and turn to glass just before they finally *shatter* into a million pieces. I could barely see what I was doing and I was terrified that I might lose him in the drifts. I was utterly terrified that I might slip and *hit him* with the shovel and have to find a way to tell you that I lost our son's body in the snow and how we'd just have to wait for the thaw and *pray* we'd find him before a fox uncovered him and dragged him away for her dinner! So you see, all I could think of was *you*. You and Pearl and poor, dead Gregory and what the bloody hell we're going to do now."

His rage had slowly descended to a scratchy whisper. "Never in a million years would I have asked or expected you to stand out there with me, but I thought you might have cared about me enough...or...or found it in your cold heart to at least *think about me*. Why weren't you with me out there, Isabel? *I needed you inside me*."

From the bedroom, Pearl began to wail again. I finally raised my head to look Edward in the eyes. There were no words I could utter, nothing I could do to tell him how sorry I was. He stared back with a hundred years worth of pain in his watery eyes.

He turned to face the direction of Pearl's screams. "I'll get that," he said quietly, leaving the room with a rush of cold wind.

I covered my face and contemplated how useless and selfish I had been. In the end, I only served as the cocoon for the creature we called Pearl. The child that had truly belonged to us was gone. I'd failed to protect him. I'd failed to be a good mother. I hoped that someday, when Gregory came back as some beautiful little sparrow or a magnificent oak tree, that he would forgive me.

(March)

I prayed that Edward would forgive me as well, and in time he did. In that brief, terrible moment after the children were born, everything between us changed. The sheer cruelty of what I'd done to him, how I'd neglected him, seemed to make us even (almost). At least that's how it felt to me (almost). I was the cold brutal monster and he was, in that frigid moment, more human and vulnerable than he'd ever been since his dreadful childhood.

The role of victim did not suit him as well as it always had me. He felt as responsible as I for Gregory's demise, but spent little time punishing himself. Though he rarely spoke of it, I would catch him, at least once a day at the kitchen window, entranced by the landscape. And always he was looking in the direction of the grave. Edward had always known loss, but as his lust for the fusion of science and religion grew, he became numb to the idea. Loss was inevitable, not worth tears or words. He'd forgotten or perhaps evolved out of what it was to actually feel loss or pain until the day he buried our son in the frozen ground. He understood loss as the things we'd known about the house and the quarry and our family unfolded before us—things greater than the lot of us.

And then there was Pearl.

Despite our ugly little situation, I should make it known that I never *hated* Pearl. For me that would have been tantamount to hating angels or goblins or any sort of make-believe creature. Pearl was never real to me.

Edward, on the other hand, worked very hard at being a decent father to her while she was still too young to do any damage. He also worked very hard at keeping an emotional distance between them. Of course, for Pearl, there was no real attachment to either of us. We were merely her means of survival until she was able to fend for herself.

In most ways, she seemed to be normal child, crying when she was hungry or needed to be changed. These, however, were her only reasons for crying. She never cried out of fear or loneliness. She never cried to get our attention or affection. If just *once* she'd cried out for me—really cried out for me—no tricks or manipulations, things might have been very different.

It bothered Edward a great deal that I didn't hold her very much. He said that he couldn't see the harm in treating her like our own while she was so young and helpless, but he was slipping under her spell, with her big violet eyes, her pale pink lips, and her feathery locks of brown and blonde streaked hair. She really was a striking child. She looked like neither of us.

Shortly after her birth, we moved her bassinet back into my old bedroom. I said I really didn't care where we put her as long as she couldn't watch us throughout the night.

Then there was the issue of my relationship with Edward. Truly, it had been a tremendously blurred line for so long that it was a bit of a relief to finally choose who we would be to each other.

For quite a few weeks, Edward did not touch me or look me in the eye. When we spoke, it was formal and only out of necessity. He could no longer keep me out of his head at will, though, and this served only to reinforce the severity with which I'd hurt him. Every time he found himself near me—which was not so often—his mind would overflow with thoughts of pain and desperation. He felt as though he was suffocating under the weight of his grief and it was I who held him there. I didn't blame him for turning away from me. I could barely look at my own reflection.

The snow lasted forever, keeping us trapped indoors with nothing but our tension and pain. There was a time when Edward would have been immune to the cold, but these days his defences were down and he relied on the house to keep him sheltered, unstable as she was. I ignored the house most days. It wasn't difficult as I was consumed with the incredible heartbreak of Edward's withdrawal. There were times that his mere presence would drive me to tears. Never had I missed anyone more than him. Not even Gregory, who I missed with an intensity I never thought possible.

I was utterly disgusted with myself. My hair had grown to the middle of my back in ragged strands, knotting into long tangles and clumps. What little weight I'd gained was gone and had taken a few extra pounds of meat with it when it left. I rarely bathed or changed out of my nightshirt...it was Edward's and it was the only way I could feel him any more. I don't know how long it would have carried on this way, I don't know how many more wretched hours without him I could have survived. I didn't care what role he played. I just wanted him back.

Most nights he stayed awake, reading in his study or staring out of the kitchen window at the glowing white earth. Every few nights, however, he'd come upstairs to check on Pearl. He'd whisper to her and more often than not I couldn't understand what he'd said. Eventually he'd settle back into the chair and remain there until morning in his usual half-catatonic state. That ritual ended the night I had the worst nightmare that I can ever recall.

Edward was whispering to Pearl. I heard the wind beating itself senseless against the vast window and the sound of blood rushing from my head as I sat up.

"What was that sound?"

Edward turned to face me. "What sound?"

"Don't you hear it? It sounds like growling."

"It's probably the wolves. Go back to sleep."

I nodded and fell back into the blankets. The noise was growing louder. I pulled the covers tighter, rolling away from the window. The moon reflected off the snow banks, casting a bitter white light through the window.

Another sound came from the garden. It was the sound of crying. I flew from the bed, throwing myself to the window. I saw the wolves, a pack of wolves closing in on their imminent kill. They circled and stalked around the prey as it cried, paralysed with fear.

"Isabel, where did you put the baby?" Edward asked quietly.

"She's right there. You were just whispering to her. Telling secrets."

"Not Pearl. Where did you put Gregory?"

"Edward," I choked, "Gregory's dead."

He looked at me with disgust and horror. "How could you say such things? Gregory's not dead. He was right here. Now where did you put him?"

I couldn't believe what he was saying. "I didn't put him anywhere. He's dead. You buried him, remember?"

"Have you lost your mind? I did no such thing. Now tell me where you put the baby! Where did you put Kate?"

"Kate?"

"What?" he snapped. "Who's Kate?"

"You said Kate!"

"No, I said Gregory! Now tell me where he is!"

There was a piercing bark and another cry. It was the cry of a baby.

"Oh god! Gregory!"

I ran with all my might, down the stairs, through the hall and to the kitchen. Edward was shouting for me to wait, which made no sense at all. There was no time to wait.

As I threw the French doors open, a tiny avalanche fell at my feet and a frigid burst of wind tore through, sending a million snowflakes into my eyes.

In that moment, in that second, when I hesitated in order to clear the snow from my eyes, the wolves descended upon Gregory, tearing him to bits.

I screamed until I was raw, running through the snow towards the gruesome scene. The wolves were scattering now, grabbing any remaining pieces of my son as they fled.

I fell to my knees in the trampled snowdrift. I could no longer feel my feet or my hands, nor could I see anything around me clearly, save for the red ribbons on the snow.

"Isabel!"

I was shaking uncontrollably.

"Bel! Come on Bel..."

I felt light, like I was moving involuntarily.

"Isabel, come on, love. Come on, back inside with you..."

Edward never said in so many words that he forgave me, but he held me by the fireplace for the longest time, still and silent except for the occasional spark and crackling of the wood. I knew then, as did he, that it was time to decide who we were to each other, once and for all.

"If you are to be my daughter again," he quietly began, "then there will be quite a few changes to be made. Separate rooms." He cleared his throat. "Other things...you know..." he took a deep, uncomfortable breath.

"Edward..."

George Scott is my father...

"No. Please listen to me. If you want me to be your father, then I'll do everything

I can to be just that. I owe you that much, at least. I can't change what I've done, but I won't touch you...I won't..."

...and when he puts his arms around me it feels nothing like this...

I didn't pause to contemplate my words. They spilled from my mouth without reserve. "I'd probably die if you never touched me again..."

My mouth was on his before I could finish speaking. And that was how we buried the incestuous truth under three feet of snow, believing that by April it would simply melt away.

⤳

The first thing I did that spring was cut my hair. I didn't bother to go about things the proper way, I just took the shears to anything that didn't lie flat. When all was said and done, there was an ankle-high mound of knots and tangles by my feet and I was looking a bit less feral.

I washed our clothes and the linens. We'd emptied the house of nearly all the debris and kept the windows open, even with the night chill of early spring rushing through the rooms. The windows in Pearl's nursery remained closed at all times since the wind usually blew in from the woods, and as we know, the woods is where the quarry lived. The winds came from her forest and each night they came knocking for the child.

⤳

Pearl dreams of warmth. Pearl dreams of the swirling sea and of the many arms of her mother. She dreams of the strength in which her mother holds her, with flowing tentacles constricting like snakes around her tiny arms and little rabbit legs. Pearl dreams of home and of being devoured by the great, deep red mouth of her mother. She can hear her mother's voice. In the hum of the layline, she hears her mother calling her name.

⤳

No matter how good Edward was to me in that first year after the birth, I could never quite move beyond his suggestion that perhaps Pearl was a normal child and it was I who had the sickness. This was devastating to me, that I might be so crazy that I'd imagine our own daughter to be a monster, and a hole in the ground to be haunted.

I wish with all my heart that I could tell you how we grew to love Pearl. I wish I could say that as the months went by it became evident that the girl was, indeed, a normal child—*our* normal child—and I could lovingly recall all the times I brushed her silky hair and tied it up with ribbons, all of the picnics and parties...but I can't. And although there were times when Edward was quite good at pretending to be a loving father, he couldn't deny his mistrust of her once she took to walking. He went to great lengths keeping his eyes on her at all times, carrying her from room to room, even if he was only to be gone for seconds. It was nothing new for him to sleep with his eyes open, though in the past I questioned if he was seeing anything or not. I didn't wonder any more; he was keeping watch now.

The list of lies that we struggled to adhere to was ever growing and changing depending upon the company. I kept in touch with George, ringing him every few weeks and even visiting him once after the children were born. It was a rather sad occasion, as I was still mourning the loss of *both* of my stillborn children and the subsequent distance that grew between their father and myself. This was also why it really wasn't a good idea for George to visit. I assured him, as time went on, that I was working through it and that things would ultimately be fine. I would just need some time.

Edward handled Dr Hausner, telling him also that we lost both children. Remembering to act as my father proved to be much more difficult, as we gave it very little thought any more, but Edward did a passable job. Hausner was, at first, a bit more persistent than George, strongly suggesting that I be examined again. He never said as much, but it was apparent to Edward that the doctor was bothered by the fact that we'd delivered the babies at home. James believed, deep inside, that the girl child might still be alive had she been delivered at a hospital, which really could be interpreted as James believing himself to be a more competent physician than Edward.

Hausner also questioned the whereabouts of the children's graves, at which point Edward confided in James with a mock confession. He confided in the suspicious doctor that we had taken it upon ourselves to bury the children on our own property. He assured James that, indeed, he was familiar with the laws and procedures of mortuary science, but felt that given the state of the foetuses (one demise at approximately sixteen weeks, the other at twenty-eight, he said, sounding so very clinical) it would be unnecessary for them to be treated the same as a fully formed cadaver. And really, hadn't I been through enough? He couldn't bear to watch his daughter suffer through all of that ritual and ceremony. In the end, Hausner warily accepted this.

It was a great deal of effort to maintain these stories, especially as Pearl got older, but since neither of us knew exactly what was to become of the situation, we decided that one more deception would hardly make a difference. And that was how we lived for the next two years.

A few months after Pearl's third birthday, Edward installed a lock on the outside of her bedroom door. The windows had been under lock and key since she was an infant, but as she grew more adept at things like gates and doorknobs, Edward felt it necessary to take further precautions.

She made the nightly task difficult for him, forever pleading with him in her little honeysuckle voice to *please* not lock her in. She said she was afraid, but not of the dark or the winds or things that most little children are afraid of. No, Pearl—a child who had never seen a television programme and who could have no concept of monsters or bogeymen—Pearl was frightened of much more terrible things. Little Pearl had her own highly advanced mythology to draw from. She had horrific undersea creatures with thousands of arms and teeth, vicious hybrids of wolves and people and foxes, she had growling darkness and amorphous destruction and ghosts...hundreds of angry ghosts. These things were living in the forest, she'd cry to Edward, and when that didn't work, she'd claim they lived in her room. It took Edward much longer than I to become immune to her manipulations.

Pearl's weakness was that she had the intellect of a demigod confined to the brain and body of a toddler. She was nowhere near her full potential—fortunately for us—and her designs only worked for so long before becoming ineffective. Edward eventually settled into the role of the stern, yet caring, father. I would hear him at her door—

"I'm sorry, love, but this is how it's got to be..."

My approach was different. I never spent much time playing the part of her mother, and Pearl learned quickly that she would find little empathy from me. When she tried to convince me one night that the sea monster and all of the other frightful things had moved into her room, I decided to engage her in rational debate.

"How can a sea monster live in your room? It would certainly need water to live, don't you think?"

She climbed onto her bed and cast her eyes to the floor, thinking things through for a moment. "Sometimes she can breathe air," she whispered.

"I see. But how do you suppose all of these things can get into the house without Daddy or I knowing? Don't you think that we might notice a parade of monsters traipsing through the halls or breaking in through the windows?"

Again she paused, now staring thoughtfully at the ceiling. "They're very little." (She pronounced it "lil-ddle.")

"If they're so little, then why are you afraid of them? You could just hit them with your shoe and smoosh them like bugs, right?"

This was the part where she would begin to get impatient with me and her true colours would seep out from behind her crystalline disguise. "I won't smoosh them— they're my friends!"

"Oh, so now they're your friends? Why would you want to be friends with scary monsters?"

She narrowed her eyes and pouted with anger and frustration, but instead of dragging the story on any further, she resorted to the bizarre and obnoxious behaviour that was usually reserved only for me. Rarely did she have to go this far with Edward. He (of all people, surprisingly) didn't have the heart to provoke her. The groaning, which she got from her real mother, would come first. It was quiet and came from her throat, her lips remaining tightly sealed, reminiscent of a ventriloquist's act. Then came the barking. She'd throw herself around the bed and twist her delicate body into most unnatural positions, yelping and barking like a dog, pulling at her hair and nightgown in quick jerks. Initially it was freakishly comical, though I couldn't pretend that it was anything other than a sign of how disturbed this creature was. After the first few times, I gave up all attempts to restrain her during these fits and would simply lock her in for the night and let her wear herself down.

Again, what a dreadful mother I am to say such things of my own child...except she wasn't...and I will admit that there were times that I could barely face myself in the mirror because I would forget what she was and just see her little cherub face and those glittering amethyst eyes. I would hear that painfully sweet voice and see her reaching for Edward, standing miles above her (I have tried, unsuccessfully thus far, to forget this view of him, myself) and I would forget that it was a facade designed to control us, and that under those little bird bones lived the kin of the monster in the quarry. I would forget this...but only for a moment.

Pearl said she saw ghosts. Usually men in dirty clothes, she said. They came from the woods at night and she would see them from her window. At night, Edward and I would listen at her door as she talked to them. She would introduce herself, then ask their names and answer herself, as though she were repeating what they said: "My name is Pearl, what's yours? William? Why do you live in the woods, William? 'Cause you died there? What were you doing there? Minding the corey? Oh, well..."

In the mornings she would drink her juice and tell Edward about the men she'd met the night before.

"...and then I talked to Ronald something I don't remember and David Keesey, they minded the corey..."

"I think you mean they *mined the quarry*," said Edward.

"Uh-huh...and then I met Louis Parker and John Wheaton..."

"You met John Wheaton?" Edward asked. His eyes glimmered like stars.

"Uh-huh. He said a secret," she grinned.

"He *told* you a secret."

"Uh-huh, he told (toad) me a secret. He said that you and her (she never called me anything but 'her,' usually followed by pointing) killed (kilt) him."

"Did he now?" Edward replied. "And you say *killed,* not kilt. That's something else."

"What's kilt?"

"A kilt is something you wear if you're Scottish. You know, if someone tells you a secret, that means you aren't supposed to tell anyone else."

"But if you kill-*ed* him, then you already knew."

Edward smiled. "Well, I suppose you're right then. It's not really a secret to us after all."

(June)

Pearl weighed on my mind incessantly. I would lie in Edward's arms night after night thinking, imagining and waiting. Waiting, I suppose for her to show her true shape and devour me. But as it was, night after night, she was just a little child locked in her room, drumming her little fists upon the window and whining desperately for her mother. Most nights I would remember that it wasn't me she was crying for, but every now and then I would jump at her distant voice, wanting to go to her, until Edward would place his hand on mine and remind me gently what she was. He'd abandoned his dreams of her humanity almost entirely by then. The child haunted us worse than the house itself.

It became too much to bear by mid month. I simply could not help being overcome by terrible visions. I thought of accidents, dreadful scenarios in which Pearl would die, or sometimes in which she would lead me to my own death. And she knew. She did not trust me any more than I trusted her. Edward knew it too.

"Please don't obsess so, love," he said one day. "Little children are clumsy. They hurt themselves all the time. Accidents happen and there's only so much any parent can do." He stared at me unwavering. "I trust you'll know what to do…if something were to happen."

Then, just days before July, as though he'd seen it coming, Pearl drowned in the pool. How terribly abrupt it is to say it that way, but it is merely a fact, one that I can think of few other ways to express. If I were to dress it up with eloquent ribbons and flowery words it would be no less horrid or true.

It took but a minute, which is about how much time passed before I noticed she was gone from the kitchen table. Edward left her with me while he went to his study for "his medicine," as he called it in front of the child.

Pearl went back to her colouring while I washed and sliced fruit for her lunch. There wasn't much she would eat other than fruit, and the occasional bit of meat, so that was what we gave her. There were no sounds in the room other than the scribbling of crayons and the tapping of the knife on the cutting board.

In the back of my mind I could feel Edward sinking into the thickness of the morphine haze, searching for some quiet and for something human. For myself, I rarely craved it any more. Human conditions were rapidly becoming overrated.

Pearl sighed loudly, shaking me from Edward's chemical descent—this was how she'd beckon me in lieu of saying my name or calling me Mummy—and I asked her what she needed.

"Me an' my friends want to go outside. We want to go into the forest an' we want you to take us."

And there it was—the thing I'd been waiting for. She was not even four years old and there was the first attempt to feed me to her mother. My skin drew tight and my heart skipped.

"I'm sorry," I cleared my throat and collected myself, "but I can't take you." I did not look at her, hoping to conceal my horror.

"But I *need* to go..." she whined.

I shook my head. "Pearl, I said no."

She slammed a crayon into the table top, snapping it into several pieces, and worked up some tears.

"If you keep this up, you'll be spending the rest of the day in your room."

Ignoring my shallow threat, she got up from the table and headed toward the study.

"Where do you think you're going?"

"I'm going to get Daddy. He'll make you take me an' my friends to the forest."

"Is that so."

"Our daddy will make you. You always do everythin' he says."

I grabbed her by the arm and she squealed as though she was being led to slaughter. She wrestled with me until I placed her firmly back in her chair.

"*Don't move*," I hissed, "We'll see just what Daddy thinks of your idea."

I didn't make it to the study. Edward could hear me calling to him from the corridor. She knew. She said 'our daddy.' Something needed to be done as things were only going to get worse and I prayed Edward would intervene. Truly, I was a breath away from the her when I heard the French doors slam shut. I yelled for Edward once more and ran back to the kitchen. Pearl was gone.

I could see her running across the emerald lawn, past the courtyard already, heading toward the trees. She was also heading directly for the pool and if she hadn't been looking over her shoulder, presumably watching for me to give chase, she might not have fallen in.

I remember running to her, momentarily forgetting what she was and what she intended to do, but as I came upon her, struggling to stay above the algae and weeds, I was reminded of what she would soon become. She was gasping for breath and flailing about, tangling herself deeper into the mass, but her eyes were not those of a terrified child. They were calm and aware, the brilliant blue-violet washed away to reveal an opaque film of pale pink and grey. These were the eyes that Willa showed me once in a dream. She reached for me, but I couldn't help her, even though instinct guided my hands toward her. I remember feeling her soft, wet hair between my fingers. I stood at the edge of the pool, frozen in the ugliness of the scene before me. I knew she meant to pull me down with her.

I would, however, be a liar if I said there were no moments in which I nearly broke down and thought of saving her, and if she had shown one drop of fear or love in her eyes I would have pulled her from the black water, but there was nothing. Nothing but those monstrous, callous eyes looking up at me, void of any human emotion, dead to any compassion ever possibly shared between a mother and daughter. And that is what I remember seeing and why I did nothing while she took her last shallow breath.

Edward volunteered for the unpleasant task of removing Pearl from the water.

"Where will you put her?"

"I'm taking her where she belongs...to the quarry." There was little emotion in his voice.

"I should come with you."

"Let me wrap her up first, then we'll go."

"Check her eyes, please."

I decided against waiting for Edward inside since the house had immediately gone into what appeared to be a state of mourning. The rooms were damp and cold despite the warmth outside and she would periodically shudder and sigh, shaking only the smallest and most delicate pictures and icons from the walls. I suppose I expected violence, retaliation—something more aggressive than sorrow, but she remained still and calm in her grief and I waited with her, just as still and just as calm in my confusion.

The quarry smelled of salt and decay. I slowed down, staying several paces behind Edward and the girl. He asked me if I wanted to go back when I mentioned that I was feeling a bit sick from nerves. I let this creature's child die (or perhaps worse, perhaps I am a murderer) and I was afraid of what vengeance she might seek. But as we stood on her steep grey cliffs, she did not lash out at me. I could see a dark shape moving near the surface of the water, and it was serene and expectant. I could feel that her many arms were ready to take back what was hers. It was far more touching than I could've ever imagined, but still I was afraid.

"She won't hurt you. You've evened the score," he said. "She took your son, you took her daughter." He stopped too late.

"You think I drowned her, don't you?"

"Bel, I didn't mean..."

"No, Edward. Do you think I killed her? Tell me the truth."

I tried in vain to hear what he was thinking, but there was only static.

"You tell me. It's your conscience. Did you drown our child?"

I thought about this and found only one true answer beneath the fear and guilt. "No. *Our* child didn't drown. He was stillborn."

And we were tossing pearls into the water...I remember this. Down she went, wrapped in a sheet filled with stones. I used to dream of beautiful ghosts in the snow, rising and falling amidst the drifts, like delicate feathers. They were premonitions of coming snowstorms, or so I believed, since in the morning I would awake to see the streets blanketed in white. She fell like a cold, white ghost.

"Did you look at her eyes?" I asked after several breathless moments.

"Yes."

"What did they look like?"

He hesitated before speaking. It was never good when he hesitated. "Like the eyes of a dead child."

We stared down into the water in silence for a very long time. The sun was slipping behind the trees before either of us spoke again.

"Do you remember what you said the day the children were born?"

"Which part?"

"The part where you suggested that this was all in our heads. That none of it was real."

"I remember."

"Do you really believe that?"

He shook his head slowly, holding back a smile. "No."

"I didn't imagine it, you know. I didn't imagine what she was."

"I know."

"Even though you didn't see her eyes...the way I did, when she died?"

He took my hand in his. "I didn't have to," he looked to the sky as it pulled the last traces of light and colour down below the canopy. "I saw them when she was born."

I felt the spark within me again, the gift that had been suffocated in part by Pearl, but mostly by my own device. I decided then that I no longer had anything to fear, not the quarry or the house, not Edward or myself. I had spent more than four years yearning for Edward to be a good man while believing him to be only a monster. But now, when he spoke, I understood that absolutes could not survive him; they could not survive this place. We were never innately good people, but we were not wicked. We were just who we were, and who we would decide to be day after day. We would no longer see right and wrong, only action and consequence, and we would be better for it. I vowed I would accept the consequences of our choices, *my* choices, and move on. And in time, that is what I did.

I stared at the green water below us as it swirled into a gentle whirlpool, welcoming its daughter back home. She is destruction and she is love. She—*my carnivorous mother*—is as good a parent as either of us could have ever been.

"That's my girl," he said smiling, satisfied with my unspoken acceptance. Then he suggested that we go home before it became too dark to see.

About the Author

Donna Lynch is a writer and musician currently living in Baltimore, MD. *Isabel Burning* is her first novel and the first in a series about the Grace family. Her written works include the poetry collections *Ladies and Other Vicious Creatures* and *In My Mouth*, as well as numerous other poems and short stories.

She is the co-founder along with her husband, artist and musician Steven Archer, of the dark electro-rock band Ego Likeness (Dancing Ferret Discs), and the spoken word/instrumental outfit The Trinity Project. She is fond of all genres of music, twisted and creepy film and literature, maps, quarries and coal mines, theology, and hairless animals.

Other Novels from Raw Dog Screaming Press

Blankety Blank, D. Harlan Wilson
hc 978-1-933293-50-9, $14.95, 188p
tpb 978-1-933293-57-8, $29.95, 188p

Rutger Van Trout has problems but the worst is not that his son might be a werewolf. It's not his obsession with transforming his house into a three-ring barnyard or his wife's haunted skeleton. The complication has invaded his community in the form of a new breed of serial killer, who stalks from house to house leaving a bloodbath that would make Jack the Ripper himself blush.

Health Agent, Jeffrey Thomas
hc 978-1-933293-43-1, $30.00, 290p
tpb 978-1-933293-44-8, $15.95, 290p

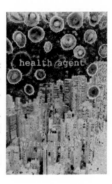

Punktown's health agents are charged with keeping the public safe from infectious disease. But for health agent Montgomery Black work is about to consume his life. The problem is a highly contagious and extremely deadly STD, mutstav six-seventy. While trying to prevent the spread of the disease Black could lose everything he cares about but there's no ignoring the suspicion that something far more sinister than the impartial hand of nature is behind the spread of this epidemic.

Sin Conductor, John Edward Lawson

Willis Lowery is just your average occupational hazards estimator until one day, while inspecting a factory, he happens across a chemical burn victim. Her name is Dusyanna, and the passion she ignites in him threatens to melt away every fiber of his morals. As he soon learns, there is no escape from her circle of degenerates, so he vows to become the devil to beat the devil.

Jesus Coyote, Harold Jaffe
hc 978-1-933293-55-4, $24.95, 148p
tpb 978-1-933293-63-9, $13.95, 148p

This docufictional novel based on the Manson murders proves that, like his coyote totem, the myths around Manson hold irrevocable power. In one swooping panoramic arc, with the bloody killings at its center, Jaffe captures the perspectives of Manson, his devotees, the prosecutors, and the victims while firing a shot against the hypocrisy of institutionalized morality.

www.rawdogscreaming.com

Printed in the United States
134853LV00001B/4/P

9 781933 293493